you don't bring me flowers anymore

REBECCA PATER

Ark House Press
arkhousepress.com

© 2024 Rebecca Pater

Cataloguing in Publication Data:
Title: You Don't Bring Me Flowers Anymore
ISBN: 978-1-7635572-0-8 (pbk)
Subjects: FIC042040 [FICTION / Christian / Romance / General]; FIC042000 [FICTION / Christian / General];

Design by initiateagency.com

To my Jason,
who always believed in me
even when I didn't believe in myself

Contents

Prologue
May
1991

"Girls, please. It's midnight. I'm tired. Can't you go to sleep now or at least pretend to and keep it down?"

"Sorry, Mrs. Mancini," Joan apologized, in that insincere way teenagers do, while rolling her eyes at Bethany. Beth's mother was nice but overly protective, always worried about how much sleep her girls got or whether they ate enough vegetables and were they dressed the way 'nice girls' should be. Joan's mother probably didn't even remember where she was tonight and, at worst, probably didn't care.

Caroline was already in her sleeping bag on the lounge-room floor as far away from Joan as she could manage. They might both be friends of Beth's, but they couldn't stand each other. Joan and Caroline's mutual dislike would probably end in insults, leaving Beth wishing that she hadn't invited them both tonight. She usually tried to keep them apart, but time was running out. Soon it would be the final exams, and then they would be off at uni and hardly ever see each other again, so she had asked them both to stay tonight when Mum agreed she was working hard enough to take a night off from studying. Both of her friends had promised to behave with each other, but Beth wasn't going to hold her breath.

To make matters worse, her mother had insisted her little sister, Jilly, join them for the sleepover. Even though she was only fifteen, she was tall and perfect, hair flowing in just that way that some girls seemed to achieve without even trying. Beth's new spiral perm was a frizzy disaster, but Jilly's hair, the darkest shade of brunette, trailed down her back in ringlets with nothing more than a wash and some mousse scrunched in.

"Anyone want some chips? I've got barbeque or chicken. Mum doesn't know, so we'll have to chuck the packets before she gets up in the morning," Jilly reminded the others. Annie Mancini had a thing about the girls eating what she called "fake food" and preferred to make everything herself. Joan grabbed a packet and started working her way through it. Like Jilly, she was one of those girls Beth envied who could eat whatever they wanted and not gain weight, but Caroline and Beth declined. Caroline had a lovely figure, but worked at it, counting every calorie that went into her body. Beth was what kind people referred to as "curvy" and the nasty ones called "fat." She had always hoped that it was baby fat that would melt away when she hit her teens. Or if she got taller like her dad, it would stretch out and hide itself in her height. Instead, she'd stayed short like her mother. Mum had been cute when she was younger, but now she looked dumpy in her daily uniform of old-lady pants and tops from shops Beth wouldn't be seen dead in. Whenever she looked at her mum, she hoped she wasn't looking at her future.

Quickly, the conversation turned to the boys at school, and Beth knew this was where the trouble would begin. "So, Joan," Caroline asked sarcastically. "Who's the flavour of the month? That is, if there's anyone left in year twelve you haven't pashed yet. I guess you could always move on to the teachers."

Joan hated the way Caroline always suggested she was easy when it wasn't true. Sometimes she wondered if Caroline was jealous of her, but then what was there to be jealous of? She was the one who was jealous of Caroline's family and their beautiful home. It was definitely time to have a little fun with her.

"There is someone new at school I have my eye on. Tall, cute, not as stupid as the others. Plays basketball. I think I caught you staring at him the other day."

Caroline began to blush. She knew exactly who Joan was talking about—Adam. Adam, who had started at their school three weeks ago. It was stupid really. Nobody transfers to a new school during year twelve. But here he was. And just *so* beautiful. Caroline had never paid much attention to any of the morons at school—boys who really were so dumb, she didn't understand how it was that, in the end, men got to be the ones to rule the world, run all the corporations, and be prime ministers. But she had taken one look at Adam as he walked into her English class and suddenly understood what all the other girls at school had been carrying on about. It was love.

"Do you mean Adam?" piped in Jilly. "He asked me out the other day. We're going to see *Silence of the Lambs* next Friday night. Sorry, Joan, but I think you might be out of luck with that one. He's all mine."

"Not likely," scoffed Beth. "You know there is no way Mum's going to let you go anywhere with a boy that old. There's no dating until you start year eleven, and if I had to wait, so should you. And even if you get it past Mum, do you think Joseph Mancini is ever going to let his fifteen-year-old daughter go anywhere with someone who's seventeen? He really will build that box he keeps threatening you with and lock you in until you're forty."

"Beth, do you think I'm that stupid? I just need a little help. You and Tom are going to the movies next week, and wasn't it nice of you to bring your little sister on your date? It's not my fault if Tom's new friend just *happens* to be at the same movie. It would be rude not to ask him to join us."

"Does Adam know about this? Or Tom? I don't think they even know each other. Tom's not exactly hanging out on the basketball courts at lunch." Tom wasn't usually secretive, and he thought Jilly was just a little kid that was always in the way when he wanted to be alone with Beth. She couldn't imagine him helping her sister out with anything.

"I don't even want to see *Silence of the Lambs*. It looks creepy. And if Dad finds out Tom was helping you, he'll ban him from the house, and I'll be alone for the rest of my life. He'll make me share that box with you, and I just don't like you enough to be locked up with you forever. "

"Of course Adam and Tom don't know. And who cares if you want to see that movie? Stay. Go. I don't care. Just be waiting outside the theatre with me when Dad comes to pick us up later. You tell Tom that's what you want to see, and I'll tell Adam what time to meet me at the theatre. You're just my cover so that neither of our clueless parents knows what's really going on. And don't even try and tell Ma or Pa what I'm planning. Don't forget what I saw in your bottom draw the other day. "

Beth knew she was talking about the prescription for "the pill" Jilly had found while she was snooping in Beth's room the other day. And now, Beth would have no choice but to help her sister. When Jilly had something over you, she had no problem using it to get her way. It wouldn't matter that Beth hadn't filled the prescription yet. It was enough for Jill that Beth had gone to see the doctor. If either of her parents found out she had done that and was considering having sex, then life as Beth knew it would be over.

The conversation hadn't gone the way Joan planned, but she guessed it didn't matter now. Caroline looked devastated at the news of Adam's date, so it was a job well done. If the beautiful Jilly had her sights set on Adam, then Caroline had no hope.

Beth was devastated for Caroline. She knew how crazy her friend was about Adam. But she was no competition for Jilly. She usually got what she wanted. Even when they were little, their parents would let her get away with more than Beth ever could. She had fought all the battles with their parents first and paved the way for Jilly to sail through life.

After Jillian's revelation about her upcoming date, the fun and energy dissipated out of the evening. The girls mumbled their goodnights to each other and slowly drifted off to sleep until only one of them was awake. Caroline had controlled herself for as long as she could, and no one heard her crying softly into her pillow until she, too, finally fell asleep.

Chapter 1
Jillian
5:02 pm 22 June 2012

For a woman who was normally in constant motion, she had never sat so still or so quietly before. She hadn't expected this kind of reaction from herself. Jillian had thought she would be the type to throw things, damage belongings, and take revenge. *Well you never know how you'll handle something until you're inside a situation*, she thought, and she had definitely never been here before. The wedding photo she had hung on the wall looked down, mocking her. She didn't recognize those people anymore: a beautiful couple looking into each other's eyes, certain that they would be together forever. Their future stretched out before them, full of promise and hope. If she took a picture of those two foolish people now, it would reveal broken vows, broken promises, a crushed heart, and dashed hope.

She heard the garage door shudder open. Her husband had told her weeks ago he would get someone out to take a look at it, but like most things he said, nothing ever came of it. That's what he was like: full of grand schemes and talk, but there were never any results. Jill dragged her eyes from the wedding photo on the wall to the rest of the room. It was all hers. From the leather couches and the rugs to the artwork and carefully chosen lamps, she had picked them all. Chris had moved into her home straight from his parents' when they married. That should have been Jill's first clue. It wasn't a good sign when a man in his thirties was still living at home. He brought nothing more than an old car and bag upon bag of expensive clothes with him. In their two years of marriage, he hadn't added anything to her home, and today, she decided he hadn't added anything to her life either. How had she ended up here? They say love is blind, but in her case, it had made her into a fool, and she hadn't seen him for what he really was: nothing more than a waste of her time and love. Perhaps if their courtship hadn't been so short, things would have been different. After a few months, he had proposed, and she was so infatuated with him, she had overlooked the little things that usually had her send other men packing.

She heard the front door open. His footsteps echoed in the quiet house. The light outside was starting to fade, and she saw a flood of illumination as he went through the house, calling her name and flicking on switches. She wouldn't normally be here this early in the evening, but he had walked past her car and knew she was home.

"Jill," he called into the empty bedroom. He made his way through the house until he found her sitting in the dark on her favourite chair.

"There you are, Jill. Why are you sitting in the dark?" He walked towards her, intending to kiss her the way he always did when he got home, but she stretched out her arm and put her hand up to stop him. Ignoring her warning, he bent down and kissed her cheek.

Jill flinched at his touch and pulled her body away from his. She couldn't imagine ever letting him touch her again.

"Baby, what's wrong?" he asked. "Are you sick?" Even Chris, who was normally too self-absorbed to notice anyone else's needs or troubles, could recognize that something wasn't right here. Maybe she had received some bad news from the doctor. She'd had so many tests recently that he couldn't keep up with them.

"Your phone rang this morning," she said, speaking for the first time in hours, as she waved the phone in her hand towards him. "I answered it. I hope you don't mind."

"Not my phone, Babe." He fumbled with his pocket and pulled out his mobile. "See," he said, holding it up to her.

"Are you sure? I found it in the funniest place. It was hidden under your car-cleaning gear in the garage. It took me a while to find it. It kept ringing and ringing. At first, I thought I was going insane and hearing things. But I finally tracked down the source of the noise. If it's not yours, then whose is it?" She held the phone out and threw it gently towards him.

Fear shot through Chris as he reached out and caught it. How could he have been so stupid? He thought he had taken every precaution to avoid discovery. The phone bills were being sent to the office, and he only turned it on once a day, after Jill had left for work, to check for messages. But here he was, after only having the phone for one week, found out because of his own incompetence. He must have left it on that morning after he had charged it overnight.

Jill could see the struggle on her husband's face. He had always been good at keeping secrets, and if he was ever found out, he had a talent for sliding out of trouble unscathed. But this time, he couldn't come up with any reason to have a second phone, and if she'd answered it, then she probably already knew. With no defence, he stayed silent and waited for the axe to fall.

"Nothing to say? I would have thought you had so much to tell me. Such wonderful news should be shared, not kept to yourself. But as you seem incapable of speech, why don't you let me help you out." Jill paused as Chris fell into the chair opposite to her. All his usual bravado and confidence had fled, and he knew he was a man whose meal ticket was about to be clipped.

"So there I am, hunting high and low to find the source of the ringing, and you can't imagine how surprised I was to find a phone I didn't recognize in my own garage. I thought I'd better answer it in case someone had lost it. Instead of being someone trying to track down their lost property, on the other end was a woman who said, 'Hey, Chris, it's me.' I thought that was a little strange considering the only other woman in your life apart from me who has the right to identify herself as 'me' is your mother, and it definitely wasn't her calling. Instead, I got to have the most informative conversation with *Meg*. She seemed nice, by the way. So helpful, filling me in on what you've been up to lately. And just in case you're wondering, your baby's due on February 15."

"I don't know what to say, Jill. You know how much I love you. I need you to know this was nothing more than a horrible mistake. I never wanted you to find out."

"Well, thank you for trying to spare my feelings." Chris hardly recognized her voice. It was so cold, so clinical. "But I'm a reasonable person. Maybe you have an explanation for how someone other than me ended up pregnant with your child. Were you caught up in a terrible tornado with a stranger? All your clothes were torn off, and then the wind pushed you over on top of her?"

"Jill, please. You can't really want to know the details. It happened, and I've never been more sorry about anything in my life."

"But I'm a solicitor, Chris. I like to hear all the facts."

Chris rubbed his hands over his temples, stalling for time as he tried to formulate the right words.

"Do you remember when I was away last month at the launch of that new wine down the peninsula?"

"If I recall, you told me it had been boring, and you wished you had been home with me. I guess you didn't tell me everything."

"Please, Jill, don't make me do this."

"Why not? You're doing so well. Now I know the where. I just need to know the why and the how."

"Fine." He sighed. He fixed his eyes on a spot on the floor, not able to look at her while he spoke, but he could feel her eyes boring into him. "Because the winery had organized accommodations for all the guests and no one was going to be driving, we were plied with alcohol. And you know what these things are like. You don't realize how much you've had because they keep topping up the glasses. I'm not sure I've ever been that drunk before. There was a woman at my table. She spent the whole night flirting with me, and I swear I told her I was married, but it didn't seem to bother her. It never occurred to me anything would come of it. We were just having fun. She kept telling me how attractive I was and touching my arm. I guess I liked the attention. These days, I feel like you're only interested in me when it's the right time of the month. I hate that I feel that way, but I haven't liked how every conversation we have seems to revolve around having a baby. Meg didn't mention fertility or doctors and treatments once. For the first time in a year, I was carefree, and I liked it. I know that doesn't excuse what happened, but it might help you to understand."

"Oh, I see. It's my fault. What was I thinking involving you in the process of trying to have a baby and asking you to take a test or come to the occasional doctor's appointment with me? You are only my husband, after all."

"I'm not blaming you. I made a mistake, and I'll have to deal with it."

"And is this the first mistake you've made since we got married? Or are you working on a whole tribe. Should I start looking for other telephones hidden around the house?"

"Of course not. It only happened once, and I'm never going to do it again. I regretted it as soon as it was over"

"Was she pretty?"

"Why is that important?"

"Because I want to know."

He knew this was dangerous territory. He had noticed Meg as soon as he walked into the room, and he had chosen to sit at her table. But he wasn't going to tell his wife that.

"Yes, she was pretty. Not nearly as beautiful as you, but attractive, and it was nice to be around someone so easy going. She reminded me of you a little, before it got so serious and stressful around here."

"So instead of coming to me and telling me how you felt, you decided to deal with your frustrations by having sex with a stranger. I hope it was good."

"I really don't remember. I was so drunk, I hardly remember getting back to the hotel. They put us on a bus at the end of the night, and when Meg asked me up to her room for a nightcap, I said yes. Now I wish I'd said no, but I had no idea what she had in mind." Chris was telling the truth when he told her he didn't have a clear memory of the night. When he woke up the next morning, he'd snuck out of the room, and after grabbing his stuff, he'd gone straight home. He'd never expected to see Meg again, and until she tracked him down through work and called him, he'd tried to pretend it had never happened. "I guess one thing led to another, and we ended up in bed together. But it meant nothing to me."

Jill stood up and began pacing back and forth. Her anger had reached its full measure, and if she didn't do something with her body, she thought she might explode. "So it meant nothing to you. You were willing to give up our life together for nothing. Do you know what that means? Me, us, our marriage and life together are worth less than nothing."

6

"No, Jill. You are everything to me. I just meant that she was no one. She's not important to me. And she doesn't need to be important to you either. Just let me handle everything, and you'll never have to talk to her again or have any dealings with the baby."

"But, Chris," she answered. "Meg is somebody. She's about to become the mother of your child. Your firstborn. That makes her very important. And it means she is always going to be in your life. So the only way I can make sure I never have to deal with her or that baby is to remove you from my life." Jill felt the last piece of calm leave her, and she knew she was about to lose control.

"Please, Jill. Can't you try and see my side of this? I told you how drunk I was. It never would have happened if I wasn't."

"That is not a good enough excuse. Not in a million years would I sleep with someone else, no matter how much I'd had to drink. And I never would have allowed myself to get into that position in the first place. You are weak. You're a weak, pathetic man, and I want you out of my house."

Chris recoiled at her words. He didn't think he deserved to be spoken to like that no matter what he had done.

"This is *our* house, Jill. I'll leave when I'm good and ready. I know you're angry right now, but when you've have a chance to calm down and see sense, you'll see we can sort this out. I don't want you to say something in the heat of the moment that you might regret later."

Jill turned away from Chris and wrenched the wedding photo off the wall. She held it above her head ,and then with all the strength she had, she threw it to the floor. Glass shattered everywhere and tiny scratches appeared on the photo where shards pierced it as they fell. Chris stepped back and covered his eyes from the flying glass, shocked by the violence.

"The only thing I regret is marrying you! I bought this house long before you came along, and it will be mine long after you're gone. You won't see one cent out of me and neither will *that* woman or *that* baby. You're about to get a serious reality check, Mr. Hamilton, because babies are expensive. And without my money keeping you in the comfort you've become accustomed to, you are in for a rough ride," she yelled, pointing her finger at him threateningly.

Chris grabbed Jill's arms in restraint, afraid she might throw something else. She pulled herself away and stepped back.

"Don't you ever touch me again! Because of you, I have to go to the doctor and find out if you've given me some filthy disease because in your hurry to sleep with some stranger, you didn't use any protection. And what if I find out that I'm pregnant? Wouldn't that be ironic? The thing I wanted most in the world just became my worst nightmare. You have two minutes to pack a bag and get out of my house. I hate you, Chris Hamilton, and I will *never* forgive you for what you've done."

Chris backed away from his wife. He knew the battle was lost tonight, but that didn't mean he would give up. He was certain that, in time, he would win her back. He had won her once even though he knew she was much better than he deserved, and he wasn't going to let her go without a fight. He grabbed a bag from the cupboard in the hall and threw in a few essentials from the bedroom before he left.

Jill waited until she heard the garage door close before she let go. She leaned back onto the wall where her wedding picture had once hung and slid down to the floor. She didn't notice the tiny pieces of glass making punctures in her pyjamas. Finally, the tears that had stayed away all day were given permission, and Jill put her head down on her knees and cried.

She remained that way for an hour, sitting alone in the dark. She might have sat there all night if the cold hadn't roused her from her stupor. She slowly got up and dusted the glass from her legs. All she wanted was to be alone, but she had made a commitment to go tonight, and she intended to keep it. She would have to make an excuse for Chris that sounded reasonable because tonight couldn't be about her and what had gone on here today. It was already half past six, so she hurriedly threw on some clothes and did her best to cover her tear-stained face. As she put on another coat of makeup, she looked at herself in the mirror and tried to understand why it had been so easy for her husband to choose to be with someone else. She knew it had been a difficult time not being able to get pregnant, but even with all the fertility worries and last year's tragedy, despite everything, before today, this had been the happiest year of her life.

Chapter 2
Beth
5:04 pm 22 June 2012

Beth stood in front of her open wardrobe. No matter how long she stood there, and no matter how hard she wished, there was nothing she could do. She didn't own a magic dress that was going to make her look thinner. She had a full wardrobe, but most of the clothes didn't fit anymore, even when she wore them with that underwear that promised to "suck it all in." All it really did was push the rolls of fat either up or down her body. And if she actually managed getting into it, forget about eating or trying to go to the toilet. Once it was on, it stayed on. She knew that it was time to give in and clean out her wardrobe, but getting rid of the smaller sizes—and, to be honest, they weren't that small—would be admitting defeat.

She needed to wear something nice tonight. Caroline would expect her to make the effort, and tonight wasn't the night to let her best friend down. She brushed her hand over a pretty dress she had fit into a few years ago, and then sighing, she pulled out a pair of black pants and a pinstriped blouse that she hoped would look all right. The last time she'd put it on, the buttons had been close to popping open. At least she wouldn't have to try and wrangle herself into her jeans tonight. It took about two hours of wear to stretch them out enough to be comfortable, but when she had worn them last week, they had dug into her stomach for the whole day. If something didn't change soon, she would have to go up a size. And unfortunately, that would make her a size twenty, not the desired twelve she used to be. The awful thing was she had thought she was so big back then. Now she *wished* she was "that fat."

Beth had never really taken to cooking. At home, her Mum had done it all, and the boarding house where she lived during uni provided all her meals. They were so bad, it was the first time in her life Beth lost weight. When Tom came to visit her, he couldn't believe how much difference losing a few kilos made on her short stature, and he'd spent the whole visit complimenting her. When she and Tom got married, she'd learnt to put together a few meals, but they got into the bad habit of bringing home takeaway because they were both so busy working.

By the time Beth was pregnant with Lochie, the kilos had already started to creep on. Caroline had been sick when she was pregnant and had lost weight, but Beth sailed through each pregnancy without throwing up once. Or, more to the point, she ate her way through each pregnancy. With the first one, she was decided she was going to get fat anyway, so why not enjoy it? It became a convenient excuse to eat whatever she desired. It never occurred to her that a baby only weighed about three kilos when it was born and certainly didn't account for the fifteen kilos she had put on by the time she gave birth. Taking a pair of jeans to the hospital had been a silly mistake, and she ended up going home in her maternity pants. She hadn't been able get her legs into the jeans, let alone her butt. And her stomach seemed to have taken on a life of its own when she moved. A week after Lochie was born, someone asked her how much longer she had to go with her pregnancy. She had been mortified and embarrassed, lying and telling the person that she was due in a few weeks. In the hospital, the nurses had assured her breast-feeding would help her take off some of the weight, and if she took the time to take the baby out for a walk each day, it would help get rid of the rest. Nobody told her she would be so tired that walking to the mailbox would be exhausting, forget about making it around the block. And breast-feeding made her hungry.

Sarah was born three years after Lochie, and Nathan came along another three years after that. By the time he was born, Beth no longer recognized herself as the girl she used to be. The weight gain had slowed down after the babies but still continued. Nathan was ten now, and at about a kilo a year added since he was born, she knew had to do something or face the fact that her life might be shortened. But her worst fear was that Tom would leave her.

He hardly looked at her anymore. Well, could she blame him? Going into shopping centres was a nightmare. Beth had noticed how the shop windows showed her reflection as she walked past the shops. Rows and rows of shinning windows, revealing her misshapen backside, and when Beth saw her stomach from the side, she wondered why people didn't ask if she was pregnant. Tom never said anything to her about her weight; well, almost never. But the other day when Beth had been about to leave for church, he had looked her up and down and said, probably without meaning to be cruel, "That does not look good."

Beth made it to the car before she started crying, so Tom never knew how much he had hurt her. It didn't help that she knew he was right. She had tried that morning to wear something other than the stretchy black pants and the long flowing tops she usually favoured. When she had tried the skirt on at the shops, she could see it didn't suit her, but it had been so pretty on the hanger that she convinced herself it was the fault of the terrible lighting and the bad mirrors in the fitting room that made her look bad, not her body. That morning had been the first time she had worn the skirt, and when she took a look at herself in the mirror and saw the awful reflection, it had been too late to go back and change. Nobody else said anything, but when she got home, she threw the skirt in the bin. She hadn't bought anything new since.

After finishing her makeup while trying hard to only look at the parts of her face that she had to—she hated focusing on her double chin and her puffy cheeks—Beth dressed in the clothes she had settled on and went in search of her family.

She found Lochie stretched out on the couch watching an old episode of *Seinfeld*. He wasn't dressed for tonight, and he didn't look like he had any intention of following the instructions his mother had given him an hour ago, so Beth knew she was about to get into a fight.

"Lochie, were leaving in half an hour. Go and put something decent on. And brush your hair. You look like you stuck your finger in a light socket." Lochie was sixteen and had very set ideas about what looked good. Beth, like most mothers, didn't like her son's style or taste. His hair swooped all over his head, held there by some sort of expensive wax that felt like glue. Long and pointy in the front, she secretly thought he looked ridiculous and longed for the days when she had been able to instruct the hairdresser. He had recently started making noise about dying it black, and even his father, who usually said, "It's just hair. It'll grow out," had forbidden it. Chances were he would come home one day with it done, and then what were they supposed to do? Shave his head while he slept? And his hair was just the tip of the iceberg. His clothes always seemed to have a slightly dirty look about them no matter what detergent she used, and they smelt like he had just picked them up off the floor after wearing them once or twice already. Once a week, Beth checked his room and collected a basket of washing that he hadn't bothered to put out. She often wondered what would happen if she just stopped doing that. Would he eventually decide his clothes were just too far gone, even for him to put up with, and put them in the washing? Probably not. He would just con his dad into buying him some more, and one day, he would trip on a pair of jeans and suffocate under the pile of filth on his own bedroom floor.

"Mum, seriously, this is fine. Nobody cares anyway what I wear, and you oldies never notice us kids once you've had a wine or two. I've told you I don't want to go tonight; it's going to be weird."

Beth breathed in and exhaled loudly. All three kids had expressed their opposition to tonight. Nathan didn't really seem to understand but always agreed with his big brother, whom he adored, no matter what he said or did to him. Sarah was only going without kicking up a huge fuss because she had developed a crush on Michael. Not that Beth understood it. No one had heard that kid speak for a year, and he was much too old for Sarah anyway. Lochie and he had been friends in the past, but Michael had pulled away from everyone in his life, including her son. She just hoped Sarah wasn't going to be too sensitive when he ignored her. That's if he even showed up tonight.

One battle lost, Beth went in search of the other two. Nathan was playing on his iPod, but he was dressed and looked relatively clean. Beth 1, kids 1, she moved on to Sarah, who was still in her bedroom. When she opened the closed bedroom door, Beth groaned. What was that girl wearing now, and where had she gotten it from? If Tom saw her in that dress, it would give him a heart attack. She had piled on the makeup, and it was not pretty. Beth sat down on the bed, leaned over to the iPod dock, and turned down the volume. It sounded like One Direction to Beth, but she could be wrong. All those bands were the same. Finally able to be heard above the racket, she braced herself for another round with her thirteen-year-old daughter.

14

"Love, I'm sorry, but there's no way I'm letting you go out tonight in that. Where did you get it from?" Rolling her eyes at her ancient mother, Sarah tugged at the bottom of the black dress she was wearing, trying to make it look longer than it was.

"I borrowed it from Karen, Mum. You said tonight was important, and we had to make an effort. Well, I'm making an effort. I don't have anything else this nice, just jeans and T-shirts, and you said no jeans."

Beth was already up off the bed, looking through Sarah's wardrobe. At least she wasn't a pig like her brother, and it was easy to see a cupboard full of nice clothes, pretty dresses, and skirts, ones that came past her knees, unlike the dress Sarah had on right now. She guessed it was not Karen's dress at all but probably belonged to her older sister, who didn't know the girls had borrowed it.

Beth pulled a pretty floral dress off the hanger. Nobody would mistake her daughter for a hooker in that, and paired with that nice cardigan, she would be warm enough. Sarah took one look at her mother's face and knew she wasn't going to win this time. And there was no point trying to get Dad's help. He didn't stop her doing what she wanted most of the time, but he was really weird about what clothes she wore. She couldn't wait until she was eighteen. Then she was going to wear anything she wanted, and nothing Mum or Dad said would stop her. Her parents held all the power for now. Eighteen was still four years and nine months away. She was counting down the days, wishing she would wake up one morning and find the years had flown by during the night, and she was suddenly legal and in charge of herself.

After she had changed into the horrible dress her mum had picked out, she sat back down at the mirror to finish her hair. But unfortunately, her mother wasn't done with her yet.

"Sarah, I simply can't let you go out with all that makeup on your face. You're so pretty, you don't need it anyway. If you like, I can show you how to do it properly." Sarah snorted with disbelief. What would Mum know about makeup? She hardly ever wore it, and even tonight when they were going out for a special thing, she looked so bland. Sarah always thought Beth was like a bowl of vanilla ice cream without any toppings or sprinkles. It was all right on its own, but with something added, it was so much tastier.

"Mum, I know what I'm doing. I'll take some of the eye shadow off, but that's all. I don't want to look boring like you. Colour looks good on me." She held out a tube to her mother. "Did you want to borrow my lipstick? It might make you look, um, a little brighter. And I think I just heard Dad come in. Maybe you should check, OK?"

Every time one of her children talked to her like that, Beth felt herself become a little less. She wondered if she was becoming invisible, and no one would even notice if she was gone. And it seemed to be happening more and more. It felt to Beth like her children thought she was some sort of elderly relative, with no power in her own home anymore, just someone to humour occasionally when they needed a favour. Most of the time, punishing them didn't seem to have any effect. They either ignored her, or if she pushed the issue and played hardball, they would just go to their dad and tell on her like *she* was the child and *they* were the parents. Tom liked peace and often gave in, proving to the kids that Beth was more of an honorary figurehead in the family and didn't really have any authority at all. Beth tried to remember what her parents used to do to get her to behave, but really all it took was for one look from Mum and that was that. If she ever tried to disobey, her dad would make it very clear that whatever Mum said was law. Lucky Mum. It must have been wonderful to have that kind of support from her husband. Beth put down the lipstick Sarah had handed her.

"That's not really my colour, but thank you so much for the suggestion. Wipe your face off, and don't make me send your father in here." Sarah poked her tongue out at her mother's back as she left the room, and Sarah slammed the door behind her.

Beth walked to the kitchen, hoping it had been Tom who Sarah had heard. Beth looked at her watch. Six fifteen—not too bad. She had asked him to be home by six but knew that was never going to happen. He was always the last to leave work. Being the boss didn't leave him much choice. After year twelve, Tom had started an apprenticeship in his father's business. He took over the plumbing company after his father retired and discovered that his dad had been running at a loss for at least a year, so Tom had inherited debt, not the thriving enterprise they had expected. By working every possible hour and taking every job no matter how small, Tom had turned the business around within a year, and now it was a thriving enterprise. He had staff to do most of the dirty work now, and he focused on the paperwork side of things.

"Hey, Hun," he greeted her, throwing his keys and wallet on the messy bench. He leaned over and kissed her on the cheek. He looked tired and dirty; she guessed it had been one of those days. "I'm going to need a shower before we go. I'm sorry I'm late. Bart called in sick again today, and I had to cover all his bookings. I think I'm going to have to let him go if this keeps up. I can't believe how hard it is to find good staff when so many people are unemployed." He shook his head, thinking about how frustrated he was constantly dealing with other people's excuses and problems. It had been a busy day, and all he wanted to do was sit on the couch and veg. Instead he had to get dressed up for a dinner he had been dreading all week. He ran his fingers through his hair, pushing it back off his dirty face. Bart had been booked to unclog the pipes of an old tank, and it had been dirty work. "I won't be long. Give me ten in the shower, and then we can get going. Are the kids ready?"

"Ready enough. You might want to give Sarah a once-over before we leave the house. We might need to scrape off her face and make her put on some more clothing. I tried, but she doesn't listen to me. You might be able to get through to her."

"I'm sure it's not that bad. You're too hard on her."

"Thanks for your support, Tom. I really appreciate it." Beth reached into the fridge and pulled out a bottle of white wine. "Go have your shower. It'll give me a chance to have a drink before we go. I know you think you had a bad day, but dealing with adults can't have been as frustrating as dealing with a class of feral ten year olds. And then our three were just as bad when they got home." She poured a full glass and took a sip as Tom looked on and frowned.

"So I guess I'm designated driver tonight again. I thought last time you said you'd drive next time we went out. "

"Please, Tom. You know how I feel about this. She's my friend, and I don't know what to say to her. Being a little relaxed might help." Tom didn't say anymore; he just turned and headed for the bedroom, frustrated that Beth always seemed to "need to relax" these days. Most nights by 9:00 p.m., she was so relaxed that she fell asleep on the couch, and he ended up going to bed alone—again.

Twenty minutes later, Tom was ready, and all three children had been assembled in the kitchen. The drive wouldn't take long, and they wouldn't be too late. Tom could see that Sarah looked very pretty in a floral dress, and he didn't know what Beth had been talking about. They'd had never really agreed on how to deal with their children, but these days, they hardly agreed on anything at all. As they got into the car, Beth, who had made it through two glasses of wine while she waited for Tom, made a request. "Please behave tonight. Remember why we're doing this."

"The only reason I'm going is because we might get a decent dinner," said Sarah. The kids all grinned at each other in agreement while Beth heard "Amen to that" muttered by Tom under his breath.

Another criticism, thought Beth. How much longer could a person go on like this? Between her ballooning weight, the way the kids treated her, the way Tom ignored her, and the awful event of last year, Beth thought this had been the most depressing year of her life.

Chapter 3
Joan
6:07 pm 22 June 2012

J oan was beyond frustrated. The builder on the medical centre project was questioning her plans again, and Joan had spent all afternoon out on the site. It was a common problem between the two professions. Builders often said that architects knew nothing about building a practical structure. Architects found builders to be a bunch of know-it-alls who couldn't read a plan if they tried. It happened on most projects, and Joan was usually able to defuse the situation with a bit of charm and her ability to convince people that they weren't actually wrong—just lacking the right information. This time, it hadn't worked and she had been ready to take a hammer to the head of the stubborn foreman who was questioning her design. She doubted it would have made a dent though. Nothing had been resolved, and she would have to prepare herself for round two on Monday. The slab wasn't even down, and they were already trying to tell her that not only did she have it wrong but so did the surveyor and the engineer. Ignoring the experts, the construction company had decided that the footings didn't need to be quite so deep and were contesting the plans that all three professionals had worked on together. But there was no way she was going to yield on this. Getting the foundation wrong would compromise the whole project, and Joan didn't fancy being the star of a *60 Minutes* story if the building collapsed.

Hurrying to her car and hoping that she wasn't going to be late, Joan entered the address into her GPS. If she was late, Caroline would think she had done it on purpose. The last thing she wanted after the day she'd just had was for Caroline to spend the whole night making little digs at her organisational skills. All Joan wanted to do was go home, slip into a bath, and then eat dinner in bed. She didn't understand why she had even been invited tonight. It had probably been Beth's idea, and not wanting to cause any conflict for her friend, Joan had agreed to attend, but a little part of her had also said yes out of respect. She had been just as devastated as everyone else, and it would be good to remember the anniversary with them. Every time she thought about cancelling, she remembered that it had been kind of Caroline to invite her.

Ten minutes into her trip, the phone rang, and she hit talk without checking the caller ID.

"Joan, it's David Saunders here from Saunders Construction. Have you got a sec?" *Just fabulous*, thought Joan. *Another argument with another* man. *Why do they all think a woman can't be just as competent as they are?* She was no feminist, but Joan did expect to be taken seriously at her job. She had graduated from the *same* university as all the men in her class and had achieved better marks than most of them. Nobody had given her a *pink* degree at the end and expected her to design doll houses and children's cubbies.

"I'm driving, David, so I might go through a dead spot. Hopefully I don't lose you." *Yeah, I might lose you on purpose*, she thought. "What's up?"

21

"Joan, I just got off the phone with Phil from the site. He told me about the trouble there today. I just wanted to let you know I've gone over my copy of the plans, and I totally agree with you. Changing the depth of the footings would be dangerous, and I've told Phil to follow your specifications to the letter."

"Really?" Maybe one of these builders had a brain in his head after all. "That's great, David. You've just saved me from the torture of having to spend another day on site with Phil. He seemed so sure that you had told him to make the change. I was going to call you first thing Monday and try to convince you that you had it wrong. "

"Look I'm sorry about, Phil," David said. "I have to be careful on this job. The budget is tighter than normal, and I told him to keep costs down. What I really meant was for him to keep an eye on things and make sure that nothing from the site went missing and that the boys didn't slack off when no one was looking. I never would have allowed him to compromise the safety of the building. I've told him as much, but I think in future it would be best if you and I sorted out any upcoming issues ourselves. You know how foremen can be, especially if they're told they're wrong by a pretty woman."

"Pretty woman? Was that your observation or Phil's?" she asked, her antenna going up a little. Joan couldn't imagine Phil having anything nice to say about her—or anyone else for that matter. She hadn't had to deal with such an annoying old bugger in a long time, and she was pleased to hear she wouldn't have to again.

David laughed as he replied. "My observation. I won't tell you what Phil called you. I'm sorry you had to put up with him today. He's an old grump, but he keeps the boys motivated. When he's not being difficult, he does good work. I'd be lost without him on site." David hesitated, unsure if it was appropriate to ask the next question, but he'd chickened out last time, so he went for it anyway and hoped she wouldn't think he was overstepping a line. "How about I buy you a drink to make it up to you?"

That took Joan by surprise. She had no trouble doing business outside of the office, and often some of the best work was done when people were a little relaxed and in a different environment. She didn't think she and David needed to meet up now that the issue had been resolved, but in the interest of client relations, it was probably a good idea to say yes. And it wasn't like it would be unpleasant. Joan had only met David Sanders twice, but both times she had certainly noticed him. How could she not? In his early forties, he had that look she always found difficult to resist. He was incredibly attractive, if just ever so slightly rough around the edges, and she'd been surprised at how funny he was. But she had put him out of her mind. It was never a good idea to get involved with anyone at work, and a man like that would always have someone waiting for him at home.

"Sure. That sounds fine. I'm back in the office tomorrow. I don't normally go in on a Saturday, but Phil's call changed my plans, and I have to catch up on today's work tomorrow. Give me a call then, and we can set up something...as long as you don't bring Phil."

"I have no intention of inviting Phil along. You're not free tonight are you? We could meet anywhere that suits you." David knew he was being pushy, but she had said yes, and he didn't want to give her time to change her mind. He had wanted to ask her out the first time he'd seen her, and he had spent the whole meeting afraid to meet her eyes in case he gave himself away.

"Sorry, I can't make it tonight. I've got a dinner at seven, and I might not get there on time as it is."

"Ah. Hot date, then?" Disappointed, David wondered if she had misunderstood his invitation and really believed he'd asked her out to make up for

Phil's behaviour today. He didn't want to waste his time if she was involved with someone.

"I wish" replied Joan. "More of an obligatory thing, and I'm not looking forward to it at all. I'd rather be home in bed."

"Now that sounds like fun." Confused, Joan could hear a smile in his voice and wondered if she was reading the conversation wrong. Maybe this wasn't about work. "I wish I could join you. Goodnight, Joan. I'll call you tomorrow about that drink." David hung up and silence filled the car.

Did I hear that right? thought Joan. *He meant join me in bed not at the obligation, didn't he?* Surely he wasn't that cheeky. Still unsure by the end of the conversation, she ran it over and over in her head. *I must have heard him wrong.* Out loud she said "You're losing it, girl. He's just trying to be funny."

At least the work situation was resolved. A huge weight had lifted off her shoulders, and she felt freer than she had all day. Joan had been working for the last two years in Melbourne and was trying to raise her profile in the industry there. She had risen to the top of the small firm she worked for in Sydney, where she had started working straight out of university, and had earned a very good reputation in the ten years she had been there. But the move back to Melbourne to work for a much bigger company with much bigger projects had been a risk. She knew she could do the work and was ready for the challenge, but she had left a life she loved and lots of friends. But it had turned out to be the right decision, as her boss was finally giving her some more important projects. Maybe one day she would realize her dream of having a firm of her own.

After high school, Joan had left home as fast as she could and travelled all over the world, working in whatever job she could get when she needed money. It had been her time travelling through Europe that had given her a love for architecture. She had not known what it was she wanted to do with her life and was so relieved to discover there was actually something out there she was drawn to. She was in the process of deciding to return home and finding out how to go to uni as an older student when she got the call to come home. Her mother had finally achieved her lifelong goal of drinking herself to death, and there was no one else to organize the funeral.

It had been a sad, small affair. Beth and her family had been the only ones there for her. Joan had always thought she would be glad when her mother died. The process of picking the casket—the cheapest one available—and finding a church that would have the funeral for a women who had never set foot in a building dedicated to God had been exhausting, but she had been able to remain emotionally detached. Few mourners turned up to the service. Margaret Webster was not a woman with a lot of friends, and the ones she did have would have been more likely to turn up if she had had the funeral at the local pub.

It was when Joan entered the church and saw the casket at the front of the chapel that she finally felt some emotion. But it was not sadness or grief that she felt. She was flooded with overwhelming anger. She could hear the minister's voice, but nothing he said made sense.

"Loving mother of Joan." No, that was not her mother. Her mother had been a horrible excuse for a human being and had loved no one, probably not even herself and definitely not her only daughter. Joan didn't remember a time as a child when she wasn't hungry. She was still ashamed of the way she had learnt to con food out of the kids at school or get invited to their houses after school and would "hang around" until dinnertime. There were some very kind mothers who included Joan in their homes as much as possible, but most children were told to stay away from her. She never looked particularly clean, and her clothes were hand-me-downs several times over.

Her mother might never have had enough money to feed and care for Joan properly, but she always had money for cigarettes and booze. And she didn't seem to mind sharing them with the degenerates she let into their home. The only good thing Margaret ever did was make sure that none of her friends went near her daughter, and when Joan woke up in the morning to get ready for school while her mother slept it off, not once had any of them ever stayed the night. The only time a man had looked in Joan's direction, he had been told to leave, and Joan never saw him again. At least she felt safe from that kind of abuse in their home. The fourth-floor unit in a state housing block was crammed with the kind of furniture most people threw out for the council collections. But as she got older, Joan did her best to keep the place clean, the same way she tried to keep herself and her clothes clean. She didn't do a very good job, though; she needed someone to show her how to do it and to provide the necessary materials, like soap and a washing machine. Joan never understood why someone from the government didn't come and take her away. Sometimes she wished for that, even with the stories she saw on TV about foster children being abused in homes. But no one ever came, probably because her mother never hit her, just neglected to love or care for her. Under her own steam, Joan made it to school most of the time and tried her hardest not to draw attention to herself.

Joan never knew her father, and her mother didn't ever talk about any other relatives she might have been able to count on. So Joan did most of her raising herself. It became easier when she was old enough to get a part-time job. Working after school and weekends at the local fish-and-chip shop provided her with an income. She was able to buy the school books and clothes she needed and, most importantly, save for her escape. Margaret didn't know about the job because Joan was afraid her mother would take the money Joan earned to boost her meagre dole payments. And that was why, with nothing but a short note of explanation, Joan left home as soon as she graduated from high school, with her passport and just enough money in her pocket to get to New Zealand. Joan's first job there was picking fruit on a strawberry farm. From there, she saw the rest of the world one country at a time. She didn't give her mother a second thought until she got the phone call three years later from Beth. And after the funeral, she had hoped never to think of her mother again.

Joan had often worried that she would turn out like her mother, but so far so good. She had a self-imposed two-drink limit, but she rarely even drank that much. Experience had taught her to become more careful about the men that she dated. She hadn't always been like that. She had a bit of a reputation as a teenager for being a "sure thing." This wasn't strictly true, but the boys at school usually got further with her than the other girls in her class. With no one telling her what was right and what was wrong, she had very few boundaries, but she quickly learnt not to believe everything she heard from the boys at school and, later, the men that she met. She had a few flings while overseas but never anything serious, and that's the way she had wanted it to stay.

After she settled back in Australia and started uni, she was much too busy studying and working to date much. Over the years, she developed a pretty good screening system for the men she did see. By the third date, she knew whether she was interested enough to continue seeing a man, but most of them fell by the wayside.

The first date was almost no indication at all of what someone was truly like. Most people were on their best behaviour, trying to impress. She always assumed most of what they said was only partially true and that they would have to revise their stories later. The second date often revealed if they were cheap, broke, "between projects right now," (code for unemployed), or just dull. If they told the same stories about themselves on the second date or talked about the one that had gotten away, they were out. If they ever suggested going back to her place after dinner, then they absolutely had no chance.

The third date was the crucial one. By now, they had let their guard down a little. This was when you found out if their mothers still ironed their shirts for them and made their lunches every day because they still lived at home. This wasn't so bad in their early twenties, but as they approached their thirties and beyond, this was a major red flag—or the ones who wanted lots of children and a house in the suburbs. Great for many women but that life wasn't for Joan. She never wanted to be that responsible for another human being and understood how easy it was to "stuff it up." She always thought it was selfish to have a baby she didn't really want just to make another person happy. And as she got older, so did the men, which meant it became even more important by the third date to weed out the ones still living with their mothers in their forties (eek!), the divorced men who were bitter and trapped in vicious custody battles, and the men who were separated and might go back to their wives. There were also the married men who were testing the waters and seeing what was out there, and then there were the serial cheaters. She could usually spot them a mile away, but in one instance, a man had happily told her he was married and looking for something on the side on their first date. She had stood up and left the restaurant without looking back. Only one married man had slipped through the net, and thankfully, Joan had never slept with him. They had made it to the seventh date before he got a call in the middle of a movie from his wife, letting him know he was needed at the emergency room immediately. Their eleven-year-old son had appendicitis. He never called again.

And although Joan never wanted children, she did want someone. She was thirty-nine now. She had been out there and seen the world. She was a success at her chosen career, and she relied on no one to provide for her, but friends were no longer enough. She wanted to come home at night to someone who knew her better than anyone else on earth and who had missed her while she was gone. Where she was going to find that rare man, she had no idea. She wanted a decent man who could actually fall in love and stay that way—one who wasn't burdened down by exes and disappointment or someone who was terrified of making some sort of commitment. Now that would be a truly mythical creature. With everything that had happened this last year that had kept her friends distracted and sad and with her inability to meet anyone worth spending more than one evening with, Joan realized that this had been the loneliest year of her life.

Chapter 4
Caroline
6:23 pm 22 June 2012

Caroline surveyed the formal lounge, smoothing a cushion and straightening a picture above the mantle that had dared to move. The bar was stocked with people's favourite drinks, and crystal glasses reflected the light thrown from the chandelier. Flowers adorned the dining-room table, which was set for her dinner guests. When everything looked perfect and she had made sure the fire was ready to light later, she began the final walk through the house, as she always did before she had guests. She never left anything to chance, so starting in the foyer, she made her way through her extensive home until she ended up in the kitchen.

Looking at the list on the bench, she was satisfied that almost everything had a red line drawn through it. Caroline liked lists. Every morning, she sat down with her cup of tea and wrote down the tasks that needed completing for the day. She also had lists for the coming week and the month. The largest and most important list was the one for Christmas, compiled at the start of October. Not one detail was overlooked, from the cards she had designed and made exclusively for her to the kind of paper the presents would be wrapped in. Every year, the cards matched the gift wrapping, and people were now in the habit of checking with Caroline about what theme she had chosen before they brought presents into her home. By December first, the house was completely decorated, cards were ready to send, and the presents were wrapped and under the tree. There were never any last-minute gifts to purchase, and Caroline refused to go near a shopping centre in the last two weeks of December except to buy food. The menu for Christmas dinner was written, and new recipes had already been tested in November. But the most important event was the Christmas party that Caroline threw every year on the first Saturday night in December. Business associates, neighbours, and friends were invited. It was considered an honour to be asked to the Andersons' annual party, and if somehow a person fell off the list of invitees, then he or she would spend the next year trying to get back on.

The menu for tonight had been a challenge even for Caroline, who felt she was capable of cooking almost anything, but she had decided the occasion deserved her very best. She hadn't always been a good cook, but when she saw how pleased Adam was by exquisite food, she had taken every class she could find and practised until she could make any meal he desired perfectly. If Adam ate something in a restaurant that took his fancy, she would track down every version of the recipe until she found the best one. Once she had that recipe, it was carefully copied down and hidden away from prying eyes. Caroline almost never shared her recipes, especially the ones that she had played around with and could make even better than the chef who invented them.

Tonight, her dinner guests would start with lobster thermidor. That would be followed by duck a l'orange with honeyed baby carrots, potatoes dauphinoise, and green beans in a garlic and butter sauce. These two courses didn't present too much of a problem. Most of the preparation had been done over the last two days and came down to timing and, of course, not overcooking the duck. Choosing to make chocolate soufflés for dessert might not have been her best idea, but they had always been a family favourite and were served on special occasions. They needed to be prepared and cooked fresh tonight. All the ingredients were carefully measured and ready to go, but it meant Caroline would need to work fast between the entrée and the main course to get them in the oven so that they were ready for serving at nine o'clock. She knew she could do it. She had practised last week, and the dessert had been finished right on time. Adam had suggested that if she insisted with going ahead tonight, she should have gotten some help in, but that wasn't Caroline's way. And there was always the chance that tonight would prove too much for her, and she might be grateful for the time alone in her kitchen. She hoped that would not be the case, but as always, Caroline accounted for every situation, even the unlikely ones.

Caroline studied her new kitchen, thrilled with how it had come out after she redesigned it six months ago. It was everything she had wanted. The benches were made of a heavy stainless steel that made cleaning a breeze. It was cook's kitchen, where she had a place for every appliance ever invented. The new butler's pantry meant that she could hide the mess if she needed to—not that this ever happened. Caroline discouraged guests from visiting the kitchen if she was cooking, and the indulgence of two dishwashers meant that as soon as one was filled, she could turn it on and start filling the next one—no dirty dishes waiting on her bench. Adam had argued with her about needing two identical appliances, but she had gotten her way, and he had later conceded it was a good idea when they entertained.

Adam. Caroline didn't know what to do about Adam. She had fallen in love with him when she was seventeen, and she had only fallen deeper as the years had gone by. She heard other women talk about how they had become bored with their husbands and craved something new and exciting. This had never happened to Caroline. Until last year, she had woken up every morning knowing she was blessed to have Adam as her husband, and she spent her days making him as happy and comfortable as she could. She was very aware that he was no longer happy, and she didn't know how to fix it. Their lives had changed forever, and instead of coming together and sharing their grief the way they needed to, Adam had pulled away from her. She thought back to a year ago as she checked her watch. It had been almost this time that the doorbell rang, and life as she knew it was over. Her reaction had been predictable, but Adam's had not. She hadn't realized that someone could become so cold, so closed up. And day by day, they had drawn apart until their interaction took on a businesslike nature. They talked about their son, Michael, and Caroline's latest decorating project. They talked about his job and the state of the economy, but Adam never once asked her how she was coping or if there was anything he could do to help her. Each time Caroline tried to ask him what he needed or offered him her love and support, he shut her down and drew himself away a little more. Caroline knew at the moment that she was alone, but it didn't stop her from hoping that one day Adam would come to terms with what had happened and let her back into his life. She was ready to begin the healing process, if that was possible at all. Tonight was going to be a big step for her. Exactly one year on, she needed to get on with her life. It would be impossible to forget nor did she want to, but it was time to stop fantasising that it had never happened and that their lives were still the same. Tomorrow morning, she intended to wake up and feel ready—ready to continue with life.

She heard the front door open, and Adam's voice got louder as he moved inside. "I'm home. Six-thirty, as requested. Are you here? Caroline. Michael. Dad's home." Caroline stepped out of the kitchen and into the hall so he could see her.

"Hello, darling. Michael's upstairs in his room. He told me he wasn't going to come down for dinner, so I was hoping you could have a word with him," Caroline requested.

Adams hand reached up to his dark, wavy hair and ran his fingers back through it. He always did that when he was stalling for time and looking for an answer. *Should I do what she's asking?* he thought. The last thing he wanted was to have a confrontation with his son when he actually agreed with him.

"Why should he come down? He's made his feelings about tonight very clear, as have I. I don't see how having people here tonight is going to make us feel better, and there is absolutely nothing to celebrate. It was a ridiculous idea, and you've guilted me into agreeing to this dinner, but leave Michael out of it. He's seventeen years old, and if he wants to be alone, then let him. I'll check on him, but I'm not talking him into doing anything he doesn't want to." Adam took several steps up the stairs, hoping to end the conversation with his wife.

"Adam" she quietly called out.

"I know. Get changed and be down here by seven. I'm a grown man. I think I know how to behave by now," he spat out, wishing she would just leave him alone.

"No. I was just going to ask you if you wouldn't mind lighting the fire. It's ready to go, and I thought it might give the room a cosy feel tonight."

"Well, it wouldn't be any good if people didn't feel cosy, would it? Have to have everything perfect for our guests tonight." He continued up the stairs, not caring about anything that was going to happen tonight.

"Never mind. I'll do it myself," she said to Adam's retreating back, not sure he'd heard her and sure he didn't care about what she had to say if he had. Caroline blinked away her tears. This was not the time to cry, but later she would need to. She didn't know what she had done to deserve such hostility from her husband. When he bothered to speak to her, he looked through her. His eyes would stare at her face, but there was no connection, and she wondered if he had any love at all for the woman he had been married to for seventeen years. When they first met at school all those years ago, she thought he had been the kindest person she had ever known. He included anyone who was interested in hanging out with him, and almost everyone was because of his ability to make them feel good about themselves. He had made some of the most tedious classes fun to be in because he knew how to have a joke with the teachers without taking it too far. Caroline had craved fun, probably because she knew she wasn't any at all. She grew up in such a serious environment. Her parents were so driven and focused only on achievements and "reaching one's goals." Caroline was expected to go to a top university and become something important, like a doctor or a lawyer. If they could have afforded it, Caroline's parents would have sent her to a private school. It pained them that illness had turned them into a one-income family and that their dreams for both Caroline and her brother would have to be achieved with a public-school education instead of the exclusive one they had planned and worked towards. She still thought of them as sad, small people. They lived a quiet life in the tiny unit they had moved into once their children had left home. Her father had spent so much time and money trying to find a cure for her mother's illness that they had not been able to afford to stay in the big family home she had grown up in. Nobody knew what was wrong with her mother—chronic pain from an unknown cause. Most doctors they saw came to the conclusion that it was all in Esther's head and referred her to a psychologist. Caroline's very proper father Edward had no patience for that kind of ridiculous notion, and Esther remained undiagnosed and unable to work. Caroline had noticed that her mother's health had improved once her husband retired and focused all his attention on her, and Caroline believed that the doctors had been right and that her mother was just looking for attention.

To a girl like Caroline, a boy like Adam had been a breath of fresh air. He teased her the same way he did the other girls in their class and didn't taunt her for being too serious or stuck-up. Most people thought she was a control freak, but that wasn't true. She just liked things to be ordered. She had desperately hoped to catch Adam's eye in a romantic way, but she never did at the time. He seemed happy to keep their relationship only on friendly terms. When he started dating Jilly Mancini, she knew she had no chance. Even though she was younger, Jilly was wild and beautiful, and every boy in school was after her. Nobody else ever turned Caroline's head or made her heart race the way Adam did. Caroline finished high school without ever having a boyfriend. It wasn't because she wasn't pretty—a few brave boys had tried and failed. She just wasn't going to settle, but her slim figure and long, blonde hair hadn't been enough to lure Adam. While everyone else at school was getting perms and wearing heavy makeup, she adopted a classic look. As she grew older, she had honed her style until she became the envy of the women who met her, and many a friend had tried and failed to emulate her look. She was finally considered the woman to be, even though in high school, she was the one most likely to be forgotten.

Caroline was twenty the next time she saw Adam. She had resisted her parent's attempts to force her to attend a uni and get a degree; instead, choosing to work as a receptionist for a fashionable interior design company. She was completing a TAFE course in decorating part time while still living with her parents. She was desperate to leave, waking up every morning to their disapproving stares when she headed out to work, reminding her how let down they felt by her choices. It had been completely by chance that Caroline and Adam met up again. Caroline had been heading into the city on the train, and Adam had been on his way to a job interview at an investment firm for an internship while completing his degree. She hadn't even noticed him, her focus on the latest edition of *Vogue Living* magazine. When he sat down opposite her and asked if she was Caroline Clancy, she knew right then when she saw who it was that she had been given a second chance. She was going to do whatever it took to keep him forever. She had never forgotten Adam, and any man she dated had been compared to him. So far, none had even come close to the lofty standards that had been set in her mind. For the first time ever, she asked a man for his phone number, and he gave it to her immediately. Whether this had been a good or a bad thing for Adam, he would never know. Life isn't like one of those choose-your-own-adventure books, where you pick the ending you want, they had all read as children. If you didn't like the outcome in the book, you could go back, make a different choice, and see if that was a better ending to the story. Real life wasn't like that. The chance meeting with Caroline had propelled him into a completely different life than the one he had envisioned for himself, but he didn't know anything different, and except for the last year, it had been wonderful.

That meeting had changed Caroline's life as well. She was in a relationship with the man of her teenage dreams. When she was with Adam, she felt like a better version of herself. He made her take chances she never would have on her own, and for the first time since she was a very little child, when all the life and laughter in her had been pushed down and suffocated by her oppressive parents, she learnt how to have some fun. She knew she was not the only girl in his life, but she never mentioned it, afraid to come across as possessive, and Adam never talked about anyone else. But after a few months, they seemed to disappear, and she knew she had his full attention. But no matter what she did or how unsubtlety she indicated that she was interested in a future with him, he never made any kind of formal commitment to her, and he never said he loved her. When he started talking about moving to Sydney, where he thought he would have better opportunities, he never once suggested her going with him. Caroline knew she was running out of time. So for the one and only time in her life, Caroline did something so underhanded and so calculated, she was still filled with shame whenever she allowed herself to think about it, which was not often. She never told Adam the truth, and she didn't even tell Beth, who knew everything about her. It had been the oldest trick in the book. Women throughout history had used it as a way to secure a man, and Adam had completely believed her when she told him the pregnancy was an accident. Everyone did because Caroline never lied. Well, almost everyone. Adam's mother absolutely believed that Caroline had orchestrated the situation, and until the day she died two years ago, she had brought it up at every family event, her anger and hatred running deep. She constantly reminded Caroline that her son's long-dead father had come from a rich family, and Adam deserved a wife of a much better class. She had wanted someone better for her beloved son, but Caroline always denied the accusations made by Vera. While Adam didn't step in between his mother and Caroline the way she wished he would, he always believed his wife had told him the truth.

Adam asked her to marry him the minute she told him about the baby. There was no discussion about giving the baby up or recriminations about being careless with contraception. From the age of ten, he had grown up without a father, and he wouldn't do that to his own child. Together they had lived the loveliest of lives. They had been poor at first but tried to look on it as an adventure. Caroline didn't care where she lived. She would have gone anywhere Adam went, but luckily that had only been up. The success of the stock market during the '90s had given Adam, who had become a stock broker, a very comfortable lifestyle. When Adam's paternal grandfather died ten years ago, naming him as the benefactor instead of passing his wealth to his daughter-in-law, whom he despised, it had left Adam very well off.

Adam's grandfather had never understood why his only son had married such a bitter, mean girl, and he couldn't stomach the thought of her receiving even one of his hard earned pennies.

The inheritance meant they could buy the home they had always dreamed of in the prestigious suburb of Kooyong. Caroline spent her days being a mother and a very happy and loving wife. She decorated their home beautifully, staying away from trends, preferring her own elegant but comfortable style. Adam could find no fault with his life. Caroline showered him with love and affection, and in return, he did his best to love Caroline the way she wanted. It hadn't been what he had planned for his life, but he knew he was a lucky man. When they looked around at the other couples they knew, plagued with divorce and infidelity, problems with their children, or money issues, they couldn't imagine that anything could interfere with the perfect life they had built together. Oh, how wrong they had been.

Caroline now knew something was going to have to change and quickly. She could feel him slipping away from her. A baby had bonded him to her once, but even if it was a possibility now, she didn't think that would work again, and she didn't want him that way.

With everything in the kitchen under control, Caroline walked through the house. It was five minutes to seven, and people would be arriving very soon. She stopped in the lounge and put a match to the ready fireplace—the finishing touch to the perfect room. It was satisfying to survey her beautiful home. In the last year, every room had been redecorated. Caroline had worked every minute of the day and most nights until she fell into bed exhausted. Adam had stopped commenting on the money she had spent very early on in the process. There was no stopping her, and anyway, all his energy went into getting up each day and breathing in and out until he could go to bed and hide away from the world and his family, wishing everything could go back to the way it had been when his life had been perfect.

Actually, that was not strictly true. There was one room in their house that had not been decorated. No one was supposed to go in, and nothing had been touched for a year. But Caroline couldn't think about that today. Maybe tomorrow. The doorbell rang for the first time that evening, and as she made her way to the foyer to greet her first guest, Caroline realized that no matter how hard she had worked and no matter how much she had rushed through each day, wishing for it to end, this had been the longest year of her life.

Chapter 5
Isabelle—one year ago

I can't tell you how excited I am. Mum is finally letting me out on my own. Without her or Dad. No one else's mum is going to be there either. Just me and my bestie. I always call her that. I heard it on *Big Bang*, which is the coolest show. It's what Amy calls Penny. I'm not allowed to watch *Big Bang*. It was on TV at home once, and Mum came in and watched it with me. It wasn't even halfway through before she turned it off and said, "Isabelle, I never want to have that show on in my house again. It is not appropriate for a twelve-year-old girl." Mum doesn't think there's much left that is appropriate for me, and sometimes I worry I might actually die of boredom, and I think about watching it anyway. But if I break the rules, Mum gives out one of her punishments. She actually has a rules list, and if I watched that show after being told not to, I would be banned from TV forever. Now I watch it at school on Heather's iPod. Her Mum lets he do anything she wants, but my Mum says that's because she's divorced and she's compensating. I don't really know what that means but I could do with some compensating around here sometimes.

So me and Heather (Doesn't she have the coolest name? Mine sounds like something out of those old books Mum likes to read.), we're going to the movies this afternoon and then were going to have afternoon tea at a cafe on Camberwell Road. We're going to Gold Class at the Rivoli theatres, which means those big chairs, and people bring you snacks and drinks if you order them. When Mum and Dad go to the movies, they only ever go to Gold Class because Mum says it's more comfortable, but I don't think she likes being stuck in the dark with all those people. Michael says she doesn't like regular people. Heather's Mum is paying for everything, and when we're finished, we can call her on Heather's phone (I have to wait to get one when I'm older because I don't go anywhere alone. Whose fault is that anyway, Mum?), and she'll bring me home.

Heather's mum said I can call her Jo, but when Mum's around, I call her Mrs. Donaldson. I wonder why she calls herself Mrs. because she's not married anymore. Mum's so weird with names. She makes all the kids of her friends call her Auntie Caroline because she thinks it's more respectful than just Caroline. And kids from school have to call her Mrs. Anderson, even Heather, and sometimes she laughs at Mum and I laugh at her too for being silly, but then when Heather's gone, I feel bad. I just wish Mum knew how hard she's making my life. Everyone says their parents embarrass them, but I think Mum does it on purpose.

Sometimes at school, if Mum's been helping in the class, which she does as much as she can, the other kids tease me and call me Miss Anderson. I'll tell you what Mum doesn't like being called: ma'am. Some guy called her that in the shopping centre once, and boy, did she get cross. I asked her why, and she said ma'am was what you called old ladies. I wouldn't tell her this, but I was thinking, *News flash, Mum, you are an old lady*. And she won't let us call ourselves anything else, like Izzy or Mike. I really like Izzy. It's much more fun than old-lady Isabelle, but Mum said if she had wanted me to be called that, then it would be on my birth certificate. My dad's so nice because when I was a kid, he called me his little Izzy Bee. I'm too old for that now, but when Mum's not around, sometimes he calls me Izzy because he knows I like it.

Michael, my brother, did I tell you about him? He's a pretty good brother for a boy; he has a special name for Mum. He calls her Lady Caroline, but never to her face. I'm not sure what would happen to him if she ever heard that. Dad heard him say it once, and he smiled but told Michael that if Mum ever heard him say that, he would be out on his ear. Now that's a stupid thing to say 'cause it makes no sense. Mum's always complaining that our generation can't speak English, but we understand each other just fine. It's the old people with stupid sayings that are hard to understand. I asked Dad what "out on his ear" meant, and he said Mum would be very cross and have to kick Michael out. That would be bad because I'd be alone here, and there would be no one to have any fun with. Michael lets me listen to music in his room sometimes with him, except that I don't really like it because its rap, and I don't think rap is cool. I think if Mum knew the words to the songs, she'd throw out his iPod, but she wouldn't really kick him out of the house. She said we could live at home for as long as we want to. The songs Michael likes have lots of swears in them, and Mum hates swearing. Swearing is definitely on the rules list. Michael says he can't wait to move out so he can have parties and eat toasted sandwiches for dinner every night. That would not be good. If he lets me, I'll go and visit Michael at his new house, but I'll come home for dinner. Mum might be serious all of the time, but she's the best cook I know.

We try really hard to get out of going if Beth ever asks us to dinner. She's a very bad cook, and me and Michael wonder why she's so big. If she tasted her own food, wouldn't that put her off eating? Then she could lose weight. Not that I would ever say that in front of Mum because Beth is her bestie, not that she would call her that. Beth has two besties—Mum and Auntie Joan. She's not my real auntie, but I have to call her that if Mum's around. That's not a lot because Mum doesn't like Joan much. I'm not sure why because I think for someone so old, Joan is awesome. She's so pretty, and she wears the best clothes. She's not married, and she has no kids, but once she told me if she did have a daughter, she would want her to be just like me. So it's almost worth going to Beth's for a horrible dinner just to see Joan. Once Michael called Mum Lady Caroline, and Joan heard it. She laughed so hard that she started snorting, and some of her drink spat across the room. That was gross but funny to watch, and it made me like her even more.

Anyway back to the movie today. We were going to see *Bridesmaids*, but Mum looked it up on Google and said no way. So instead we have to see *Spy Kids*, which is so embarrassing, but at least it in Gold Class. I'm so over having to watch movies my mum approves of, but it's worth it to go out. Sarah, that's Beth's daughter, saw *Spy Kids* and said it was for babies. She thinks everything is for babies. I once heard Mum tell Dad that Beth and Tom needed to get Sarah under control or she was going to be a nightmare before she was fifteen. If anyone asked me, I'd tell them she's already a bit of a nightmare. We used to be friends when we were little, but now she teases me and calls me little Izzy Bee, but not nice how Dad used to. I wonder if Beth would let Sarah see *Bridesmaids*. She probably would unless Mum found out and told her the rating. Then Beth would say no cause she always listens to Mum, and then Sarah would be really mad. She already doesn't like Mum much.

Don't get me wrong. I love my mum. She's just a bit hard to get on with and expects us all to be perfect like she is. I don't think she's ever made a mistake. That's her favourite word in the world: "perfect." She's very beautiful with long, blonde hair. Dad says I look just like her, so I guess I must be pretty too, but it's hard to tell. Boys like Heather more than they like me.

Mum says that's good, and I should hold out for the best one like she did with Dad. Mum has a lot of fancy clothes that look nice on her, but they don't look very comfortable. There are all these new fluro T-shirts in the stores, and I tried to talk her into buying one, but she said if she didn't wear it the first time around, there was no way she was going to wear it now. She said they were from the '80s. That was last century, which was a really long time ago. She's always worried about looking old. Michael said it's because when I was born, they had to do an operation or she might have died. I can't remember what it's called. A hysto-something, and he said she's worried it will affect her hormones and make her look older than she is. I looked it up on the net once, and that's why there are only two kids in our family. Although Mum's always telling us we are the perfect family, so she might not have wanted anymore anyway.

My granny—she died last year—she was always talking to Mum about when Michael was born. Granny gets really angry about it, which I don't understand because she loved Michael, and I thought she would be pleased Mum and Dad had him. Dad once told her to stop bringing up old stories that weren't true. I'm not sure what they were talking about. Parents do that a lot—talk about stuff, and we only find out half the story. I do know that Mum didn't like Granny though. She wasn't very sad when Granny died, and she didn't cry at the funeral. Dad was sad, but he didn't cry. I've never seen him cry, and he once said crying wasn't something real men did. He did say lots of nice things about Granny, like how she had raised him alone after his dad died. I guess that's why I only had one grandad and two grannies. We don't see our other granny or granddad much, and they don't seem very interested in us. Dad's mum was always asking us over, and I think she would have lived with us if she could have. But that would be weird because her and Mum did not get on. Michael said that on the morning when we found out Granny had died, he heard Mum singing that song from the *Wizard of Oz*, the one about the wicked witch dying. I think he made that up. Mum's not that mean.

Oops. Better go. I hear the doorbell. That will be Jo, and I can't wait another second for today to start. I'll let you know how it was all later.

~~~

I'm back. The movie was okay but going to Gold Class was ace. They treated us like grown-ups, and the ticket guy was so cute. He called us both "young lady," which is pretty stupid, but his boss probably makes him. It's really busy at the café on Camberwell Road where we're having afternoon tea. We got a seat outside so we can see all the people going by. I'm having a brownie and a hot chocolate because it's pretty cold out here. At least it's not raining today. Lots of people are around, so Mum has nothing to worry about. No one's going to kidnap me from here.

Jo is coming soon. Heather rang her and told her which café we are at, and now she's just talking and talking. She likes a boy at our school called Devon, and that's all I ever hear about, but it hasn't stopped her from pointing out every cute boy who walks past our table. If they look at her, she flips her hair and smiles at them. I wonder what Devon would think about that. I don't really like any of the boys at school. Sarah's big brother is kind of cute, but I don't think he even knows I'm alive. He's fifteen, so he's too old anyway. I might take Mum's advice for a change and wait for someone a bit like my Dad—someone special.

I can see Jo now. She's walking down the street towards us but not quickly. She must have seen something in the shoe shop she likes. She has a lot of shoes. Heather let me look in her wardrobe once, and there were, like, a million pairs. I don't know how she walks in any of them. They're very high and pointy.

She just saw us and waved. I was about to wave back, but all of a sudden, people seem to be yelling and running. It must be that car. It's going very fast, and I think it's on the wrong side of the road. Its horn is beeping, but I don't know why it's beeping at us. He's the one that should be getting on the right side of the road. It looks like its heading straight for the footpath. I think I need to move fast because the man driving it looks like he might be asleep. I'm trying to move but my scarf is caught on the chair, and when I try and tug, it pulls around my neck. Heather is screaming at me, and I'm trying, but I can't get free.

I can hear people yelling all around me. When I open my eyes, there is a man cutting open my shirt. I should be embarrassed with all these people watching, but I hurt too much. It's very hard to breathe and not like when I get asthma sometimes, but like something heavy fell on me. The man who cut open my shirt is talking to me. I can see his face, and I'm trying to listen over all the noise. He asked my name, and I know it's Isabelle, but I can't seem to say it out loud. I must be crying because my face is all wet. When I try and lift my arm to wipe it, I can't make it move. I try to talk again, but all that comes out is sort of a moan. The pain is not so bad now, so I must be all right. And I think maybe I'm floating. The man is saying he's given me some drugs to stop me from hurting. That's good. I can hear Jo in the distance, and someone is crying. If it's not me, it's probably Heather. I'm so glad she's my bestie. I hope it's forever, like Mum and Beth. I can't see anything anymore. I guess I have my eyes closed, and it doesn't hurt, but I can feel something pushing on my chest. Everyone around must be gone because I can't hear them anymore. Even Heather. Boy, are we going to have a story to tell when we get back to school, and I promise to tell you all about it too.

I don't like it how I feel so alone right now.

And so tired.

I wish my mum was here.

Chapter 6

Caroline straightened her back and whispered, "Show time," to herself as she always did when she had guests. She opened the door with a welcoming smile on her face, only to feel it disappear when she saw who her first guest was.

"Oh, Joan." She hesitated before stepping aside and making space for Joan to enter through the door and into the foyer. "Welcome to our home. This is your first time here, isn't it?" She leaned over and gave her a perfunctory kiss on the cheek, wondering for the hundredth time what had possessed her to invite Joan when she hated being anywhere near the woman. But Beth had insisted, and when Caroline said no, Beth had looked her directly in the eye and asked, "What would Isabelle have wanted?"

"It is. And it's beautiful." Joan did a 360-degree turn, taking in the high ceilings and the imposing chandelier that hung from what had to be the most ornate ceiling rose she had ever seen. It had been dark and cold outside, but the moment she stepped inside, she felt warm and welcome. She recognized the elegance of the intricate parquet floor and the original artwork that adorned the walls. No expense had been spared here, but she didn't feel like she was in a museum but rather a much-loved home.

Joan followed Caroline through to the formal lounge on the right while taking in the imposing staircase that led upstairs. The beautifully restored floors extended to the lounge room, and Joan saw that the rugs on the floor wouldn't have been out of place in a stately home in Europe. A roaring fire was situated between two sets of doors that were closed, but Joan could see that they opened out to the large patio that had been lit up to highlight the extensive gardens. Joan could imagine the wonderful parties that had been thrown outside in the summer, not just by Caroline and Adam, but by the other families who had lived here over the century that this house had stood.

"How old is this house?" Joan asked, in awe that someone she knew could live in such luxury. "I'm guessing late 1800s."

"1893 to be exact," she heard from behind and turned to see Adam standing in the door way watching her. "Hello, stranger," he said, taking quick strides towards her and enveloping her in his arms. He kissed her gently on her cheek and then pulled her tighter into his hug. She could smell the alcohol on his breath and stepped back. She hated the smell of scotch—her mother's drink of choice—and still found herself repulsed by it.

She held Adam at arm's length. He was still desperately handsome. Looking at him was like looking at a movie star from a long-gone era. He was greying a little at the temples, but it certainly didn't make him look any older—not that she had ever been interested. He had always been a little too polished for her, but they had become great friends in school. Joan had never understood how Caroline had snagged him when he had never shown any romantic interest in her when they had all been at school together. But then Joan had always seen Caroline as the ice queen and didn't know what Beth saw in her either. Joan had thought Beth was joking when she told her that Adam and Caroline were expecting a baby and were getting married. She had always wondered if the baby had been more planned than

Adam believed, but it was none of her business, and she had always kept her thoughts to herself.

"Hello, Adam. Still gorgeous as ever. Caroline should be careful someone else doesn't snap you up." As soon as the words left her mouth, she wished she could scoop them up and shove them back in. Old habits die hard, and she had never been able to resist messing with Caroline.

"Now, Joan. You'll get me in trouble if you keep talking like that." Adam smiled but didn't look at his wife. He knew that she agonized about other women making advances towards him, and it had happened on the odd occasion, but he always made it clear that he was married and not interested. "This is your first time here, isn't it?" he asked as he walked behind the bar, picking up a decanter and refilling the empty glass he had been holding in his hand.

"It is. You must have an amazing decorator."

Adam raised his glass towards Caroline who had been standing quietly watching the exchange between her husband and the woman he knew she despised. How could he be so familiar with Joan—kissing her, hugging her, and laughing with her—when he hadn't touched his own wife in months?

"Caroline did the whole thing. Every room in this house has been decorated to complete perfection by my clever wife," he said, but the tone of his voice was not one of pride. The tension in the air was thick, and Joan wished she could disappear into the floor. Adam took another swallow of his drink while Caroline stood silently, offering no defence for her husband's bad manners.

Do something, Joan thought to herself and turned back to Caroline. "Well it's beautiful. You have a real talent for decorating. Do you do this professionally? Because if you don't, you should. I get asked all the time for recommendations from clients, and I'd be more than happy to tell people about your work."

"Thank you, Joan, but I'm much too busy here to trudge around antique stores helping clueless people find *just* the right table. I'm a mother and a wife, and that keeps me very busy."

"And besides," Adam piped in from the bar as he poured his third drink for the evening. "If Caroline was out working all day, when would she have time to spend all my money? And what would we do if the entire house wasn't redecorated every year? Imagine how deprived I'd feel if I had to sit on the same furniture two years in a row."

Joan had never seen Adam behave so appallingly to anyone before, and she was shocked that he would speak to his wife this way—so rude, so bitter. Desperate to change the subject, Joan asked Adam if he would mind getting her a glass of wine.

As Adam poured Joan a glass of chardonnay, the doorbell rang, and Caroline left them alone to answer it. *Please be Beth*, Joan silently begged as she settled on a stool next to the bar.

"You were very harsh with her, Adam."

"I'm surprised to hear you defend her, Joan," he replied. "Last time I checked, you weren't exactly a fan of my wife's."

"I'm not, but I've always been a fan of yours, and no matter what, you were always a gentleman." She pointed her finger towards the glass he had half drained in the last two minutes. "Maybe you should lay off those or at least slow down. I can't imagine what you've been through in the last year, but drinking won't help, and nobody deserves to be talked to that way."

Adam set his drink back down on the bar, picking up the decanter and slowly pulling out the stopper. He tilted the bottle in his hand and refilled the glass to the top. When he was done, he set the decanter back down and picked up the glass. He took a sip, not breaking eye contact with Joan the whole time.

"I'm a big boy, Joan. I think I'll decide when I've had enough." He knew he was being rude, but he was past caring. Why did everyone think they had the right to tell him how he should behave and how he should feel? It had been going on for a year, and it was enough already. People needed to mind their own business.

Opening the door, Caroline had never been more grateful to see Beth. Falling inside to get away from the cold, Lochie and Sarah threw out a hurried hello before they brushed past their parents going in search of Michael. Or maybe Joan. For some reason, children always gravitated towards her. Caroline had never understood it, especially when Joan didn't seem interested in having children of her own. Isabelle had adored Joan. They had met at Beth's house. By the end of the night, Isabelle and Joan were fast friends, and Caroline couldn't help but feel jealous of the way her daughter chattered and laughed with Joan. She had been aware that sometimes Isabelle rang Joan to talk, and she was always asking her parents to invite her to the parties and dinners they frequently held.

After allowing Caroline to kiss him, Nate disappeared off after his brother and sister. Tom nodded hello and followed his son in search of a drink and, hopefully, some decent male company. One look at Caroline and Beth could see the tension in her face. Most people wouldn't recognize it, but Beth had known her for over thirty years, and she knew when Caroline was upset.

"Are you okay? We can just go if this is too much."

Caroline shook her head. "I'm fine. But Joan's here, so I'd appreciate it if you kept her entertained tonight and out of my way like you promised."

"Sure," she said as she followed Caroline to the lounge. Beth had thought this whole night was a big mistake and that Adam, Caroline, and Michael should have spent it alone, but Caroline had been adamant that this was the way she wanted to spend tonight. Caroline excused herself, saying she needed to check something in the kitchen, and sent Beth in to the lounge. Beth sat in Joan's recently vacated seat and asked Adam for a drink.

Tom was sitting on the couch with Joan, and they were already deep in conversation. Joan was the next best thing to finding another man to talk to. Tom had taken one look at Adam and his seething expression and decided a quick hello would be enough. They hadn't been close friends in school and were only thrown together because of their wives' friendship. It wasn't like Tom didn't like Adam and Caroline, but being in their house was daunting, and he was always terrified of breaking something expensive. Joan was much more relaxed, and he enjoyed talking to her. Only half listening to the story she was telling him about a family she had met while she had been travelling around Greece, he was distracted by the two at the bar. Adam already looked a little worse for wear and with a glass of something that looked like scotch in her hand, he could see that his wife wouldn't be far behind. Tom had nothing against someone having a few drinks, but he had noticed recently that Beth seemed to be at least half way to drunk most nights. He was becoming concerned about her recent habit. He didn't know why she was drinking so much, but he knew that if it didn't stop, he was going to have to address it soon. That was a conversation he wasn't looking forward to. He couldn't see how it would end well—probably the same as all their interactions these days, with angry words, accusations, and no real outcome. But tonight certainly wasn't the night to bring it up. If Adam and Beth carried on the way they had started, he thought they could always put them in a corner together, and they could keep each other entertained.

The doorbell rang once and after a moment, it rang again. Adam looked out over the room and saw that Caroline was nowhere in sight. She was probably in the kitchen checking on dinner, so he stepped from behind the bar and headed for the front door. When he opened it to Jill, he thought he'd never seen her look more dishevelled. Years ago, she had morphed from the wild teenager she had been into an adult who always dressed beautifully. Tonight, her blouse clashed with the skirt she had chosen and her long ringlets had been hastily drawn into a messy ponytail. Her face was thick with makeup but beneath it, her eyes were swollen and red. It looked like she had been crying. He looked out the door, waiting for his friend.

"Where's Chris? Is he still parking the car?"

Jill had spent most of the drive over trying to invent a plausible explanation for why her husband hadn't come but couldn't come up with anything better than an emergency with his parents. Anyone who knew him would never believe that he was still at work, and Adam was the only friend who had stuck by him, so she couldn't use a friend as an excuse.

"He's really sorry, but his mum's not well. She insisted that he came over. You know how he is with her. Always goes running when she asks, so it's just me tonight. I hope that's okay."

"That's weird. He texted me at about five to check that everything was still on for tonight." He pulled out his phone from his pants pocket and checked for any new messages. "I wonder why he didn't let me know he wasn't coming," he said when he saw that there wasn't one.

Jill shrugged her shoulders, pretending she had no explanation while she watched Adam close the door. From behind, she could admire his broad back and slim waist. She had always loved how tall he was. It had been hard for her to find a man taller than her. Chris had matched her height but Adam had always towered over her. She had liked how it made her feel petite even when she knew she really wasn't. When he turned around, he could see her staring at him and wondered if he had something on his face. He brushed his hand over his cheeks and lips. Watching him, Jill remembered that there had been a time when those lips had been hers to kiss.

She reached up and gently kissed him on the cheek. She could smell his aftershave and breathed deeply. He stepped away from her. He knew he'd had a lot to drink and that his judgement probably wasn't very good, but that type of kiss hadn't felt the same as it had when her sister had kissed him hello earlier. She smiled and linked her arm through his.

"Remind me why we broke up again, Adam?" Jill asked, her voice taking on a flirtatious tone.

Adam shook his head, remembering back twenty-two years. "If I recall, it was because you dumped me, and I was heartbroken when you did."

"Well, I must have been out of my mind to let you go. If Caroline ever gets sick of you, give me a call."

Adam disentangled himself from Jill and, with a hesitant laugh, said, "I wouldn't let Caroline hear you talk like that if I was you. Joan's here, so she's already in a bad mood. And I doubt your husband would like to hear that kind of talk either." Adam had no idea what had brought this on. He and Jill never talked about how they had been a couple all those years ago, especially not in front of their spouses. It wasn't a secret, but Caroline had always felt a little threatened by Jill and was uneasy when Jill was around her husband. But once his old friend, Chris, had started dating her and they had married, Caroline seemed to relax. Two years ago, the couples had started spending more time together. That would have to change if Jill continued flirting with him—unless he had misunderstood her. Maybe Joan had been right. Perhaps he should lay off the drinking tonight and just focus on getting through dinner.

What is wrong with you? Jill thought to herself. *Flirting with a married man hours after kicking your own husband out of home for being a cheat.* She knew she had embarrassed Adam and that she had embarrassed herself. When they walked into the lounge together, Caroline, who had returned from the kitchen, saw that her final guests had arrived and announced that dinner was served. As the others found a seat, she pulled Jill aside.

"Where's Chris?"

"I'm sorry, Caroline, but he couldn't make it tonight. He sends his apologies, but something came up last moment."

Caroline was sure that Jill wasn't telling her the truth, but she didn't have time to think about it now. Beth was still at the bar, helping herself to another drink. Adam was seated at the head of the table, and Caroline gave a quiet sigh of relief when she saw that he had switched to water. As she began to serve, Michael slipped into the room and took the vacant seat beside Lochie. Caroline leaned over, kissed the top of his head, and quietly whispered in his ear. "Thank you."

He nodded and whispered back, "She belonged to me too, Mum. She would want us to be together." Gently squeezing his shoulder, she stepped back, hoping to catch her husband's eye. Maybe Adam wouldn't be so angry if he saw that Michael was okay with tonight, but he appeared to be in deep conversation with Tom and never looked in her direction.

Caroline served the lobster, and soon the room fell quiet, except for the sound of Ella Fitzgerald singing softly in the background and the odd murmur of pleasure at the delicious dinner. When her guests had finished the first course, the noise level in the room increased as people fell into conversation. Jill leaned over the table to Beth, who was sitting opposite her.

"Are you busy tomorrow morning?"

Beth shrugged her shoulders. "Not really. Nate's got Auskick, but Tom's taking him. Why?"

"I need you to come with me to the doctor tomorrow."

"Isn't that your husband's job? And where is he tonight?"

"I'll explain tomorrow. I'll pick you up at nine, all right?"

"Fine, but you better call me at eight to make sure I'm awake." Beth looked Jill over, thinking how odd she was dressed tonight, and it looked like she'd put her makeup on in the dark with a trowel. She didn't have time to think it through as a glass clinking loudly caught her attention.

Caroline rose and tapped her water glass to catch their attention. When she saw that all eyes were on her, she began the short speech that she hoped she could get out with no tears.

"I want to thank you all for coming tonight. You all know why we're here—to remember our beautiful girl, Isabelle. I asked each of you to join us..." she said as she looked to Adam and then to Michael "...to say thank you for all of your love and support over the past year. I hope each of you know how important you were to Isabelle and how much comfort you have brought to our family. I know I couldn't have made it through this year without you. So please join me in a toast as we remember her tonight."

Each person picked up a glass and raised it in remembrance. Silently, they reflected on how they had felt when they heard the news. It had come as a terrible shock to them all, and no one would disagree that a gap had been left in their lives.

Adam knew the right thing to do would be to stand and say something, but he couldn't bring himself to join in with this farce of an evening. This room full of people he was forced to spend this horrible night with thought they were sad. They had no idea how sad a person could be. Every time he walked past her closed bedroom door or found something in the house that had belonged to Isabelle, he crashed into the knowledge all over again that she was gone. Nothing would ever be right again, and he had no idea how he was supposed to raise a glass in toast to his lovely girl and then move on. It wasn't possible.

Caroline had hoped that Adam might say something. He had refused when she asked him earlier, but she thought he might have changed his mind. Instead, he sat silently at the head of the table with his head bowed, fiddling with the linen napkin he held. She pushed her chair back and began clearing the plates to a trolley that had been standing in the corner. When she was done, she caught everyone's attention again.

"I'll be out with the main course shortly, but I need to spend a little time in the kitchen finishing off dessert. Please help yourselves to the bar, and if you can't find what you want, ask Adam. He'll be happy to help you." She waited for him to respond, which he did with an imperceptible nod, but she could see he had no intention of helping her tonight.

Beth, who was always willing to help, even if she wasn't very good at it, called out to Caroline. "Would you like a hand in the kitchen?" Before Caroline had a chance to reject her very kind but terrifying offer, the room erupted into unanimous agreement.

"I'm sure Caroline has it all under control," "Don't let her near your kitchen," and one person even called out, "Please no."

Caroline laughed for the first time that evening. Thankfully, Beth had consumed enough alcohol that she didn't take offence, but it didn't stop her from sticking her tongue out at the whole table. Caroline pushed the trolley down the hall as she heard laughter spill out from the room. Thank you, Beth, for breaking the ice, even if you didn't mean to. She was delighted to hear everyone having a good time. Tonight wasn't meant to be sad, and Isabelle would have thought the situation was hilarious. She had hated Beth's cooking.

Chapter 7

Jill knew she couldn't leave without apologizing to Adam. She found him sitting near the front window, staring out into the darkness. He looked so sad and alone. As the evening had progressed and everyone else had started enjoying themselves, he had withdrawn from the conversation until he stopped speaking all together. When she approached him, he didn't notice, and it took a light shake of his shoulder to get his attention.

"Adam, I'm going."

"'Night, Jill," he said with a weary smile.

"I just wanted to apologize for earlier. I don't know what I was thinking. I shouldn't have flirted like that."

"Don't mention it. This whole night has been strange. I'll be glad when it's over."

"Can I get you anything? Do anything for you?"

"Can you bring her back?" he asked, his voice breaking as he turned back to the window, dismissing Jill.

Having nothing to offer him, she headed back to the dining room to say her final goodnight, wishing she had a way to make his pain disappear. Caroline seemed to be holding up all right, but the old saying "time heals all wounds" wasn't working for Adam. If anything, he was getting worse as time went by.

After saying goodnight, she slipped out quietly. The drive home was uneventful, and she was back in Brighton in fifteen minutes. She let herself in to her dark home. *This is my life now*, she thought. No one to come home to. No one waiting up to see how my day was. The house was silent except for the ticking of a clock. She flicked on a lamp and settled herself on the couch. Maybe some TV could keep her company. Switching between channels, she had two choices. There was a football game on, but she had no interest in that, and one of those ridiculous romantic comedies that she usually didn't bother with. It had already started, but missing the beginning wasn't a big deal, and she could already predict the ending. Two people meet. They fall in love, have a misunderstanding, but at the end, they would rediscover each other and drive off into the sunset together, all happy and sparkly. Two beautiful people whose lives would work out perfectly. Urgh! She turned off the TV in disgust. She couldn't watch those two idiots anymore. Why did women always fall for that rubbish? She was certain that those ridiculous movies were responsible for most of the dissatisfaction women felt with their own lives. How could real life possibly live up to the romantic standard set by Hollywood? She saw it a lot at work—marriages breaking down because of people's unreasonable expectations for each other. Why did they always believe there was someone better out there who could fulfil their needs? And now she was about to join the sad world of divorce. She didn't even want to think of what it would be like out there. A single woman again, but now she was older. And with every day that went by, her chances of having a baby were slipping away.

Climbing into her unmade bed, she felt a chill. She would have to invest in an electric blanket now that there was no one else to warm the bed at night.

Jill lay awake for hours, reliving the confrontation with Chris. Each time she replayed his feeble excuses and imagined him touching another woman, her bitterness and anger embedded themselves a little deeper. It was almost two before she fell into a troubled sleep.

~~~

Joan had left for home shortly after Jill. The evening had taken a pleasant change in direction when Caroline started telling stories about Isabelle. Beth, who had way more to drink than she should have, had a lot of funny stories of her own, and soon the room was erupting in laughter. Joan hadn't known Isabelle for very long, but she had loved spending time with her when she could. She had been funny and kind, and Joan had seen a lot of her father in her. Adam had disappeared straight after dessert, but Joan couldn't blame him. He'd been quiet all through dinner, and Joan's heart broke for him. She couldn't imagine trying to live under the weight of that kind of loss.

When she got back to her terrace in Collingwood, she turned on the TV. The first channel had some stupid rom-com on, so she flicked over to the football match. She had learnt long ago that those kinds of movies played no part in reality. That kind of romance didn't exist in real life, and she was probably about to get another taste of disappointment from David Sanders. She hadn't been able to stop thinking about him all night, but she was sure it had been a waste of time. A man that good looking and successful was bound to have someone, and that someone was probably some bouncy twenty-something named Tiffany.

Joan directed her attention back to the football game, trying to distract herself from thinking about David and the possibility that something might actually happen with him. She had probably misunderstood him when he had asked her out. Back to the game Joan, she thought and stop imagining something that isn't there. It wasn't her team playing, but she was always happy to watch any game. This was a good one. Hawthorn was killing Essendon, and soon she was yelling at the telly. She had missed footy while she had been overseas. She watched until the game ended, and after checking that her house was locked, she headed for bed.

She slipped into her warm bed, grateful for the electric blanket that switched on automatically every night. It had been a very cold winter, and sleeping alone meant there was no one else to warm up the bed. As she drifted off to sleep, she thought about the game she'd just watched. *I really should try to get to the MCG to see some live games this year*, she thought. Her house was within walking distance after all. *Now I just need a man to go with. Maybe if drinks work out with David I could invite him.* Unless of course he was a Carlton supporter. If he was, then they definitely had no kind of future together.

~~~

Tom and Beth were the last to leave. Tom had been ready to go for an hour, but Beth had been impossible to move. She and Caroline had been exchanging stories about Isabelle, and it was good to see them laugh together. Adam had taken himself off earlier, and Tom decided to leave him to it. Sometimes a man needed to be on his own. He had no idea how he would cope if something happened to one of his children. He looked in the rear mirror at Sarah, who was arguing with Lochie about Michael. Her brother had taken great delight in telling her that Michael would never be interested in a little kid like her and had his eye on a girl from school. Lochie had seen a picture of her on Michael's phone and took extra pleasure informing his sister how pretty the girl was. And she was sixteen, so Sarah had no chance. Tom knew he had to have a bit of a chat with her at some stage about boys, but he had been under the false belief that she wouldn't be interested for a few years yet. Tonight, Tom had been given a taste of what the teenage years would be like with his daughter, and he knew he wasn't ready.

Beth was quiet as Tom drove them home. She hoped she hadn't embarrassed herself too much. As she began to sober up, she wondered why she kept doing this to herself. In the past, she drank sometimes, but lately she had been drinking far too much. She knew she was going to have a hangover tomorrow, and she could already feel the nausea settle in her stomach.

When they arrived home, Tom carried Nate, who had fallen asleep in the car, to bed. Sarah and Lochie disappeared off to their bedrooms. Sipping a glass of water, Beth settled herself on the couch and turned on the TV, finding that one of her favourite movies was halfway through. It didn't matter because she'd seen it so many times, she almost knew it off by heart. *I wish I had a life like those two*, she thought as she watched the story play out. That was true love. Why couldn't Tom be like that with her?

Sitting down on the couch beside her, Tom picked up the remote and started flicking through the channels.

"Hey, I was watching that," she exclaimed, reaching across to pull the remote from his hand.

"You've seen it a thousand times. It's a stupid movie, and I can't sit through it again." He found the football game he had been looking for and saw that his team was getting killed.

"Well, I guess I'll go to bed and watch it there then," she retorted as she stood up from her seat. Tom didn't even bother responding, instead screaming at the screen and issuing orders to the players like they could actually hear him. She shut the door to the bedroom behind her to block out the yelling from the lounge room and changed into her favourite nightie. Made of flannelette, it always made her feel cosy. She propped up the pillows and turned on the TV in the bedroom. She knew she should really go and clean her teeth, but skipping one night wouldn't hurt, and it's not like Tom was going to bother kissing her goodnight.

When Tom came to bed half an hour later, Beth was passed out with the TV still on. *No chance tonight then.* He sighed, disappointed again. How long had it been? A few weeks at least. He considered waking her up, but when he saw that she was wearing that awful nightie, he took that as an indication that he would get a no even if he tried. He changed into boxers, not needing pyjamas. Beth was like a hot water bottle. They had never needed an electric blanket, no matter how cold it was. He lay there for a few minutes, listening to her breathing. *How long do I have to put up with this?* he considered. *I love Beth, but I'm so lonely.* Before he drifted off to sleep, he wondered if she was too.

~~~

"I'm off to bed," Adam announced as he put the guard in front of the fire, which had begun to die down. Caroline had been clearing the last of the glasses from the bar but stopped to look at her husband.

"I'll only be a few minutes. I just need to get these in the dishwasher, and then I'll be up too. Do you think you could stay awake until I get there? I'd like it if we could spend some time together. We haven't done that for a while."

Adam knew what she meant by "spend some time." It had been months since they'd had sex, and the last time it had been so mechanical and awkward that he hadn't wanted to try again. Instead he kept putting Caroline off with excuses of being too tired or going to bed early to avoid her. He didn't know why he felt that way. Most men would be thrilled to have such a beautiful woman pursuing them, and there was no denying that she certainly was beautiful. He heard a lot of men complaining that once their wives had children, they lost interest. That had never happened with Caroline. She had always made their physical relationship a priority, and she had never given him any reason to complain. But when Isabelle died, something changed. It didn't happen straightaway, but over the year, he had slowly withdrawn from her until the thought of even holding her hand filled him with revulsion. He knew it wasn't fair to her. He had always been the centre of her world. His rejection had hurt her deeply, but he couldn't fake it. He didn't want her anymore.

"I'll try, but I'm really tired," he answered as he climbed the stairs. He could feel her eyes on his retreating back and wondered again what he was going to do. Maybe he needed to leave. Permanently. That would put them both out of their misery.

As Caroline watched Adam disappear into their bedroom, she felt her heart sink. She missed her husband—missed the way he used to kiss her and tease her when she was being too serious. She'd tried everything she could think of to entice him, but nothing she did worked. She returned to the thought she constantly had these days—maybe he had found someone else. Every time she imagined him touching another woman and having someone other than her touch him, it made her sick. She clung to the knowledge that he hadn't done anything that would suggest he was having an affair, except his complete rejection of her, of course. Maybe it was time to consider getting some help for them both she decided as she finished loading the dishwasher. She was about to turn out the light when Michael appeared at the door.

"Mum, have you got a minute?"

"Of course," she responded. It had been so long since Michael had spoken more than a few words to anyone that there was no way she was going to tell him no. After Isabelle had died, he started spending hours alone in his room. He said he was studying, but she knew he was making excuses. He had gone silent the same way his father had and did whatever he could to avoid conversation with her. She sat down and waited for him, not wanting to push. He pulled out a chair and sat down opposite her.

"I'm not sure what to do about Sarah. I think she might have a little bit of a thing for me."

Caroline smiled, thinking about how Sarah had followed Michael around all night. "You picked up on that, did you? She definitely has a thing for you."

"Do I need to do anything about it?"

"No. I think it will pass. Unless you like her?"

He rolled his eyes at his mother. "Yuck. She just a little kid. She's the same age as Isabelle."

"She's not really a kid, so be careful not to hurt her feelings. You could break her heart if you're not careful."

"Isabelle was never like that. I don't think I ever heard her talking about boys."

"But she would have started. Heather wasn't necessarily the best influence, and she was boy crazy."

"I miss her, you know. I thought she was a pain, always hanging around and annoying me, but now it's so quiet here. I wish I could hear her chattering away about something silly." He stopped talking for a moment, trying to find a way to put his thoughts into words that made sense. "Sometimes I wonder if what happened was my fault."

This surprised Caroline more than anything she had heard in a long time. "No, Michael. How could it possibly be your fault?"

"Because I pushed you into letting her go that day. She was always telling me she felt like a little kid, and she was desperate for some freedom. But if I'd minded my own business, she'd still be here."

What a burden to be carrying around, she thought. *My poor boy.* No wonder he had retreated so far away from her. Not once had she considered that he might feel responsible.

"Michael, look at me." She waited until she saw that she had his full attention. "You were not responsible. I decided to let her go out and don't think I haven't spent every minute of the last year regretting that. What if I'd said no or insisted on picking them up after the movie instead of letting them go out after? I've driven myself crazy second-guessing my decision. But in the end, I always come to the same conclusion. No one is to blame here. I can't even blame the driver of the car. He was dead before he hit her, and his family is missing him the same way we miss her. It was a horrible, tragic accident. It has changed our lives forever. I would give up my own life without hesitation if it meant bringing her back, but it doesn't work that way. So I'm trying my best to work out how to live the rest of my life with part of it missing."

Michael leaned back into his chair before he continued. "I just keep thinking about what she would have been like when she grew up. She would have been a great mother. You know how she was around babies. Now you'll never get to be a grandmother."

"Why? Do you think you won't want children one day? Don't get me wrong. There's no need to hurry, but one day maybe."

"Because what if something happened? Like with Isabelle."

Caroline understood his fears. Isabelle's death had proved she really had no control over her life. She wondered if there was someone or something out there playing with them like puppets on a string, and people had been created only for its amusement. Caroline had never really believed in God, but if it turned out he did exist, she hoped she would get the opportunity to ask him why he had taken her daughter from her, decades before he should have, stealing away Isabelle's opportunity for a future and a family of her own.

Putting her own thoughts into words, Michael asked, "Do you ever wonder where she is now?"

"Every day. If you ask Beth, she'd tell you Isabelle's in heaven. I don't know if that's true, but it's an image I've held on to this year—that she's happy somewhere, not missing us too much."

"I don't know if I believe in God either. How can I believe in a god who would let Isabelle die? "

"I simply don't know. When I asked Beth the same question, she said 'If you have an eternal view of life, then death is not the end, just the beginning of the next stage.'"

"Something to think about, I guess." He stood up and pushed his chair out. "I'm going up now."

"I'll come up with you," she said, standing to join him.

"Do you think Dad will be all right? I worry about him. He never says anything about Isabelle, and I tried to talk to him once, but he shut me down."

"I'm sure he'll be okay. He just needs some time. He adored her, and he's missing her just as much as we are."

They walked up the stairs together, turning out the lights as they went. At her door, he kissed her goodnight, something he hadn't done in years. "Thanks for listening, Mum."

"Anytime. I'm here for you, Michael. Whatever you need. I love you very much."

"I love you too," he called over his shoulder as opened his own bedroom door.

Caroline quietly opened her door and found the room dark. She went into the en suite and changed into her pyjamas. As she slipped into bed, she considered waking Adam. He had his back turned to her and the covers pulled up tight around him. She wished she could slide in behind him and share his warmth. Her side of the bed was cold, but then it was always cold these days. She turned her own back to his, afraid that if she did wake him, he would only reject her again. How long were they going to stay this way—two people who had become strangers to each other?

Adam stayed as still as he could while Caroline prepared herself for bed. He breathed slow and deep, hoping that she would think he was asleep. When she hopped into bed, he felt her hand hover over him for a second, and then she withdrew it and turned away. He relaxed a little, relieved that he had avoided her again. He didn't have to make excuses or see the hurt look in her eyes that he was responsible for every time he rejected her. Another long day had gone by where he didn't have to talk to her. What would be the point of talking anyway? He had nothing left to say.

Chapter 8

Out of habit, Jill rolled towards her husband's side of the bed as she woke, hoping for his warmth. Instead, she found an empty space where Chris should have been. They had always had a ritual on Saturday mornings—breakfast in bed and a chance to catch up with each other after the busy week. Jill regularly worked late nights and was usually drained by the time she made it home after dealing with other people's problems all day. Saturdays were sacred. No talk of clients or lawsuits. Just her and her husband dreaming together about the future and imagining what their lives would be like when children came along. Sometimes they didn't make it out of bed until lunchtime.

For the first few seconds of consciousness, she didn't remember what had transpired the previous day. But when she slid over and found the bed empty, her body registered that something had changed, and then her brain caught up. He wasn't here anymore, and he wasn't coming back. She glanced at the clock and saw that it was only six o'clock. She could try to go back to sleep, but she was quite sure that wouldn't be possible. There were four hours to kill before her doctor's appointment, and it was much too early to go to Beth's.

She threw back the covers and headed for her en suite. She hadn't bothered to take off her makeup last night, and her mascara had run during the night. *Not a pretty sight*, she thought. Reaching into the cabinet for makeup remover, she saw Chris's moisturiser. In the past, it had amused her how he was always trying new products to keep his skin looking young. When she had discovered that he actually went for monthly facials, she'd laughed so hard, she cried. He'd been furious at her for the way she teased him about going to a beauty salon and had sulked for a week. Not wanting to run into his belongings every time she entered her bathroom, she grabbed a suitcase from the hall cupboard and started throwing his stuff in. It only took five minutes to clear the room of him, but she couldn't believe how many beauty products he had. What sort of man used a hair mask for hydration and insisted on having his own hairdryer? Once she started, she couldn't stop, so she headed for the wardrobe. She filled five large suitcases with clothes and shoes. Not all of them had come from the bedroom wardrobe. Always complaining that the bedroom didn't have enough storage, he had taken over the one in the spare room as well. There had been plenty of hanging space for a normal man, but her vain clotheshorse of a husband had been obsessed with his appearance and spent most of his wages on new clothes.

Why on earth did I let him get away with that? she thought. He never had his wages banked into their joint account, insisting that he keep his money separate. It hadn't stopped him from taking money out of the account she got paid into any time he felt like it. More than once, she had become overdrawn when he had taken a large sum of money out and didn't consider that it was needed for things like paying the mortgage or food. Thinking that she better change the internet banking password so he wouldn't have access to her wages, she stopped packing and logged on to her bank. She would be able to change the password online, and on Monday, she would close the account. It only took a few seconds to login in, but it took a lot longer for the swearing to stop when she saw what he had done. He had taken one-thousand dollars out of the account yesterday from an ATM. He'd probably done it straight from leaving the house last night. One-thousand dollars was the daily limit, but she didn't put it past him to go back today and take more out. She moved the money left in the account to one that he didn't have access to. With the password changed, he wouldn't be able to get at it on the internet. Toxic—that's what he was. Not only was he a cheat, but now he was a thief as well. *Is that what I meant to him, just a bank account?*

Furious, she started checking every cupboard in the house. Half an hour later, his huge CD collection was boxed up and sitting outside along with the suitcases she had filled. There wasn't much else of him in the house. Not caring how early it was, she sent him a text informing him that all his belongings were out on the driveway, so he'd better come and collect them today if he didn't want them stolen. Later when she left, she would make sure every dead bolt and chain was locked, and she would climb out a side window at the back of the house that he would never think to check so he couldn't get in. She wanted all evidence that he had ever lived in her home gone, and she never wanted him to step foot through her door again. She even went through the kitchen cupboards, removing his protein powder and his boutique beer from the fridge. Satisfied that he had been completely removed, she headed back to her bathroom for a shower. With great satisfaction, she spread her own products out over the counter where they used to be before he moved in. Now all she had to do was tell her sister and her mother what had happened. At least her father would never have to know how much of a failure her marriage had been.

Chapter 9

"I'm late. I'm late. I'm late," Joan sang quietly to herself as she pulled into a park in a side street near the Esplanade Hotel. In typical Melbourne fashion, the sun had come out and so had all the people. The "Espy" was packed, so she was relieved when she saw David had been able to secure a table in a quiet corner. Sitting at the bar didn't make for good conversation.

Joan gave a little wave to acknowledge that she had seen him. As she approached the table, he stood up and leaned towards her to kiss her cheek in greeting as she stretched out her hand to shake his. Not the start David had been hoping for, he corrected himself and took her hand in his own.

That was awkward, Joan decided. It wasn't normal practice to start business meetings with a kiss. Maybe she should take that as an indication that he wasn't thinking today would be about work. He pulled out a chair for her, and as she seated herself, he pushed it back in. *I like this*, she thought. Gentlemen seemed to be very thin on the ground these days. Not that she believed men should take all the blame. Gender equality had confused several generations of males, and now they didn't know what the rules were. Should they open doors and pay for dinner or would that offend? Joan never had an issue with being treated like a lady. A man who opened the car door always scored big points. A man who initiated a date and then gave her the bill at the end of dinner did not. Once on a first date—not her choice but a set-up—the man had pulled out a calculator and added to the last cent how much her share was. Joan had been the one to leave the tip that night, and when he called a week later to see if she was free, she declined. Letting a girl know just how cheap you are is not a good move, especially on the first date.

Sitting back down, David couldn't help but stare at her. *How is it possible that a woman this attractive even had time to see me today?* he wondered. *She must have someone in her life that keeps her busy.*

"Hey, Joan. I'm glad you had the time to catch up today. I hope I'm not dragging you away from anything or anyone important?"

"No. I was free, and it's such a beautiful day. I'm happy to be out of the house."

"Good. I just wanted to make sure there were no hard feelings about Friday? Phil's a stubborn, old goat. And he's never been interested in keeping contractors or suppliers happy. I guess that extends to architects as well. But it's important to me that our working relationship is harmonious. With any luck, we'll get to work together on other projects."

"Thanks, but don't worry about me. I can handle Phil. I just wanted to make sure no one cut corners that could lead to disaster down the track. I can see now that you won't let that happen."

David took a sip from the beer he had ordered earlier. He'd been so excited when Joan had agreed to meet him when he called her this morning that he had been unable to focus on anything at home. He had walked instead of driving to the pub to get rid of some of his nervous energy. He would have preferred to meet for dinner last night but wasn't sure he would have had the courage to ask her out again if she turned him down. He thought he had more chance of a yes if he asked her to meet for a casual drink. Realizing that she had nothing in front of her, he jumped up.

"I'm so sorry. I've completely forgotten my manners. What would you like to drink?"

After asking for a white wine, Joan watched David as he headed to the bar. While his back was turned, she took in the considerably good view of her afternoon companion. He wasn't too tall. Probably about five-feet, eleven-inches, but he had broad shoulders and it certainly looked like he could keep up on a building site. He was wearing a cream cable-knit jumper and the collar just brushed the bottom on his hair. It was a dark-blonde tangle of unruly curls that fell on the back of his neck. For a second, Joan imagined being able to run her fingers up from his strong shoulders and through those curls. "Mmm" she sighed quietly. As he turned back towards the table with her glass of wine and another beer for himself, she took in the rest of him. His face was a little rugged, just the way she liked, and he was unquestionably good to look at. His green eyes were fringed with dark lashes, and she decided he was definitely her favourite kind of man. There was nothing effeminate about him at all. Joan found the current trend for men getting facials and even Botox laughable. When Beth had told her that Jill's husband, Chris, got monthly facials, the two of them had laughed so hard at the image of him slathered in mud with a towel wrapped around his head that they had ended up howling, with tears running down their faces. Sometimes she wondered where all the manly men had gone. Probably scooped up by sensible women who hadn't left it this late to find a husband. It was slim picking out in the single world, and Joan was becoming very tired of the looking. She had always resisted online dating, but soon that might be her only option.

Heading back to the table, David saw that Joan had been daydreaming, but she had been looking in his direction. *I hope that was about me.*

"So do I stack up?" David asked as he sat down and put Joan's glass of wine in front of her.

"Huh?" She had been so deep in thought she hadn't realized he'd returned to the table, and he'd caught her completely off guard.

"I saw you giving me the once-over. How do I stack up?" Grinning at her, Joan knew she'd been caught, but at least he couldn't read her mind. If this was just a work thing, then she was in trouble because she didn't think she'd been able to sit in meetings with him again without being able to imagine touching him. Hoping to hide her real thoughts, she responded indignantly.

"I wasn't looking at you like that. I was admiring your jumper. It's very nice." She could feel the heat rising up her neck and knew she was doing a terrible job at lying.

"Well, I'm very glad you like my *jumper*. I picked it out especially to wear today, and I would have been very disappointed if you hadn't liked the look of my *jumper*." He was enjoying her embarrassment. And it gave him hope. She wouldn't have been looking if she wasn't just a little bit interested.

"I do like it; it goes very nicely with your jeans." David raised his eyebrows and tutted at her.

"So you were looking at my *jeans* too. And did you like how my *jeans* looked." By now, he wasn't even pretending to hide his amusement at Joan's embarrassment at being caught perving on him.

Blushing a deep red, Joan's brain screamed at her to shut up. She had two choices. Try and make a graceful exit or steer the conversation back to why she was here. She didn't think she had it in her right now to make an excuse to leave, so change the subject it was.

"We should get down to the reason we're here. I'm really glad you agree with me about the footing on the building. It could have been a disaster if Phil had gotten his way."

David took a swallow of his drink, put his glass back down, leaned forward, and placed his hand on hers. "Joan, I think maybe you've misunderstood the reason I asked you for a drink. I did want to apologize for Phil's behaviour on Friday, but I have no intention of spending the afternoon talking about work. I don't do business on the weekend. I thought I made it pretty clear on the phone the other night that my interest in you was of a more, shall we say, personal nature."

Trying to hide her delight, she felt her embarrassment slip away. She had gotten it right when he had called on Friday. But she wasn't going to make this easy for him.

"Personal, huh? How do you know I'm not married with six delightful children at home?"

"Apart from the fact that you have no rings on your wedding finger, I asked around about you. I'm still not sure if you're seeing someone, but I do know you're not married. And I can't imagine six children ever being delightful." His eyes widened, and a sliver of fear went through him. "You don't want six kids do you?"

Enjoying his discomfort but not wanting him to get the wrong idea, she put him out of his misery. "No, I don't want six kids. I don't want *any*. They were never part of my plans, and if I did, don't you think I've left it a little late?"

"As a man interested in spending more time with you in the future, there's only one way to answer that. You don't look any kind of 'too late.' And I think a determined woman like you would find a way to have children if that was what she wanted."

"Well, then. As a man who wants to spend more time with me, why don't you tell me a couple of things about yourself? Unlike you I haven't been asking around about your situation."

"What would you like to know?" David asked.

"Married?" Might as well find out before she let her heart get any more involved than it already seemed to be.

"No. And I'm not divorced either. I was engaged once, but it was called off."

"Your choice or hers?"

"Hers. Not something I like to talk about. Next question."

Joan paused for a few seconds, trying to figure out how to compose her next question. She didn't want to sound like one of those desperate women who saw every man she met as a potential husband, but she was genuinely interested in what he would say. She didn't want to waste her time on a man who was only looking for a one-night thing or someone he could call up when he was looking for sex.

"Can I ask why you never got serious with anyone else after your engagement?"

"Hmm. I guess I just never met anyone who was worth getting serious with. I've dated a fair bit over the last ten years, but I never met anyone I wanted to spend the next thirty of forty years with. I'd rather be on my own than with someone who was *just good enough*. Does that answer your question?" he asked.

Time for a change of subject, Joan decided, before she came across as desperate instead of just interested. "It does. How did you end up owning your own building company? It's hard work breaking into the market *and* making any profit in this environment. What made you want to take the risk?"

Comfortable ground, David thought. Any more questions about his love life, and he would have had to reassess his first impression of Joan. The few times he had met her, she had never given off the air of desperation that he often saw in single women in her age bracket. Careers cemented and biological clocks ticking, when they looked around at their prospects, most discovered that the best men were either off the market or divorced with kids, not looking to start another family. So a reasonably successful, unattached man like himself was an attractive option. His sister was always trying to set him up with single mothers from school. Some of them had been great, but he had no interest in raising someone else's children when he didn't even want any of his own. Plus a lot of the time it seemed so messy with custody issues and parents fighting amongst themselves about how to raise their children. Getting stuck in the middle of that sort of situation sounded like a nightmare to him.

"I worked for one of the majors for five years. I was a site manager, and I got sick of seeing the stupid mistakes being made because the head office only cared about the bottom line instead of delivering quality work. And then at the end of the build, they spent too much money redoing work that should have been done right the first time, not to mention frustrating the clients. How many times have you heard people say they'll never build again after dealing with a bad builder? And the way they start out with a reasonable price and then charge astronomical amounts for small variations is highway robbery. So I found some contractors willing to work with me. I had enough cash saved up to get started on my first house. After building a few spec homes, I had someone approach me to build for him off his own plans. It grew from there. A good reputation goes a long way. The medical centre is the biggest project I've done so far."

"I imagine you have a lot riding on getting this project right. You said the profit margin was pretty tight." Joan remembered this from their conversation the other night.

"It is, but if we can get it finished on time and nobody makes any major stuff ups, we'll do all right out of it. I'm going to be out on site most of the time. I find the boys work faster if I'm there, and because I know your plans inside out, I'll be able to put a stop to any mistakes before they happen."

"What do you think of the design? I know the owners loved it, but I'd appreciate your perspective. You're the one who has to build it."

David took another swallow of his drink. He caught the attention of a waitress and held up his glass for another. He pointed to Joan's empty glass, but she declined another wine and asked instead for a Coke. He took his time with his reply because he didn't want to sound like he was flattering her to score points.

"Actually, I think it's really clever. I liked how you used inexpensive materials for the build but in a way that doesn't look cheap. Just because it's not a very high-income area is no reason for people to have to put up with an ugly building. And there's nothing worse than being sick and having to wait in a cold, utilitarian environment. The drawings I saw of the waiting room gave an impression of warmth, and having so many different services under the one roof will be good for the community."

The waitress bought their drinks over, and David took the opportunity with the break in the conversation to change the topic.

"We've ended up talking about work, which I didn't want to do. It's my turn to ask you some questions now. I know you're not married and have no children hiding at home. Parents? Siblings?"

"Okay. Mother, dead. Father, unknown. No brothers or sisters that I know about, but you never know. My father could have children all over the place, and I'll never meet them."

"So you know nothing about your father? Didn't your Mum tell you anything?" David couldn't help but feel sympathy. His parents had just celebrated their forty-fifth wedding anniversary and still loved each other very much. He saw them most weeks and couldn't imagine not having them around anymore. It looked like he and Joan had a completely different upbringing. That probably explained why she came across as so independent and strong.

She had no choice but to be that way. That was one of the things he had been attracted to when he first met her. She didn't seem needy.

"All I have is a name. Jonathan Morgan. I don't know if it's real, but it's on my birth certificate. I got a copy for my passport when I turned eighteen. And I have a box of papers that I found when I was going through all my mother's things after she died. She must have meant for me to have it because she wrote my name of it. I kept it, but I've never looked inside."

"Aren't you even a little curious? I can't imagine not looking to see what was inside. It could answers all your questions. And even if your mother's box doesn't tell you anything, you could find out on your own. Why don't you Google his name, and see what you come up with? Everybody deserves to know their father."

"Well not every father deserves to know his daughter. I've done fine without him, and I don't understand why everyone seems to think I should be looking for him. I have no desire for a reunion with someone I've never met." Joan had heard it all before, and it frustrated her that everyone else thought they knew what was best for her.

David threw his hands up in surrender. "I'm sorry. I didn't mean to upset you. I just thought you would be interested in finding out about your history, and one day, it might be important if you get sick or need a kidney."

"I know about my history. I had a deadbeat mother who didn't care about me. What were your parents like? Nice people who loved you. Plenty of food and a clean home? Someone who cheered you on and helped you achieve your dreams? People like you can't even begin to imagine what it's like growing up hungry and alone. I had *nothing*. But I survived and nothing in a box could ever change what my life was like. And as for my father, why on earth would I want to track down some man who might not even know about me? Showing up on his doorstep unannounced could ruin his life. Or worse, what if he did know? How would finding out he abandoned me before I was born help?" Joan could hear her voice beginning to sound hysterical and tried to calm it down before she continued talking. "I don't want to know him. I don't need to know him." Her voice returned to a normal pitch as her heart rate slowed. "Could we drop it, please? It's not a happy subject, and we've been having such a nice time." Joan picked up her drink and took a sip. David, surprised at how quickly the afternoon had turned, sat quietly, afraid of saying anything in case he made things worse than they already were.

The pub was getting fuller by the minute, and the sound of happy people laughing all around the two magnified the silence at the table. Joan knew it was up to her to try and rescue the afternoon. She took a deep breath and gave David a forced smile. "Sorry to sound a little crazy. It's just that the subject is a bit personal, and I prefer not to think about it if I can."

"Don't be silly. I shouldn't have asked. You know men—always putting their foot in it." David was just relieved Joan hadn't stormed out or worse—cried. He never knew what to do when a woman did that.

They switched the conversation to recent movies they had seen, but the lighthearted mood of the afternoon was gone. When they finished their second drink, Joan decided that it would be a good time to extract herself. They hadn't been able to return to the easy, flirty atmosphere of earlier, and Joan knew it was entirely her fault. David had asked if she wanted another drink, but she said she needed to get going. He stood as she got up from her chair, but this time, he didn't try to kiss her and she didn't bother to offer her hand. David did ask to walk her back to her car, but she declined. What would be the point? She was sure she would never hear from him again on a personal level, and now work would be awkward. And unlike other times when she knew it wasn't going to work out but hadn't minded, Joan felt hugely disappointed. David was…she couldn't even think of just one word to describe him. He wasn't just attractive. Lots of men were, but she could imagine snuggling up next to him and never wanting to leave. He was ambitious but not in a ruthless way. He genuinely cared about the people he worked for. *If only I hadn't sounded so nuts at the end*, she berated herself. *I know he meant well. Sometimes men just have a way of thinking every situation needs to be solved. And what he didn't realize was that he had hit a tender spot.* Joan had been thinking for the longest time about finding her father. So far she hadn't been brave enough to start. *Sometimes it's better not to know the truth*, she thought as she unlocked her car.

David couldn't believe he'd been so insensitive. She was the first woman in such a long time that he had met that didn't make him want to run away after fifteen minutes. She was the kind of person his mother would have called "sassy." Self-assured and confident. *You're so stupid*, David he admonished himself. *It was going so well, and she looked so beautiful.* He groaned out loud. *You didn't even tell her how good she looked today. That's dating 101. What kind of an idiot are you? And then to ruin it by bringing up her parents and pushing her. If you'd just shut up and listened instead of offering your opinion, we could have moved on to something lighter. Now she probably thinks you were judging her. She was clearly very sensitive about her parents and rightly so. You're going to have to apologize because what happened was completely your fault. Even if she decides she never wants to see you again, you still have to work with her.*

David settled the bill and started his walk home. He had been so full of energy when he had set out earlier, but now he felt drained and wished he'd brought his car. He didn't notice the people around him enjoying the winter sun. All he could think about was that he had blown it. They had only spent an hour together, but it had been the best hour he'd had in a long, long time.

Chapter 10

Beth rummaged through her handbag, trying to find the ringing phone. *I really must clean this out,* she thought. Finding it, she saw on the caller ID that it was Caroline. Hitting answer, she didn't even get a chance to say hello before she heard an unexpected voice on the other end.

"Beth. It's Adam. I really need you to come here as soon as you can."

A frightening chill ran through her. Last time she received a phone call from Adam was when Isabelle had been killed. Beth had been serving dinner for the kids at about six when the phone rang. She'd been surprised when she saw it was the Anderson's number because Caroline never called during dinner. It hadn't been Caroline, but Adam, and when he had asked her to drop everything and come now, she had. He had refused to answer her questions, just told her she was needed. Instructing Lochie to call his dad and watch his brother and sister until Tom got home, she'd driven as fast as she could, desperate to get to their house.

The entire drive, Beth's imagination ran wild with the terrible possibilities. If it had been one of Caroline's parents, she would have been sad, but they weren't close, and she would have called herself. Beth wasn't aware of any suspicion of serious illness in the family, and all four of them were in perfect health.

But when Beth finally pulled into the driveway of her best friend's house, she was unprepared for the police car parked near the front door. This wasn't bad news. They would only be here if it was the worst news. If there had been an accident and there was hope, she would have been called to the hospital, not their home. Beth felt her hands start to shake, and then it descended down through her entire body, and she was unsure if she would be able to make it from the car to the house, unsure if she wanted to. She pulled in behind the police, and stepping out, she waited. When she saw the front door open, she saw Adam shake the hand of a tall police officer and then the younger female officer who followed out of the house. Beth gently closed her car door behind her and watched as the police officers returned to their vehicle. Both nodded in her direction, but neither of them offered an explanation for their presence. She climbed the stairs, never taking her eyes of Adam his face white and strained and when she reached the top of the landing there was only one question to ask.

"Who?"

"Isabelle."

Beth felt her legs crumble beneath her. Adam reached out and caught her underneath her arms, lifting her back to her feet.

"Beth, I need you to keep it together. Caroline needs you to keep it together."

Beth nodded, unable to speak as she found herself propelled forward to the lounge. Caroline looked so tiny sitting in the corner of the huge couch. Michael was curled up beside her, his head in her lap. Beth took a few steps towards her and then kneeled down in front of her best friend, taking her hand.

Caroline raised her head and saw who it was.

"Oh, Beth. She's gone. My baby girl is gone."

"I know. I'm so, so sorry.

Caroline's tears returned, and seeing her cry, Beth was no longer able to hold her own back. They sat there together for a long time, crying silently. There was nothing that could be said. Time had seemed to stop.

Later, returning from his office where he had been making calls, Adam beckoned Beth, and she quietly rose and stepped into the hall with him. In a whisper she asked, "Adam, what happened?

"The police said she was hit by an elderly driver. He was either dead or close to death before the accident. They think his foot wedged on the accelerator, so the car kept going." Beth clamped her hand over her mouth, trying to stop the fresh flow of tears that wanted to escape. What a waste. What a tragic disaster.

"What happens now then?"

"I just got off the phone with a funeral home, and they said they will organize with the hospital to collect her." He stopped talking then and bent over at the waist, with his hands leaning on his knees and his breathing erratic.

Beth reached out her hand and placed it on his arm.

"It's okay, Adam. You don't need to explain."

After a minute, he stood up and shook his head like he was trying to shake the truth off himself.

"Her body. They will collect her body. We'll be able to decide tomorrow when we want the funeral." He pointed towards the lounge room.

"How is she?"

"She's devastated. Adam, I'm sorry. That seems like such an inadequate phrase, but I am."

"Thank you." He leaned back against the wall of the hallway and dropped his head into his hands.

"I can't believe this is real. Tell me it's a mistake. Tell me it's not my daughter but someone else's child, and it's their life that's been destroyed forever, not mine"

"I wish I could. I can't, but I can stay as long as you need me."

Nodding, he headed for the lounge. "I need to check on Michael."

"And I need to call Tom." She had heard her phone ring several times but had ignored it. Tom would be worried, and she'd given no explanation to her kids, hadn't had one to give, just run out of the house.

Adam closed the door behind him. She couldn't hear the conversation, just murmuring and then more crying. She pulled her phone out, walking towards the kitchen for privacy.

"Beth, thank goodness you called. I've been frantic. Where are you?"

"I'm with Caroline. There's been an accident."

"Is everyone okay? The kids said you ran out without telling them what was going on."

"No, not everyone is all right. Isabelle has been—" She paused, hating the words she knew she would have to say over and over each time she had to tell another person. "She's been killed." Finally alone, she was able to cry the way she needed to. Not in quiet sympathy, but in fury at what had happened to such a lovely girl. Beth had been the fourth person in the world to hold Isabelle, only behind the doctor and her parents. Hugely pregnant herself with a daughter of her own, she had stayed with Caroline throughout the labour, and when she was rushed to surgery half an hour after giving birth for an emergency hysterectomy, Beth had sat with Adam for an hour while they waited for the doctors to tell them it was going to be all right.

Tom sat silently on the other end for minutes, waiting for Beth to speak. He could hear her crying, feeling helpless. He waited for her, not knowing how he could help.

"Tom."

"I'm here."

"I need to stay tonight. Can you please take care of the kids for me?"

"For as long as you need. Do you want me to come?"

"Thank you, but no. But could you call Jill? And Joan? She adored Isabelle, and she would want to know."

"I will. What shall I tell the kids? What do I say?"

"I don't know. Just take care of it, please."

"Okay. Will you be home tomorrow?"

"I'll try. I'll let you know if there's anything else you can do."

"Call me anytime. I love you, Beth."

"I love you too, Tom."

It had taken three days before Beth made it home. She had stayed until the doctor had come and given Caroline a sedative to get her to sleep. For days, she had wandered around the house, lost and exhausted, refusing to eat and unable to rest. For the first time ever, Adam had to organize something alone. Caroline couldn't even comprehend that a funeral was required. When Beth arrived home at midnight on Sunday night after Caroline had finally fallen into a deep sleep, she crept into Sarah's bedroom. Beth crawled into bed with her, hugging her tighter than she ever had before, feeling grateful she wasn't the one who had lost her daughter and, at the same time, guilty that she felt that way.

"Beth, are you there?" Adam's voice drew her back to the present and broke through the panic that had settled on her.

"Adam, what's happened? Is Michael all right? Has something happened to Caroline?"

"Michael's fine. He's already left for school. But something's wrong with Caroline. I don't know if she's ill. She's been in bed for days. I left her alone on Saturday because I thought she might be tired from all the work she did for Friday night's dinner, and then yesterday she told me to leave her alone. And now when I went into see if she was all right, she was crying. No, worse—she was sobbing. I don't think she's eaten since Friday night, and even though I've taken her a jug of water and a couple of cups of tea, I don't think she drank anything. I don't know what to do. I've never seen her like this. Well, not since…you know when."

"All right. You need to calm down, and I'll get there as soon as possible. I have to drop the kids off at school. You wait with her, and I guess I'll be there in about an hour," Beth said, thinking it was lucky she wasn't working today.

"I'm sorry. I can't stay. I have a staff meeting first thing in the office, and then I have a client coming in at ten. I really need to be at both. I'll leave the key under the mat, and you can let yourself in."

"Adam, I really think you should stay home. What if she needs you, or if she's just waiting to be alone so she can hurt herself?"

"No. I'm sorry, but I have to go. And she'd never do anything like that. If you can get here as soon as possible and call me when you find out what the problem is, I'd really appreciate it. She won't talk to me anyway, so I can't help her." The line went dead. She couldn't believe that he had actually hung up on her.

"Kids!" she yelled. "Hurry up. We have to leave early. Caroline's gone crazy, and apparently it's up to me to save her." Lochlan appeared in the kitchen, looking sleepy and only half-dressed for school.

"Not surprised. I told you she was going to lose the plot one day."

"Well, thank you for your opinion and your heartfelt concern. Now get your skates on. I need to get out of here." It took another twenty minutes for Beth to get all three children ready and in the car. After dropping them at school, she fought the peak-hour traffic, wishing Caroline didn't live so close to the city while fuming at Adam. She had always thought they had the perfect marriage, but she had noticed lately that there was a disconnect. They had barely spoken on Friday night. It was understandable. Losing a child would have a devastating effect on any marriage. But Beth had hoped they would come through the other side reasonably intact. *I must have missed something*, she thought. *I didn't realize it was so bad. How could he leave her alone for two days without trying harder to find out what was wrong?*

When she finally arrived, Beth found the key to the front door under the mat and let herself in. It was deathly silent in the house, and Beth hoped her previous prediction about Caroline doing something drastic was wrong. Maybe she was asleep. But as she got to the top of the stairs, she could hear crying. Beth knocked on the door to Caroline's room.

"Go away, Adam."

"It's not Adam, love. It's Beth. Can I come in please"? It took a few seconds before she heard the faint response: "Okay."

When she entered, Beth saw that the room was dark, and it smelt like it had been closed for days. She could make out Caroline's slight shape huddled under the doona. She lowered herself gently onto the edge of the bed and pulled back the covers a little to reveal Caroline's face. Beth had never seen her usually lovely friend look so awful. Her hair was matted and greasy. Her face was blotchy and red from crying, and it looked like she had lost weight since she had seen her only three days ago. She took Caroline's hand in hers. It was cold, and her skin felt dry and thin. What could have happened to bring about such a drastic decline in such a short time?

"Love, has something happened? With Adam maybe? He called me this morning to come, but he didn't seem to know what was wrong. Do you think you can tell me?"

Beth waited quietly for a response. Caroline turned slightly towards her, wiping away her tears. Then in a whisper, her voice hoarse, she spoke. "I thought I was okay. I made it through a whole year. I got through her birthday and Mother's Day. I managed Christmas without her and did my best to make it a happy day. And I really, really thought that if I could survive all the special days and events that she should have been at for a whole year, that it would start to get easier. I expected to wake up on Saturday morning and be able to move on with the rest of my life. But it didn't happen. Instead when I woke up, I felt such an overwhelming heaviness inside I couldn't do anything but cry. I thought I'd survived the worst of it." Caroline stopped talking then, pulling herself up, leaning on the pillows, and resting against the headboard.

"And now all I can think about is all the other milestones I am never going to get to experience with my daughter. I won't see her finish high school or fall in love. I'll never get to go to her wedding, and I'll never get to play with her children. I've been robbed."

Beth considered her response, choosing her words carefully. "I think maybe you're finally feeling the grief you need. I expected this once the funeral was over, but you seemed to bounce back so quickly. Too quickly, I think. You kept yourself so busy and focused that you never gave yourself the chance to grieve properly. It might not feel like it right now, but I think this is a good thing."

"You do?" Caroline asked. "You think staying in bed all day and weeping uncontrollably is a good thing? I haven't looked after my family, I haven't eaten or showered, and I feel like I'm in a deep dark pit with no way to climb out."

"You won't feel like this forever. But you have suffered an extraordinary loss. And in your effort to cope and get through, you haven't given yourself permission to deal with just how shattering the death of a child is. You've bottled up all your pain and loss, and now the seal has been broken. You had to release the pressure, and it looks like it's all happened at once. For the past year, you've been doing everything in your power to avoid it. You've completely redecorated your house. You still host dinners and volunteer at that op-shop. You've gone about this year like nothing changed, when, in

91

fact, nothing will ever be the same again. You have to give yourself a chance to heal."

"Well, I have to tell you I have absolutely no idea how to do that. She's not here. She's never going to be here. It's not like we had a fight that I need to repair. I can't fix this." Caroline started to cry again. Long, hot tears streamed down her face. "I have always been strong and in control, and yet here I am, free falling. I don't know how to stop this."

"I doubt you will ever get over this completely. But if you face your pain, then maybe, bit by bit, it might start to fade. You will always have the scars, and you will always miss Isabelle. But I really believe talking about it instead of pretending it never happened and just trying to go on with life is the only way to move forward. You can always talk to me. You *need* to talk to Adam. He's probably going through similar feelings, and men tend to act like nothing's wrong. You could always talk to a professional or find a support group. And then maybe, day by day, little by little, it should get easier to cope. And then one day, something will happen that makes you happy, and that will be okay. You shouldn't feel guilty because you're still alive. Don't forget you have years and years ahead of you for wonderful things to happen. You have an amazing son. One day, he'll get married and have children of his own. They will never replace Isabelle, but they could bring you a lot of joy."

Caroline gave Beth a faint smile, remembering the conversation from the other night, and shook her head.

"Michael told me on Friday night that he was never going to have children. He sounded very certain."

"I wouldn't worry about that. I've never met a teenage boy who thought he was going to have children. But they must change their minds at some point or there would be no one left on earth. I, for one, am looking forward to my children having some of their own, not because I have any great desire to be a grandmother. But it will be wonderful revenge for all the torture they're putting me through at the moment." Beth started to laugh. "I can't wait to see Lochie try and change a nappy. Hopefully he has a boy, and then he can see what it's like to be peed all over. It was like he knew when I was dressed to actually leave the house."

"That would be nice." Michael had been a beautiful baby, and she was sure his would be too. "And if Michael never has any kids, I can come and play with your grandchildren."

Beth nodded. "You absolutely can, but I have it on very good authority that Michael's madly in love. That's always the first step."

Happy to see a faint smile from Caroline, but knowing she was a long way from better, Beth asked, "Have I been any help today? Do you need another day or two in bed?"

"I don't think so. I feel like some of the heaviness is gone. I'm glad Adam called you. You're a wise old lady."

"I wouldn't be calling me old if I was you. Your fortieth isn't that far behind mine. Now do you think you might be able to get up? Maybe have a shower, clean your teeth. If you think you'll be all right, I can go downstairs and find you some breakfast."

"Do I look that bad?" Caroline asked.

"It's not just how you look," said Beth, screwing up her nose. "You don't smell the best."

"Nice bedside manner. Do you talk to everyone like that?"

"No," said Beth, pulling back the covers and helping an unsteady Caroline out of bed. "Only you, love."

Chapter 11

Beth stood in front of Caroline's perfectly organized pantry, looking for something she could give her for breakfast. It was full of food, but there wasn't anything ready to eat, not even a box of cereal, but she knew Caroline wouldn't eat it even if there was any. The fridge offered up eggs and neatly stacked containers of fruit and vegetables.

"Fabulous," Beth muttered to herself. "I'll have to *cook* something." Preferring to put off that task for as long as possible, she took a seat at the small table and retrieved her phone from her bag. She found Adam's number and tapped the screen to connect.

"This is Adam," he answered.

"Hey, it's Beth. I thought you might want to know how it went."

"Is she all right? I would have stayed and waited for you this morning, but I really had to get to my meetings. Is it the flu?"

"No, it's not the flu. Caroline's just had a few bad days after the anniversary. It hit her harder than she was expecting. What she really needs is to talk to you. I also think it might be a good idea to look at getting her some professional help. She's up and taking a shower now. I'm going to get her to eat some breakfast, and if she wants, I'll take her to the doctor. He might be able to give her a referral to a therapist."

"Thanks, Beth, I really appreciate you coming. I'll make sure I'm not late tonight, and if she needs to go and see someone, I'll take her myself this week, I promise."

"Are you sure? I have the time today, and I think it could really help," Beth said, not trusting him to do what was needed for Caroline.

"I said I'll do it. And you're probably overreacting anyway. She's been fine. I can hardly tell if she even misses Isabelle these days as it is." His tone changed from mild concern to anger instantly, and it confirmed for Beth that Caroline wasn't getting the support she needed.

"Do you really believe that? She adored Isabelle. She's just trying to manage the best way she knows how."

"We're all managing the best we can. What makes her so special?" Beth heard other voices at the other end of the phone and after an abrupt "I've gotta go," Adam hung up on her. *Maybe he's the one who needs the most help here*, Beth thought as she got up to put the jug on to make tea and took a couple of eggs out for scrambling. Even though everyone was always telling her she wasn't much of a cook, she was sure she could manage the simple dish. Fifteen minutes later when Caroline walked into the kitchen, Beth was serving the eggs onto a plate and had poured the tea.

She didn't understand. The eggs had been kind of watery, so she had left them in the pan to make sure they were definitely cooked. But when they had started to burn, she pulled them off the heat and could only hope they tasted better than they looked. Putting the plate in front of Caroline, who had taken a seat at the table, Beth noted that she was looking much better than she did when she had found her earlier that morning. Caroline took the fork in her hand and started to eat the meal in front of her. After only two bites, she put the fork back down on the plate and took a long drink of tea. She looked up at Beth and pleaded, "Please don't make me eat this. Haven't I been through enough?"

"Don't be silly. It can't be that bad." But Caroline nodded her head and pushed the plate away. "That bad?" asked Beth.

"It's runny and chewy all at once."

Beth sighed. "I tried. I would have made you some cereal, but I couldn't find any. And I know you don't eat toast. I know I can make that. There's no food in this house."

Getting up from her chair, Caroline started to pull ingredients out of the fridge.

"There's plenty of food here. You just need to know what to do with it. I'm going to make some more scrambled eggs. Would you like some?"

"Sure why not?" Beth gave in, disappointed with herself. It was getting a bit ridiculous when she couldn't even cook an egg. She watched from her seat as Caroline melted a sliver of butter in a clean pan. She cracked four eggs into a bowl and then added two spoons of pure cream.

"I thought you used milk, not cream?" As Caroline added a pinch of sea salt and gave the eggs a quick whisk, she answered Beth's question. "I prefer cream. It's a much nicer flavour. Milk makes the eggs watery, which probably explains why yours were running all over the plate. How much milk did you use?"

"I don't know. A lot more than the amount of cream you put in." She wrinkled her nose in disgust when she saw that Caroline added a handful of baby spinach to the pan along with the eggs. "I hate spinach. It always tastes slimy."

"Beth, have I ever fed you slimy food?"

"No," Beth conceded.

"Then trust me. And besides, the way you eat, you probably need the vitamins. I'm surprised you don't have scurvy. Within three minutes,

Caroline handed Beth a plate that held no resemblance to what she had made earlier.

"It's not fair you know," said Beth after she had finished the best eggs she had ever eaten. "You cook like a chef, and you eat butter and cream and never put on any weight. I'm eating cereal with no-fat milk every morning, and I'm getting fatter by the minute."

Caroline ran her eyes over Beth. It did look like she had put on more weight, but Caroline would never have mentioned it. But if Beth wanted to talk about it, then Caroline was happy to offer her some advice. But she would tread lightly. The last thing she wanted was to cause her friend embarrassment.

"Are you concerned about how much you weigh?"

"Of course I am. Look at me. I know I'm disgusting. Tom won't look at me anymore. No one looks at me. It's strange how the bigger you get, the more invisible you become. And it's not like I'm not trying. I don't even eat that much, and I try to pick all the right foods. All low fat, but nothing helps, and I keep piling on the weight."

"Did you ever think that low fat might be the problem? Most of those foods are packed with sugar to make them taste good."

It's so easy for you, Beth thought. Caroline had never needed to worry about her weight.

"You know, I tried no carbs as well. I lost some weight, but as soon I ate normally again, the weight went straight back on. I've tried just about every diet under the sun, but I could never stick to them because I was so hungry. And I won't drink those shakes. I had one once. I nearly threw it up. It was like drinking chocolate-flavoured glue."

"Do you want to lose weight?" Caroline asked. When Beth nodded, she continued. "Stop eating low fat, stop eating anything with the word 'diet' in it." Caroline stopped talking for a second, trying to decide if she should tackle the biggest contributor to Beth's weight gain. "And you have to stop drinking."

"I hardly drink at all. I doubt that has anything to do with my gaining weight."

"I think it's a huge factor in your weight gain. Alcohol affects your metabolism, and when you drink, you eat more. I've been concerned for a while about how much you're drinking, and I don't think I'm the only one."

"I'm not an alcoholic." Beth's voice rose in protest. "Far from it."

"I know you're not. I'm not suggesting that you are. But you have to admit that you do drink a lot more than is good for you. You never used to have more than one or two, but recently, it's increased to a lot more. Imagine the damage you're doing to your body. I really believe if you cut out alcohol and make some simple changes to your meals, you will find yourself losing weight."

"I'm really not an alcoholic." Beth tried to find the right words to make Caroline understand. "I just like how that first drink of the evening makes me feel. Much calmer. And when I feel calmer, I don't worry as much about all the things going on around me."

"Like what?"

"The kids. Raising teenagers is hard. And I feel like I'm doing it on my own. Tom's so busy at work, and when he is home, he either shuts down and doesn't talk to us or he gives in and lets the kids do whatever they want. So at the end of a horrible day, I have a couple of drinks to block out the noise of the kids fighting and to stop myself feeling so lonely. The sound in the house recedes a little, and life becomes bearable for a while."

"Why didn't you say something? I think we've both discovered today that it's important to have someone to talk to."

"Caroline, the last thing I wanted to do was burden you with my problems, especially over the past year. I can't imagine that you want to listen to me whinge about Sarah."

"You're right. It might have been hard to listen to, but I would have. And what about your marriage? You can always talk to me about that."

Beth poured herself another cup of tea, trying to formulate an answer that would make sense.

"I love Tom. And I guess he still loves me. But we've drifted so far apart, it's as if we're just roommates. We live together, raise our children together, we even have sex sometimes, but we aren't friends anymore. I feel like I could be replaced with another woman, and as long as she looked similar to me, he wouldn't even notice."

"Are you sure it's that bad?"

"We were best friends, Caroline, and now we hardly speak. And when we do, it's usually because we're fighting—over the kids, over money, over all sorts of silly things. And it's become such a habit, it's the only way we communicate anymore. I'm sure the real reason is because I've put on weight. And I can't blame him. I'm disgusting, and I wouldn't want to be with me either."

"I don't know if I believe that. Tom chose you all those years ago when you were already a bit bigger than the rest of the girls at school. You were always cute and curvy, and you're still cute and curvy. "

"Then why doesn't he look at me anymore? Why did he say what he said the other day?" Beth dropped her face into her hands and started crying.

"What did he say, Beth?"

"About a month ago when I was on my way out, he looked me up and down and said to me, 'That does *not* look good.' That's when I knew how disgusting he thinks I am."

"Did it look good? Not you, but what you were wearing?"

"Well, not really. If I'd had time, I would have changed." She wiped her tears away. "I threw the skirt out when I got home."

"You know, he probably thought he was doing you a favour. He handled it badly, and his words have caused you a lot of hurt. But do you tell him, if he puts on something that doesn't match or looks terrible, to get changed?"

"Always. He has terrible taste."

"There you go. He was only doing the same for you."

"So," asked Beth, "you don't think he's given up on me?"

"No, Beth. I don't think the problem is that he's given up on you. I think it's that you've given up on yourself. Think about this: Men are very visual. When was the last time you gave him something to look at? Don't forget I was there when you bought that awful flannel nightie. I tried to talk you out of. It was hideous. What's he supposed to think if you come to bed in that every night? That you're making yourself available and that you're interested in him, or are you saying I'm covering myself up in my flannel suit of armour so don't bother coming near me?"

"But I'm not interested. I don't want to have sex. I don't want to put on something sexy. It would look horrible, and the last thing I want to advertise is how awful I look. I'm so embarrassed by myself that it's killed any desire I had in me. I know sex is important to men. It's not like I say no when he wants to. I just try and get it over and done with as fast as possible."

"How do you think that makes him feel? Do you think he enjoys knowing you'll let him, but you have no interest and hope he gets done as soon as he can? It sounds like you're providing a service, not engaging in romantic and intimate time with the person you promised to love forever."

Beth considered, trying to put herself in Tom's shoes. "I guess he doesn't feel that good. Maybe like he's using me. But it's not even about him. George Clooney could show up and say 'How 'bout it?' and I'd turn him down. I can't fake my feelings. I'm just not interested anymore. And let's be honest.

No matter how much you talk about what I wear, I can't believe that Tom would want to look at me anymore."

"Well, imagine coming to bed to that attitude every night. What's he *supposed* to do?"

"It's not like he's making any effort either. He doesn't talk to me; he hardly helps me with the kids. I can't remember the last time he took me out to dinner or brought home flowers for me. Why do I have to be the one to make all the effort?"

"So you don't want to stay married?"

"Of course I do. I just wish it could go back to the way it was before we got so busy and the kids took up so much of our time and energy."

"Then you're going to have to stop worrying about scoring points and who's wrong or who's right. You need to give up your right to be right and do something constructive. Don't worry about what he's doing. You need to make the first move."

"So your suggestion to fix my marriage is to come to bed in something lacey and initiate sex? I'll look horrible."

"Beth, the problem isn't what Tom thinks about how you look but what *you* think about how you look. So for yourself, do something about it."

"That might be true, but I don't know how to get myself back. I'm going to be forty this year. I've failed every time I've tried to lose weight. I'm not sure I can be bothered anymore. As much as I want to look good and be healthy, I don't think I can do it. I've had three babies. It's really hard to recover from that. Men don't have to get fat and stretched out until they feel like they're going to pop. I bet if men were the ones having babies, liposuction would be paid for by Medicare."

"You're probably right," Caroline said, agreeing, "but how much more weight have you put on since you finished having kids? If you lost just *that* weight, it would make a huge difference to your appearance and your health.

You say you love Tom, but your actions don't back that up. Don't you think he's worth making the effort for?"

"That's so easy for you to say. Look at you. You're gorgeous."

Caroline felt like a fraud giving out marriage advice when she knew hers was in shambles. She could walk around in four-inch heels and nothing else all day, and Adam wouldn't be interested. But then, Tom and Beth hadn't had to face the kind of trauma she and Adam had been through. And she was sure with a little more time, things between her and her husband would be right again.

"I think it's very important that you try, and give him a chance. He might be just as worried as you about what's going on and not know how to fix it."

"What if nothing changes? What if I do try, and he doesn't care or even notice?"

"It won't happen. Tom's not like that. Think about why you chose to marry him. And be specific."

Beth thought back to when she had met Tom over twenty years ago. Like any teenage girl, she had first been attracted by the way he looked, but after awhile, when she got to know who he was and what he was about, she knew he would be a good husband. He was honest and stable, which was something Beth really valued. She never caught him looking around to see if there was someone prettier, so she was sure he would be faithful. And he was very protective of her. When they got engaged, he had a plan to provide for her and any children they had. She knew he would do anything he had to keep her safe. He reminded her a lot of her father.

"*You* were there when we met. I loved how sensible he was. Jill was always happy to go out with guys with flashy cars and cool clothes. I was never interested in that sort of thing. I wanted someone I could have a family with."

"So of *all* the men in the world, *he* was the one who filled the needs and desires you had for husband. So imagine if he came home next week and told you he wasn't going to work anymore. He was going to shut down his business and watch TV all day. If you wanted to pay the mortgage or buy food for the kids, it was up to you. He was just too tired to make the effort. He wasn't sick or injured. He hadn't lost his job. He just didn't want to do it anymore. How would you feel about that?"

"You know I'd be furious. He would be letting me down and not holding up his end of the bargain."

"What you're doing is no different. You need a husband who shows you love by providing for you and your children. He needs a wife who boosts his masculinity. So when you hide away and make sex a job on your to-do list, it says, 'I don't love you' and 'You aren't worth the effort.' We all have needs, Beth, and just because his are different than yours, it doesn't make them any less important or valid. It's not fair to get a ring on your finger and then just coast for the rest of your life. Marriage is hard work, but the payoff is worth it. So if you need to lose weight to get yourself to a place where you can feel good enough to give him what he needs, then that's what you're going to have to do."

"I don't know where to start Caroline. I've tried, and I've failed."

"Then you try again, and I'll help you any way I can. The first thing you need to do is learn to cook a few meals. Good proteins and lots of vegetables. Don't cut out all the carbs, but make better choices about the ones you do eat. If you get rid of the sugar and the alcohol, that's the best start you can make. And eat real food, not those awful packaged meals you live on. You can't tell me they actually taste good."

"Of course they don't. But they're easy, and I can't ruin them. You saw today. I can't even make scrambled eggs."

"You're a smart girl, Beth. You saw me cook them today, and I have no doubt you could go home and make them yourself. So if you start your day with an easy meal like that, you're on your way. Lunch is simple. Salad with some protein, and, in winter, you can easily make a healthy soup. Just skip the bread, and you won't get hungry in the afternoon. And stay away from anything processed. Fresh vegetables only. I'll teach you some simple recipes and help you plan some menus. But you need to take it seriously. You won't lose the weight in a month. It's taken years to put it on, so take each kilo as a victory."

"Caroline, you shouldn't be worrying about me. You've suffered such sorrow the last few days and, before that, the last year. You should be concentrating on yourself, not worrying about me and my marriage. I'm sorry. I shouldn't have said anything."

"Yes, you should have. And before you got into such a state. Yes I've had a hard time and I need to do some damage control in my own marriage, but talking to you has been cathartic. For the last three days, I've been going around and around in my head, and it's been good having something different to focus on."

"And you're really going to talk to Adam?"

"I heard you this morning, Beth. I can't bottle my feelings up anymore. I don't think Adam should either. I'm going to make him talk to me when he gets home, and then we can figure out what we need to do together to get through. But helping you will be fun. I'm looking forward to seeing you get healthy."

"Then for you, I'll try."

"No, not for me. For you. And for Tom. It'll be worth the effort."

"I don't really have a choice, do I? Imagine me learning to cook. Nobody will believe it. The only time my kids eat vegetables not out of a packet is when they come here."

Caroline looked at Beth and made sure she had her attention.

"I meant what I said about the drinking. You can't continue on. It's ruining your health, and I got the feeling from Tom on Friday night he wasn't too happy about it. You're going to have to find another way to cope when you feel stressed."

"It'll be hard. I've come to rely on it."

"Well, you can't anymore. And think of your kids. What sort of example are you setting for them? Do you want them to think your behaviour is normal?"

"Ouch. That's harsh. Do you talk to everyone like that?"

Smiling genuinely for the first time that day, Caroline pulled Beth to her feet and hugged her. "No. Only you, love."

Chapter 12

```
Where were u the other nite
Didn't Jill tell you
Said at yr parents
Have you got time to meet
Usual place
Yep. 6:30
Cu then
```

Needing some Dutch courage, Chris arrived at the pub early to get in at least one drink before he saw Adam. He hadn't told anyone what had happened with Jill, and he knew Adam was going to be furious. When Chris had asked Adam to set him up with Jill three years ago after seeing a photo of her with Beth, Adam had refused at first. He told Chris that he definitely wasn't Jill's type. She preferred men with goals and ambition, and he drifted from job to job and still lived at home with his parents. But Chris had nagged him until Adam relented and arranged for them to be at the same party. But Adam had made it clear that he wasn't setting them up, and it was up to Chris to introduce himself and see where the night took him.

And it had been easy. She was already thirty-four and starting to wonder if she would ever get married. He spent the evening by her side, charming her with his easy nature and telling her about his big plans for making a fortune as soon as he got his big break. He told her how important he thought it was to get married, but he had been waiting for just the right girl. She was not only more beautiful in real life than the photo, but when he found out that she was also a successful solicitor who owned her own home, he decided that she was definitely "the right girl." After that first night, Chris spent every dollar he had on expensive dinners and gifts in an attempt to impress her, never letting Jill know his real financial situation—that he was close to broke and in debt. After four months together, he proposed marriage, and when she said yes, he knew he would be on easy street from then on.

Charming her parents proved to be much harder than it had been with her. Jill's father was instantly wary, and her mother wasn't interested in how good looking or attentive to her daughter he was. She wanted to know how he was going to provide for Jill, and when he told her the same ideas for making money he had told Jill, she pulled each one apart and highlighted what a fool he really was. Luckily for him, Jill was so in love that she laughed off her parents' concerns. Ten months after their first meeting, they were married, and his future was secure. He'd be happy to let her have babies, and he would stay home and take care of them. Didn't they spend most of their time at school anyway? And she could keep him in the comfort he intended to get used to.

But he had blown it, and for a one-night stand he barely remembered. It had been a horrible week. He missed Jill. In his own self-centred, what-can-I-get-out-of-this fashion, he did love her. Their life together had been great for the first year. The fertility problems in the second year had put a dampener on their sex life, but he had tried his best to go along with what she wanted and to be supportive. He'd come to the conclusion that babies wouldn't be so bad and would cement her to him forever. Now he was living in a horrible hotel room piled high with all his stuff. She'd locked him out of the house and blocked all his access to the bank accounts. He needed this situation to end as fast as possible, and he hoped Adam might have an idea on how to make that happen.

Adam arrived and ordered his drink at the bar before sitting down. He took one look at Chris's face and knew something was very wrong. He normally looked like he'd stepped straight out of an advertisement for hair product. Today his clothes were rumpled, like he'd slept in them, and he didn't look like he'd shaved in a week. Anxious about what he was going do to solve his financial situation now that Jill had cut him off, Chris had called in sick for the last week and had really let himself go. He felt like his life was spinning out of control, and he had convinced himself he was the victim of two women. What he didn't realize was that he was a victim of his own stupidity.

"What happened to you? You look terrible."

"I know. It's been a tough week. So you really haven't heard yet?"

"I haven't heard anything. Seriously, what's going on? You lose your job or something?"

"No. My job is fine. I've lost my wife."

Adam leaned towards Chris, shaking his head but not surprised. He had been waiting for this day. "What did you do?"

"I slept with someone. Jill found out last Friday and kicked me out."

"Are you out of your mind? What on earth would possess you to do such a stupid thing?" Adam exploded. "I thought you were happy with Jill. This woman must be really something to get your attention. How long has it been going on?"

"I'm not having an affair. It was just a stupid one-night stand. Remember that wine thing I went to for work? She was there and spent the night coming on to me. I'll admit I enjoyed the attention, but I swear I had no intention of sleeping with her."

Adam had always known Chris was weak. But he couldn't believe that he would be this stupid. He should never have agreed to let him meet Jill. She deserved better than ending up with a lazy opportunist like Chris. He was nice guy most of the time and fun to hang out with, but his judgement had always been lacking. He was a follower, never a leader. Adam didn't think he had ever done something quite this stupid though.

"So you had a one-night stand with some random chick. Were you ever going to see her again?"

"Absolutely not! When I woke up the next morning, I was horrified. I hardly even remember it 'cause I was so drunk. I got out of the room as soon as possible and didn't expect to ever hear from her again."

"Then why did you tell Jill?"

"I didn't tell her. Meg, that's her name, she told her."

"Well you must have made quite an impression for her to track down your wife and tell her. Does she want to have some sort of relationship with you? Tell me you weren't stupid enough to hook up with a psycho. She hasn't gone all 'fatal attraction' on you has she?"

"No. I bought a separate phone that I was using to communicate with Meg. Jill heard it ringing. She answered it, and Meg was *kind* enough to fill her in."

"I don't follow. You had no intention of seeing this woman again, yet you bought a phone so you could talk to her. You're not making any sense, Chris. "

"She's pregnant, and she says it's mine."

Adam's mouth dropped open in surprise. "You idiot."

"I know."

"What do you expect me to say? Way to score? How could you sleep with a stranger and not use protection?"

"I told you I was drunk. I wasn't really thinking things through in the heat of the moment."

"And Jill knows she's pregnant? What a kick in the guts for her. How long have you guys been trying for a baby?"

"A year."

"You've been trying for a year with no luck, and then you sleep with someone else once, and bam she's pregnant. Are you sure it's yours?"

"I have no idea. I've made it very clear I'm not going to pay for anything until I know for sure if it's mine. I have to wait about seven months until it's born. Then we can do DNA testing. And if it's not mine, maybe Jill will get over it and forgive me. I have no intention of just walking away."

"What does Jill want to do? Is she talking divorce?"

"Yep. She messaged me to pick up all my stuff on Saturday when she was out, and I haven't heard from her since."

"So she knew before she came to dinner?"

"Yeah. Sorry about that, by the way. But I didn't think Jill would be happy to see me there. I wanted her to have some time to cool down, and I needed to figure out what I was going to do about all this. Have you got any ideas?"

Adam shook his head. Chris didn't seem to understand how bad this was, and Adam knew Jill. She wasn't exactly the forgiving type. At least now he understood why she had behaved so strangely on Friday night, but there was no way Adam was going to mention that to Chris. It would only make matters worse.

"I don't think you can. I was surprised she took you on in the first place. I can't see her giving you a second chance."

"Would you consider talking to her for me?"

"You've got to be kidding. Even though we're mates, there's no way I would ever have let someone like you near my daughter, and I'm not going to help you with Jill. If you want her back, you're going to have to figure it out on your own."

"Some mate you are."

"Don't forget I knew Jill before I knew you. I intend on staying out of this."

"Your call, but if you change your mind, I could use the help. I'm going to get another drink, and then we can switch to a new topic. You want one?"

Adam nodded, his glass empty.

"Do you mind shouting? I'm a little short."

Adam dug into his pockets and found a twenty. This was typical of Chris. He never seemed to have any money. Adam watched him at the bar, flirting with the barmaid as he ordered their beers, and when he saw Chris pocket the change, he decided after this drink he would leave. He didn't want him leeching off him all night.

Returning to the table, Chris put down the beers and settled back into his chair.

"So how was Friday night?"

"It was fine. You know Caroline. Dinner was perfect."

"Yeah. It would have been nice to be there. And you're doing all right?"

Adam shrugged his shoulders. It was the question people kept asking that he had no real answer to. If doing all right meant wishing he could disappear into a deep, dark hole and never speak to another person ever again, or removing the part of his brain that reminded him every minute of every day what he had lost, then sure, he was just fine.

"I'm hanging in there. What else am I supposed to do?"

"And how's Caroline? I haven't seen her since the funeral. She looked like she had been holding up really well that day."

Adam hated thinking about that day. Caroline had woken up the next morning after the doctor had come and sedated her, and it was like someone had thrown a switch. One day, she was hysterical, and the next, she was her old self. Calm and in control. She carried herself on like she was hosting a business dinner, not attending her daughter's funeral. She greeted everyone and thanked them for coming. He never saw her cry, and when they lowered the coffin into the ground, she stood by silently. He hadn't wanted to cry. He'd wanted to vomit. He'd wanted to throw himself into the filthy hole in exchange for Isabelle and beg God to return her alive. But he, too, had stood there, with his eyes closed behind the dark glasses he wore in the bright winter sun, unable to watch.

"She was all right up until Saturday morning. I found her crying in bed, and she stayed there all weekend. Beth came over, and I don't know what she said, but at least she got her out of bed. But now she's gotten all clingy, trying to get me to go and see a therapist or something."

"Are you going to go?"

"No way! If she wants to go, I won't stop her, but I told her there's no chance I'll be going. So now she's refused to go without me. Typical female guilt trip. She's driving me nuts, following me around, telling me I have to let my feelings out."

"It sounds like she's worried about you."

"Well, she doesn't need to be. I'm so sick of people offering their advice and torturing me with their pop psychology."

"I know I haven't turned out to be the best husband, but I do know enough to know that women need to talk. Maybe you should just listen to her and at least go once to the therapist. It might help you both. And if it doesn't help, at least it will get her off your back."

"You know, I'm so sick of that rubbish." Adam banged his fist onto the table, startling the people sitting near them. The bartender looked over, looking to see if there was going to be any trouble. Adam lowered his voice and gained control of himself.

"I could talk about the accident every day for the rest of my life, but it's not going to bring my daughter back. She's gone forever. Everyone has their opinion of what I should do and how I should cope. Unless it's happened to you, you don't know what it's like. At least Caroline had left me alone, but now she's gotten in on the act as well."

"Mate, I'm sure Caroline's not trying to tell you what to do. She probably just needs to feel connected to you. And if she doesn't feel connected to you, she might find someone else who will listen to her. You don't want to end up alone like me."

"Why not? It can't be that bad. No one hassling you, no one probing your brain to find out what you're thinking. Sounds all right to me."

"No way, man. I had a good thing going, and I blew it. Now I'm living in a dumpy hotel room, facing a divorce, and I'll probably have to pay child support for the rest of my life for a kid I don't want with some girl I don't know. You've got it good, and you should do whatever she wants to keep it."

"I don't know. Maybe. But at least I'm not as stupid as you. I think you better plan on living in that hotel for a long time. It's gonna take a lot more than a bunch of flowers to win Jill over. You really are a jerk."

"Tell me about it."

Adam stood to go to the bar. He changed his mind. Why not stay a bit longer and shout a few more drinks? It's not like he wanted to go home.

"Another drink?"

"Bring two. I'm gonna need them."

~~~

Several hours later, while weaving his way back to his hotel, Chris decided it was time to bite the bullet and call Jill. The worst that could happen was that she would hang up on him. Finding her number, he dialled.

"Hello," Jill mumbled while checking the time on the clock next to the bed. It was 10:30 p.m. Not that late, but with no one to come home to, Jill had found herself working late each night and then falling into bed so she didn't have to think. She was exhausted, but it was better than spending a lonely evening at home feeling sorry for herself."

"It's me. Did I wake you?"

Sighing, Jill replied, "What do you want, Chris?"

"I just wanted to see how you are." Pausing, he decided he might as well go for it. "I miss you."

"Whose fault is that, Chris? And you shouldn't be talking to me. Jeremy from the office is handling the divorce. You can contact him or get your solicitor to do it if you need to communicate with me."

"I don't have a solicitor, and I'm not going to pay someone to tell you how sorry I am. I was just hoping you had reconsidered. I could be home in about twenty minutes. I don't have to stay. We could just talk and see if we can't find a way to sort this out."

"Are you hard of hearing? I couldn't have been more clear. This is over. We are over. You need to find yourself a lawyer and leave me alone."

"Please don't make me beg, Jill. I regret what I did to you more than anything. Don't you miss me just a little? I could come home and remind you just what it was you loved so much about me."

"Chris, you're drunk and disgusting. Every time I think about you ever touching me again, my skin crawls."

"Don't be like that, baby," he slurred.

"Don't call me baby. I'm not your baby. I was nothing more to you than your teller machine, and that's come to an end."

"What do ya mean?"

"You stole a thousand dollars out of my account. You're a thief."

"No, I'm not. That was my money too, and I needed it to pay for somewhere to stay."

"Then pay for it out of your own bank account."

"Marriage means you share your money. I would have given you money if you needed it."

"Hardly. In our marriage, what was mine was yours and what was yours was yours."

"It's not my fault you earned more than me."

"Yes, it was. You're a loser, Chris. Why don't you go home to your mother, and then you'll never have to pay for anything again. Is that where I should have your mail forwarded to? Your mummy's house?"

"Don't do that. I haven't told them yet."

"Why not? Don't you think your mother will be thrilled? She's going to be a grandmother."

"I don't think this is what she had in mind," Chris mumbled. He hadn't even begun to think about how he was going to break the news to his parents. They adored Jill, and his father loved to remind him he was punching above his weight with her. They had spent years being frustrated with the choices he made, and they were right when they said she was the best thing that had ever happened to him. Telling them he was having a baby with a stranger was going to give them another reason to be disappointed, and he didn't think they would bail him out like they had other times. When he'd

115

moved out, his father had taken him aside and told him he better make it work because they couldn't afford to help him financially anymore.

"That's not my problem, Chris. Get yourself sorted and find some legal representation. Don't call me again. I'm done with you."

Jill hung up and then threw the phone against the wall. The force she used exploded it into pieces and left a hole in the plaster. It probably wasn't the most mature thing she'd ever done, but it made her feel better for a minute. He had ripped her life apart, but here he was, calling her like what he had done was no big deal. She had found out this morning that *she* definitely wasn't pregnant. She hadn't been as relieved as she thought she would be. As big a mistake as she knew it would be to have a baby with Chris, it had probably been her last chance. Now every month would go by, and there would be nothing to look forward to. All the tests except for the HIV one had come back clear. It would be a few months before she would find out about that one.

After about an hour, Jill finally fell back asleep. It wasn't very restful, though—full of dreams about Chris coming to visit her to show off his new baby and her clothesline full of baby clothes she'd never get to use.

~~~

After Jill hung up, Chris walked back to the hotel. Tomorrow he would have to call his parents. He'd also have to find somewhere more permanent to live. He had gotten used to living well beyond his means, with Jill paying most of the bills. A solicitor was also going to cost him a fortune. At least that was a one off. The most expensive thing was going to be paying child support for the next eighteen years. It just didn't feel real to him, but the gravity of the situation was slowly beginning to sink in. His life as he knew it was finished. He was about to become a single father, and even though he couldn't even imagine the baby, let alone a growing child, he wasn't selfish enough to let the kid grow up without knowing it's father. He thought about how sorry he had always felt for those dads out on the weekends, filling their children with McDonalds and dragging them to places like the zoo in an effort to spend some quality time together. Now he was about to become one of them.

Chapter 13

Why did Phil have to be such a pain? If he could just follow the plans to their exact specifications, then David wouldn't have to be making the phone call he had been dreading. It had been ten days since the disastrous "sort of a date," and David had picked up the phone and started to dial Joan's number so many times that he'd lost count, but every time, he hung up before it connected. And then a week had passed, and it got too late to be acceptable to ring and apologize, except that now he was left with no choice. He had to ask a question that could save him a lot of money. He dialled her number and waited.

Joan's phone had been ringing all morning. She was dealing with a particularly obnoxious couple. They wanted a million-dollar house for half the price and couldn't seem to comprehend that every time they moved a wall or added another bathroom, the cost was going up, not down. It wasn't like they didn't have the money. They were completely loaded, and for some reason, that made them think they were geniuses. It didn't matter how many times Joan went over the plans with them and tried to show them that what they wanted wasn't going to be functional—they thought they knew best. At this point, they would end up living in a rabbit warren that Joan would be ashamed to put her name on. The floor plan was becoming so disorganized that the owners would have to hand out a map and a compass to their guests when they came to visit unless they wanted people getting trapped in the library—a round room that had a secret door on the inside "just for fun"— instead of finding the powder room.

When her phone rang again, she grabbed it and checked the caller ID. She let out a quiet groan when she saw who it was. Could her day get any worse? She was tempted to let it go to voicemail and deal with it later, but that would only delay the inevitable. At some point, they were going to have to speak to each other, and now was as good a time as any.

When the phone kept ringing and ringing unanswered, David decided he must have really offended Joan if she wasn't going to answer. *At least this way, I can leave a message*, he thought. *Much less uncomfortable, and I'll suggest she email me her response.* He was so busy preparing what to say in the message that he was completely caught off guard when Joan answered.

"Hello." She was greeted by silence and tried again. "Hello." Still nothing. *Must be a bad connection*, she thought. She was about to hang up when she heard his voice.

"Ah, Joan. It's David from Saunders Construction. I was just about to leave you a message." *Always email*, he reminded himself, trying to remember why he had called. Just hearing her voice was enough to distract him.

Joan waited for him to continue, but when the silence lingered, she decided to take matters into her own hands.

"I can always hang up, and you can call again. I promise not to answer, and then you can leave a message. But if you need me to respond to whatever you need to ask me about, I'd have to call you back. If I left you a message and you didn't get the answer you wanted, then you'd have to call me again. That could go on all day."

"No, Joan." *Great, I've made her mad again, and in only twenty seconds,* he decided. *Just get this over with.* "That won't be necessary. Phil has a query, and it's time sensitive. Do you have a few minutes to talk it over?"

"Sure. What's your *expert* foreman sure that I have wrong this time? Does he think the building would get better ventilation without a roof? Or perhaps he thinks the space would have a more open feel without any internal walls, including the bathrooms." Her voice dripped with sarcasm. It had been a long and frustrating morning, and every time someone questioned her judgement, it pushed her closer to the edge. But she needed it to not be David she lost it with. He already thought she was nuts. No need to confirm it. She pulled herself up. *Be calm,* she thought.

"It's the slab. He wondered if it actually had to be quite that depth. It looked a lot to me too, so I thought I'd check before we poured next week."

"Actually, that's not a bad question." She flipped into architect mode, glad her voice sounded more reasonable. "I thought the same thing, but the company who did the soil testing was adamant. Council agreed, and there's no way you'll pass your inspections if you change the depth. Tell Phil I'm sorry, but he's going to have to follow the plans to the letter this time. It would have saved you a bit in the budget if you could have reduced it."

"No kidding, but safety first, right? Thanks for your time."

"It's no problem, David. That's what I'm here for." Joan paused, trying to gather her courage. She had wanted to ring David so many times last week and apologizes, but she was still embarrassed by her reaction to his simple question. "Listen, about Sunday—" she started to say but was cut off by David.

"I wanted to talk to you about the other day," he began. They both stopped at the same time, realizing they had cut each other off and waited for the other to start again. After a few seconds, it was obvious no one was sure who should continue first. After waiting a few more seconds, David made a suggestion. "Ladies first."

"Okay. I just wanted to say how sorry I was about Sunday. I don't normally carry on like that. I don't know what got into me."

"I do. I was being nosey and opinionated. If I'd minded my own business, then you wouldn't have had anything to be upset about. I'm the one who needs to apologize."

"Good," Joan continued. "So we're both sorry. You know what I'm really sorry about? I'm sorry it ruined our afternoon. I don't know if you noticed, but I was having a wonderful time. Well, until I decided to do my impression of a drama queen, that is. It's been a long time since I spent time with someone I liked quite as much as I like you."

Leaning back in his chair and smiling, David felt lighter than he had in days. He had thought he had completely blown it with Joan, but maybe there was a chance.

"I couldn't agree more. You are the most interesting and, may I say, the most beautiful woman I've met in a very long time. It would be silly for us to not try again."

"Well, the last thing I want is to be silly. What did you have in mind? Coffee or lunch sometime?"

"Nope. Definitely dinner. And soon. Would Friday night suit you or is that too short a notice?"

"Friday sounds perfect. Where would you like to meet?"

"How about your place? I'll pick you up. Seven o'clock okay?"

"It is. But what if the night goes badly? History should tell you I can be quite volatile, you know. What if you ask me something I don't like?" Joan asked, hoping he could hear the smile in her voice and pick up that she was having a little dig at herself. Not everyone got her sense of humour, and more than once she had been met with blank stares by a man who thought she was serious.

"I'll take my chances, but I'll do my best to not ask you anything that will induce violence. I'll see you Friday night."

"Friday night, then. Bye, David."

"Bye, Joan."

~~~

Joan had floated through the rest of the week. Even the most obnoxious clients couldn't spoil her elated mood, and when her doorbell rang at exactly seven o'clock on Friday night, she was more than ready for the evening to begin. Skipping out of work early had given her time to make sure she looked her very best. When she opened the door, she could see that David had gone to just as much effort. His usual jeans and work shirt had been replaced by a checked blue-and-white shirt and a navy pair of slacks. He was holding a bunch of oriental lilies.

"Hi, Joan. Wow, you look amazing." Despite the cold weather, she was wearing a knee-length dress with capped sleeves. The deep blue matched her eyes, and the light fabric hugged her in all the right places. She had finished off with heels that accentuated her slim legs, and he could see she probably worked out. He wouldn't mind joining her one day, at least on the warm-up anyway. He could help her with her stretches.

"Hi, David. Come on in. I'll just find my bag, and we can go." David happily followed her through to the kitchen, barely noticing how beautiful her home was, instead captivated by the view she provided. Dragging his eyes off her, he looked around and saw that her home reflected what he knew about her. The space was smart and elegant. Most terrace houses were small and had pokey rooms. She had obviously had a lot of work done to open it up.

"Your house is beautiful. From the outside, you can't tell it looks like this. I can see your fingerprint all over it. I'm guessing you did all this yourself?"

"I designed all the changes but had all the work done. I'm not nearly as handy with a hammer as you are. The outside is next summer's project. There's not a lot I can change except to put a new coat of paint and clear out the gardens."

Handing the flowers to Joan, he said, "These are to say just how sorry I was about the other day." She received them with a smile but decided it was time to let the matter rest.

"We need to stop apologizing to each other. Let's just forget what happened and go and enjoy our evening." She picked up the bouquet and began arranging the flowers in a vase.

While Joan was taking care of the flowers, David wandered around the room, appreciating the casual style and picking up pieces Joan had carefully chosen. Most weren't expensive. She wasn't a woman who cared about labels or trends. She knew what she liked and was just as happy to spend fifty dollars on a print as she was to spend thousands on an original piece of art as long as it made her feel good. Tonight's dress was a perfect example of that. She'd bought it from a chain store. It wasn't expensive, and it didn't come with an exclusive label. But when she put it on, she knew it suited her, and it made her feel feminine. Finished with the flowers, she picked up her coat and her bag—a knockoff Chanel she'd bought on her last overseas holiday in Asia. She knew some women would be able to tell the difference, but she didn't care. Why spend thousands of dollars when you could spend fifty? It did exactly the same thing.

"Shall we?" David asked, seeing that she was ready.

"I'm right behind you," said Joan as she followed him back down the hall, not minding the view at all.

~~~

David had chosen a French bistro on Malvern Road for dinner. As usual, it was packed with diners, all jammed in together. The noise of glasses clinking and people laughing would make deep and meaningful conversation difficult, but it was the kind of place where you spent the evening people watching and whispering to your companion "Turn around now. They look familiar. Do we know them or have we just seen them on TV?" The waiters were all French and full of their own importance, and Joan guessed the wine list would be expensive, and the food on the menu would be difficult to pronounce. It was perfect.

It had been years since Joan had enjoyed a real French meal, and she enjoyed talking David through the menu, explaining what everything really was. Her French was rusty, but she could still get by. David rejected the calf's liver and chose prawns and the eye fillet. Joan had wanted to choose the snails, but after seeing David's horrified expression, she settled instead for the scallops—although she couldn't see why one was gross and the other was acceptable—and the rack of lamb. While they waited for the first course to arrive, they entered into a lively discussion about who had the best taste in music. Joan had been more of a Duran Duran fan as a teenager and still enjoyed listening to the latest music. David preferred the Australian classics, such as Cold Chisel and Midnight Oil, from his teenage years and had very little interest in anything recorded after 1995. When Joan pulled out her iPod to show him the wide range of music she listened to, he couldn't believe she had over a thousand songs on the little device. When he admitted he didn't own an iPod and still kept it old school with a CD stacker in his ute, she told him he was a dinosaur, and it was time he entered the new century. At least they both agreed that rap was awful and lamented the degeneration of the modern teenager. They were laughing over how tempted David was to drop a pencil down the pants of one of his apprentices who loved showing his underwear to the rest of the world when he stopped midsentence, staring in the direction of the door.

Joan turned around to see what had caught David's attention. A family was standing next to the reservation desk, talking to the maître'd. The husband could have graced the cover of *GQ*. He was tall and slim with his hair greying at the temples. His casual clothes screamed money, and he conducted himself like the world had been created for the sole purpose of giving him somewhere to live. The two children, both in their early teens, looked bored. It was clear that eating at such an expensive restaurant was an everyday occurrence for them, not the special treat it was for lesser mortals. But it was their mother who took Joan's breath away. Her blonde hair fell in gentle waves around her exquisite face. Her figure made Joan wonder if she was a model because she was tall and incredibly slim. She was wearing a V-neck dress in soft plum and lace that Joan had seen in a magazine last month. But instead of a knockoff like Joan's, she was sure it was a genuine Collette Dinnigan. Remembering the price, she knew it cost double her weekly mortgage payments. The woman didn't bother looking around the restaurant at the other diners. Why would she? There couldn't possible anyone here more important than she was.

David dropped his eyes away from her and started to eat the prawns that had been placed before him. Joan dragged her gaze away from the family and back to David, upset by his interest in them. No matter how gorgeous someone was, didn't men know it was rude to stare when they were with someone else? She ignored the plate in front of her, hoping for an apology from David or at least an explanation, but neither was forthcoming. She wondered if tonight was going to go the way of their first date—a disaster. At least this time it wouldn't be her fault.

David concentrated on his entrée. He didn't think she'd seen him. She was almost seated when a waiter collided with a diner who had stood up unexpectedly and sent a tray of drinks flying. The sound of breaking glass caught her attention, and she looked across the room. David lifted his head at the same time to see what the commotion was about when their eyes met. Fifteen years disappeared in a moment. She hesitated and then leaned across to her husband, whispering in his ear and motioning towards David. Standing, she started to walk towards David and Joan's table.

Feeling the presence of someone standing next to her, Joan looked up expecting to see the waiter. Instead she was looking at the most perfect face she had ever seen outside of a magazine. The skin was like porcelain—so very perfect—except this was a living, breathing person that no one had airbrushed. Confused, Joan began to feel like she was in some sort of art-house movie that she didn't understand when the woman began to speak to her date.

"David. I thought it was you. It's lovely to see you. You look just the same."

David took his napkin out of his lap and placed it on the table, standing as he did. The stranger stepped towards him and reached up, kissing him on his cheek.

Her lips felt cold against David's flushed face, and he wished the floor would open up and swallow him. All these years, and he'd never run into her once. And now today, when he was with another woman, here she was.

"It's been a long time, Charlie. I'd ask how you were, but I can see for myself. It looks like life is treating you well."

"I prefer Charlotte now."

"Of course you do. How are your parents?"

"They're good. The same. And what about you? Are you married? Children?"

"No and no."

"I'm surprised. You were always the marrying kind."

"Things change, Charlie," he reminded her, refusing to use the name she had always said she hated. "I changed. Someone changed me." Joan saw Charlotte flinch as David sat back down, and her face blushed at his words. There was obviously a history between these two people. Hoping to end the uncomfortable silence that had descended on the table, Joan put out her hand in greeting.

"Hi. I'm Joan." Good manners dictated that Charlotte take it, and she introduced herself.

"Nice to meet you. I'm an old friend of David's." Charlotte had barely noticed Joan before. So distracted was she by David and the instant feeling of regret for the life with him that she had rejected. She looked Joan over, noting that she was a beautiful woman. But her well-trained eye could see that she wasn't very well dressed, and her purse was the knockoff of the original Charlotte carried with her tonight. She looked down at David, who was busy finishing his entrée and trying to pretend she wasn't there. Charlotte turned back to Joan. "Well, I should go. It was nice to meet you. I hope you enjoy the rest of your evening." She turned on her well-shod heel and returned to her table.

Joan could see that David's hand was shaking. His face was drawn, but she wasn't sure if it was caused by rage or despair. Charlotte had clearly been someone important to him at one time. Joan was desperate to ask but didn't want to push. It didn't sound like Charlotte had been in his life for a long time, but the effect she had had on him was disturbing, and Joan wondered if he might still be in love with her.

David put his cutlery down and looked at Joan. She looked confused, and as much as he wanted to, David decided there was really no way to ignore what had just taken place. Besides if he intended to have any kind of relationship with Joan, he was going to have to explain sometime. He might as well get it over with.

"Do you remember I told you I nearly got married?"

Joan's eyes widened with surprise as she realized what he was telling her. "To Charlotte. You two were engaged?"

"Thanks. So you think I'm not in her league either?"

"No, it's not that. She just didn't seem your type. I guess I don't know your type. I just meant I thought you might prefer someone a little more down to Earth. Not quite so—" Not wanting to insult someone she had only met for a few minutes, Joan stopped talking.

"She wasn't always like that, and she never looked that flawless when we were together. But she was beautiful. When she agreed to marry me, I thought I was the luckiest man on earth. What I didn't know was she was just waiting for someone better to come along."

"I very much doubt her husband is better than you," she declared, looking over at him. He was sniffing and swirling a glass of red wine while the waiter stood by. "He looks like a waste of space to me."

David had never met him, but watching him now, he had to agree. "Unfortunately, she didn't think so. She met him about two months before we were supposed to get married. So while we were picking menus and sending out invitations, she was seeing him. His name is Carl, and he's from a very rich family. They made all their money about a hundred years ago in real estate, and now they live off trust funds. I doubt he's ever had to work a day in his life. Charlotte decided to take her chances with him, and one week before the wedding, she called it off."

"And left you heartbroken."

"She left me with the half of the bill for the wedding. We also had to sell the house we had bought together because I couldn't afford the mortgage on my own. But yes, she also left me heartbroken."

Interrupted by the waiter bringing out their main course, they both stopped talking. At least this explained why such an eligible man wasn't married. He had been hurt. Deeply.

Picking up his fork, David asked, "Do you mind if we don't talk about this anymore? I've tried very hard to forget, and seeing Charlie was not what I was expecting tonight."

"Of course we can." Joan took a bite of her meal and was instantly back in Europe. "How's your dinner? Mine's incredible. I haven't eaten anything this good since I was in France."

Soon Joan was regaling David with funny stories about her travels throughout Europe. After they finished their dinner, they both decided to skip dessert. There hadn't seemed to be a lot of food on their plates, but they were both full. David paid the bill and then helped Joan on with her coat like the gentleman he was before they stepped out into the cold. When they left, Joan noted that he didn't look in Charlotte's direction, but Joan couldn't resist. She saw a woman who looked sad. Neither she nor her husband were talking to each other, and the children looked to be squabbling. Charlotte looked up and caught Joan's gaze. She gave her a wan smile and lifted her hand in good-bye. Joan smiled in response and wondered what Charlotte was thinking. Perhaps she was regretting her decision in letting David go. Joan hoped she would never be that foolish.

On the drive home, Joan insisted on switching the radio from an oldies station to something from this decade and began to sing along. She sounded terrible, but David enjoyed seeing her having fun. If that was the worst thing about her, he decided then she was as close to perfect as a woman could be. By the time they reached Joan's house, David's previously happy mood had returned. He left the car idling—a clear sign he wasn't looking to come in. He leaned over and kissed her lightly on the lips.

"I had a wonderful time tonight, Joan. I'm hoping we can do this again."

"I'd like that very much, David."

"I'll call you soon then. And about Charlie—I got over her a long time ago. It was just a shock to see her, so please don't read anything into my reaction. I haven't thought about her in a very long time."

"Okay."

"Good. I'd hate for you to misunderstand. I'll see you soon."

"I'm looking forward to it," she replied.

"Wait there." David opened his door and walked around to her side. He opened the door for her and offered her his hand to help her out. He kissed her once more, on the cheek this time, and then watched as she walked to her door.

Joan let herself into her home and locked the door behind her. *How to find out someone's secrets quickly*, she thought. *I just hope he's telling the truth when he says he's still not in love with her.* If he'd been pining for her all these years, then she had no chance. And she very much wanted a chance with David.

When he saw that Joan was safely inside, David returned to his car and pulled out of her street. Running into Charlie like that had been a shock. And it had brought back all the old feelings, not of love but of humiliation and rejection. It had taken years for him to get back into the dating world after her, and he had never found a woman he trusted since. But hiding away and keeping everyone at arm's length wasn't the answer. He wasn't sure if it was just that enough time had gone by or if it was Joan, but he knew it was time to give love another chance. He pulled over to the side of the road and took out his phone. It's probably too soon to call her. *Maybe a compromise*, he decided as he started typing.

R U free 2moro

I could be persuaded

Movie?

Sounds perfect

I'll call you 2moro

Looking forward to it

Nite

Nite

Chapter 14

It shouldn't be this hard to get three children ready every morning, but by the time Beth finally had them in the car, she felt like she'd already done a day's work. Getting them out of bed in winter bordered on impossible, and it didn't matter how much she yelled and reminded them what they needed for school, most days she didn't get out of their street before she had to turn the car around and go back for something. Today she saw that Lochie didn't have his tie around his neck. She could turn around to get it, but she would be late for her appointment. *Bugger it*, she thought. Another out-of-uniform detention for him it was.

Tom had left early this morning, so she hadn't seen him. But she had reminded him about their dinner reservations last night and put a reminder on his phone for two hours ahead of the time she needed him home. No excuse was acceptable.

She found it hard to believe that today they would be celebrating seventeen years of marriage. Going in, she had always had the expectation that it would last but then, didn't everybody? To be able to say, "I've been married to the same person all this time" was a huge accomplishment. Look at poor Jill. She had only managed to last two years. Beth knew how lucky she was.

It had had its ups and downs like all marriages, but what Beth had never expected was how slow and how quick time could go all at once. Having a baby within the first year of marriage meant they never had the time to consolidate themselves as a couple. One day, they were two people in love, and the next, they were a family with all the responsibility that goes with that. And when Tom took over his father's business, their lives got even more hectic. Most days passed by in a blur, with each of them wishing only for a quiet minute to themselves and a decent night's sleep. But inside of the crazy busy days were the hours that never seemed to end—the days when Sarah was teething and cried continuously or how when Nate turned one, he refused a day nap. Unfortunately that meant that at five o'clock he started screaming with exhaustion and then fell asleep, only to wake up three hours later ready to play all night.

When all three kids finally made it to school, Beth thought she might get a chance to breathe. Instead she started emergency teaching at a few local schools to help take the financial burden off Tom. They didn't really need the money now, but it gave her a chance to escape the house and see other adults, which she desperately needed, because if Beth thought raising babies was hard, she was completely unprepared for the joys of raising teenagers. It hadn't been too bad with Lochie until he turned fourteen. Overnight he became impossible. She often wondered if all parents had to deal with the soul-destroying abuse she seemed to receive daily or if she was the only one. Suddenly she had become some sort of idiot who had no life experience and didn't understand anything. Every word she spoke was taken as an insult, and her eldest son believed himself to be a mature wonderful example of humanity who just had the misfortune of being dropped off to the wrong family at birth. He'd only recently started to behave like a reasonable human being again, but the relief of that was overshadowed by Sarah. When she turned twelve, Beth's sweet, kind girl disappeared and was replaced by a boy-crazy alien who thought she had the right to dress anyway she wanted and made "less is best" her motto. It didn't help that it was becoming impossible to buy anything decent in the shops. Beth had seen the early summer clothes and noticed that most of the shorts and skirts for girls could easily be confused for a belt, they were so short. Beth didn't know how she was going to drag Sarah through her teenage years with any modesty. Probably kicking and screaming no doubt. At what point had parents lost control and children had taken over the world? Beth had missed that memo. She was grateful every day for school uniforms when she tugged down the dress that Sarah always hitched up with the belt to make it shorter. There was only so much a girl could do to make navy plaid look inappropriate. Nate was still at that age where he loved his parents, but Beth knew it wasn't far off before he, too, thought they were his enemy. Sometimes Beth wondered if there would be anything of her and Tom remaining by the time he turned eighteen. Someone would have to come and scrape what was left of them off the floor and try and reconstitute them back into the people they used to be.

Half an hour later, Beth was ensconced in a chair at Caroline's hairdressers with the strangest woman critiquing her hair. She was broomstick thin with jet-black hair cut into a severe bob and dressed in clothes designed for someone twenty years younger. Beth had already been nervous about putting herself in the hands of a stranger, but Caroline had insisted Harlow was the best. Now she was just plain terrified. She had no desire to leave here two-hundred dollars poorer and looking like a short, fat version of Cruella de Vil.

Her mind was put at rest when after about five minutes of lifting and dropping her hair, tutting as she went, Harlow suggested colouring it about two shades darker to a light brunette and then highlighting it with caramel overtones. She also suggested taking a few inches off and adding layers around her face to create movement and accentuate her deep-brown eyes.

Beth agreed, thinking if it was too awful she could always tie it back in the usual ponytail, and no one would notice.

It took one cup of coffee, two magazines, and about three hours until she was done, but the time was well worth it. When Beth saw the completed style, she was thrilled. Her hair did indeed fall in soft layers around her face, and the colour wasn't that different from her own, just richer. It reminded her of melted chocolate cascading down her back. As Harlow removed the cape, she shook her head from side to side, watching herself in the mirror. She felt magnificent.

Harlow stood back from her work. Another masterpiece. She caught Beth's eye in the mirror and asked, "You like?"

"I definitely like. Thank you."

"I want to see you back here in eight weeks. We can't have you letting yourself go again."

Beth nodded her agreement as she paid the astronomical bill. Maybe she could find someone a little closer to home and a little more reasonably priced, but at least now she knew it was possible for her to look pretty. Now she just needed to find something to wear tonight that made her feel as good as her hair did.

A few minutes of driving took her to her next destination. Caroline was meeting her, insisting that she needed the help. She'd told Beth it was to boost her confidence and offer her a discerning eye, but Beth knew it was probably to make sure she actually went home with something new. Beth had steered Caroline away from her usual shops that were full of snooty sales assistants who acted like they were doing you a favour if they let you purchase something from their exclusive store and only carried clothes for women who had an "eating optional" policy. After combing the Internet, Beth had found a place that catered to bigger women who wanted to dress in clothes other than floral tents.

Caroline was already inside when Beth arrived. She was pulling clothes off racks and handing them to a shop assistant who was looking more than a little harassed. The poor girl probably didn't understand why a woman with Caroline's figure was in there when they didn't sell any clothes small enough for her. Beth snuck up behind her and, in a put-on haughty voice, imitated every shop assistant who had been cruel to her over the years.

"Excuse me, madame. I don't believe we can help you. You're much too skinny to be in our store. Perhaps, madame, would prefer to try somewhere more suitable."

Caroline swung around ready to put whoever was brave enough to speak to her that way back in their place when she saw that it was Beth. Her eyes lit up with delight, and she pulled her friend into a warm hug, careful not to mess up her hair.

"You look amazing. I can't believe how pretty you look. I told you how amazing Harlow was."

"You did. You didn't tell me how weird she was, though. The woman scared me half to death."

"Who cares if she's weird? She's an artist, darling," she said, affecting a French accent. Now let's shop."

Soon Caroline had Beth in and out of different pants and skirts, and even got her to try on a dress, but they both agreed a little more weight needed to be lost before Beth could carry it well. She had lost five kilos so far. Not earth shattering, but it had already begun to make a difference. The clothes she had been stuffing herself into fitted properly again, and Beth had even begun looking at some of the other items in her wardrobe that hadn't seen the light of day in two or three years. The good food choices—Caroline refused to let her use the word "diet"— she was making had not been easy. For the first three days, she had suffered through screaming headaches that didn't go away no matter how much Panadol she took. When she came close to quitting, Caroline insisted it was just her body suffering from sugar withdrawal. She had made it through, and now she was starting to notice that she had more energy and was less moody. It had been a huge change having to make a shopping list every week, and sticking to it had been difficult, but the cooking hadn't been as hard as she first imagined. Once a week, Caroline came over and taught her a new meal. Beth had discovered cooking a roast was easy, after years of thinking that people who could do it had to be amazing cooks. The kids had even adapted to the changes in the house. Their favourite meal turned out to be grilled chicken with a warm red onion and tomato salsa. Caroline had promised that next week they were going to cook spaghetti and meatballs. Beth would have to do without the spaghetti, but Caroline promised Beth she wouldn't even notice. She still missed eating chocolate, especially at night while watching TV, but even that craving was disappearing. Early on, she had pointed out to Caroline that studies were always saying chocolate was good for your mood, and some even said it aided in weight loss. Unmoved, Caroline pointed out they weren't talking about Cadbury dairy milk but organic cacao powder. Beth didn't think sitting down to a movie and a spoon full of raw cacao powder sounded very tasty.

The hardest change for her had been giving up alcohol. Every day for the first few weeks, she had craved a drink, especially when the children were being even more obnoxious than usual. For the first week, she had been irritable, not knowing what to do with the empty hand that usually held a drink at night. The way she missed it highlighted to her that it had been a problem, even if she hadn't seen it, and she was grateful to Caroline for bringing it to her attention before it became too hard to stop. She hadn't been perfect. She had given in a few times, feeling ashamed of herself the next morning, and she had never told Caroline. But it *was* getting easier, and sometimes when she thought she might throttle a child, but instead of reaching for a bottle, she locked herself in the bathroom with a book and had a long, warm soak in the bath. It didn't have quite the same effect, but at least she couldn't hear them fighting in there.

After about an hour of shopping, Beth wasn't sure if she would actually have the energy to go out tonight. Caroline had been like a whirlwind, making Beth try on outfit after outfit. But they had been successful, and Beth now had a beautiful ensemble for the evening ahead. They had settled on a pair of chocolate pants that fell straight from the waist and were long enough to accommodate a pair of heels to add some height. The top was a beautiful scooped-neck blouse that wrapped around her waist and accentuated the curve that was slimmer than it had been. It was a soft caramel, almost the colour of her highlights, and shot through with strands of turquoise thread to add a little interest.

Beth stood in front of the full-length mirror, admiring herself for the first time in years. She was still carrying most of the weight, but wearing clothes that fit her properly and suited her shape made a huge difference. Her face was already looking thinner, and she could finally see that she *was* pretty. Her confidence in herself was returning, just a little drop at a time, but it was beginning to amount to something significant. Now if she could just get Tom's eyes off the footy and on to her, maybe he would see the same changes in her that she was seeing in herself.

Caroline suggested a quick lunch before Beth had to go and collect her children from school. They found a busy café nearby and, after ordering two chicken salads, Caroline turned the conversation to Beth and how she was going.

"I can already see a difference. How much weight have you lost so far?"

"On Monday morning, it was five kilos." Beth smiled, proud of herself as she remembered seeing that the digital numbers on the scale had dropped into a lower decade.

"And you're only weighing yourself once a week?"

"Yes, Mum," she lied. Beth couldn't help it and had been weighing herself every morning. On the days when the scales gave her the grim news that she had put on a few hundred grams, she thought about quitting, but overall, the numbers were dropping, so she hung in there.

"I think it's time to add some exercise. It will help you build muscle, and muscle burns fat. I have a book in the car I want you to read. Instead of doing hours of cardio, you do short bursts of high-intensity exercise to raise your heart rate. You will have to work harder, but for a much shorter time."

"Oh, goody. Can't wait." Beth remembered jumping around the lounge room to Jane Fonda aerobics videos when the kids were little. They never helped no matter how often she did them, and they left her feeling silly and worn out for the rest of the day.

"Don't be like that. It's good for you."

"If you say so."

"I do. Has Tom said anything about the changes you've made?"

"He's enjoying the food. I don't think he noticed that I've lost any weight yet."

"He will. It's obvious in your face. "

"I know, and I'm excited by the prospect of losing more."

"And what about that terrible nightie? You aren't still wearing that, are you?"

"No. You'll be pleased to know I threw it out."

"Excellent. Now I don't want details, but are you making a bit more of an effort in the bedroom?"

"I am. I think it kind of took him by surprise, but he isn't complaining. I just wish he wasn't so distracted. I think something's going on at work, but he hasn't said anything." She took the last bite of the salad the waitress had brought over earlier and then checked her watch.

"I better get going or I'll be late for the kids."

"Well, don't let them annoy you tonight. Good mood, please."

"I'll do my best."

"Pamela will be at your place at five-thirty, and I insist you take heaps of pictures for me."

"I will. Thanks for all your help today. I would have been lost trying to find something that worked, and I would never have picked that top for myself."

"Well, if you've got it, flaunt it. Tom's going to think you look hot tonight. Have fun."

~~~

As promised, a makeup artist that Caroline used if she had a special event on arrived at half past five. Sarah was mesmerised by the cases of eye shadow and cream. She watched her mother transform from ordinary to beautiful. She could hardly believe that it was her mum. Clever shading made her cheek bones appear more prominent and helped her face look slimmer. Sarah asked question after question, and Beth decided it had been worth the money for Sarah to see that you didn't need to paint your face in thick layers to look pretty. It took about half an hour, but when Pamela was finished, Beth felt like a movie star. Maybe she could pick up a few tips from Pamela too. She still looked like herself, but much fresher and younger. As she dressed, Beth realized that Tom should have been home and in the shower by now. She decided she'd better give him a call. She pulled out her phone from her bag and saw that she had a missed call and a text. She had turned off the ringer at lunch and completely forgot to turn it back on. Both were from Tom. *Probably telling me he's running late. Typical.* But when she read the message, she realized just how wrong she was.

Sorry babe gonna have to cancel tonite. Emergency.

Dialling his number, Beth's fury grew while she waited for him to answer. She had been talking about dinner for a week. She had spent all day preparing, and it was their wedding anniversary. What could possibly be more important?

"Hey, Beth. Did you get my text?" he answered before she had a chance to speak.

"I did. Are you out of your mind? We have important plans for tonight."

"I know, and I'm sorry. We'll have to reschedule. I got a call from the hospital. A pipe burst in the basement car park, and it's a flood down there. It could take hours to fix, and we have to do it now."

"Can't John go? He's your after-hours guy this week."

"Nah, it's his kid's birthday, and I already let him go. He's going to take any calls that come in after nine tonight, but the hospital can't wait. I'm sorry to let you down, but we can go on Friday night. It would have been nice to get out, but another night's just as good. You call the restaurant and reschedule, and I'll see you later tonight."

Beth stood in the middle of her bedroom, staring at the silent phone. Tom had hung up on her. She slipped of the heels she had been wearing and put on her slippers. She joined the boys on the couch but couldn't follow what they were watching. Disappointed didn't even begin to cover how she felt. She had been working so hard to improve their marriage and had gone to so much effort for tonight, and he'd blown her off for work. What was the point of trying to change when her husband didn't even notice? When the doorbell rang ten minutes later, she took the money she'd given to Lochie and answered the door for the pizza delivery. She sat with the kids, eating her first takeaway for about six weeks, as silent tears slid down her face until all the makeup was washed away. Understanding that something was very wrong with their mother, the children remained subdued for the rest of the evening and quietly went to their bedrooms to do their homework without arguing. Once Beth was alone, she looked into the fridge and from the back pulled out a bottle of white wine. She found her favourite DVD and sat herself down to watch. *Sleepless in Seattle* had seen her through many lonely evenings, and it would have to do it again. She twisted the top off and poured herself a drink. She kept the bottle close by. She had no intention of stopping until it was empty.

~~~

It was eleven o'clock when Tom finally finished the job. The leak had been easy to find, but getting it fixed without turning off the water to a major institution was difficult. He was making a note in his invoice book about how many hours to charge for when he wrote the date down for the first time that day. He knew it was important, but it took him a minute to realize what that day was. Oh no! Their wedding anniversary. Beth normally reminded him every year, and he would buy her flowers and a cheesy card, but they hadn't made a big deal of it since their tenth year. That explained why she wanted to go out to dinner tonight. Why hadn't she said what the occasion was?

Stopping at a twenty-four-hour supermarket on the way home, Tom managed to buy a card and a sorry-looking bunch of roses. They were slightly brown on the edges but still better than nothing. He hoped his wife was in a forgiving mood, but when he pulled up, he saw that all the lights were off. He snuck into the house, not wanting to wake anyone, and found Beth asleep on the couch with the credits to one of those movies she liked—they all seemed like one continuous waste of time to him—playing on the TV. As he leaned over to retrieve the remote from the coffee table so he could turn of the TV, his foot hit an empty bottle on the floor. He picked it up and put it on the bench. He made his way through the dark house to the bedroom. He couldn't help but feel disappointed about the empty bottle he'd found. He had noticed that she had cut back her drinking to almost nothing. It had been so nice lately. He hadn't commented on the changes she'd been making, but he had noticed. He even thought she'd lost some weight. He had never minded too much when she put it on, but he didn't like how affected her. *And now he'd gone and stuffed up. I better get some sleep*, he thought, *because I'm going to have a big morning tomorrow. I also better get some earplugs because I see a lot of yelling in my future.*

Chapter 15

When Beth woke the next morning, she found herself still on the couch. Tom was sitting on the coffee table, facing her, with a cup in his hand and another one beside him. As she sat up to accept the drink he held out, her stomach rolled. Too much wine last night when she wasn't used to it anymore combined with the greasy pizza turned out to be a bad combination. The old familiar feeling of a hangover washed over her as her head began to thump. She accepted the coffee, not saying anything to him, curious to see if he even knew what he had done yesterday. A bunch of very sorry-looking roses were in a vase and sat on the table next to Tom, and he picked up an envelope and handed it to her.

Beth took a sip of the coffee and then opened the envelope. It was an anniversary card, and inside was a handwritten message.

Dear Beth,

I'm so sorry we missed our dinner last night. I promise to make it up to you. Happy Anniversary

Love Tom. Xxx

Before she had a chance to respond, Tom continued on from the card.

"I really am sorry. I completely forgot what yesterday was. I thought our dinner plans were just a chance to get out of the house. I didn't realize until too late that it was our wedding anniversary."

"You forgot?" she asked, her tone bitter. "Gee, you can't imagine how important that makes me feel." Beth could feel last night's tears returning, and she wished Tom would just go away and leave her alone so she could cry in private.

"Beth, why didn't you tell me? If I'd known, I would have made a special effort to be home. You've always reminded me in the past. Why not this year?"

"Because I already have three children. I don't need another one. Every time I have to remind you about something that's important to me, it diminishes it. Do you know how sick of having to make sure you do the right thing I am? You have the footy fixture memorized. You don't have any problem remembering your mother's birthday. Why don't you make an effort for me? Am I that unworthy of your consideration these days?"

"No, you're not unworthy. I love you. You're my wife. It was an honest mistake, and if you'll let me, I'll make it up to you."

"What with? A bunch of flowers that look like rejects from the petrol station. You used to bring me flowers all the time for no reason. If these are a reflection of how much I mean to you, then we have a serious problem. "

"I know they look tragic. There was nothing open last night except the supermarket, and I forgot to put them in a vase."

"It's not the flowers, Tom. You didn't remember. I made it so easy for you. I made the reservations, and I reminded you over and over. All you had to do was show up, but you couldn't even bother to do that."

"I told you I forgot." Tom didn't want to wake up the kids, but he was finding it hard to keep his volume down. Why did she always make him feel like he was the only one who did something wrong in their marriage? He hadn't been too happy with her in the past few years either. "I don't understand. You never seemed to mind telling me when things were coming up before. You know how much I've got going on at work. I can't fit anything else in my brain."

"Well, guess what? I've always minded. I hate that I'm such a low priority for you. I hate that you have absolutely no clue about what to buy me for my birthday or that my Christmas present is always some joint thing for the house that I have to suggest. I'm not asking for you to follow me around all day, throwing rose petals at my feet. But I wish you would take a bit of time to consider what's important to me. All I am to you is a babysitter and a house cleaner. You take me for granted."

"Are you serious?" Tom stood up and shut the door to block out the sound of his yelling. "When was the last time you considered me? Your only interest in my work is whether we're making enough money. I'm the boss. I *had* to work last night because if I didn't do the job, we would have lost the hospital contract. I've put on extra staff to cover the work, and I can't just fire them if it falls through. Yes, I should have asked someone else to cover the shift, but I forgot Paul had asked for a few hours off, and it was too late to get someone else to do it. Do you have any idea what's going on in here?" he said, pointing at his head. "Can you even begin to comprehend the pressure I'm under every day to make sure this all works?"

"How would I know? You never talk to me anymore about work, or anything else for that matter. So don't you dare make this my fault," she fired back at him in an angry whisper.

"Poor Beth. Stuck with such a bad husband. You think I take you for granted. Back at ya, baby. I'm nothing more than a walking cheque book to you. I'm sorry that I forgot it was our anniversary, but you could have reminded me. Instead you let me walk into a trap. You knew I'd forget. Well, at least now you can play the martyr and tell all your friends what a terrible husband I am. Don't forget, love—you're not so perfect yourself. I might have a few complaints of my own. "

Shocked by her husband's accusations, Beth couldn't respond. That wasn't what she thought at all. She never wanted to trick Tom. She had just wanted for him to remember on his own, thinking it would demonstrate that he still loved her and was interested in their marriage. She'd done everything to jog his memory short of outright telling him. Now *she* was the one copping the blame.

Seeing the hurt look on her face, Tom wished he could take his words back. He'd noticed a huge change in Beth lately and seen that she had been making an effort. What was the point of going over old ground?

"Forget I said that. I didn't mean it."

"Yes, you did. I want to know what you meant."

Tom paced in front of the TV, trying to figure out a way to get out of this, but he didn't think it was possible. Beth could be like a pit bull. Once she grabbed onto something, she wouldn't let go, and he had given her something to grab onto.

"I just meant that we haven't been very close the last few years. And I'm not blaming you alone. It's both of us. I'm busy. You're busy. We have the kids."

"Which is why I planned a dinner out last night. So we could spend some time together. Do you know what I did yesterday? I spent most of the day getting ready. I had my hair done. I even went shopping and bought something new to wear. I thought an evening out would give us a change to reconnect. I guess my expectations were too high."

Sighing, Tom sat back down at the table, leaned over, and took Beth's hands, his anger disappearing instantly when he saw how disappointed she was.

"Your expectations weren't too high. I stuffed up and forgot. It would have been really nice to go out. And thank you for making an effort." Looking at her properly for the first time that morning, he could see that her hair was different. It was a bit hard to tell after she had slept on it all night, but he could see it had been pretty.

"Is that a new top? I don't think I've ever seen you in it before."

"It is. I wanted to look nice for you. Instead I wasted money on something you're never going to see."

"Yes, I will. We can reschedule. Let me make the reservations and organize everything. I know it'll be a few days late, but it's the best I can do."

"What's the point, Tom? The moment has passed, and I don't think I want to try again." All the fight left her then. "I feel so let down."

"And you should. I've been a colossal idiot, but I desperately want to make it up to you. Please let me?"

Beth looked at Tom, and not the way she usually did. It's funny how when you live with someone for so many years, you stop looking at them properly. She thought he was still as handsome as the day they met. He wasn't too tall, which suited Beth, but he had strong, broad shoulders, which she loved. They always made her feel like he could protect her from anything. His face had aged a little over the years, but whose hadn't? He was beginning to go grey, and even though he complained about it, Beth liked it. It made him seem like more of an adult. When you're married to someone you've known since you were seventeen, sometimes it was hard to think of them in those terms—not as a teenager anymore but as a man.

"All right. I'll go, but please don't stuff it up."

"I promise I won't. Friday night?"

"Okay." Beth hesitated, not sure if this was the best time to bring this up, but while they were clearing the air, she might as well. "Tom, what did you mean about work? Is something going on that I don't know about?"

He shook his head. "Don't worry about it. It's my problem, and I'm dealing with it."

"How can you expect me to understand your pressures if you won't talk to me about them? I want to know."

"It's nothing major. We're just so busy. You'd think that in this economy, things would be slowing down, but we're not."

"Isn't that a good problem to have? Put on more staff, and then you're problems solved."

"I am. I'm looking for someone to start ASAP. But it's not just the jobs. When I started working with Dad, it was just me and him. Now there's staff to deal with and the office. We used to handwrite invoices, but now everything's on computer, and you know how much I love them. I have to deal with the unions, and they love making it hard to get my guys on some sites. And every month the paperwork keeps piling up. I have to know every rule and regulation, but each time I think I've got it right, the government changes the rules again. I have to deal with GST, and PAYG, and BAS. I swear, if they throw one more acronym at me, I might explode. I'm completely snowed under."

"Can you hire someone who takes care of all that stuff for you? If they dealt with the wages and the invoicing, it would take a lot of pressure off."

"I can get someone in, but I'm not keen on them having access to the bank accounts. And while the guys are generating money and covering their wages and costs, having someone in the office is just a drain. They aren't going to pay for themselves."

"I get that. But if you don't have to do the work in the office, you can be out on site more, and that would increase revenue wouldn't it?"

"Yes, it would. The thing is I don't want to do it anymore. I hate plumbing."

"What?"

"I really, really hate it. It's never been what I wanted to do. If I'd gotten a better score on my exams, I would have gone to uni like the rest of you. I was so jealous when you all went off and started your lives. Instead I had to stay at home with my parents and work for my father. I never had a choice. I couldn't study, and you remember how bad the job market was back then. My father offered me an apprenticeship, and it was a reliable trade. People always need plumbers, but it wasn't what I had in mind for myself."

"I had no idea. You never said anything. Ever. Even when we were in school, you never mentioned it. I thought you were happy with the idea of going to work with your dad."

"Not really. But I only scraped into year twelve. I resigned myself to the idea that I wasn't going to get into uni anyway so I didn't try. By the time I decided what I wanted to do, too much of the year had passed, and I couldn't catch up."

"I'm a little afraid to ask. What is it that you wanted to do?"

"Promise not to get upset? It's not exactly a huge money spinner."

"I'll try, but you're starting to scare me. With all your complaints about the government, you aren't thinking of becoming a politician are you?"

"No, I have no interest in going into politics. But I do have something specific in mind. I've been thinking about it for a long time, decades really, and what I really want to do is teach."

"What, like at TAFE? Teach plumbing."

"No. Like at a high school. I'd like to be a history teacher."

"Tom. Why? Teaching is awful. I hate it."

"I know you do, but half the time you're only babysitting a class. You don't get to see the kid's progress as the year goes by and get to actually know them and help them learn. I think if you taught the same class all year, you might feel differently about your job."

"Maybe. But you can't just decide to get a job teaching. You have to go to uni for years and earn a degree. If you did it part time, it would take eight years, and we'd never get to see you. It would be worse than it is now."

"I know. I'm not suggesting I go part time."

"Full-time study and a full-time business. That's impossible. If you think you're stressed out now, imagine adding classes, and exams, and assignments. You can't do it."

"I know. That's why I'm considering selling the business."

"Are you out of your mind? We can't live on my income. I know you said I think of you as a walking cheque book, but I really don't. But we do have three children and last time I checked, they expect to eat every day and have somewhere to live. I'm kind of fond of the concept myself." *Great*, Beth thought. *The last thing I need right now with two teenagers is a husband going through a midlife crisis as well.*

"I've never neglected my responsibilities. Do you really think I'm going to start now?"

"No, of course not. But why do you need to sell? What if you put someone in to run the day-to-day aspects and oversaw them? That way, we would still have some income."

"Because if I don't trust someone to work in the office while I'm there, do you really think I'm going to hand the whole thing over to someone else and expect them to handle all that responsibility? They could run the whole thing into the ground or quit, and then I'd have to take it over again. If I sell, all the pressure is off me so I can concentrate on uni, and I think we'd make a really good profit."

"Are you sure? Who's going to buy it?"

"I've had a couple of offers already. The contract with the hospital has given me something worth selling. The contract is with the business, not me personally. Anyone buying us out would take that over. And don't forget we have a big customer base in the area. Our reputation is worth a lot."

"How much would you get? Surely not enough to live on for four years while you study?"

"You'd be surprised. I'm thinking of getting a proper valuation done so I know if I'm being offered a fair price. But I don't want to use the money from the sale to live on. I would still work part time, but probably just on the weekends. Instead of having to pay a guy a fortune to work on a Saturday, I could be the one getting double time. And our mortgage is almost gone. But before we make any decisions, I need to find out what it's worth and make sure it's a viable idea. I'm not going to put us into debt to do this."

"Have you really thought about what being a teacher entails? I've never had to go out and be a plumber, so I can't compare which job is worse, but I think being a teacher is one of the hardest jobs there are. Day after day of kids who have no respect for you and would rather be anywhere else but school."

"Maybe. But there are hardly any male teachers out there. You agree that a lot of teachers are just doing a job. I want to teach, and I think I could make a difference."

"I'd rather you tried to make a difference in the lives of your own children."

"If I was teaching, I could. I'd be around a lot more, and I wouldn't have to be on call all the time. We could actually take a holiday together. When you and the kids are off from school, I end up working because that's when my staff take their holidays. I didn't even get Christmas day last year because I couldn't get anyone to agree to cover emergencies."

"And you're really, really sure this is what you want to do?"

"It is."

"Okay then. If it's what you want, then we'll find a way to make it work."

Tom's face lit up. He had never thought Beth would even consider letting him do this, let alone support him in it. Women. Always full of surprises.

He leaned over to the couch and hugged his wife. "Thanks for listening to me and for saying okay. I know this is a huge change and nothing's going to happen yet. I don't even know if a uni will take me, but I do know something's got to give. This job is killing me, and it's keeping me from my family. I don't want that anymore."

Hugging him back, her mind swirling with the possibilities, Beth wondered if this might actually be a good thing. She wanted her husband to be happy, and she could see that right now, he wasn't.

From the corner of her eye, Beth saw the clock. It was almost 7:00 a.m. Tom was already late for work, and if she didn't get the kids up, they would never get to school on time. She was working today filling in for a grade-six teacher. She'd taught the class before, and the children were little horrors. Maybe Tom should come to work with her one day and make sure teaching was what he really wanted to do. One day of trying to teach twelve-year-old boys English might be enough to send him back to smelly drain pipes. Pulling away from him, she stood up and was about to head down the hall to wake up Nate. He took longer than anyone to get ready. But Tom grabbed her hand and looked into her eyes.

"I'm really sorry I wasn't here last night. I wish I could have seen you all dressed up. And don't think I haven't noticed the effort you've been making in the last few weeks. It's obvious you've lost some weight, and I really like the attention you've been giving me lately. You know, in the bedroom."

"Well, I haven't minded it too much either. I guess I forgot how nice it could be, and I promise next year to remind you when it's our anniversary. I just have to accept that there are some things you aren't good at, but you make it up in other ways."

"No need. I've put a reminder in my phone for your birthday and our anniversary so I won't forget next time."

"That's a good idea. Now to make up for those really sad-looking flowers. Please tell me that I can be the one to tell Lochie that you both might be going to uni together at the same time. It's not often I get to give such good news this early in the morning."

"You're a naughty girl, Beth Fraser. First tell me I'm forgiven and that you accept my apology."

"You are, and I do. But you still owe me a dinner out with no excuses this time."

"Agreed. Now can I watch while you deliver the good news to son number one?"

Chapter 16

Adam scanned the restaurant, looking for his lunch date. He wasn't sure getting involved was the right thing, but when Jillian called, she had sounded so worried and so desperate for his help. He should have told Caroline. If she knew he was meeting Jill alone, she would have been upset, and it would only make things worse. Since he had moved out of their bedroom and into the guest room last month, she had become even more suspicious of him. He knew she thought he was having an affair. Why else would a man refuse to sleep with his wife? He hadn't made a big deal of the move. One night, he'd told Caroline he wasn't feeling well and offered to take the guest room so his sneezing and coughing wouldn't keep her awake. Instead of returning to their bedroom when he was "better," he slowly moved his belongings into his new room and hoped Caroline would accept it. He never gave her an explanation, and she never pushed him to come back. But he had found her checking his phone, and he had found credit-card statements and phone bills out on his desk after he had filed them away. It looked to him like she wanted him to know that she was suspicious.

He wasn't having an affair. It was, in fact, the furthest thing from his mind. And what would be the point? He had nothing left to give of himself. When Isabelle had died, he might as well have died too. Her very existence had brought him more happiness than he could have believed possible. Yes, he loved his son, Michael, and was proud of the man he could see him becoming. But Michael's conception had forced Adam into making decisions and taking on responsibility that he hadn't wanted and didn't feel ready for at the time. Isabelle had been a completely different story. She had been planned, and he had looked forward to her birth. He was older and ready to become a father that time. When the doctor had placed the tiny baby girl in his arms minutes after she was born, it had only taken seconds, and for the first time in his life, he truly understood what it meant to love someone. And she had felt the same way about him. Isabelle had adored her father. She waited for him to come home every night, sitting with him on the couch, telling him every little detail of her day. Sometimes her incessant chatting would drive him crazy when all he craved was a little peace, but he always listened and spent as much time with her as she wanted. The most important thing was for Isabelle to know that he loved her more than anyone else in the world.

The gaping wound left by Isabelle's death was now covered over with deep scar tissue. It was hard and ugly. Somehow Caroline had managed to stay afloat, filling her days and nights with friends and caring for their son. In his rational moments, he knew she missed their daughter just as much as he did and grieved daily for her, but his rational moments were becoming few and far between. He resented Caroline's ability to move past the initial shock and carve out a new way of living. It was nothing close to what her life had been, but at least it was bearable. Adam was still so devastated he could not see a way forward or any reason to continue on. He never seriously considered suicide. That was for cowards. But if something came along that took him from this life, it would be a relief. But relief never came; instead, he spent his days reliving the moment he opened his door to the police and everything changed.

So every day that Caroline got a little bit stronger, Adam moved a step further away from her. And each time that she touched him or looked at him with love or affection, he grew colder and more resentful, believing that she must not have loved Isabelle as much as he had. She couldn't have or she would be a reflection of what he had become.

He saw Jill seated in the back corner of the restaurant. She was talking to the waiter, and when she noticed him, she raised her hand in a welcoming wave. He made his way over to her, negotiating the maze of tables, and seated himself. After placing their orders with the waiter, Adam looked at Jill, wondering if it would be best to tell her the truth or lie a little. He decided to go with the lie. "You look well. How are you holding up?"

"Liar. I know I look terrible. Lack of sleep and hate will do that to a girl."

"That bad, is it?" Adam asked, not really wanting to know the answer. Chris knew he was meeting Jill today and would grill him later for every word she said.

"Yeah, it is. I'm trying to get over it and move on, but I'm just so very, very angry. And every time he calls, I'm reminded all over again why I'm in this position."

"He's calling you? How often?"

"It depends. Sometimes once a week. Sometimes five or six times a day. I stopped answering the calls, but he always leaves a message. A few weeks ago, the letters and the flowers started. At first, it was annoying but now, it's starting to scare me. What concerns me the most is that none of the letters were delivered by the postie, and none of the flowers were delivered from a shop. The flowers are always waiting for me on the porch when I get home, and the letters are always shoved under the door. That means he's coming to the house. I changed the locks as soon as I told him to leave, but I'm beginning to get scared at night. Sometimes when I arrive home, I see his car parked on the street. He doesn't approach me, but I don't feel safe. I'm considering getting a dog or at least an alarm for security, but that seems so extreme. If you could just ask him to back off, he might listen to you."

"I don't know, Jill. I'd rather stay out of this, not take sides."

"Please, Adam. You're his friend, and he respects you. Maybe he'll listen. Otherwise I'm going to have to involve the police, but I worry that might make things worse. You hear stories of men losing it, hurting their wives when they don't get what they want."

Adam really didn't want to become involved, but if Chris was thinking about doing something foolish, then wasn't it his responsibility as a friend to try and stop him? It might be uncomfortable to approach Chris, but if he didn't, Jill could end up hurt, and his mate could end up in jail.

"I'll speak to him. I'd rather not, but I can see this is bothering you. I can't imagine anything would come of it. Chris has never hurt anyone, and he would never hurt you. He's probably just missing you and wants you to know how much. But I don't like that he's hanging around the house, watching you. That does sound creepy. He hasn't made any threats, has he?"

"No. Not at all. It's a lot of 'sorrys' and 'I miss yous.' Which is why there's not much point going to the police. He hasn't done anything illegal, but it is scaring me."

"What does your solicitor say?"

"He suggested trying to take out an AVO. He thinks it will help with the divorce and force him to stay away but often they don't work, and I don't want it to end up on his record. Unless he actually threatens me, it's not a path I want to go down."

"So you're still going ahead with the divorce?"

"Absolutely. I don't want him anywhere near me. I know some people manage to work through adultery, but I can't. I don't want to spend my whole life looking for secretive behaviour, checking emails and texts, and listening in on phone calls. It would be a horrible way to live, never fully trusting, always expecting him to do it again. Chris promised me he would never ever go near another woman again, but his words meant nothing. He promised that when we got married. For me, trust is the glue that holds a marriage together. Without it, the relationship is a farce. I deserve better than to live a half-life waiting for him to do it again, and he isn't worth having to live that way. When I found out what he'd done, my feelings for him died. I have no need or desire to try and resuscitate them.

"Jill, people make mistakes. And it was just a one-time thing. Why don't you hold off on the divorce for a while and see if your feelings change?"

"Once, a hundred times. What's the difference? I can't imagine anything would change my mind. It's over. I just wish I didn't have to wait so long to get dissolution. We have to be separated for a year. And don't forget that by then, the baby will be born. He might want to start a life with it and Meg."

"I doubt that will happen. He wasn't very happy with Meg, and he blames her for your marriage breakdown. He has no interest in her, and I don't think he's given the baby much thought either. He's only thinking of you."

Jill shook her head as the waiter put their salads down in front of them and refilled their water glasses. "Typical Chris. Blaming someone else for his problems. He used to do that every time he lost a job. I felt sorry for him at first, but after the third time he was fired and had all the same excuses, I started to wonder if he was the problem. I would have been better off if I'd never met him."

"Ah, well, you have to blame me for that," Adam confessed as he picked up his fork and took a mouthful of his salad.

"Why? You didn't set us up, did you?"

"Sort of. He saw some photos Caroline had of you and Beth, and he asked about you. When I told him you were single, there was no going back. He harassed me constantly for a chance to meet you. That's why Caroline invited you to our Christmas party that year."

"Do you know I never knew that? I just thought it was odd that I received an invite. Caroline had never asked me before."

"Are you surprised? With our history, the last thing she wanted was you hanging around unattached. She did tell me not to try and set you up, but I didn't listen. She's always tolerated Chris for my sake, but she thought he was a bit useless. She was right again, I guess."

"Well, she was right about Chris, but she had no need to worry about us spending time together. We dated over twenty-two years ago, and I've never seen you look at anyone else."

"Maybe you should tell her that, then. She thinks I'm playing around."

Jill stopped eating and put her fork down. She would have never believed that he would be unfaithful. She always thought of him as one of the good ones. But if a man like Adam was playing away, then what hope was there? Why couldn't men be happy with the person they had chosen? How could trading in one wife for another be any better? She did understand that things sometimes went wrong in a marriage, especially when it came to sex, but that had never been a problem with her and Chris. That was one of the reasons why she found it so hard to understand why he had cheated on her. She had never said no to him. She had never wanted to, but she guessed some men couldn't help themselves and wanted something more, probably for the ego boost and to prove that they were still attractive to the opposite sex. Unfortunately, her job gave her a front row seat to see the damage that was done because of adultery, and now she had firsthand experience. The fallout from an unfaithful partner was widespread. Unplanned pregnancies and disease affected the adults involved, but Jill felt sorriest for the children. Broken homes left children with part-time parents, sometimes living in poverty, and with disappointed and confused feelings. Nobody ever came out the other side unscathed.

"Please don't tell me you're cheating on Caroline? Because if you are, I don't want to sit here and have you give me your excuses why. I don't want to hear it."

"Of course I'm not cheating."

"Then why would she think you are?"

Adam hadn't come to lunch today with the intention of becoming the topic of conversation, but he had brought it up, and now he felt like he owed her an explanation.

"I've moved into the spare room."

"Can I ask why?"

"I don't know. I don't really understand it myself. I just don't want to be around Caroline anymore."

"But she must have done something to make you feel that way."

"She wants me to see a therapist. I've told her no, but she won't let it go."

"Is that such a bad idea? People are worried about you and how you're coping with Isabelle's death."

"So you're all sitting around discussing me? Is Caroline in on this gossiping?"

"Nobody's gossiping about you, and Caroline hasn't said a word. She never would. But after the anniversary, Beth and I were concerned. What's wrong with getting some professional help?"

"How about I don't need it?"

"Adam, you're not moving forward. You're wallowing in your own pain. Is that how you want to live the rest of your life? Stuck in your grief and loss? Don't you want to eventually be happy again?"

161

"'Happy.' What a stupid word. Why do people expect to feel happy? Life is painful. What is there in this world to be happy about?"

"Adam, at some point you need to find something worth waking up for every morning. You shouldn't want to spend the rest of your life this way. Do you think that if you try to have a good life, you'll forget Isabelle? You won't. That's not how life works. Right now, you're carrying your grief like a shield and using it as an excuse to shut everyone out, but Caroline is the last person you should be doing that to. She knows how you feel. She's been through the same thing. Wouldn't it be better if you could go through it together?"

"She doesn't understand. She wants to move on and forget Isabelle. I can't do that. I don't want to."

" That's not what she wants. She's just trying to get on with her life. You're not even forty yet. Are you content to live the next thirty or forty years alone, pushing everyone away and suffering this self-imposed misery? Isabelle wouldn't want that kind of life for you. Maybe it's too soon for you, but some day you're going to have to decide that it's time to live again."

"You sound just like Caroline. Time to move on. Still a life to live. Blah blah blah. None of you know what you're talking about!" Adam yelled, standing up and throwing his napkin on the table, pulling out his wallet. He threw down a fifty and turned, heading for the exit. The tightly packed room barely slowed him down, and waiters and diners skittered out of his way as he crashed through the front door. The concierge chased after him, asking if everything had been all right with the meal, but Adam put his hand up, shutting down any conversation.

Stunned and a little embarrassed, Jill waited a few minutes to be sure Adam had left and then called for the bill. She didn't envy Caroline if that was what she was dealing with at home. Jill had never seen Adam angry, let alone so out of control. All those years ago when they had been dating, he had been such an even-tempered guy. He'd always been a gentleman, treating her with respect and never raising his voice. And when the inevitable had happened and her father found out she was going out with someone two years older, he'd handled the interrogation from Joe Mancini with a style and grace beyond his years. When Jill decided to end it after five months, her father was more upset than anyone. There hadn't been any real reason to break up. Adam hadn't done anything wrong, and she still liked him a lot. But at sixteen, it was time for a new adventure. He hadn't pushed her and accepted her decision. He was young too. When they met five years later at Beth's twenty-third birthday party, there had been no hard feelings, and they had remained friends ever since, albeit with a nervous Caroline watching on. Jill just hoped he could find a way to live with the hand he had been dealt before he permanently pushed away everyone in his life, including his wife and son.

Adam stormed down the street and back towards his office. Why couldn't people let him be? He wasn't asking for sympathy, and he never burdened people with how he felt. He just wanted to be left alone. People on the street moved out of his way, fearing he might knock them down. The restaurant was only a few minutes from his office, but at the speed he was walking, he was back at work in half the time it normally took. It only took one look from him for his assistant to decide the messages she had for her boss could wait awhile. He had been so nice to work for when she started three years ago, and even when his little girl had died last year and he was sad, this had still been the best place she had ever worked. He had been the best boss she had ever had, but lately he had become impossible. His moods were explosive, and she and the other staff had to tiptoe around him, desperate not to make a mistake in case it set him off. Maybe it was time to start looking for another job.

The walk back to work had done Adam no good at all. He was still furious that Jill had spoken to him like that, but he had made a promise to her and intended on keeping it. He dialled Chris's number from memory and waited for him to answer. It only took two rings; he had been waiting for the call.

"Hey, mate. How did it go at lunch? Is she gonna take me back?"

"You really are a fool, aren't you? No, she's not taking you back," Adam barked into the phone. "Leave her alone. She's ready to get the police involved. Stop calling her, stop sending notes and flowers, and stop going to the house." He slammed the phone back into the cradle and fell into his chair.

Adam sat for a long time. Nobody knocked on the door. His phone didn't ring. It gave him time for his anger to dissipate, and he felt his heart rate slowly begin to return to normal. He knew he was going to have to apologize to Jill. He wasn't sorry at all, but it was the right thing to do. She was the one who had poked her nose into his business, but he should have handled it better, but not now. Later, when he wasn't so angry at her. But he wasn't going to apologize to Chris. He'd made a huge mistake and put Adam in the middle of his problems.

Adam buzzed through to his assistant, Kate. She brought the handful of messages that had been left for him while he was out to lunch and the new ones she taken after he had returned. Kate had thought it best not to put any calls through while Mr. Anderson was in such a state. She handed them over and waited for his next instructions.

"This is quite a pile, Kate. When did all these come through?"

"While you were out to lunch."

He flipped through the message slips, finding one from his biggest client. It was marked 2:00 p.m. "I was here when this call came in. Why didn't you put it through? You know I've been trying to get a hold of Donald for three days."

"You seemed, umm…" Her voice trailed off, not sure how to explain she didn't think he was in any frame of mind to talk to such an important client when he'd returned from lunch. The call had come in shortly after she heard him yelling on the phone.

"I seemed umm what? Just get him back on the telephone and put the call through immediately. And don't ever hold my calls again unless I tell you to. Got it?"

"Yes, Mr. Anderson." Kate scurried out of his office, mentally writing her resume as she went. It was definitely time for a new job.

Chapter 17

"So spill. I want to know all about this new man of yours," Beth said as she set a cup of coffee down in front of Joan. "Although the way you won't let us meet him I'm beginning to wonder if he's real, or are you just ashamed of us?"

Joan picked up the drink and took a sip. She grimaced at the taste. Caroline might have been able to teach Beth to cook a few meals, but she hadn't been able to convince her to buy a decent coffee machine.

"Yes, he's real, but I can't bring him over here and let you serve up this coffee to him. It wouldn't be fair."

"Very funny. Stop changing the subject. I want details."

"There's not a lot to tell. It's early days yet," Joan answered, being deliberately cagey. She had never been one of those women who ran around telling everyone they knew that this could be "the one" after only a few dates.

"Joan, you've been going out for over three months. I can't remember you sticking with someone for this long in years. You usually have one date, maybe two if they pass muster, and then you still give them the flick."

"That's not true. When I was in Sydney, I was with Ryan for five months. It didn't work out, but that was pretty long term."

"Get back to me after you've been married for seventeen years. *That's* long term."

"Well, most of us don't meet our future husbands in high school. You and Caroline ended up with the only decent guys at that school. I could only attract the ones after a good time."

"You brought that on yourself. If you'd said no once in a while, maybe someone a bit more sensible might have asked you out."

"Are you calling me loose?" She laughed, remembering the term Mr. Mancini used to call girls he thought had no morals.

"If the shoe fits," Beth said, teasing. Her dad had always liked Joan and never said anything to her about her string of boyfriends. Beth had always worried that Joe would decide Joan was a bad influence and ban her from the house, but he never did. He ended up being the closest thing to a father that Joan ever had. When he passed away two years ago from a heart attack, Joan had been just as devastated as his two daughters.

"Can I at least see a picture of him? If he's managed to hold onto you for this long, he must be some kind of heartbreaker."

"He's very attractive, all right? Is that what you want to hear?"

"Nope. I want to see for myself. Now give me your phone. You must have a photo of him on there."

Deciding it was easier to just give in, she handed the phone over. Joan almost never talked about her relationships even to her closest friend, but this time she wanted to. If she wasn't *with* David, she was *thinking* about him. No man had ever held her attention the way he did, and for the first time, she understood what all those ridiculous love songs were about. She felt like someone had stamped a huge smiley face on her heart. If this wasn't love, then love didn't really exist.

"He's your screen saver. Ooh, it must be luv," teased Beth, fluttering her eyes and making kissy faces into the air. "He certainly has that rugged outdoors thing going on, doesn't he?"

"Give me that," Joan said, grabbing her phone back and putting it back in her bag. "If you could see how silly you look doing that, you'd stop."

"Don't be shy. Come on. The most excitement I get around here is discovering someone else unloaded the dishwasher. I need to live vicariously through you."

"I doubt that's true. Don't forget I was here ten minutes ago when Tom left. The way he kissed you good-bye, it looks like I might have to live through you."

"Why? I thought things were going well with David."

"No, they are. Very well actually. He's nice. He's *very* nice." She paused, thinking what an inadequate word "nice" really was. "Actually he's the most delicious man I've ever met. I'd spend every minute of the day with him if I could."

"Are you serious? I've never heard you talk about anyone like that. It sounds like you're in love."

"I'm not going to tell you I love him if I haven't even told him yet."

"But you do. I can see it in your face when you talk about him. Does he feel the same way?"

"I have no idea. I hope he does. He seems just as happy as I am when we're together. We like the same things—art, and movies, and football. He's a Collingwood supporter too, which, of course, makes everything perfect."

"Oh, good grief. Who cares about that?"

"I do. I have no intention of being in a mixed marriage. It's black and white all the way."

"Did you say the M word?"

"I did, didn't I? I don't think I've ever said that before." She smiled, remembering the bridal magazine she'd been flipping through at the supermarket the other day.

"Has he mentioned getting married?"

"No. Neither of us has. We haven't even, you know, slept together yet," she whispered in case one of Beth's children was in hearing distance.

"You haven't? I must say I'm surprised. That's not your usual style."

"Thank you very much. I'm not the kind of girl you seem to think I am. I don't jump into bed with every man I meet."

"I know that. I'm sorry I didn't mean to insult you. We're just so different, that's all. I'm a one-guy kind of girl. I always knew Tom was it for me. I couldn't imagine letting anyone else near me."

"Well, were not all religious nuts like you. That whole one person for life thing is just ridiculous. How on earth are you going to find out if someone is worth sticking with if you can't try before you buy? Once you're married, you can't get a refund. You're stuck with them."

"If you feel that way, what's stopped you from going for it with David?"

"I guess at the start I always had in the back of my mind that we need to work together. If it went wrong, then it would be really uncomfortable. I couldn't imagine having to continue working with him for the next six months if we'd slept together and then he dumped me. It would be agonizing every time I had to see him, and I think he felt the same way in the beginning."

"Is that the only reason you waited? Because of work? Are you sure there isn't something else? Once this building is finished, there's a good chance you'll never run into him again in a professional capacity."

"No, it's not just that. I've hesitated because in the past, it hasn't worked out for me. I've slept with men quicker than I probably should have, and before you know it, it's over. I discover they were only looking for a fling.

And I met the woman David was engaged to. She was so beautiful, I don't know how I'll ever live up to that. He's told me that he's completely over her and it was a long time ago, but I'm not even close to being in her league. But each time I see him, it's getting harder to say good-bye at the end of the night. Just kissing him is so addictive. It's a bit like being sixteen again, but I'm not sixteen and neither is he. It's time to move this thing along, and I really want to. I can't worry about work or Charlotte anymore. He suggested we stay in tonight, and you know what that means."

"Are you sure that's a good idea? Why don't you wait until you know how he really feels about you?"

"I don't think this is just a fling for him. He's talking about plans in the future. He's asked me to the Boxing Day Cricket. It's a family tradition, and I'll get to meet his sister and his parents. And Christmas is over two months away. He must be serious if he's planning that far ahead." Joan had been delighted when David asked her. She had never been invited to meet a man's parents before, and she knew that for him it was a huge step. He hadn't let anyone meet them since Charlotte.

"I agree that sounds serious. Meeting someone's parents is a big deal, but it's not a commitment. And you know I think sex should only happen within the confines of commitment, the biggest commitment of all—marriage."

"You know, you're about the only person who believes that. Yes, I wish I'd been a little more discerning about who I slept with in the past, but I don't feel like that with David. He's not going to hurt me or leave me."

"Joan, can I be honest with you?"

"Can I stop you?"

"I know you think my beliefs are old fashioned, and I bet you think that if I hadn't met Tom so early, I probably would have slept with guys I didn't end up staying with. But one thing my parents taught me was that sex isn't just a fun way to spend an evening. It's a serious thing. Every time you do it, you join yourself to that person. It's not just a physical thing; it's also your soul and your emotions, and that is much too important to share with just anyone. Think about how you feel the next day after you've slept with someone. Yes, it might have been nice at the time, but how does it work out for you?"

"It's never worked out, and I've regretted that. But I'm certain it's different this time."

"How can you be? You know how you feel about him, but you have no idea if he loves you. What if it turns out he doesn't? You will be devastated. Don't you want to make sure first before you give yourself to him?"

"Let me tell you about David. He's wonderful and kind. He gets my sense of humour, and we laugh so much when we're together. He's hard working, and honest, and very, very sexy. I can't think of anything else I could want in a man. I'm a good judge of character, and I trust him. He isn't going to hurt me. It's just too early for us to start making formal commitments, but I think it will happen in time. I'm not going to blow it by rushing him and forcing his hand."

"You're right. You shouldn't rush him, but you shouldn't rush yourself either. Why don't you wait? If you're not ready to get married, then you're not ready to be having sex together."

"They are two completely different things, Beth. We're adults. He's forty-two years old, and I'm thirty-nine. What you're suggesting is ridiculous. We've waited long enough, and I don't want to wait anymore."

"Joan, you're my friend, which means I get to tell you what I think." Beth paused, aware that she was about to step on some toes. Joan never mentioned her parents. She acted like she had been dropped from the sky at eighteen, fully grown and alone. "You never had parents that gave you boundaries. Your mother didn't care what you did, and you didn't know your father. That's not normal, and it's definitely not a good way to grow up. Most kids have someone in their lives to teach them what's right and wrong. You didn't have that. You had to grow up mostly alone, and to be fair, I think you've done an awesome job. I admire you and the life you've made for yourself so much. You are strong, independent, and a beautiful person. But you should have had someone there cheering you along and letting you know how wonderful you are. A mum and dad's job is to let their children know how precious and valuable they are."

Beth reached over and took Joan's hand. "Look at me." Joan raised her head, and Beth could see tears forming in her friend's eyes. "I'm sorry that no one ever said this to you when you were a child, but I'm going to say it now. You are valuable. You are a wonderful, unique human being. You are lovely, and you deserve someone who will love only you for the rest of his life. You don't have to settle for anything but the whole package. Love and marriage. It's not too much to expect."

Joan pulled her hand away, wiping her eyes. No one had ever spoken to her that way. No one had made her cry since she was a little girl. Joan had been building her defensive walls since she was tiny, and they had done a good job during the last thirty-nine years. They had kept people at a distance and let her live life on her own terms. No one had ever gotten away with trying to tell her what to do or what decisions she should make. But then, no one had ever cared enough to try or was close enough to feel like they had the right. Joan discovered she didn't like it much—having someone poking around and prodding into all the dark places she didn't like to think about and questioning her self-worth was painful. It was time to shut this conversation with Beth down.

"Beth, no one feels like that anymore. Having sex with someone doesn't take away my value. You really are a drama queen."

"Look, I know you think I'm out of date. I don't care. Everywhere we look today, we're bombarded with sex, but it's not making anyone happy, not in the long term anyway. People think they can do what they want, and as long as no one gets hurt, it doesn't matter. What they don't seem to realize is that they're hurting themselves. Look at Jill. Her marriage is over because her husband decided to sleep with someone else. He decided to be selfish. It was only one night, but his life is ruined. So is Jill's. And for what? A few minutes of pleasure he says he can't even remember?"

"I agree with you about Chris, but I'm not doing the same thing. I'm not married. Neither is David. I don't see anything wrong with sleeping together if that's what we both want. Besides how long do you think he'll wait around? And even if he decides he doesn't want to get married, I'd rather have what he's willing to give me than nothing at all."

"So you're going to sleep with him to try and hold onto him? If he really loves you, he'll wait. He might not like it, but he won't walk."

"Beth you're delusional. It's been over twenty years since you were out there. The world has changed. You don't have to deal with the modern world the way I do. You have someone. It's so easy for people like you with your perfect marriages, giving out advice to us lonely single girls. But we don't want to hear it, and I've finally found someone I might have a shot with. It's not like I'm settling for someone so I won't be alone. I love him. There, I said it. And I'm certainly not going to risk losing him over some outdated morals that no one, including me, believes in anymore except you."

"The world might have changed, Joan, but it certainly isn't for the better. Just ask the children of teenage mothers and broken relationships. How much do you think they would love to grow up in a traditional home with two parents? How much would you have loved to grow up in a home with a father?"

"I grew up just fine. There's no need to worry about me," she lied.

"I'll always worry. I only want the best for you. And trust me, my marriage isn't perfect. We have rough patches, but because we have the commitment of marriage and a bond that we never shared with any other person, we didn't give up or find someone more to our liking. Recently I've had to take a long hard look at myself and make some changes, but it was worth it. You need to find someone you're willing to do that for and someone who is willing to do the same for you. And if he doesn't want to make that kind of commitment, then isn't it better to find out now rather than later? Keep a man waiting, and you'll find out just how devoted he is to you, not just what he can take from you."

"He won't be taking anything from me. And I want him too. It'll be us together."

"For how long? I still think if he won't wait, he isn't the kind of man who will want to spend the rest of his life with you. Isn't that ultimately what you want?"

"Yes, that's what I want, but being together now doesn't mean that won't happen permanently later. Some people live together and never get married, but it's for life. And everybody has sex before they get married."

"Maybe. But how many different people were they with before they settled down? People treat sex like a sport. This isn't all a game."

"Beth, I know you care about me and want me to be happy. But in the end, it's my decision. And if I was you, I'd be careful who I talk to like this. You sound kind of judgemental.

"The last thing I want to be is judgemental. I'm just an old lady with a lot of experience. It's up to you whether you take it or not."

"Well, I think I'll pass. Maybe you should concentrate on your own kids instead. Do you tell them the same rubbish you've been telling me?"

"I do. And they roll their eyes at me and carry on, but when the time comes, I trust they'll remember what I've taught them and that they'll think it's worth waiting and they are worth waiting for."

"Come on. You didn't wait until you got married. You and Tom jumped the gun."

"I know. And we both wish we hadn't. The guilt of what we did stayed with me for years and affected our marriage."

"Why would that affect your marriage? You didn't have any old baggage or have to worry about being compared to other women from Tom's past. What you're saying doesn't make any sense."

"I know you won't understand this." Beth paused, trying to find the right words without sounding like she was preaching at Joan. "The Bible is clear. God intended sex only within a marriage. I knew what I was doing was wrong, but at the time, I just didn't care. And I felt so bad for not waiting that when even after we were married, I still felt like I was doing something wrong. I have moved on from feeling that way but not until after I had asked God for forgiveness. And even then, once he had forgiven me, I had to forgive myself."

"I don't know, Beth. I know how all that God stuff is important to you, but I don't believe it. As long as no one is getting hurt, what's the difference?"

"But someone is getting hurt, Joan. You are. And while you can never go back and change the past, you can make a choice not to continue on the way you were. Imagine a relationship where you knew you were valued for who you are, not just for what you let some man take from you until he's done. Hold yourself to a new set of values that were created to protect you. Isn't it worth at least thinking about?"

"Well, you talk a good talk, Fraser. And, yes, what your describing sounds ideal. Perfect, in fact."

"There you go. Maybe I'm not completely wrong."

"Oh, you're still wrong. You're a dinosaur. Extinct."

"Hey, not nice. I know there are other people who think the same as me."

"Yeah, people's grandmas." Looking at her watch, she decided it was time to get going. She had a lot to do before tonight.

"Wish me luck?" she asked, kissing Beth's cheek.

"Just think about what I said before you jump into anything you might regret."

"Trust me, Beth. The last thing I'm going to be thinking about tonight is you."

Chapter 18

David took one last look in the mirror, pleased with what he saw. He noticed he looked more relaxed these days, probably because he couldn't stop smiling. He gave Joan all the credit. He never felt like he had to put on a mask with her. He was who he was, and she accepted him for that. In the past when he'd dated other women, he often found himself spending time with someone he had nothing in common with and trying to find something, no matter how small, to create a connection. Some women were bitter because of past relationships that hadn't worked out, and they judged every man they met based on the one who had let them down. Others weren't bitter, just desperate to find someone to love them. Instead of being themselves, they agreed with everything he said and loved everything he loved. Luckily he had become skilled at discerning when he was being lied to and steered clear of those women. He didn't want to waste his time with someone only to find out later that she was a fake and that nothing she had said was true. He certainly didn't want to be someone's last chance at marriage. If he was ever going to take the plunge, it had to be with someone special, someone he could trust.

That's what he liked—he wasn't ready to use the word love yet—about Joan. She was the first completely honest person he had ever met. If she loved something, then she really loved it. If she didn't, then she was upfront and told him. He had already discovered that she would never go camping with him. It was one of his favourite pastimes, but she had made it clear if he wanted to spend a night away together, it would have to be in a fancy hotel. Speaking of which, he was beginning to wonder if they would ever get to spend a night together. They had been seeing each other for over three months now and so far, nothing had happened in the bedroom department. But he was a forty-two-year-old man, and he had certain expectations. At the moment, he felt like he was in a backwards version of *The 40-Year-Old Virgin*. He had hesitated at first because of their working relationship, wanting to make sure things would be going further than a few nice dinners out before he took the risk. He didn't think it was an issue anymore. Seeing her was the highlight of his day, and what they had was more important than work. And he was sure he had convinced her that he no longer felt anything for Charlie. Whatever it was, they had always stopped before things went too far. He knew it wasn't a lack of attraction to each other. She was quite possibly the hottest woman he had ever known. There was something about a brunette with blue eyes and legs that seemed to go on forever. Every time he saw her, he was astounded nobody had snapped her up years ago, and he was thrilled she wanted to be with him. But it wasn't just the way she looked, which was sublime. It was her. She was feisty and funny. He loved her quirky sense of humour, and he couldn't remember laughing this much with anyone else. He never had to wonder if she meant what she said. It was impossible for her to lie. She would make a terrible poker player. He always knew what she was thinking.

He could definitely see that she could be his last stop. But he had thought that about Charlotte, and he had been wrong. But this time, he was older and plenty wiser than he had been, and he knew that at some point, he'd have to trust his instincts. His instincts told him Joan was the right girl for him. It was definitely time to take the next step and make sure they were as compatible physically as they were mentally. And he was sure she was thinking the same thing. When he had suggested dinner at her place and a movie on the couch, she had agreed immediately. He didn't think he could have been clearer about his intentions if he'd sent her a written invitation, and she hadn't said no. She had even offered to cook. As far as he was concerned, tonight it was all systems go.

~~~

When Joan opened the door an hour later he couldn't help but whistle—probably too many years on building sites—but there was no other reaction that could convey how good she looked. Skinny jeans were complimented by knee-high boots, and the plunging nature of the top she had chosen couldn't help but draw the eye. He pulled her in for a long, welcoming kiss, and then, smiling down into her beautiful eyes, he said, "You look good enough to eat."

Gently pushing him away, Joan smiled. "Dinner first, me later. I've been slaving in the kitchen all afternoon, and I'm not going to have the first meal I make you ruined because you can't have a little self-control."

"Oh, and how 'bout you? You can wait all evening?"

Joan stopped walking towards the kitchen and turned back towards David. She loved the way his green eyes were smiling at her in an obviously suggestive way. Meeting him in the middle of her hallway, she wrapped her arms around his hips, tucking her hands into the back pockets of his jeans and tilted her head up as if she was about to kiss him. She could smell mint on his breath and the musk aftershave he preferred. She moved her mouth closer to his ear, and after gently biting it, she whispered, "Just barely."

~~~

Dinner hadn't been complicated, and it certainly hadn't taken as much time as she had intimated. Pasta carbonara from a recipe she had picked up while working as a waitress in a small restaurant in Santa Nicola near Rome, along with herb—definitely not garlic tonight—bread and a salad. Simple but delicious. Never one to cook anything sweet, Joan had picked up some macaroons on her way home from Beth's. She had spent the day trying to forget everything her friend had said to her but found herself disturbed to discover Beth's words weaving their way into her thoughts, even during dinner. She did her best to ignore them and concentrate on David. As they flirted and laughed, she decided Beth didn't know what she was talking about. David wasn't planning to hurt her any more than she planned on hurting him. If anything, it would bring them closer together. Stacking the dishwasher together, they negotiated her small kitchen, "accidently" getting in each other's way, almost dancing as Alicia Keys played quietly in the background. When they were finished, the job taking longer than it should have, David brought two glasses of wine to the couch, where Joan was waiting for him.

"So what movie have you picked for tonight? I know this is supposed to be a romantic evening in, but please tell me you haven't picked some chick flick. Nothing annoys me more than having to watch Meg Ryan fall in love and then out of love, only to discover she was in love all along."

"Not likely. I actually didn't get a movie, if you don't mind. I thought we might do something else tonight."

Finally, thought David. *I was right.* He mentally checked his wallet, remembering that he had definitely added a couple of condoms before he headed out for dinner.

"I'm sure I could be persuaded to skip the movie for whatever you had in mind. Did you want to stay here on the couch or did you have somewhere more comfortable in mind?"

"No, I think here's fine. We could probably use the table, but this is good."

David raised one eyebrow, considering her suggestion as he looked over to the small table they had just eaten dinner on. He thought that was a little strange, considering she had a perfectly good bed in the other room. And the couch would be fine if that's what she wanted, but he wasn't a teenager anymore. He couldn't see the point if there was a bed available. He had found that a little mood lighting and a comfortable bed got more desirable as he got older.

"We could always take this to your bedroom. Or am I rushing you? Whatever suits you is fine with me."

It dawned then on Joan that David was suggesting they head for bed now. She was quite sure the evening was heading in that direction, even with all of Beth's ridiculous interfering, but it was only eight o'clock, and she had something else in mind first.

"Hold on there, cowboy. We'll see how the night pans out, but I actually had something else planned for now. There's no hurry, is there?"

"Speak for yourself. I'm not sure you quite understand what you're doing to me sitting there looking so…" He struggled to find a word to describe just how attractive he found her, but he settled on "hot."

"Well, blame yourself. This was your idea in the first place." She motioned towards the coffee table, where a shoe box sat. It was tied with a satin scarf and, in black marker, *For Joan* was written on the lid.

181

"This is the box I found when my mother died. I've never looked inside, so it could turn out to be a complete bust, but there might be some info about my father in it. I didn't want to look in it alone and since you were the one who got me thinking about him, I was hoping you wouldn't mind being with me."

Great, thought David. *Instant mood killer*. He hadn't been expecting the evening to take such a serious turn, but it was a small box. It was probably filled with cute baby pictures of Joan and old school reports. Apart from their first date, Joan had never talked about her father, and when she mentioned her mother, it was rare and tinged with loathing. He couldn't help but be curious about her life when she was a child, and maybe the box held some answers.

"I'd love to help you. But don't think for one second I've forgotten the reason for a cosy night in."

"Oh, I doubt you'll let me forget." She smiled as she winked at him. She lifted the box onto her lap. When she had found it in the back of her mother's wardrobe after her death, she had been tempted to throw it away. It had been Beth who convinced her to keep it. She had pointed out that Joan never had to look in it if she didn't want to, but if it was gone, then she could never change her mind. She pulled at the edge of the ribbon, and the bow untied easily. She set the scarf and the lid aside and looked in.

The box was almost empty. She rifled through the few things it did hold. It looked like a few paper cuttings and a photo. Sitting on top of the pile of papers was an envelope with her name. She picked it up. It had probably been sealed at one time, but the glue was old that it no longer held. She looked at David.

"Should I look inside?"

"It's why we're here, isn't it?"

"I'm nervous." She held the envelope out towards David. "You do it. I can't."

"Are you sure? It could be private."

Nodding, she continued to hold it out.

He took it from her and, looking inside, pulled out one piece of folded paper.

"Do you want me to read it?"

"It's why we're here, isn't it?"

David opened the page and saw that it was indeed a letter addressed to Joan. He cleared his throat and then started reading aloud.

Dear Joan,

It's been a few years since I've seen you. I don't know where you are anymore but unless I hear otherwise, I guess you must be okay. Sometimes I see Annie Mancini at the shops, and she keeps me up to date. Last I heard, you were in Germany, but that was over two months ago, so who knows. You could be anywhere by now. I need to write this to you now as time is running out. I have nowhere to send it, but hopefully it will get to you at some point.

I was recently admitted to the hospital. Not surprisingly, they told me I have advanced liver disease. There's nothing they can do for me, and the only thing I can do for myself is to stop drinking. We both know that's never going to happen. I can't see the point in continuing on. I should want to live for you, but you have no need for me. You were self-sufficient from the beginning. I'm sorry I wasn't much of a mother to you.

I wanted to love you, but every time I looked at you, I was reminded of how you came about. My parents wanted me to give you up, but when you were born, I ran before they could take you away. That's why you never met your grandparents. They weren't very nice people, and they never believed me when I told them what happened. They were ashamed and didn't want anyone to know I had had a baby. As for your father, let me just say he was not a good man, and you are much better off never knowing him.

I wish you all the best for your life. I'm sorry I didn't love you the way you deserved. Mum

David looked up from the letter, wondering what Joan's reaction would be. He could see why she had struggled so much with her mother. It was pretty short on love and emotion. It made him grateful for his parents, who always loved him unconditionally.

"Well, that didn't tell me much. She didn't mention how she met my father, who he was, or the circumstances of my birth."

David handed the letter to Joan to look at for herself and reached into the box. He found a birth certificate, which confirmed that Margaret Webster was her birth mother, and her father's name was Jonathon Morgan. She had been born in Ballarat on the third of March 1973. He filed that date away, noting it would be her fortieth next year. *Better not forget that one*, he thought.

"What else is in the box?" she asked, tossing the letter and the birth certificate aside. She'd needed one years before when she had applied for her passport and had ordered a new one at the time. David pulled out a very old-looking yellow form. It looked like a carbon copy, and the top said Victoria Police Crime Report.

"This looks important. I think you'll want to read it yourself? It might be private. It looks like some sort of form from the police."

"No, you read it. It's probably nothing."

Trying to be careful with it because it looked so old, David read further down the page. The complainant was Margaret Webster, and the accused was Jonathon Morgan. The alleged offence was sexual assault. The complaint was dated 17 June 1972, but the offence was recorded as having taken place on 27 May 1972.

"Um, Joan. I really think you should be the one reading this," he said as he handed the form over. She read aloud what he had already seen and then moved to the lower half of the page. In old type was a paragraph titled "Details of Complaint":

Miss Margaret Webster (18) of 27 Baker Street East Ballarat alleges that at approximately 8 o'clock on the evening of 27th May 1972, she was raped at work by her employer Mr. Jonathon Morgan (approx. 30) Managing Principal of Morgan Partners, where she was employed as a junior secretary. According to Miss Webster, there were no witnesses as all the other staff had left for the day. Miss Webster did not make a complaint at the time of the incident and has since left the employment as junior secretary of Morgan Partners. Miss Webster is now pregnant and alleges Mr. Morgan is the father as a result of the alleged incident. It is my recommendation that further investigation is required before any charges are laid.

The form was signed and dated by her mother and the officer who took the complaint. There were no other details of what had happened or whether any formal charges were laid.

Joan could feel David's eyes on her. He looked as shocked as she felt. In all the many fantasies she had conjured up as a child, never did she imagine that such a horrible event had been responsible for her conception. She found it difficult to equate the mother she had known with a teenager who must have been terrified and alone.

"Well, I guess this sort of explains the way she lived. I'm not sure how I would have coped as a young woman having to go through such an experience. I wonder what happened with the police. If she'd told me, I might have understood better, maybe not thought so harshly of her. She never said one word about any of this."

"Would you want your child to know she was the product of a rape? I can see why she kept it a secret."

"If it's true, then you're right. I feel sick just thinking about it. I can't imagine growing up with that hanging over my head."

David took her hand in his, hoping to comfort her. "We can stop if this is too much for you."

She shook her head. "We might as well get this over with. What else is there in the box?"

He pulled out the few remaining items. "Just some newspaper clippings." He removed them, along with a photo of a woman holding a baby. He flipped it over and saw it labelled and dated: Me and Joan, April 20 1973.

The woman who must have been Joan's mother was pretty, but she looked nothing like her daughter. She was tiny with long, blonde hair. He passed the photo to Joan and moved on to look at the newspaper articles. The paper clippings didn't have any dates. The first was an article about a "local accountant and up and coming land developer Jonathon Morgan" who had made a donation to help build a new wing for the local hospital. There was a photo of two couples attending the local charity dinner. The caption read "Jonathon Morgan and his wife Emily with business partner Gerald Caine and his wife Lisa." The second article looked a lot newer. It was of a much older Morgan with his wife and a woman in her twenties in a wedding dress beside her new husband. The caption underneath was "Daughter of local entrepreneur marries prominent doctor." What struck David about the photos was how much Joan looked like Jonathon Morgan and, in the later picture, like his daughter. He had no doubt that the girls were sisters. They both had the same colouring and height. Every feature from their slim nose to their high foreheads and full lips were almost identical. None of their mother's looks had been passed down. It was all him.

"It's a picture of your father, and there's also one of his daughter. I guess that means you have a half-sister."

"That's assuming he is actually my biological father. She could have made the whole story up in an attempt to take the blame off herself. My father could be anyone."

Handing the pictures over, he said, "If you look at these, I don't think you'll have any doubt that your mum was telling the truth. You might never know if it was consensual or forced, but this man has to be your father. You look just like him."

Instantly, Joan could see the resemblance. First in the man she could easily see was her father and then in her sister. *Half-sister*, she corrected herself, her thoughts running wild. *I wonder if we'll ever meet. Can you imagine?* Turning up on someone's doorstep and announcing that their father had raped her mother over forty years ago wasn't the best start to a relationship. He must have avoided being charged by the police and continued on with his life. Country towns didn't usually describe convicted rapists as "local entrepreneurs." *I wonder if he's still alive*, she thought. He must be in his early seventies now. From the style of the dress, Joan guessed her sister had been married in the early nineties. She looked young, so that probably put her around her midforties now.

"Can you imagine," asked David, "what it must have been like looking at you every day and seeing the face of her attacker? It must have been terrible to be reminded every day of what happened to her."

Joan hadn't made that connection, but it certainly explained her mother's hostility towards her. For the first time, Joan began to feel sorry for Margaret Webster, the adult. When she had decided to keep her baby, she had no idea that it would turn out to look so much like its father. The daily reminder would have been agony. It didn't excuse the way her mother had ignored and neglected her, but it did throw new light on why she had trouble loving her daughter.

"Are you all right? Is there anything I can do for you?" David could see that the evening didn't have much of a chance to revert to the earlier romantic mood, but that was understandable. This wasn't the time. Everything that Joan had believed about her life had just been turned upside down.

"I'd really like some tea if you don't mind." She handed him back the glass of wine she had been sipping from earlier. "Is it all right if I just sit for a bit? This is a lot to absorb, and I'm not sure how I feel. I just need some time to think."

"Of course you do. I'll make the tea, and you do what you need to do." David headed to the bench and filled the jug. He could still see Joan from where he was. She held the baby picture of herself and her mother in one hand and the picture of her father and sister in the other. After finishing the tea, he added a couple of the macaroons to a plate and brought them to the coffee table. He handed Joan a mug and settled in beside her on the couch. Taking a sip of his drink, he thought to himself, *Ah, tea and cookies. Definitely* not *the food of love.*

Chapter 19

"Hi, girls," greeted Caroline as she stood up and waved to get their attention. Saving a table in a busy café at this time of year had been almost impossible, and she was relieved Beth had finally arrived. Why couldn't she ever be on time? Arms laden with shopping bags, Beth looked dishevelled and exhausted. She unceremoniously dumped the bags on the floor and fell into her chair, lay her forehead on the table, and loudly declared, "I hate Christmas."

Jill was much less dishevelled than her sister, but it was obvious that she had lost weight recently. She had already been thin enough, and this new weight loss left Jill's face gaunt and her clothes baggy. She only carried a few bags which she placed under her chair as she took a seat. She took a sip of the water Caroline had already poured and responded to her sister's pronouncement. "You don't hate Christmas. You love Christmas. You just hate the thirty days leading up to it."

Beth raised her head and glared at Jill, "No, I've decided. I'm over Christmas. It's nothing but a ploy to rid me of all my money and prove what a failure I am. Every year, I set out with the best intentions to write a list and buy my gifts early. I think to myself, 'What would Caroline do?'" she mimicked in a mocking voice. "And then I end up doing nothing. And here I am yet again. One week until Christmas. The tree is finally up, but this year Nate and Sarah decorated it for me, so it looks like it was done by a bunch of drunken monkeys. Nate did something to the setting on the lights, and we can't change it, so they don't even flash on and off anymore. These pathetic offerings are the first of the gifts I've managed to find," she said, gesturing to the bags on the ground, "and nothing's wrapped. I hope nobody's expecting any cards this year 'cause it ain't gonna happen." She took a deep breath, clenching her fists out in front of her chest. "And if I hear one more Christmas carol, I might just stop dead still in the middle of the shops and start screaming. They're supposed to make you feel all happy and festive, but all I hear is, 'You're running out of time, your running out of time.'"

"Why don't we have some lunch, and then I can help you shop this afternoon if you want?" offered Caroline.

Beth contemplated shopping with Caroline. They had a slightly different take on what a budget was for. Beth needed to stick to one, and Caroline thought they were something set by the government once a year that didn't really mean anything. But she could use the help before she murdered some shop assistant who didn't have what she wanted and seemed completely disinterested in helping her.

"Are you sure you have nothing else to do this afternoon?"

"I was done weeks ago. And with the Christmas party held last Friday night, I'm as free as a bird."

"Show off," Beth retorted, but she was smiling. "I'll take it."

"Good. Now I guess you're wondering why I've broken my no shopping centre the week before Christmas rule and asked you to meet me today. I need some advice, and you two are probably my best bet."

"As long as it has nothing to do with helping you pick a gift for someone, I'm happy to help. Otherwise you're on your own. I'm tapped out."

"Are you sure you want me here?" Jill asked. "If this is personal, I can always get lunch somewhere else and meet up with Beth later." She wasn't exactly close to Caroline, and she had never sought Jill's council in the past.

"No, Jill. You're exactly the person I wanted to talk to. Let's order lunch, and then I'll explain."

The three women discussed the various items on the menu and what would be best for Beth. As much as she would have loved to choose the chicken schnitzel sandwich with chips on the side and a chocolate milkshake, she resisted. She was doing so well with the changes to her diet. And with the hope of wearing something pretty on Christmas day, she didn't want to find any of the kilos she had worked so hard to lose.

"The Thai beef salad looks good. Just ask them to leave out the noodles, and you should be all right," Caroline suggested, looking up from the menu. "So how's it all going? You look amazing."

Beth grinned, thrilled with the compliment. "I feel amazing. I put on some size-sixteen jeans yesterday, and they were too loose to wear. You two skinnies can't imagine what that feels like, but it was marvellous. I've lost thirteen kilos so far."

"If things are loose, maybe you should buy some new clothes. I'm betting your smaller jeans are years old and will be completely out of fashion. I think the last time you were in a size pair of fourteen jeans, *Friends* was on TV and the waists came halfway up your stomach."

"I don't even have any. I gave up on ever fitting into them a long time ago and threw them out. But I'll wait until the sales after Christmas to buy anything new. I haven't got the energy to worry about clothes with everything else I have to do this week."

"So you're going to poke around in that hideously outdated wardrobe of yours and just pull out something you already have to wear on Christmas day?" Caroline asked, horrified. Every year, she had something new and fabulous to wear at her Christmas party, and the same thing went for Christmas day. She would never put on something…old.

"I did see a dress I liked this morning," Beth conceded. "I was thinking about going back and trying it on. I guess one new thing couldn't hurt."

"Perfect. We'll add it to the list, and if that doesn't suit you, I'm sure we can find you something else."

Jill had noticed how much nicer her sister had been looking lately and the effort she had been making with her hair and makeup. But the changes weren't just physical. Her attitude had also changed. She no longer dragged herself around like a useless lump, feeling sorry for herself. She was becoming more like the bubbly girl she had been when they were teenagers.

"I had wanted to lose twenty kilos by my birthday, but I don't think I'll quite get there. But I have to say, I'm proud of myself." Jill and Caroline gave each other a furtive glance, hoping to steer Beth away from discussing her upcoming fortieth birthday. Tom would literally kill them if they let anything slip.

"And has Tom finally noticed how much weight you've lost?" asked Caroline.

"He has, and he's thrilled, not necessarily with how much weight I've lost but that I'm happier with myself. Feeling better about how I look and taking some pride in myself certainly puts a girl in the mood, if you know what I mean. He hasn't been complaining about that."

"Beth, there's a good chance I'll never have sex again, so it would be helpful if you could keep it to yourself. I never thought I'd be jealous of you, and yet here I am. You've been married all these years and still at it. I couldn't even make it three months past my second anniversary before my husband got sick of me."

The waitress came over, and the three paused their conversation to place their lunch order. When she left, Caroline took a deep breath and tried to compose herself. It was wonderful to see Beth and Tom so happy, and she felt partially responsible for that. But Beth's happiness just highlighted her own problems.

"So is it all right if I unload on you two?"

Both Beth and Jill nodded, curious at what Caroline had to say. It was unusual for her to ask anyone for help in her organized world, and she was always very private.

"Of course you can. We're here to help," Beth offered her voice, full of empathy.

Folding her hands in front of her, fingers interlaced in an effort to stop the shaking, Caroline began. "I think Adam might be having an affair." Her voice broke a little, but she inhaled, trying to stem any tears that might dare to show themselves. Saying it out loud to people was so much more real and devastating than just thinking it to herself. "He's hardly ever home, we never sleep together, and that's been completely his choice, not mine. And he moved into the spare room months ago."

Beth was shocked by this revelation. Caroline hadn't said a word to her. She had guessed there were some problems, but this was far worse than she had ever imagined. "Do you have any proof? Have you seen any evidence that there's actually someone else?"

"No, I don't have any proof. I've checked his phone bills and the bank statements to see if I could find any hotel charges or unusual purchases. But don't forget, he's a rich man. He could easily have other credit cards I don't know about or even be paying cash. And if it's someone from work, why would he need to make calls? They would see each other every day. His assistant, Kate, was pretty cute. She just recently quit her job, which was has made me suspicious. I rang to ask Adam a question, and his office phone was answered by someone called Susan. She said she had been working as Adam's assistant for two weeks, but he never said a word to me. If he's having an affair with Kate, she could have left before people guessed what was going on. For all I know, he's set her up in an apartment somewhere, and she's living off my money. That's why I asked you here today, Jill. It's happened to you, and I thought you might have some ideas of what to look for."

"Caroline, I don't think I'm much help there. The first clue I had that Chris had cheated was when I took the phone call from the girl he'd cheated with. When I saw him the next day after the event, he was the same with me. There were never any overt signs, like lipstick on his collar or smelling like someone else's perfume. I was so completely oblivious that I've been wondering recently if that was the first time. I'm sure if he hadn't made her pregnant and had got away with it, he would have done it again. He was never really sorry that he cheated, just that he was caught. But you don't need to worry about Adam. I know for a fact that he's not having an affair. He told me he absolutely isn't, and I believed him. If anyone would be suspicious of men at the moment, it's me, but I'm sure he was telling me the truth."

Directing her full attention towards Jill, her gaze steely, Caroline asked, "And when would you have talked to my husband about this?"

"At lunch about two months ago." *Oops*, thought Jill, seeing the surprised expression on Caroline's face. That idiot didn't tell his wife they had met up. Here she was thinking she was helping, and she had just made it worse.

"Why were you meeting for lunch?"

"It was completely innocent. I swear. Chris was starting to harass me about taking him back and because he and Adam were friends, I thought he might have a word with him. And he did. Chris has backed right off and stopped calling and writing letters. Adam was a huge help."

"That still doesn't explain why you know he hasn't been unfaithful. How does asking for his help segue into a discussion about his fidelity?"

Jill did not want to answer that question. Nobody ever wanted to know that their husband or wife was going outside their marriage to discuss problems they were having, especially with someone of the opposite sex, and definitely never with an ex. Adam hadn't planned on confiding in her, but Jill didn't think that would matter to Caroline.

"We were just chatting, and he mentioned that you thought he had someone else. He denied it, and I'm sure it was the truth."

Caroline paused, thinking through this new revelation from Jill. "So my husband knows I think he's cheating on me and instead of denying it, he's happy to let me continue thinking that. What makes him think that's what I suspect?"

"Um. Look, it was ages ago. I have to think back."

"Well, please do. I'm very curious to find out what my husband's been saying behind my back."

Beth could see the situation was spiralling out of control. Jill was her sister, but it was a little hard to take her side at the moment. She had warned Jill off Adam, but it didn't look like she had taken her advice. And Beth hadn't heard a thing about any lunch between them.

"Caroline, I'm sure it was an innocent meeting. Jill just needed some help."

Caroline's angry stare swung towards Beth. "Did you know about this? Is everyone sitting around discussing my marriage?"

"No, I had no idea," she assured Caroline. She turned to her sister, furious at her for putting her in this situation.

"Jill, what were you thinking going to Adam? If you needed help, you should have come to me or Tom. He would have happily talked to Chris and got him to back off."

"I wasn't thinking anything except that I needed help. In my opinion, Adam was the best man for the job."

Caroline flicked her fingers in front of Jill's face. "Focus on me, please. You haven't answered my question. Why did my husband tell you I thought he was having an affair?"

"He didn't really say. He just said he knew you suspected him and something about moving out of your bedroom. I asked him why and suggested he could do with some professional help. His reaction was almost violent. I got the feeling he's becoming unstable. He yelled at me and stormed out of the restaurant."

"Are you sure? Are you sure you aren't the one he's having an affair with? This could all be a way to put me off track. Don't think I didn't notice you hanging off him the night of Isabelle's anniversary. I chose to let it slide then, but I'm not going to let this continue."

"Hang on there," Jill said, pointing her finger at Caroline. "Yes, I did flirt a little that night. I'm sorry about that. I had just received the most devastating news of my life, and I was feeling like the ugliest woman on earth, but I had no intention of doing anything. It meant nothing; it was just a knee-jerk reaction to being so completely rejected. I just needed a little reassurance from someone that I was worthwhile. And do you know what? Adam brushed me off. He couldn't have been less interested. And even if he had been, I would never start an affair with a married man. I know how dangerous that is, and how heartbreaking it is for everyone involved." Jill took a deep breath, trying to calm herself down. She detested being accused of something she hadn't done. As a solicitor, she saw how dangerous false accusations were.

"I'm sorry. I didn't mean to accuse you of anything. I'm just frightened. I know things with Adam aren't right, but he won't talk to me or let me help him. But it doesn't sound like he had any trouble confiding in you."

"It wasn't like that, Caroline. I had to drag it out of him. He was reluctant to talk about anything with me. For what it's worth, I think he needs help.

He doesn't seem to be handling Isabelle's death at all. Could you suggest getting some counselling to him? He certainly didn't want to hear it from me."

"Jill, don't you think I've tried that? I've begged him to go and talk to someone with me or on his own if he prefers. I've made him several appointments with qualified councillors, but he just cancels them and refuses to go. If he's at home, he sits in front of the TV all night, watching documentaries. Heaven forbid he watch something that made him smile or laugh."

"He did say he had no right to ever be happy again. It's like he thinks if he's laughs or enjoys something, then he's not honouring Isabelle's memory."

"Well, I understand that. I felt the same way for a while. Beth helped me to see that it's not true. And until I realized that, I was stuck. I just need to try again with Adam and make him understand."

"I'd be careful if I was you. He didn't want to talk about it with me, and he was really volatile. I've never seen him angry with anyone before, but at lunch, he was completely out of control."

Caroline stood up from the table to leave. There was no point in putting this off. Adam needed to know she understood how he felt. She knew he was going to be home this afternoon. He said he had a few things to take care of. If she caught him unawares, it might be to her advantage.

"Where are you going?" Beth asked. "We haven't had our lunch yet."

"I'm sorry, girls, you're on your own for the rest of the day. I have to get home." She turned to Jill. "Thank you. You've been very helpful, and I appreciate it. I know I can get Adam to talk to me. I'm sure you tried, but I'm the one he's married to. I'll make him listen to me."

Chapter 20

The whole drive home, Caroline rehearsed what she would say to Adam. She was desperate for him to understand that she knew how he was feeling. She had been there, and it wasn't until she acknowledged just how badly she was coping with Isabelle's death and let her grief out instead of bottling it up that she started to recover. She had woken up on the morning of the funeral determined not to make a scene and to hold herself together the way she always had. And for a year, that was what she did every morning—woke up and told herself that she couldn't change the circumstances so she just had to get on with it. Making a show of herself and looking for sympathy wouldn't help her. She had told herself that if she did it long enough and pretended that everything was all right, then her life just had to go on as it had and that eventually it would become true. Breaking down the day after the first anniversary was the best thing that could have happened to her. Every tear that she cried those three days helped to wash away the lies that she had been telling herself. She still had a long way to go. There were many days where she had to force herself to get out of bed and go through the motions of being a wife and a mother. And every day that she felt like she couldn't go on, that life wasn't worth living,

Caroline remembered all the other people in her life that she loved. She had friends she could count on. Michael was a wonderful son and although things weren't right with Adam for the moment, she loved him deeply. She hoped every day that he would look at her and see that she was there for him and wanted to be with him. Every night when she went to bed, she didn't look on the day where he had ignored and avoided her as a failure. She counted it as being one day closer until he made the same breakthrough she had, and then he, too, could be on the slow road to recovery. At least for him, it wouldn't be as lonely as it had been for her because she would be beside him. If she could just find the right words to get through to him, maybe that first day could be today. If there truly was no one else in his life, then there was nothing standing in their way.

She pulled her Mercedes into the driveway and saw Adam's car backed up to the porch with the boot open. As she was about to get out of her car, Caroline saw the front door open. Adam stepped out, dragging a suitcase behind him, and, at first, didn't see her. When he turned towards his car and picked up the suitcase, he saw her out of the corner of his eye. He stopped and dropped the bag back on the landing.

Adam looked like a little boy who had been caught in the act of stealing from his mother's purse. He stood still, not knowing what he was supposed to do—continue putting the bag in his boot or take it back inside. He halfheartedly raised his hand in greeting, leaving the bag where it had fallen and waiting to see what would happen next. Caroline remained in the car, watching him, but didn't wave back. He could see the confusion on her face and wished he had started a little earlier in the morning. Deciding there wasn't much point trying to hide what he was doing, he picked the bag up again and slid it into the back of his car. It was almost full with his belongings.

Caroline turned off her car and opened the door. None of what she was seeing made any sense. Adam hadn't said anything about going away for business, and he didn't have time for a holiday. He kept telling her how busy he was and how much work needed to be done before the office closed for the Christmas break. Most nights, he dragged himself home exhausted and went straight to bed.

Stepping out of her car and quietly shutting the door behind her, Caroline knew something was wrong. Something big was about to happen, something she didn't know about. She walked up the drive towards the steps that led to the front landing. She could hear the thumping of her heart pounding inside her head, and as she got closer to Adam's car, she saw that the boot was full of suitcases. Definitely not a holiday.

When she reached Adam, a walk that felt like it took an eternity, she didn't think she should kiss him like she normally would in greeting, although she had stopped trying that recently. Every time he avoided her kiss, even on his cheek, it confirmed what she already suspected. He couldn't stand being touched by her anymore, even in the most generic way. They stood there together at the front of their house for seconds, hours, days—no one speaking, just looking into each other's eyes, trying to gauge what the other was thinking.

Eventually Caroline broke the connection turning back to look into his car once more.

"Going somewhere?"

Adam didn't know how to make his words come out. How do you tell someone who has been nothing but the best to you that you're leaving them? That even though they haven't done anything wrong, you can't bear to be near them anymore? It wasn't supposed to happen like this. He had planned making his escape in private, with nobody watching or catching him. Caroline was supposed to be gone all day. She'd told him she wouldn't be back until late afternoon, so he had organized his day around her movements. He was just going to slip out of the house, leaving a note so no one worried about him, and then call in a few days.

"I thought you were going to be gone all afternoon."

"I was. My plans changed. I came home early. I needed to talk to you." She gestured towards his packed car and examined the guilty look on his face. "It looks like I got here just in time."

Adam pulled an envelope from his back pocket and held it out to his wife. Caroline's hands remained at her side. If he was going to leave, she wasn't going to let him skulk off into the night like a coward without telling her why. Adam stepped forward, taking her rigid arm, and tried to put the letter into her hand. When she refused to close her fingers over it, the envelope fluttered to the ground. Adam leaned over and picked it up before the wind caught it.

"Please take it," he pleaded. Adam extended out his arm again, but Caroline ignored it. "It'll explain everything. I have to go. Someone's expecting me."

"I don't care if you're having tea with the Queen of England. I can see you're leaving, and I want to know where you're going and I want to know why."

"Can't you please just let me go? I've written it all down. It's easier this way."

"Easier for whom? You? I don't care if it's easier for you. I deserve an explanation for what's going on here, and I expect you to give it to me. Now we can do this out here or we can go inside. You choose."

Aware that he wasn't going to be able to leave without explaining himself, Adam stepped towards his car and closed the boot. Turning, he headed for the front door, stepping through into the house, feeling like a man walking to his own execution. He had thought this was the right thing to do and the right way to do it—put everyone out of their misery and try to start his life again. Alone.

Caroline followed him through the door and closed it quietly. They each took a seat in the lounge facing each other. The Christmas tree stood in the corner. Tall and beautiful, laden with decorations collected over many years by both of them, it mocked Caroline, reminding her of the many family Christmases when they had exchanged gifts and laughed at the terrible jokes in the crackers while they ate dinner together, often with friends joining them. Caroline always went to extremes to make sure Christmas time was the happiest part of the year. This year, Adam planned to spend it alone with nothing more than the TV for company. He stared down at his shoes, unable to meet the hurt look on his wife's face. He knew this was going to be bad. He was going to cause her more pain, and she had already been through enough. But so had he, and it was time to think of himself and what he needed. He couldn't stay here, pretending for her or even for Michael, and he was sure they would be better off without him.

"Is Michael home?" she asked, almost reading his mind. Neither of them wanted their son to overhear what was going to be said. He had been hurt enough too.

"No. He went to a movie with some kids from school. Do you really think I would do this if he was here in the house?"

"I don't know what I'm supposed to think of you anymore. I'm racking my brain to imagine what I must have done to make you want to leave me without so much as a good-bye."

"I was leaving you a letter. I told you that would explain everything."

"Forget the letter, Adam. I don't want to hear about it anymore!" she yelled, her self-control failing her. "I'm never going to read it. I want to hear from your mouth why you're doing this." She wasn't hysterical yet, but she could feel it coming.

"What can I say? I'm leaving you." He paused. "I'm leaving us."

"So there is someone else. I wasn't sure, but today Jill had me convinced I was wrong."

"Caroline, listen to me. There is absolutely no one else. I'm not leaving you because I'm in love with another woman. I can't even imagine looking at another person right now. This really doesn't even have anything to do with you. I just have to go. I can't be here anymore. Our life, what we used to have, is over. Pretending every day that things are fine is killing me. I'm suffocating here in this house. Maybe on my own, I can try and carve out some sort of existence for myself and just forget I was ever here."

Caroline resisted the urge to scream or even to cry. It wouldn't help, and at least he was talking to her for the first time in eighteen months. At least she'd gone with her instincts and come home when she did. There was time for her to fix this.

"Adam, I understand exactly how you feel. We both lost the most precious thing we had together. Our daughter is gone. She isn't ever coming back." She hadn't wanted to, but tears slowly slid down Caroline's cheeks. "But trying to get through this alone isn't the answer. We need each other now more than ever. I need you more now than ever. And we still have Michael. Even if I didn't love you as much as I do, I would try for him." She leaned across to take his hand in hers. "Won't you try just for him if you can't do it for us?"

Adam pulled his hand away from her, unmoved by her words. "And what are you suggesting? We keep living here together, two people trapped in a house until when? Until he finishes high school? Until he gets through uni? Or would you prefer to wait until he's married with children of his own, and then you'll let me go? Why wait?"

"You make our lives sound so horrible. We've hit a snag. I'll admit that it's a huge one. What I don't understand is why it's made you pull away from me. We love each other, and we should be relying on each other to pull ourselves out of the pit we've fallen into. I'll do anything it takes. And if we can't help each other, we can get outside help. Tell me what you want me to do, and I will do it willingly."

"I've told you a million times that I don't need some professional poking around in my head, filling it with useless information that doesn't mean anything and telling me how to feel. Can't you listen? Can't you hear me for a change and understand? If you want to waste your money on something so ridiculous and self-serving as counselling, then you go ahead. But you don't need it. *You're* doing just fine. I can see you've already moving on. Well, I can't move on, and I never want to!" Adam was screaming now. "And *you* don't need to fix me either. I'm not one of your projects, Caroline. There's nothing wrong with me!"

Caroline couldn't believe the venom in his voice. In eighteen years. he had hardly ever raised his voice to her. He had always been the kindest of men. But angry now, Adam launched out of his chair, knocking the occasional table beside him to the floor. A vase of Christmas lilies tipped over, and water soaked into the carpet. He paced around like a caged animal, desperate for freedom from his prison.

"Why won't you just let me go?" he asked, stopping when he reached the window. "You won't be alone long. You're beautiful woman. Any man would be lucky to have you, and you deserve better than me."

"But, Adam, I don't want anyone else. No one else will do. I loved you the minute I set eyes on you. You are *it* for me."

Still staring out to the world beyond their window, Adam felt himself calming down. He could hear in her voice that she still had hope that he would stay. She really thought she could convince him that this was just a glitch, and they would continue on together, and if she worked hard enough, she could glue all the shards of his broken soul back together.

"That can't be true. There's hundreds, thousands of men out there who would be perfect for you. This is your chance to find someone better than me. You have to know I only married you because you were pregnant. I stepped up and fulfilled my responsibility. I know you didn't do it on purpose to trick me like my mother said, but it forced us into a situation I never expected or wanted. We never would have been married if it wasn't for Michael. Now we can rectify that, make a better life for ourselves." Adam sunk into the chair that sat beside the window looking out on the world. *Have I said enough*, he asked himself? Any other woman would be screaming and throwing things at him by now, telling him to get out. Why was she putting up with this, letting him talk to her this way? But she sat silently on the couch. He knew he was hurting her, but it was the only way he could make her understand, and nothing he had said to her was untrue.

Caroline rose and stepped towards him.

"You don't mean that, Adam."

"Yes, I do. You need to believe me."

"Are you telling me that you don't love me? That you never loved me?"

Adam didn't answer. He didn't want to answer. This was the question he had never thought too long about. What was love, really? If it was affection for another person, then yes, at one time, he had loved her, but he had never felt that lightning bolt that knocks you off your feet that people described. That one moment when you knew you couldn't live without them. So he stayed silent. The only sound in the room was the ticking of the clock on the mantle. He could hear the faint sound as cars drove by and a bird, happy in the warmth of the summer day, chirping in the distance.

Minutes passed by. The world could have ended, and Caroline wouldn't have noticed. All that she cared about was that right now, *her* world was ending.

"Adam, please. Answer me. Are you telling me you were never in love with me? Not even a little?"

Lowering his voice to a whisper, afraid to hear his own words, Adam finally gave his wife an answer. "I don't know."

Caroline felt like her brain was expanding pressing against the inside of her skull. If it could she thought it might explode.

"So the last eighteen years have been a lie. Isabelle's death has just given you a good enough reason to leave. She was the only thing keeping you here all these years."

"No. That's not right. I have been happy. I'm just not anymore."

Caroline turned to face her husband. She didn't think there was anything she could do to make him change his mind. She was going to have to give up any self-respect she had left for herself and take a chance. No matter what he had said to her, she knew he was worth it.

She took a few steps towards him until she stood directly in front of him. Caroline knelt down and looked up towards his face. She put her hands to the back of his head and turned it until he was facing her and their eyes met. She leaned forward and kissed him ever so gently on the lips. Just for a second, she felt him yield beneath her touch.

Adam had thought Caroline was going to hit him. When she kissed him instead, he was so caught off guard that his body responded before his mind had a chance to take control. It had been so long since he had allowed another human to touch him in any way, and he could feel himself begin to reawaken. His lips began to move beneath hers, and his hand longed to reach out and touch her. His body was taken over with a longing that he had squashed down and chosen to resist for over a year.

But when his head took over, it screamed at him to stop. *You don't want this.* He pushed Caroline's shoulders away, and their connection was broken.

"What are you doing?"

"I'm making the first move," she answered.

"What?"

"Haven't you ever watched a movie where you can see two people about to make the biggest mistake of their lives and walk away from each other? I always believed that if one of them took a chance and kissed the other one, then they would see they really did love each other."

"Have you lost your mind? This is no romantic story. This is our own personal tragedy." Adam stood up out of the chair. He looked towards the coffee table and gestured towards the letter he had left their earlier.

"If you don't want to read it, that's up to you, but there's also something in there for Michael. Tell him I'll call him tomorrow, and if there's an emergency, call me on my mobile. Adam strode towards the door, grabbing his keys from the hall stand.

"Where are you going?" Caroline called to Adam's retreating back. "In case Michael wants to know."

"I've rented an apartment in the city. The landlord's waiting for me, and now you've made me late."

"So you planned this. You didn't just wake up this morning and decide to go. You've been working on this for a while?" She felt her body turn against her and then nausea rising and threatening to make her physically sick. He meant this. He really, really meant this.

Not feeling it was necessary to answer, Adam yanked the door open and then slammed it behind him. The latch didn't catch and the door banged back and hit the hat stand. Valuable old glass shattered on the parquet floor as the door continued to swing in the wind. She heard the sound of his car door slam, and then his car roared out of the driveway, scattering stones beneath his tyres.

Caroline caught the door and closed it behind his retreating car. There was no point trying to chase him. He had said his piece, and she had heard him. She finally understood. He didn't love her, and she was sure he was never coming back. She bent down and started to collect shards of glass off the floor. One of the pieces cut her thumb, and soon blood was flowing down her hand and onto the floor. *How fitting*, she thought as she watched it dripping and forming a puddle. *My heart's bleeding out. Now my body is too.*

Chapter 21

"This is yummy. Are you sure you don't want the rest?" Joan asked, dipping her spoon yet again into David's chocolate mousse.

"It's all yours. I can't eat another bite." David was always astounded at how much Joan could eat and never gain any weight. When he was younger, he'd been the same way, but as the years crept on, he noticed so did the kilos. When he started spending more time looking at plans of buildings instead of constructing them, it had become worse, and he was forced to take up jogging to keep trim. Assuming that Joan must be a workout queen because of her slim build, he had asked her to join him in an early morning jog one Sunday, but she had snorted in derision and told him that if he wanted to run around in circles with all the other crazy people running around in circles, he was welcome to it. She would be curled up in bed until ten, but he was welcome to join her for lunch if he wanted. Lunch wasn't quite the invitation he was looking for; he was hoping for the curled up in bed, but that seemed to have been put permanently on hold.

"I don't know how you stay so slim. You tell me you don't exercise, and that's your second dessert for the night. You must have magic metabolism."

"Well, that certainly didn't come from my mother. When I was little, she was tiny, but by the time I left home, she was just about as round as she was tall. Who knows, maybe I inherited it from my father."

"Any decisions on whether you want to meet him and your half-sister?"

"I still don't know if I want to meet him. Some days I think I do just so I can look into his eyes and see if he really is the monster he must have been to do what he did. I do know I'd like to meet my sister. I just don't know how to manage that without upsetting her and ultimately running into my father. But I think I am coming to terms with it all. It's just hard to comprehend how one small piece of information can completely change your perspective about someone. I spent years hating my mother. I used to wish someone would come and take me away. I hated having to see her drunk every day and feeling so neglected."

"Is that why you hardly drink?"

"I guess it is. I made a decision when I was a teenager to never end up like her. I don't mind other people drinking; it's just not for me. One glass of wine is more than enough."

"I still find it appalling that you had to live that way. You should have been out playing and learning, not worrying if there would be a next meal. It sounds like you raised yourself."

"I did mostly. Sometimes teachers would help me out by slipping me extra school supplies. I learnt to shop at op shops when I needed something. I would take money from my mother's purse. Just small bits at a time so she wouldn't notice. Not that there was ever much in it. And along the way, there were some kind mothers too. Beth's mum and dad kind of adopted me as their third daughter when I was about thirteen. I learnt more from Annie Mancini than anyone else. She taught me how to clean a house, how to cook some basic meals—that sort of thing. I always wished I could live with them, but I understood that their own children were their first priority. And to this day, Beth is still my best friend in the world."

"I'd like to meet her sometime. I'm beginning to wonder if you're keeping me a secret. I haven't met any of your friends."

"I'm not keeping you a secret. I just didn't want to push you before you were ready. I do think you two would get on well. I could ask her if I can bring you to dinner one night. She's dying to meet you, so I'm sure she'll say yes."

"Sounds like a plan. Has she got a family?"

"She's been married forever. She met Tom in high school, so we've all know each other for years. They have three kids that Beth wants to do away with most of the time, but I adore them. Their house is crazy and chaotic, but I'm always welcome. I'm going there for Christmas lunch, and I bet when I get there, Beth will still be deciding what we're going to eat. Hopefully her mum's going to be doing most of the cooking."

"I wish we could spend Christmas together. I thought about asking my parents if I could bring you, but that seemed like too much pressure to meet them that way. The cricket will be better. Less formal."

"I think the cricket is a perfect way for us to all met. Besides we're not really in that space yet where I should be going to special events."

"What space is that?" David questioned. He began to feel slightly anxious. He hated these conversations with women. Where's this leading? What are your intentions? Where's this relationship going? They always seemed to want a time frame on when you would be taking the next step.

"The space where two people are in a committed relationship."

"Joan, I don't know if you've noticed, but we seem pretty committed to each other. I haven't seen anyone else since I met you, and I assume you aren't looking for anyone either. And it has been five months that we have been seeing each other."

"Of course I'm not looking. We've just never talked about the future. If we even have a future. I have no idea what you're thinking."

David leaned away from the table in his chair, putting distance between them while he looked for the right words.

"You know how much I love spending time with you. We're together as much as we can be. I wish we could be together a lot more. There's nothing I'd like more than to take you home right now and spend the night with you, the whole night so we can wake up together. That's what I'm thinking. We could be out of here and back at your place in fifteen minutes. Doesn't that tell you how I'm feeling? Isn't that enough for now?"

Joan felt her heart drop. She knew where this was going. She had been here before—yet another man who found her attractive, enjoyed her company, and wanted to sleep with her but didn't think she was worth taking that last leap for. Did she have the word "easy" stamped on her forehead?

Mirroring his earlier action, she, too, leaned away from him in her chair. She shifted her gaze from his face that had been staring intently at hers to the other diners in the room. They were surrounded by happy families and couples enjoying each other's company. It was three days until Christmas, and people had that festive glow on their faces. It broke her heart to know that this year, like every year, she would spend Christmas with wonderful friends, but there would be no one who loved her exclusively. There wasn't going to be anyone to wake up beside on Christmas morning or anyone to give her silly gifts she didn't want or need but loved anyway because they had been chosen especially for her.

"David, I won't sleep with you. I want to desperately, but I'm saying no."

David pretended he hadn't heard most of what she had said and focused on the "I want to desperately" part of her last statement. She was the one woman in years that he had considered worth waiting this long for, had seen her through the heartbreak of finding where she really came from, and she was saying no to him. No way was he giving in to what she had decided without a fight.

"Look, Joan. What's stopping you? *You* want to. You just told me so yourself. There's absolutely no doubt that *I* want to. Unless I've completely misread you, it wouldn't be your first time. We're both consenting adults with no other entanglements. I can't see any problem with it. If I haven't been clear enough in the past, you turn me on more than anyone I've ever known. "

"I want more."

"What more could you want? I'm all yours."

"Sure for now. But how long is that going to last? I've heard it before. 'I want you,' 'you're so sexy', "we'll be together forever', 'trust me, I really care about you.' Do you know what I want to hear? I want to hear someone tell me 'I love you' and mean it."

David closed his eyes for a second and sighed.

"Don't you think it's a bit soon for that? I need more time. I'm not some moony-eyed teenager mopping around and telling every girl that looks in his direction that he's in love with them. I'm a grown man, and telling someone you love them is a serious thing to me. I won't be forced into making that kind of commitment if I'm not ready or I'm not sure."

Joan could see the disappointment on his face. She didn't want to be the cause of that. What she really wanted was to grab his hand and drag him out of the restaurant back to her place. But she couldn't go down that path again, not even with David.

"Trust me, David. The last thing I want to do is push you or force anything on you. I'm just letting you know how I feel. In the past, I was happy to sleep with someone I liked and found attractive. But recently, I've been reassessing my life. In the last eight weeks, so much has changed for me. I've found out that I was the product of a rape. That was a huge shock. I always believed my mother must have slept around and become pregnant by accident. I don't know why I thought that because although she had a lot of friends at the house while I was a kid, she never had a boyfriend and she never let any men stay over. I probably overheard someone say it when I was little. It was unusual for a kid not to know who their father was back in the seventies and eighties, and people talk."

"So because of what happened to your mother forty years ago, you're swearing off men for the rest of your life. You want to end up sad and alone like she was?"

"No, I'm not swearing off men, especially you." She smiled, trying to lighten the situation, which had gone from a casual evening out to the most important and difficult conversation she had ever had.

"I just don't want to settle for less. I can't do the casual sex thing anymore."

"So what are you saying? You're not willing to move this relationship forward unless we what? Get engaged? If I put a diamond on your finger and give you a wedding date, you'll think I'm sincere?" Joan shook her head, and David, who had just taken a swallow of his drink, choked and sprayed beer across the table. "You're not going to have sex until we get married. That's ridiculous. Its 2013, not 1813. That's not how it's done anymore, and it's certainly not the way I intend to live my life."

"But it's how I intend to live mine." Her voice was quiet but firm, and he believed she meant it.

"Joan, what you're expecting is unreasonable. I don't know of one man who would go along with such a crazy idea."

"Well, I happen to think I'm worth expecting unreasonable for. Nothing about love; real love is logical or fair. Expecting to feel the same way about someone forever and making the decision to tie yourself to them for the rest of your life makes no sense when you really think about it. But that's what I want."

"Why?" David could hear a whining tone to his voice that he didn't like, but he didn't understand at all where this conversation was heading. "It's not like the virgin fairy can come back and return your virginity to you."

"No, but I wish she could. I wish I'd made better decisions in the past. All I can do is make good decisions now."

"I just don't know how to respond. You never said a word to me before."

"I never used to think I deserved it before. But recently, Beth made me understand that I have value and that no one else was going to treat me with respect if I didn't treat myself that way. I've realized that when sex is done the wrong way, it can cause permanent damage, and I don't want to start off anything with you the wrong way. Sex ruined my mother's life and although I'm not suggesting in any way that you would want to hurt me knowingly, you could. If I gave in to make you happy—and yes, I would be happy too, but only in the short term—to discover later that you didn't love me and decided to walk away, then I would be devastated. I'm sorry, David. I'm making a stand for myself. If somebody wants me, they need to want me permanently."

David knew when he had lost. And this was one of those times. "I haven't met Beth, but I can tell I already don't like her." David rested his cheek in his hand and leaned his elbow on the table as he looked at Joan. He smiled faintly at her. "I wish you weren't being such a woman about this. I thought you were different."

"I'm sorry to disappoint you, but that's what I am, David. I'm a woman. It takes some of us longer to get here, but most of us want the same thing— love, marriage, someone to grow old with. All the old clichés are true. No one wants to be alone. This is just the first time I've decided I'm not willing to settle for less."

"So what happens now? Do we keep dating and see if this develops into something more? It could take me years to be ready for marriage. But who knows. I might eventually give in out of desperation because let me tell you if there was anyone that could sway me, it would be you."

"As tempting an offer as that that is David, you're not ready, and I don't want you that way. Blackmailing you has never been my intention." Joan stopped talking, wishing she didn't have to say it, but she saw no other way. "It seems we're at an impasse. You know what you want, and I know what I want. Unfortunately, they aren't the same thing."

"So you're telling me it's over. That's definitely not what I want."

Joan's shoulder's sagged in defeat. "I don't see any other way. You can't hang around forever waiting for me to change my mind. And I absolutely refuse to hang around hoping you'll change yours. We both deserve better than that. Maybe we'll find what we're looking for with someone else. I can't see any reason to stay together and let time slide by while we become more frustrated with each other. I like you too much to do that to you."

Joan pushed her chair back and stood up to leave. She needed to go now before she changed her mind. She pulled her purse out of her bag to pay. David jumped up and grabbed the bill from her hand.

"Please, let me. It's the least I can do."

"Are you sure?"

"I'm sure. I'm going to miss you so much, Joan. If you ever change your mind..." He left the sentence hanging.

"And I'm going to miss you too, David."

Joan walked towards the door of the restaurant. She was grateful they had come separately. If he drove her home, she didn't think she would be able to resist him. It was nearly impossible in a room full of people, but if she was alone with him, she knew it would be hopeless. She was at her car when she heard her name. She turned and saw it was David rushing towards her.

"Wait, Joan." For a second, her heart leapt. But when he held a bag out to her, she knew she had been wrong.

"I wanted to give you this. It's your Christmas present. I almost forgot."

"David, that's very kind of you, but considering the circumstances, you don't need to give it to me."

"I want you to have it. When you see what it is, you'll see it belongs to you anyway."

He handed over the pretty red bag with Christmas ribbon tied to the handle. Joan took it and then reaching into her own handbag, she pulled out a much smaller package.

"I want you to have this too. I hope you like it."

David took the gift, standing in uncomfortable silence as he took in every beautiful feature on Joan's face.

"May I hug you good-bye?"

"I'd like that," Joan answered.

David enveloped Joan in his arms, breathing her in. *This is the last time I'm ever going to get to do this*, he thought. His mind was frantic with the realization that he would never see her or talk to her again. He desperately wanted to put a stop to this madness, but he didn't know how without giving in, and he wasn't going to do that. Joan pulled away first and kissed him gently near the corner of his mouth, her cheek touching his. Hugging him one more time, she whispered so quietly in his ear that he almost missed it, and maybe it was more for her to say than for him to hear. "I do love you."

Before David had any chance to respond, Joan rushed to the driver's side of the car and let herself in. The traffic was light at this time of night, and he didn't even have time to wave before her car had pulled out of its spot and was gone. He stood there for a long time, willing her to come back. He had never felt this kind of devastation. When Charlotte had left him, he had felt anger and rejection, but this was much worse because it was his fault. He could have stopped Joan. He could have told her what he was really thinking—how he loved her so much it frightened him. Instead he let fear and pride get in the way—fear of letting her into every part of him and then having her decide he wasn't the man she wanted and leaving him. And pride. He always believed it was up to the man to make the first move. He felt like he hadn't been given that chance. If she'd just let him have a little more time. If she had told him what she was thinking and not rushed things. But she hadn't. She had taken the decision out of his hands, and now she was gone.

He walked slowly in the direction of his car, gift in hand. Seeing a bench, he sat down for a moment and pulled the paper off the present. Inside the black box he unwrapped was the beautiful watch he'd admired in a shop window when they had been out together one day. The back was engraved with the words: *Christmas 2012, love Joan*

There was also a note written in her tidy architect print:

> *Dear David,*
> *Merry Christmas. I hope this is the first of many. I wanted you to have this so you'll never be late. That way I'll never have to spend an extra moment without you.*
> *Joan*

David stood up and continued on to his car. When he reached it and got in, he turned the engine over. The radio immediately came on, deafening him. He'd had it cranked right up on his way to dinner even though it was tuned to a station of Joan's choosing. He'd been so happy, he had been singing along with the pop music he usually hated. Now a song Joan loved was playing. She always sang along, and the more he teased her about her voice, the louder she sang. It was "Without You" by Usher, and he didn't think there was a worse song to hear right now. The words resonated with him: "If you're not here, I'm paralysed without you." He flicked off the radio and clenched the steering wheel. Losing control, he smashed his fists down on the wheel and yelled "Argh!" It wasn't supposed to be like this. What had he done?

Joan made it all the way to the end of the street before tears blurred her vision and made it dangerous to drive. She pulled into a side street and stopped the car. She had no choice but to give into the heartache she was feeling as hot tears drenched her face and ran down her neck. Eventually the tears ran their course, and she was able to calm herself down. She looked over to the passenger seat and saw the gift David had given her. She picked up the bag and pulled the tissue paper out of the top. She reached inside and felt something heavy. The bag dropped away, and she saw that it was a beautiful frame. It was silver and looked old. Inside the frame was the picture she had found with David. It was her mother and herself when she was a baby. It had been blown up, and someone had gone to the effort to restore it. It was beautiful and instantly became her most valuable possession. She traced the line of her mother's young face with her finger. "I never knew you at all did I?" she spoke aloud to a woman who had been dead for nearly twenty years. Putting the frame down on the seat beside her, she saw that there was a card. It must have slipped out of the bag when she was opening the gift. She wasn't sure she could bear to read it, but it was impossible to resist. On the front was a picture of two bunnies dressed in scarves and gloves, kissing, with a sprig of mistletoe hanging above their heads. Inside David had written a short message.

Dear Joan,

Merry Christmas. I wish we could spend it together, but I'll see you Boxing Day. I don't know what our future holds, but I'm looking forward to us finding out together.

David xxo

Knowing her future was now going to be without David, Joan was no longer sure that she had made the right decision. Beth and her ideals. "No," she spoke aloud. Stop second-guessing yourself. It was the right thing to do. She just found out sooner rather than later this time that it wasn't going to work out. There must be someone out there for her. She couldn't imagine that she could love anyone more than she had loved David, but at least now she knew she was capable of actually falling in love. This had been the first time for her. Joan pulled away from the curb and started towards home. Sick of the quiet, she turned on the radio but immediately wished that she hadn't. Her favourite song was playing—David Guetta and Usher's "Without You." Every time it came on the radio, she sang it at the top of her voice, but tonight she was too raw, and it felt too real. Now maybe it could become her anthem. "I will never be the same without you." Yep, that seemed about right. The soundtrack of her life.

Chapter 22

"Could you come here for a minute, love? I want to talk to you." Tom called from the couch.

"Just let me finish loading the dishwasher? I won't be long."

"Why don't you leave it for a minute? I don't want any interruptions, and you know what the kids are like. The second we try to have a serious conversation, they barge in and hijack it."

"Serious conversation? Is something wrong?"

"Nothing's wrong. Just come and sit."

Tom patted the seat next to his and waited expectantly. He had put so much time and effort into making sure every little detail went to plan, but it all hinged on getting Beth to agree. It meant telling her a few tiny white lies, but they were for a good cause, and hopefully she would forgive him.

"What's up?" Beth asked, lowering herself into the couch a minute later. Sitting felt good. She was exhausted after dealing with a grade-five class all week. For the hundredth time that day, she wished she'd chosen any career other than teaching. Tom must be mad to consider becoming a teacher.

"All right, I'm sitting. What's so important that it can't wait until the dishes are done?"

"I want to talk to you about your birthday. You know it's next week, and I've made a few plans for the day."

"I told you. I want to spend that day in bed under the covers, crying for my lost youth. If I stay there for the whole day, it will be like it never happened. I've decided I'm going to call the whole thing off and turn forty next year instead."

"How about instead of staying in bed all day, I whisk you away for a night? You don't have to see anyone. It'll be just me and you. I'll take you out for a fancy dinner, and then we'll spend the night somewhere nice. You can turn forty in private, and I'll even schedule in some time for you to sulk about your lost youth if you like."

Surprised, Beth considered Tom's suggestion. They hadn't gone away together since their tenth wedding anniversary. As much as she didn't want to celebrate this particular birthday, if it meant getting away for a night, then she was in.

"What about the kids?"

"Sorted. Your mums agreed to pick them up from school, and she'll stay the night."

"What about work? Can you take a day off? And I'll need to let the agency know I won't be available that Friday."

"Done and done. The boys at work know I won't be there and short of a major accident, they know they can't call me. I already let your agency know by phone and email that you're not available."

"Where will we go then? The city? It's probably not enough time away to go to the country. We can look online and book something tonight. If we leave it too long, we won't be able to get anything good." Beth started to rise from her seat, but Tom grabbed her hand and pulled her back down.

"Never you mind where we're going. That's for me to know."

"Are you telling me, Tom Fraser, that you've actually organized something? Without help?" Beth couldn't imagine Tom surfing the Internet looking for hotel rooms and making bookings. He always left that sort of thing to her. This was definitely a first.

"Yes, I have smarty pants. I can do things."

"What if I'd said no?"

"Then I would have had to kidnap you."

"I'd like to see you try. All right, I agree to your offer. But with one condition. We're going away because we want to, not because it's my birthday. I don't want to hear any mention of turning forty."

"Sorry, can't do it. We are going to celebrate all things Beth and part of that is that you've made it this far in life. You should embrace it. It's a milestone."

"It's not a milestone. It's a millstone wrapped around my neck, dragging me down. I can't be turning forty. I'm sixteen. Sixteen with my whole life still ahead of me. I haven't made any mistakes yet, and I have no cares or worries. I wish I could have stayed sixteen forever."

"You're not sixteen. You're going to be forty next week, and you're going to love it. Think of all the wonderful things that are going to happen to you while you're in your forties. The children will finish school. Think about all that responsibility lifting off your shoulders. If we get lucky, they might move out and we'll finally have some peace. Lochie could even get married in the next ten years. I don't know about you, but I'm looking forward to becoming grandparents. Revenge is sweet, and we're going to have front-row seats for the best show on earth."

Beth considered that, although the grandparent part scared her half to death. That would mean she really was getting old. And she wasn't sure what kind of parents her children would make. She wouldn't let them take care of a cat, let alone a tiny human being.

"Maybe it won't be so bad. I just don't like the idea of getting old. I hate watching my mum age."

"Your mum's as sharp as a tack. I think she does more now than she ever has. And look at you. You've lost so much weight, and you're getting fitter every day. It's going to be a long time before you have to worry about getting old and decrepit. "

"I wanted to make it twenty kilos by my birthday. I've only lost seventeen."

"Don't be so hard on yourself, Beth. That's just a number on the scales. How much muscle have you put on from exercise? If you're healthy, that's really all that matters, not a number. I'm so proud of what you've achieved."

"I feel kind of proud of myself too. The thing is it hasn't been that hard. Now that I've got used to cooking, I'm almost enjoying it, and I don't feel hungry all the time like I did when I tried other diets. I wish I'd done this years ago."

"Well, you can't change the past. You can only look ahead, which is why we need to celebrate your birthday."

"All right, but if I have to be forty, then I want a cake. Do you think Caroline will let me?"

"Forget Caroline. If you want a cake, then that's what you're going to have. If you want, I'll get you two."

~~~

Beth stood in front of her mirror, looking to see if she felt different. She looked the same as she had yesterday. Nothing had fallen off in the night, and her face hadn't sagged down to her knees. Yes, there were a few wrinkles, but they had been there the day before so she couldn't blame them on turning forty. *It doesn't matter how hard I try*, she thought. *Time still marches on. I can't stop it, and there's nothing I can do to control it.*

She finished off her makeup and then dressed in the new jeans she'd bought last week. If she was going to be forty, then she was going to look the best she could while doing it. The smell of someone cooking drew her to the kitchen, and she could hear the usual squabbling coming from her children. She had been hoping she could get through the morning without having to yell at anyone before she dropped them off at school. If that happened, she would be able to go for twenty-four hours without having to get mad or upset. That would be the best birthday present ever.

Her footsteps alerted Tom to her presence, and he quietly hissed at Sarah and Nate to quit it. When he saw his mother, Nate grabbed her hand and led her to the table. When she was seated, he leaned over and kissed her on the cheek.

"Happy birthday, Mum," he said and handed her the first present off the top of a very impressive pile.

"Thanks, Nate. Can I open this?"

He nodded and said, "This one's from me. I picked it myself, so I hope you like it."

Tearing off the paper, Beth revealed a box containing her favourite perfume, Estee Lauders' Beautiful, along with a body wash and a hand cream. She hugged Nate and told him how thrilled she was with the gift. Next, Sarah came over with a cup of tea for Beth, which in her excitement, she banged down on the table and spilled a little.

"Me next, me next," she chanted, pulling an envelope from the top of the pile and handing it to Beth.

"This was totally my idea, so don't let Dad take the credit. He thinks he came up with it, but he didn't. It was all me."

Sarah looked too excited, and Beth suspected that it must be something her daughter was going to get to use. But when she opened the envelope, she was delighted to see it was a voucher for a day with a personal shopper. It was for her favourite department store that she had avoided for the last few years because of her size. They did have a larger-women's section but every time she inevitably ran into someone she knew, and she had ended up being embarrassed. *Not anymore*, she thought. Now I can buy whatever I want, wherever I want. There was also cash attached to the voucher and when she looked, she saw it was five-hundred dollars.

Tom came over with a plate piled high with bacon and eggs, which he set in front of her.

"Happy birthday, babe. The money's from me just to help you get started. We hope you enjoy."

"Thank you, Tom. And you too, Sarah. What a wonderful idea. You know how much I don't like shopping for myself, and having some professional help will make it so much easier to get some new clothes."

"And plus, Mum, you're usless at picking out anything decent, so maybe she'll get you to buy some clothes from this century."

"Sarah," scolded Tom, exasperated at his daughter. She really needed to stop saying whatever was in her head out loud.

"Don't worry about it, Tom. She's right. I am hopeless at shopping, and I've decided I'm not allowed to get mad at anyone today." She turned to Sarah.

"I promise I'll do my best to buy something from this century. Maybe even this decade, if you get lucky."

Lochie was the last of her children to give her a gift. It hadn't been on the table because that would have given it away. He brought in a beautiful crystal vase, and it was filled with the most amazing roses she had ever seen. They were a deep scarlet with not buds like most modern roses. They were the old-fashioned kind that she so loved—blousy and full with their beautiful faces smiling at her. They reminded her of her father, who had always grown the most beautiful roses. She was going to really miss him today.

Tom leaned in and kissed her gently on the cheek. "These are from your dad's garden. I went early this morning to pick them. He would have wanted you to have them today. The kiss is from your mum, and she says she'll see you tomorrow when we get back."

Instantly Beth was overwhelmed and started to cry. She had been completely taken off guard by the beautiful gesture.

"Hey, no tears today. This is supposed to be a happy day."

"I know. I just miss him so much."

"Well, maybe this will cheer you up." Tom handed over a small blue box, not wrapped but with the trademark white ribbon tied around it. Every woman in the western world recognized that box as a Tiffany's and dreamed of one day receiving one. She pulled the ribbon open and then removed the lid. Nestled inside was a beautiful pair of earrings. Simple but elegant, they were her favourite stones—emeralds, round and surrounded by a ring of small diamonds.

"Oh, Tom." She looked up into the expectant faces of her family. She felt the tears return. She knew she was so blessed to be part of the lives of the four amazing people who stood around her. Taking the earrings out of the box, she started to put them on. "Can we afford these? They look expensive," she asked but not really caring. Apart from her engagement and wedding ring, Beth didn't own any real jewellery. She had always considered it a waste of money when there were so many other things to pay for. But now that she owned a pair of the real thing, she could see what all the fuss was about. They felt heavy in her earlobe, and they made her feel rich and special.

"Never mind the cost. You are one hundred percent worth it. Now eat up. There's still a pile of gifts over there to open."

The morning passed in a blur. She opened lots of lovely little gifts—candles, books, and even a CD of some of her favourite songs from the nineties. The kids teased her, pretending they didn't know what the antiquated thing was, with Lochie suggesting that maybe it was a coaster for her tea. Thankfully her family had stuck to her no-chocolates rule, which meant she didn't have to look at them while they mockingly called out to her, "Eat me, eat me."

When it was time to drop the children off at their schools, Beth had had such a wonderful morning, she almost couldn't bear to part with them. She leaned over and whispered to Tom so they wouldn't overhear. "Maybe we could take the kids with us. They could take the day off school. It wouldn't do any harm."

Tom whispered back as he pulled out of the driveway and headed down the street. "Fat chance. Today you're all mine."

Tom and Beth spent the morning weaving their way down the peninsula, stopping for a leisurely lunch by the beach. At two, they checked into a wonderful little cottage situated on a large property a short drive from Red Hill. It had views of the sea and even an outdoor spa. The house was owned by a funny old couple that fawned over Beth and insisted on giving them a tour of the cottage, pointing out every feature and telling them little stories about the people who had built it. After half an hour, Tom managed to move Bridget, the woman who owned the property, towards the front door and was prepared to push her out if need be. When he finally got rid of her, he locked the door in case she returned and suggested a nap before they got ready for dinner. As it turned out, they didn't get much sleeping done, but Beth hadn't minded at all. If that was what a nap entailed, maybe she should take one every day.

When she heard a knock on the door at five, Beth guessed it was probably the owner, checking to see if everything was all right. She considered not answering the door, afraid they would never get rid of Bridget and have to bring her along with them to dinner. Instead she found a lovely-looking girl standing on the step, laden down with bags.

"Hi. I'm Sally. You must be Beth."

"Yes. Can I help you?" Beth asked confused. Nobody knew where they were, and she certainly didn't know this girl.

"I'm here to help you get ready for tonight. Your husband's taking you out in a couple of hours. I'm going to do your hair and makeup." She took Beth's hand and examined it. "We should have time to do a manicure too before your reservation."

"Tom," Beth called out loudly. "There's someone called Sally here. Do you know anything about this?"

Calling out from the small sitting room, Tom answered, "Yes, I do. Just do what she says and ask for the note."

Sally pulled out an envelope from one of the bags and handed it to Beth. When she opened it, she found a letter from her mother.

> To my baby girl,
>
> Happy Birthday. I can't believe you're forty today. I'm so delighted to know the woman you have become and the mother you are. Your father and I were always so proud of you. If he could be here today, he would tell you himself. I wish you a wonderful day and have a lovely dinner tonight. Sally is my gift to you. Settle back and let her do her magic on you. Take a photo so I can see how beautiful you look.
>
> Lots of love,
>
> Mum

Sally propelled her towards the table and ordered her to sit. She plugged in hair curlers and opened bags of makeup. When she had Beth's hair up in rollers, Sally started working on her face. After an hour, she had been plucked

and combed into submission. Her nails had been shaped and painted. Tom
sat there the whole time, reading his book and not passing a comment, only
looking up occasionally. When Sally declared she was finished, Tom put the
book down, walked over, and looked her up and down.

"Not bad. I do think something is missing. Maybe you should check the
wardrobe in the bedroom. Sally will be here for a little bit longer in case you
need touching up."

Beth bounced towards the bedroom. The day she had dreaded since she
turned thirty was turning out to be the most wonderful one of her life. She
hadn't even had this kind of pampering for her wedding. Pulling open the
wardrobe door, she found the most beautiful dress hanging with a bow tied
around the hanger. It was in a lovely soft sea green that would complement
her new earrings perfectly. Sleeveless, it wrapped around and tied on the side.
The V-neckline plunged just a little but not enough to be indecent. Sitting on
the bottom of the wardrobe was a box, and when she opened it, she found a
pair of gorgeous shoes. They had a two-inch heel with delicate straps covered
in rhinestones. There was a matching handbag and another letter. She recognized the handwriting immediately. This one was from Caroline.

> To my wonderful friend,
>
> Happy birthday. I'm sure you and Tom are having
> a wonderful day. Wear this knowing how beautiful you
> are. I can't imagine my life without you in it, and I'm so
> glad we met all those years ago when we were six. Take
> a photo, and I'll see you soon.
>
> Your Bestie (as Isabelle would say)
>
> Caroline

Pulling the dress off the hanger and feeling the beautiful soft fabric, Beth could see it must have cost Caroline a fortune. She saw with dismay that it was a size twelve. She wasn't sure she'd be able to get into it. Caroline must have been a little more optimistic than she should have been. Stripping off the dress she had planned to wear to dinner, she carefully put the dress on, wrapping it around her waist and tying it at the side. It turned out to be the perfect choice. It fit her beautifully. Typical Caroline. She always got it right. Beth turned to the full-length mirror and saw how the dress flattered her. It showed the new definition in her waist and set off her curves. The skirt fell in waves below her knees and when she put the shoes on, they accentuated her legs, which had slimmed down since she had started exercising. She had never felt more beautiful in her life. Maybe being forty wouldn't be so horrible after all.

When she stepped out of the room, Tom was waiting. He had changed into a suit she had never seen before and was even wearing a tie. Tom gasped in delight when he saw Beth. Taking her hand, he twirled her around, enjoying the way she moved in her new dress. Sally primped for a few minutes, adjusting a few curls and redoing Beth's lipstick. When she was done, she took the camera Tom offered her. After a few snaps, Sally declared it was time for them to leave for dinner and started packing up all her gear.

Desperate to know where they were going, Beth began peppering Tom with questions before they even got in the car. He refused to answer, instead pretending to concentrate on his driving. They made their way down the long drive, admiring the old oak trees that stood on either side like sentries. But instead of pulling out onto the road, Tom stopped the car at the main house. Beth had admired it when they had arrived earlier in the day and was longing to look around it. She had seen the front room when they checked in but felt it would be rude to ask the owner for a tour of her home. Tom turned off the car and got out. Before she had a chance to ask what was going on he opened her door and taking her hand helped her out.

"Tom, why are we here? It's rude to bother people. They're probably having their dinner." He didn't answer, instead leading her up the stairs and opened the majestic door without knocking. It was very quiet inside, and Beth began to feel like a trespasser. Tom kept her hand in his and pulled her forward to another set of doors. Before he opened them, he very gently kissed her lips and said, "Happy Birthday, Bethany Fraser. I love you more than anything else in this world."

He pushed open the door, and from the darkness of the room, she heard forty people yell, Surprise!"

The lights flicked on, and Beth saw all her favourite people. Her mother was standing there with Beth's children, beaming. Caroline and Jill stood together, clapping. Joan was standing to the side, trying to look happy even though she was alone. Months ago, David had planned to be her date. She saw friends from church and teachers she worked with. The neighbours she liked were here, and the ones she avoided weren't. Tom must have worked so hard to pull this off. She had simply had no idea at all. She turned to him and shook her head.

"How did you do this?"

"I had a little help from your mum and your friends. I couldn't let another year go by without you knowing how much I appreciate and adore you. So…good surprise?"

She threw her arms around his neck and kissed him deeply, not caring who saw. She heard cheers from some of the adults and calls for them to "get a room." When Beth had kissed him as long as was decent in front of her guests, she stepped back a little and looked around again at all the people who had come out for her. There was a photographer taking pictures, and in the corner, she could see the most decadent chocolate cake she could imagine. Tom leaned down, catching her attention.

"The photographer is Joan's present to you. We're going to take some family portraits with the kids and your mum later. I think you should get one with Joan and Caroline too if you can get them to behave with each other. The cottage tonight was Jill's present, and we're not staying one night; we're staying for three." He paused for a second to let it all sink in. He could see that she wasn't mad even though she had always declared surprise parties to be horrendous and had made him promise on more than one occasion to never throw her one.

"You didn't answer me. Was this a good surprise?"

Beth's eyes glistened with tears, and she turned to the man who had made not only this night but her whole life possible. She reached up and stroked his cheek, taking in every facet of his wonderful face.

"Definitely a good surprise," she answered.

Chapter 23

It had been exactly fifty days since David had seen Joan. At first he had been optimistic, sure that she would change her mind. But with every day that slowly trickled by, his hope dwindled. She really, really meant what she had said. If her ultimatum had been a ploy to force his hand, she would have called by now. But he hadn't heard one word from her and with so much time passed, he had finally accepted that he wasn't going to. So here he was, alone again, spending another Saturday at the building site because he had nothing better to do.

Christmas had been a nightmare. He had to explain to his family why Joan wouldn't be joining them for the Boxing Day match. His father had laughed and said, "She's got you there, Son. Don't do it unless that's what you really want." His mother had been even less help, declaring Joan to be "a wise girl." She then spent the next hour complaining about the decline of any moral fibre in today's society and thought if more girls took a stand like Joan had, men would be forced to behave better and do the right thing, instead of treating the world like a sexual supermarket where they could sample all the goods without buying. Seeing how miserable he was, his sister, Jessica, suggested he should be waiting at the jewellery store first thing the next morning and buy the biggest engagement ring they had. When he told her to butt out, she said he either needed to man up and beg Joan to take him on permanently or stop his whining because he was ruining Christmas day for everyone. Families.

David had gone on one sad, awful date since Joan had walked away. There had been nothing wrong with the woman he had met for dinner. Jessica had insisted on setting him up with yet another mother from the school where her two children attended. Meredith was very attractive, not dissimilar in looks to Joan—Jessica knew what he liked. She had been funny and didn't spend the entire evening putting down her ex-husband like some women did. *She* wasn't the problem at all. *He* was. He broke the cardinal rule of dating and spent the evening talking about Joan. He couldn't have made the night worse, telling his date how much he missed Joan and what an idiot he had been for letting her go. Before dessert was served, she stood up from her seat and advised him to crawl back to Joan on his hands and knees before she wished him luck and left. Meredith also made the suggestion that if he wasn't willing to marry Joan, he should be kind enough to not waste any other women's time taking them out until he had managed to get her out of his system. That had been a week ago, and he hadn't been able to get Meredith's words out of his head. He knew that's what he should do, what he wanted to do. The only thing stopping him was pride, but that was disappearing with every second he had to live without Joan.

After unlocking the gate to the site, David drove his car onto the lot. It had been raining all morning, and the clouds looked like they might be about to give a repeat performance, so he grabbed his waterproof jacket from the passenger seat. He looked at the hard hat and the safety vest he always kept in the car, but rejected them. Phil had asked him to come down and take a look at the roof. They had hired a new roofing contractor, but Phil didn't think they had installed the flashing correctly on the northeast gable. When David had seen the weather report, he decided a wet day was the perfect time to check; he would be able to go inside and see if there were any leaks. But while it wasn't raining, he would get up on the roof and take a look. Phil had left a ladder for him at the spot he had an issue with, and David climbed up carefully because the rungs were wet.

He could see the problem immediately and was grateful he hadn't paid for the work yet. Something else to sort out on Monday. He sat on the roof for a bit, taking in the view and contemplating his situation with Joan. He knew he couldn't go on like this. She hadn't yielded, so it was up to him. And he wanted to. So badly. She might have moved on or her feelings might have changed, but he would have to take that risk. Today. He would call her when he got home.

As he had expected, drops started falling again. At first it was soft, but after a few minutes, it began to fall heavily. David decided this was a good opportunity to see if the ceiling was leaking. He carefully turned around, swinging himself onto the ladder, and started to make his way towards the ground. He was about halfway down when he felt his boot slip. He managed to regain his footing, and looking down, he saw the rung was covered in mud. The rain had turned the building site into a swamp, and he must have gotten wet clay stuck to the bottom of his boots earlier. Leaving the rung on the ladder dirty could be dangerous for the next person who used it, and the last thing he needed was one of his guys slipping and falling. He started to scrape his boots on the step, pushing the wet mud off as he went. There was one stubborn bit that resisted, and he gave it a good kick to knock it off. Everything from that moment on appeared to happen in slow motion. As he was kicking, his foot slipped forward off the rung awkwardly and his left knee, weakened by an old sporting injury, gave way under his shifting weight, and his whole body dropped down and then flipped backwards. As he fell backwards and headfirst towards the ground, his right foot caught the rung above, and he heard his fibula snap. The weight of his falling body pulled his leg free from the ladder, and the impact of hitting the ground knocked him unconscious.

~~~

Joan was already awake when her phone rang at eight o'clock on Sunday morning. In the past, she had always been able to sleep late on the weekends, but her broken heart woke her up early most days. Although Joan knew she had done the right thing, time hadn't diminished the longing she had for David. She spent her evenings alone, working or trying to watch television, but nothing held her interest for more than a few minutes. Being at Beth's surprise birthday party last week and seeing how Tom loved his wife so much had magnified her loneliness. Daily, sometimes hourly, she picked up her phone, desperate just to hear David's voice, but each time she put it back down. She knew if she spoke to him, that would be the end of her. The only thing keeping her from throwing herself into his arms was distance.

Her caller ID identified the person rude enough to call on a Sunday morning as Phil. *Unbelievable*, she thought. She had been thankful that he had begun to consult her on any problems on site instead of David, but that didn't mean she enjoyed talking to him. Each time he called, by the end of their conversation, she wanted to throttle him. He was such an old woman, constantly questioning her judgement and making a complete pain of himself. She was tempted to ignore his call and deal with whatever imaginary problem he had come up with this time tomorrow, but who was she kidding? She had nothing else to do, and now was as good a time as any.

"Hey, Phil," she greeted, screwing up her face in dislike. She should have gone with her first instinct and ignored his call.

"Joan. Sorry to bother you on a Sunday, but I thought this might be important for you to know. There's been a bit of an accident on site."

"I'm sorry to hear that, but I'm not sure what it's got to do with me." She rolled her eyes and sighed. "You're not suggesting it's my fault are you?"

"No, but I thought you might want to know. I don't know what happened yet, but last night, a man walking his dog passed the building and found David unconscious. The police think he must have fallen from a ladder. I'm not sure if I should be telling you or not, but I got the feeling you two had something going there for a while."

"How badly is he hurt?"

"I'm not sure. His sister called me about an hour ago to let me know it's going to be awhile before he can be back at work. He's at Dandenong Hospital."

Joan didn't wait to see if Phil had anything else to say. She hung up on him and ran to her bedroom. She grabbed the clothes she had been wearing yesterday and dressed as quickly as she could. Not taking the time to brush her hair or even clean her teeth, within two minutes, she was in her car and heading down Punt Road towards the M1. Always confident behind the wheel, Joan drove like a mad woman, grateful the traffic was light.

It took her less than half an hour to reach the hospital. She had imagined every scenario possible from a minor bump on the head to finding David in a permanent coma. She didn't allow herself to consider that he might be dying. She pulled her car into the almost empty car park and ran towards the entrance. Not really knowing where she should be heading or whether they were even going to let her in, Joan banged on the security window at the front desk.

"I'm looking for David Saunders. He was brought here last night."

"Are you a relative?"

"No, I'm his…" She stopped, knowing if she told the girl she was nothing to David that she wouldn't tell her anything. "I'm his fiancé. I've only just found out he was in an accident."

The girl put the magazine she had been reading down and started tapping on a computer. After thirty seconds, she looked up at Joan.

"He's on the second floor, but I really can't let you up. Visiting hours start at ten."

Joan had no intention of waiting until ten o'clock and sprinted towards the elevators. She hit the button repeatedly, knowing that it wouldn't bring the lift any quicker but she needed to do something constructive with her hands. After what seemed like an eternity but was actually less than a minute, the lift doors opened, and Joan rushed in and hit the button for the second floor. When the lift doors slid open, she stepped out and saw a nurses' station. The person behind the counter looked friendly, but Joan still hesitated to approach her. She knew she had no right to be here, and she was going to have to lie to find out which room David was in and if he was all right.

She smiled at the nurse, wishing she didn't look so scruffy.

"Hi. I'm trying to find David Saunders. I'm his fiancé, and I've just been told he's been in an accident. Can you please tell me how he is and where I can find him?"

She heard the questioning voice of the woman who had been sitting on a chair near the lift behind her and turned to face her.

"You're David's fiancé. That's strange. He didn't tell me he was engaged." The woman in her late thirties was very pretty, and Joan felt her heart sink. This woman looked like she belonged here, while Joan knew that *she* didn't.

She held out her hand in introduction. Not a natural liar, Joan decided it would be best to be honest with this woman. At least she might be able to get some information about his condition out of her.

"My name's Joan." She lowered her voice so the nurse wouldn't hear. "I'm not really David's fiancé. I'm just a friend. They wouldn't let me see him or tell me anything if they knew I wasn't family. I just found out he's been in an accident, and I wanted to see if he was okay. "

"So you're Joan. I've heard all about you. Being David's ex, I'm surprised to see you here."

"I'm sorry. I know I'm intruding. I'll go." She backed away from the woman, feeling heat rising up her neck in embarrassment.

"Wait. I can take you in to see him if you'd like. He's asleep, but I don't think he would mind."

"Thank you, but it looks like you have it covered. I'll leave you to it. Please don't tell him I was here."

The woman gave her a quizzical look. "Don't be silly. He'll be thrilled you came."

"I don't think so. And I'm sorry if I've made you uncomfortable. I really am his ex. There's nothing going on between us anymore. I was just worried, and I didn't think before I came here. His new girlfriend shouldn't have to put up with his old one hanging around."

The face of the woman lit up. "There's no way I'm David's girlfriend. I'm his sister, Jessica. I'm very pleased to meet you finally." Relief flooded through Joan. Not a girlfriend, just a sister.

"Is he all right? Phil rang me, but he wasn't sure how badly David was hurt. I came straightaway." Joan tucked her hair behind her ears and looked down at the dirty sweatpants and the old T-shirt she was wearing. "I don't normally look this bad. I was in a bit of a hurry."

"Phil's an idiot. I told him David was going to be okay. He shouldn't have scared you like that. I would have called you myself if I'd known you were so interested. I have David's phone. so I had your number.

240

Smiling, Jessica looked over at the nurse who was watching them both with interest. "It's all right, Chloe. I'll take Joan in to see David. They're very newly engaged, so I didn't have her number."

Jessica pulled Joan towards a closed door and put her finger to her lips, warning Joan to be quiet. There was a closed curtain around each of the two beds, and Jessica quietly opened the one furthest away from the door. Joan gasped when she saw David. His leg was in plaster from the knee down, and he had extensive bruising on his face.

"As you can see, his leg is broken. He was unconscious when he was found, so we don't know how long he was out, but he woke up in the emergency room, was able to speak, and knew who he was. He's on IV painkillers, so he doesn't stay awake for very long. The good news is that the doctors say he'll be fine. He can probably go home in a few days."

Joan felt all the tension drain from her body. Embarrassed but unable to stop herself, she burst into tears. Jessica led her back out into the foyer, and after finding a chair for her to sit on. brought her a paper cup of water and handed her a tissue. After Joan had wiped the tears from her eyes, she saw Jessica had sat down beside her and was appraising her carefully.

"He really is going to be fine. His leg will take about six weeks to heal, but it was a clean break, so he'll be as good as new. And I'm sure he'll be glad that you're here."

"I was just so worried. If anything had happened to him..." Her voice trailed off. She didn't belong here. David had his family looking after him. He didn't need her, and he had probably already moved on with his life. "I should go. I'm relieved he's going to be okay."

"Please don't go. David will want to see you. He's been pathetic since you broke up."

"He has? He hasn't found himself someone new?"

"Hardly. He went on one date, and that's only because I practically forced him. She's a friend of mine, and she said he talked about you the whole night. She left halfway through their dinner and told me I'm never allowed to try and set her up again. A blind man could see how much he misses you."

"He does? I haven't heard from him, so I didn't think he did."

"Oh, he definitely misses you, but he's a stubborn man. You really messed with his head."

"I didn't mean to. It just didn't work out."

"There's plenty of time for that." Jessica stood up. "I need to go home for a few hours and get some sleep. Mum and Dad will be here about ten. Do you think you could stay with him until they get here? He gets confused when he wakes up, and I have to keep telling him where he is. It's the drugs. They're making him more stupid than he normally is."

"I can stay. But I look awful, and I could use a shower. I don't want David to see me like this."

Jessica smirked at Joan. "If this is what you look like when you think you look awful, I can't imagine you look when you've put in a bit of effort. Maybe you should forget my big brother. You could do much better than him."

"I don't think so."

"Really? I can only see him as my not-so-smart brother. Letting you go just proves what an idiot he is." Jessica took a pen out of her purse and rummaged around until she found an old supermarket docket. She wrote something down and handed it to Joan.

"That's my number. Call me if anything changes or if you want to check on David later. They won't give you any information here because you're not family. Not yet anyway," she said as she winked at Joan. Jessica waved good-bye to the nurse and walked towards the lift. Joan stood and started back towards David's room. She quietly closed the door behind her and pulled the chair beside the window as close as she could next to his bed.

Very gently, Joan took David's hand and lay her head down on the bed next to where he slept. She knew it was dangerous for her to be here. Nothing had changed for her; she still refused to be in a casual relationship with him. And even though Jessica had told her David missed her, that didn't mean he was ready to get married or even that he might want to in the future. If she hadn't promised to stay until David's parents arrived, she would have slipped out before he woke up and saw her.

Joan didn't notice David stirring until his hand moved under hers. She sat up as his lids opened and closed a few times. When his eyes focused, and he saw who was sitting beside him, he decided he must be dreaming. The whole night had passed in a drugged blur, and he wasn't sure what was real and what wasn't. This was by far the best dream he'd had all night. He could hear Joan's voice, and she was smiling at him. He tried to focus on her. He didn't want to miss what she had to say, even if it wasn't real.

"Hey, sleepy head," Joan whispered, not wanting to wake the other occupant in the room. "Are you in any pain?"

David slowly moved his head from side to side, and in a croaky voice, he said, "No pain. Happy you're here."

"Do you know where you are?" She couldn't tell if he knew what had happened, and he didn't seem to be quite all there.

He was beginning to remember falling yesterday and knew he was in hospital. He opened his eyes again and saw that Joan was still there, and he could feel the light pressure of her hand holding his.

"Are you really here?"

"I am. But I can wait outside if I'm bothering you."

"Don't go," he said, slipping back to sleep.

Joan watched as David drifted off again, but after about half an hour, he woke up. This time, he was more lucid. He didn't know that her eyes had never left his face. He might not love her, she had decided, but she did love him, and she wanted to be able to recall what he looked like for the rest of her life. It might not have worked out, but she would always have the memory of what it had been like to love someone.

David woke to Joan's beautiful face. He didn't know why she was here, but if it had brought her back into his life, he would be willing to fall off a ladder every day. He cleared his throat and focused on Joan.

"How did you know I was here?"

"Phil called me."

"Remind me to give him a pay raise."

"I will. You need your sleep. I can go if you like. Your parents will be here soon, and your sister will be back later."

David shook his head, surprised by the pain. The painkillers must be wearing off. "Please stay. I'd rather you never left me again."

"I'll stay till your mum and dad arrive, and then I should go."

"Big plans for the day?" he asked, hoping they didn't include a man.

Shaking her head, she replied, "No. But you don't need me here. This is a time for family, not old friends."

"Is that all we are? Old friends."

"I don't know what we are, David. But I know it's not good for me to be here. It's too hard."

"Why is it too hard? I've missed you. Haven't you missed me?"

"Yes. But I can't go through all this again. A girl can only take so much heartbreak."

"Did I cause that?"

"You didn't mean to. We wanted different things, that's all. That's the risk you take with relationships. People don't always feel the same about each other."

"Did you mean it when you said you loved me?"

"I didn't say that."

"Yes, you did. I heard you that day."

"I'm sorry. I didn't mean for you to hear me. I just wanted to say it once."

"And do you still feel that way?"

"David, please don't ask me that. "

"It's just that I was thinking. If you love me and I love you, there's no reason for us to be apart anymore."

"What did you say?"

"I said I love you. I should have said it sooner. What I'm waiting for now is to find out if you still love me."

"Of course I do, David. But you probably don't know what you're saying. They have you on drugs for the pain."

"I think the drugs have worn off. I have a splitting headache, and my leg is in agony. You don't need to think that I won't remember this conversation."

"I'll get the nurse. Maybe they need to give you another dose." She was halfway out of her chair before David put his hand up to stop her.

"Forget about the pain. I'll be fine. Do you remember when you said we were at an impasse? I agree. We were. That means one of us needs to change their mind. I've decided it should be me."

"I'm not sure what that means, David. You made it very clear you weren't ready for anything permanent."

"Joan, I can't go on in this life without you. I've become a hazard to myself and others. I'm lucky I haven't been in a car accident. I've been so miserable and distracted. Look at me. I could have been killed yesterday falling off that ladder. So I think it's best if we get married. I don't want to wait. I want to do it as soon as possible. But just so you know how serious I am about this, don't you dare try and get me into bed. Until that ring is on your finger and the 'I Dos' are said, I'm completely off limits."

Joan tilted her head, trying to decide if David was serious or not. "David, why don't we wait until you're feeling better? You shouldn't be making decisions when you're in this state."

"I'm not going to change my mind. If you don't say yes now, it just means I'll have to ask you again tomorrow. If I have to, I'll ask you every day until you agree."

Joan had no intention of accepting an offer when it was made by someone not in their right mind. As much as she wanted to scream yes, that would be unfair to David when he realized what he'd done later. She hesitated, not really knowing what to say. She heard the door open and saw two people, one a man who looked very much like David and an older woman she guessed was his mother. She'd never been happier to be interrupted in her whole life.

"David, your parents are here. We can talk about this later. When you're better." She stood up as David's parent's approached the bed. She held out her hand to David's father and introduced herself to them both.

"Hi. I'm Joan. I'll go and let you visit with your son. "

David's parents looked at each other, his mother raising her eyebrow at her husband, pleased with what she saw. His father was thinking his son was a very lucky man, and his mother instantly imagined how beautiful her grandchildren were going to be.

"I'm George, and this is my wife, Daisy. Please don't leave. We're very happy to meet you."

"I'm happy to meet you to. But I should go. David's very tired, and he's still confused from the drugs."

"I'm not tired," David growled. "I've been asleep for hours. And I'd really like an answer to my question. Don't let her leave. Mum, tell her when I say something, I mean it."

Daisy nodded her head in agreement. "He's right, dear. David never says anything unless he's sure. "

"Thank you, Mum. Joan, I'm still waiting for your answer. Would you please marry me?"

Daisy's hands flew to her mouth in surprise, and she breathed in, wanting to answer for Joan. Of course she would marry David. George patted David on the arm—the closest he came to giving affection to another man, even his son.

"'Bout time, Son. Congratulations."

"Don't congratulate me yet. She hasn't said yes."

Joan could see three pairs of eyes staring at her. This wasn't quite the romantic proposal she had imagined when she had thought about marrying David. But if he meant what he was saying, then this would be the most wonderful moment of her life.

"Are you sure that's what you really want?"

"Yes."

"And you're sure you understand what you're asking?"

"I am."

"Then I say yes."

"Oh, thank goodness," Daisy exclaimed. It was well past time for David to be married, and he had driven them crazy in the last two months, moping around and missing Joan.

David sighed with relief. "Thank you, Joan. Now if you don't mind turning your backs, Mum and Dad, I'd like to kiss my fiancé."

"Don't be silly, David. I've seen you kiss a girl before." Daisy laughed.

"But you haven't seen me kiss this one, and she's the only girl I plan to kiss for the rest of my life. So a little privacy please."

"We'll wait outside," George said, pulling Daisy towards the door, delighted with his son's decision.

Alone again, Joan remembered how she had left the house that morning. She hadn't taken the time to make herself presentable at all.

"David, as much as I'd love nothing more, I didn't clean my teeth this morning. I was kind of in a hurry to get here, and I didn't have time," Joan admitted, feeling embarrassed at the mess she was in.

"And you think I've been up and about, toothpaste in one hand and brush in the other? Come here and kiss me quick before I explode. I've missed that more than you can imagine."

"It couldn't have been more than I missed you," she murmured. Careful not to touch any part of his face that was bruised, Joan leaned over and brushed his lips with hers. When her lips touched his, David couldn't imagine what had made him think he could live without her. She was definitely *it*. She was his last stop.

Chapter 24

Jill couldn't have been more surprised when she opened the door and found Chris standing on the front porch. He had a bouquet of red roses in one hand and a bottle of champagne in the other. He thrust the flowers towards Jill, and with a happy grin plastered across his face, he proclaimed, "Happy Valentine's Day!"

"What are you doing here, Chris? I told you to stay away, and besides, Valentine's Day was two weeks ago."

"I know it was, but I didn't think you'd agree to see me then."

"What makes you think I'm going to agree to see you now? Please go away and take your flowers with you." Jill handed the flowers back and started to shut the door. Chris put his foot in just before the door was slammed in his face, and Jill was unable to close the door no matter how much strength she pushed it with.

"Please give me a minute, Jill. We have something wonderful to celebrate. I came over as soon as I found out."

"Then you should have called. I don't want you in my house ever again." She continued to try and close the door, but his foot was securely in place.

"You know if I rang, you wouldn't have answered. And this is such good news, I wanted to tell you in person."

Jill sighed deeply. Opening the door a little, she looked at her soon to be ex-husband. He was still the same handsome man she had married. While the separation had left her looking exhausted and she had lost too much weight, he looked like he didn't have a care in the world. Either he hadn't missed her at all or his news was so good it had wiped away all the sorrow and regret he had professed in the countless letters he had written to her.

"What could be so important that you needed to come here and bring champagne?"

"Meg's baby was born."

Jill kicked out her left leg and connected with Chris's shin. In surprise and pain, he pulled his leg back, and Jill took the opportunity to slam the door. She locked it just to make sure he couldn't get in and started to walk back to the kitchen, where she had been making dinner. She didn't usually eat much of it, but she still went through the motions every night.

Chris stood on the doorstep. *Well done, Chris*, he said to himself. That wasn't the way that was supposed to come out. He rang the doorbell again, and when she didn't return, he started pounding on the door and calling out Jill's name. After a few minutes, he could see her shadow through the glass.

"Chris, I've got the phone with me. Either you leave or I'm ringing the police."

"I'll go in a minute if you insist. I just came here to tell you it's not my baby. I know for an absolute fact that *I* am not the father."

Jill's finger hovered above the 0 on the phone pad that she had been prepared to use. This was a curveball she hadn't been expecting. Not his baby. Her life had been turned upside down, her dreams of a child of her own had been crushed, and he was here telling her it wasn't his baby.

Jill stepped closer to the door and turned the lock. She opened the door fully, and moving aside, she made a reluctant gesture of welcome to Chris. "You'd better come in then."

Chris handed back the roses to Jill and strode down the hall to the kitchen like he had never left. It almost looked the same. There were a few bits and pieces missing, but they were at his place for now. He'd found a small studio apartment in Fitzroy to rent, but he hoped that he would be back here soon. Tonight, if Jill would have him. He was positive she would let him come home now that he wasn't going to be tied down to a baby. She wasn't so unreasonable that she would let one tiny indiscretion, especially as there were no permanent consequences, keep them apart. And he was so ready to come home. It had been almost eight months since he'd been with anyone. There had been opportunities, but he had been proud of himself for knocking them back. Jill would appreciate the sacrifice he had made for her and for their future. He opened the door to the glasses cabinet and pulled out two flutes. Setting them down on the kitchen bench, he popped the cork of the champagne and filled the glasses. The bottle of Moet hadn't been cheap, but he wanted Jill to know he thought she was worth the expense.

Returning to the potato she had been peeling, Jill's emotions were in turmoil. What would this mean for her and Chris? Did it mean anything at all? It had never occurred to her once since he had confirmed the one-night stand that he might not be the father.

"Chris how can you know this quickly that the baby isn't yours? I thought DNA testing took ages. How long ago was the baby born?"

"A few days ago. A boy. We didn't need to do DNA testing. I nagged the doctors to see if there was a way we could find out about paternity earlier, and he agreed to do a blood type test on the baby. It was just a little pinprick on his heel, and they were able to tell me straightaway. Meg's blood type is A, and mine's AB. The baby's blood type was O. That means the real father has to be either O or B type. An AB type can't produce an O-type baby. When I confronted Meg about it, she said there were two other guys who could also be the father, but she had hoped it was me because I seemed like a nice guy. I left the hospital and came straight here. If she wasn't a woman and she hadn't just had a baby, I think I might have hit her. I was angry enough. That cow tried to ruin my life!"

"I wouldn't be placing all the blame on her if I was you. Sleeping with her gave her plenty of ammo. and there was a one in three chance that it was yours. You should be feeling sorry for that baby. He may never know who his real father is."

"I do feel for the little guy. He was pretty cute, and it made me all the more sure that we should have some babies of our own. We could get started right now if you want."

"Is that what you think? That I'm just going to let you come back and pick up where we left off. The baby not being yours doesn't change what you did. You were still unfaithful."

"It was once. And while we've been apart, I haven't gone near anyone else, I swear. I made a mistake. It was the biggest one of my life, and I promise you I've learnt my lesson. I love you, Jill. You're my girl. Let's give it another shot, and you'll never regret it." Chris picked up the glass of champagne and held it out towards Jill. She put down the peeler and took the glass.

"I think I need to sit down. This is a lot to take in."

"Sit, sit." Chris guided Jill to her favourite chair. He remembered the last time he had seen her sitting in it. That had been the day he thought his life had ended. But here he was, back in his house, and he *knew* that Jill was going to let him come home.

"So what do you say? Forgive me?"

Jill took a sip of the champagne. It probably wasn't a good idea to drink too much. With all the weight she'd lost and on an empty stomach, it would go straight to her head. This situation needed her to keep a clear head. She set the glass down on the lamp table and leaned forward, looking closely at her husband who was unable to stand still, so full was he of relief and optimism. He looked like a giddy schoolboy who had just stumbled over five bucks unexpectedly. She understood why he felt this way. He thought that the roadblock to their getting back together was gone. Unfortunately, for him his news made very little difference.

"This is a huge decision for me, Chris. I have to decide whether I can trust you again. I used to trust you completely, and you made a fool out of me. And then instead of owning what you did, you tried to lay some of the blame at my feet. I agree that we were facing a tough time trying and failing to get pregnant. But that could still be an issue for us. Or what if we do have a baby and something's wrong with it? I don't think I can count on you to stay with me when things get tough."

"I never left you, Jill. You were the one who kicked me out."

"The minute you stepped outside our marriage, you left me, Chris."

"I was drunk. I didn't know what I was doing," he reminded her, still refusing to take responsibility.

"That's not a good enough excuse. You let it happen." Jill's initial surprise at his announcement turned to anger as she heard the same old garbage coming out of his mouth. How could he not get it? "Meg might have been the first to flirt, but at any time, did you change tables or tell her, 'No, thanks. I'm a married man,' and walk away? It was your responsibility to shut her down, and instead, you let the situation get more and more out of your control until you lost it all together."

"What can I do to convince you it will never happen again?"

"I don't think you can. This is about me now, and what I decide I'm prepared to live with."

"So you're saying no."

"I'm saying I need some time to think about this. Don't get your hopes up. I'm trying very hard to find a way to forgive you so that maybe one day, I'll find some peace of mind. But I'll never forget what you did. The hurt you caused will scar me for the rest of my life. It might fade eventually, but it will always be there."

"So, what? I'm just supposed to wait around while you decide how *my* life should go? How long, Jill?" Chris whined, his true nature revealing itself. Why did *she* get to make all the decisions for him? He had followed her rules and stayed away, but it was time for this exile from her life to end.

"I won't take long. But I need to be alone to think. I promise I'll call you as soon as I decide."

"You do that," he snapped. He had imagined so many times what their reunion would be like. She would throw herself into his arms, thrilled that nothing stood in their way anymore. He had truly believed that this entire split had been because she was jealous of Meg's pregnancy and his involvement. He was unable to comprehend the reality. Infidelity tore lives apart. If it was once or a thousand times, it did the same damage.

Furious, Chris glared at Jill and turned on his heel. He headed back down the hall, his footsteps heavy and quick. Jill stood up and followed him halfway down, calling after him. "Chris, I really am happy for you. Congratulations on not becoming a father."

Not stopping, Chris pulled open the unlocked door, and, furious that he hadn't got his way, shouted back at her, "Yeah, whatever." He slammed the door behind him and the sound reverberated throughout the house. He stopped on the footpath and pulled his phone out of his pocket. Finding the number he was after, he dialled. His call was answered quickly.

"You up for a drink?"

"Can't think of a reason not to."

"Meet you in ten. At the usual."

"Done."

"And bring your wallet. We're going to need it." Hanging up, Chris jumped in his car and pulled out into the traffic. Jill watched him leave from inside through the front window. She knew he was disappointed, but an angry outburst wasn't the way to convince her that she should let him come back. His exit had confirmed what she had come to believe of him in the last eight months. He was a spoilt child in a man's body. He hadn't matured the way he should have, and instead of handling problems like an adult, he used his charm and looks to get what he wanted. If that didn't work, he reverted to tantrums, like a toddler with no self-control. She was finding it difficult to see even a glimpse of what she had fallen in love with in the first place. She was just glad she realized what he was really like before they had children together. The last thing she needed was a husband she couldn't count on or trust. Maybe he had done her a favour having that one-night stand. Tonight would certainly make it easier for her to move on. It's hard to miss something that never really existed in the first place.

~~~

By the time Chris reached the bar Adam was already there. He'd already had one beer and was starting on his second. Chris waved and then headed to the bar. He ordered two shots of bourbon and brought them over to the table.

"Hey, mate. Long time, no see."

"Yeah. Listen, about the last time we talked, you know about Jill. I wasn't in a good mood."

Chris waved his apology away. "Don't worry about it. Just put that beer down and take a shot of this. Tonight I'm celebrating, and I don't want to do it alone." He pushed the glass towards Adam and picked up his own. He tossed the drink back into his mouth, and in one swallow, it was gone. The burn felt good as it descended down the back of his throat, and the warmth as the bourbon hit his stomach reminded him that he was a man. Much better than some sissy bottle of champagne. Adam picked up his glass and took a sip. He preferred scotch, and he preferred it on ice in a nice glass, but this would do. He'd had a bad day, a bad week, a bad month. Might as well drown his sorrows.

"So what are you celebrating?"

"It turns out I'm not the father."

"Well, congratulations, mate. I'm pleased to hear it."

"Me too. Another drink, I think." He headed back to the bar and returned a few minutes later with four shot glasses. "No reason going back and forth. But the next round's on you."

"Sure. So did you tell Jill?"

"I've just come from there. You'd think she'd be happy, but she wasn't. She said she still doesn't trust me and needs to think it over." He finished his third shot of bourbon within fifteen minutes and began to feel Jill and her opinions slip away. He didn't need her anyway. She was holding him back. He'd tried marriage, but it wasn't for him. Adam still had a full glass sitting in front of him.

Chris poked at the glass. "Come on. Keep up."

"Are you sure that's a good idea, drinking so much? You won't be able to drive home."

"So I'll take a cab. And you can get your lovely wife to come and get you. She's a lot nicer than mine."

Adam picked up the drink and threw it back. The first two burnt the back of his throat and took his breath away, but by the third, his mouth began to feel numb.

"She won't be coming to get me. I don't live with her anymore."

"What happened? She kick you out too? Women. They're all the same."

"Nope. I left. We were making each other miserable. So how 'bout we change this conversation? Did you order more drinks?" Adam hadn't eaten since lunch. His small apartment had a kitchen, but he had no idea how to cook. Caroline had always taken care of everything domestic. He'd eaten takeaway for the first month after moving out but quickly came to hate it, and for the first time in his life, he started to gain some weight. Sometimes he went to a restaurant, but he felt ridiculous sitting on his own. It was better when Michael came on the weekend. Then at least he had a dinner companion. He'd been contemplating ordering a pizza when Chris had called, and so here he was on an empty stomach drinking in a way he never did.

"It's your round, remember? Jack for me."

When Adam stood up from his chair, he felt the three shots he'd just had. *Better get some chips*, he thought. Soak up some of that alcohol. He could tell he was beginning to sway and put all his effort into concentrating on putting one foot in front of the other. He made it to the bar and ordered another four shots of Jack Daniels and a couple of bags of chips. The bartender poured the drinks but before he handed the tray over, he gave Adam the once-over.

"Buddy, you and your mate might want to slow down a little. I don't want any trouble, and I don't want you chucking up on my nice clean floor. Okay?"

Adam pulled a fifty out of his pocket and handed it to the man. "I promise we'll behave." Picking up the tray was harder than he thought it would be, and by the time he got back to the table, he'd spilled some of the liquid from the glasses.

"So," Chris asked. "Have you got someone else on the side? Is that why you really left home? 'Cause you had it good there. No need to go anywhere unless you've got someone better waiting in the wings."

Adam picked up his glass and decided he would try and make it last. He didn't think he was going to get anything else out of the bartender, who was keeping a close eye on them.

"There isn't anyone else. I told you. I'd just had it."

"I bet Jill's got someone else. That's why she's not going to take me back. Probably some rich lawyer at work. A man makes one mistake, and that's it—he's out. No second chances with that one."

"Hey, mate. What did you expect? *You* got someone else pregnant, remember? What else was she going to do?"

Chris picked up his fourth drink for the evening in one hand and with the other, he pointed at Adam. The massive quantity of alcohol that he had drunk in just a few minutes had hit his bloodstream, and the effect was not pretty.

"But I wasn't the father. She just tried to trick me. And why are you defending Jill? You two would make a perfect pair." Through his drunken haze, Chris remembered that Jill had once told him that she and Adam had been an item in high school. *That made sense*, he thought. Adam's gone and left his wife, and Jill won't take him back because she already found some-one else.

"Are you sleeping with my wife?" he asked, finishing off his final drink for the night. His words were slurred together, and he'd lost all sense of reason.

When Adam didn't respond immediately, Chris thought this confirmed his suspicions. He stood up and pushed his chair back, unsteady on his feet. He regained his balance, holding onto a beam for support.

"That's it!" he yelled. "You're sleeping with my wife and here you are, trying to make *me* feel bad." He projected his voice to get the attention of the rest of the room as he pointed towards Adam. "Did you hear that? My buddy here can't be trusted to keep his hands off my wife. He was my best man. I guess she thinks he's the best man now."

The bartender came out from behind the counter and headed towards their table.

"Sit down, Chris. I haven't been anywhere near Jill. I've barely seen her since you two split up."

"I don't believe you. You're a traitor, and she's no better. You two deserve each other. Maybe I'll pay Caroline a visit and see if she'd like some company, if you know what I mean. I've seen the way she looks at me. I bet she's really lonely up there in that big house. I could show her how a real man satisfies a woman."

The barman, a big guy who looked like he was used to breaking up fights, had stepped in front of Chris as he hurled his filthy suggestion about Caroline at Adam. He was still seated, and the barman didn't see him as a threat. He was more concerned about the drunk throwing around insults and disturbing the rest of his customers. By the time he realized his mistake, it was too late to stop Adam, who sprung out of his chair.

White-hot fury over took him. His pulse thumped around his head, and he lost all control at the thought of Chris ever touching his Caroline in that way.

"Don't you ever talk about my wife like that!" he roared. He reached around the bartender and grabbed Chris by the collar. Drawing his arm back, he curled his hand into a fist and pushed it forward with all his strength and all his rage. And for the first time ever in his life, he hit another human being. Once was enough, and Adam released Chris's shirt, allowing him to fall back into his chair, which toppled backwards with his weight. Chris slumped to the floor and groaned in pain. Adam raised his hands in surrender to let the bartender know he was done, and he fell back into the chair and finished the last drink sitting on the table.

"Millie," Bill the bartender called out to the women who had also been working behind the counter. "Better call the police." He took one look at Chris, chair overturned beside him and struggling to get to his feet, and amended his instruction. "Might want to get an ambulance too."

~~~

Adam waited quietly for the police to arrive while the bartender helped Chris up. The damage didn't look too bad, but regret was already setting in for Adam. He had lost control of himself. He felt a large presence looming over him, and he looked up. The policeman standing next to him was at least six-foot-three and solid. He looked vaguely familiar to Adam, but he couldn't place him. He hadn't had a lot of need for the police in the past, and he had never been in trouble.

"Am I under arrest?"

"Not yet. Your punching bag doesn't want to make a formal complaint, and there's no damage done here. You're going to accompany us down to the station and make a statement in case he changes his mind. Can you please confirm your name for me?

"Adam Anderson."

The police officer looked up from his notebook. "Do we know each other?"

"I don't think so. I've never been arrested before."

The police officer knew he had spoken to this man before. It hadn't been recently, but he was sure they had crossed paths at some point. He walked Adam out to the car and closed the door after he climbed into the backseat. His partner joined them, and they headed towards the station. It was bothering the officer that he couldn't remember this man. It was part of his job to recognize people. Searching his memory as he drove, he was close to giving up when it came to him. Not last year but the year before, he had delivered the worst news to this man and his wife. He hated having to tell people that a family member had died, but it was always worse when it was someone's child. He remembered this one well—standing at their front door, waiting for it to be answered. And when a woman had opened the door, he hadn't needed to say anything about his reason for being there. Just his presence and his request to come in was enough, and she had begun to shake uncontrollably before he said another word. But her response was normal. It was terrifying to watch, and the tragic loss of a little girl's life made him sick, but it was her father's reaction that had stayed with him. He could have been telling Adam that he was going to receive a parking fine for all the emotion he had shown. He asked practical questions and when faced with the awful recounting of the event, Adam never reacted once, thanking Mark for coming and taking his number if he needed any further information. Mark had never seen the recipient of such devastating news receive it with so little feeling. But he could see now that Adam must have just been masking his grief all along. When they pulled into the car park, he left Adam in the backseat for a minute and pulled his partner aside.

"I know this guy. I had to tell him his twelve-year-old daughter had been killed eighteen months ago. He's not a troublemaker. I think I'll just have a bit of a chat with him and see where his head's at."

"Your call, Mark. Nobody wants to make it formal anyway. Did you want to do it inside or just take him home?"

"I'll take him home. I think I remember where he lives."

Mark hoped back in the car and turned around. "I'm going to take you home. There's no need to make this official."

Adam mumbled his thanks, starting to feel like he could be sick. The shock of what he'd done had sobered him up, but he knew he was going to have a serious hangover tomorrow. And at some point, he was going to have to face Chris. The policeman turned onto Toorak Road and started to head towards Kooyong.

"Excuse me, Officer. I don't live this way. I'm in the city."

"Don't you live in Kooyong?"

"I did, but I've moved." Adam frowned, confused with how this stranger knew about him. "Sorry, how do we know each other? You do look a little familiar to me."

Mark pulled over to the side of the road and put the car into park. He turned in his seat and faced Adam. "I was the officer who delivered the news that your daughter had been killed."

"Oh." Adam remembered now. "Not the best way to meet someone."

"No. It's not a part of my job that I enjoy. I remember your wife too. How is she doing?"

"She's fine. It looks like I'm the one not doing very well."

"Have you considered talking to someone? I'm not much of a touchy-feely guy but I've seen it help people. You and Mrs. Anderson could go together."

"We're not together anymore. I live alone now."

"I see. That happens a lot. People grieve differently, and that can cause rifts and confusion in a relationship. It doesn't mean one cared less than the other. It's just that we all manage in our own way. It's just a shame that so many good marriages break down when they face a tragedy."

"Thanks for the advice, but I don't need it."

"If you say so." Mark hit his indicator and looked for a chance to pull out into the traffic. "Why don't you direct me, and I'll get you home?"

The rest of the trip passed in silence and when they reached Adam's apartment building, the police officer pulled over in a no-standing zone and turned off the car. He stepped out and opened the back door for Adam. Thanking him, Adam pulled out his keys and headed for the entrance. He was almost inside when he heard the officer call his name. He stopped walking and turned towards the officer.

"Mr. Anderson, I know you don't want any advice, but I'm going to give it to you anyway. You're heading for trouble. If you continue on the way you are, the next person you hit might not be so understanding. You could end up facing charges or worse, seriously hurt someone." The officer walked towards where Adam had stopped and held out a piece of paper to him. Adam's hand remained by his side, not acknowledging the officer's words. "This is way outside of my police duties, but I can't let you walk away without doing something. There is help out there." He tucked the note into Adam's top pocket and then turned and returned to his car.

As Adam watched him drive away, he felt himself begin to crumble. He didn't want to hear anything from the policeman or anyone else for that matter, but somehow, people's words were beginning to get through. He had to decide if this was the life he wanted. No friends, no family. Alone for the rest of his life. He missed Caroline desperately, more than he ever imagined he would, and he missed his son. Despite himself and his certainty that he didn't *need* anyone, he was lonely. As he let himself into his apartment, he looked around at the space. He hated it here. He saw his reflection in the mirror near the door. He barely recognized himself anymore, and he didn't like what he was becoming He looked down at his swollen hand. He'd hit someone. His friend of twenty years. His stomach lurched, and he ran to the small bathroom. He made it to the toilet just in time before throwing up the alcohol he had consumed earlier. When he was done, he wiped his mouth and sat down on the lid of the closed toilet. Tiredness overwhelmed him, and he placed his head in his hands, feeling the pain of the one he had used as a weapon. He welcomed the pain. It reminded him that he was alive. As he contemplated his situation, he knew he had lost all hope. He had hit it—rock bottom. That sudden realization brought with it a rush of emotion that he didn't expect, nor could he contain. Suddenly he felt himself sobbing involuntarily. It was a totally foreign experience for him. He had never cried like this before. Even when Isabelle had died, he hadn't shown much emotion; he'd remained strong for his family like a man should—or so he had believed. What he didn't see at the time was that all he had done was turn his pain inward, and it had changed into anger that had torn him apart.

He didn't know how long he cried. It could have been a few minutes or it could have been hours, but for the first time since Isabelle's death, he felt like himself again. Pulling himself off the bathroom floor, he looked into the mirror while he washed the tear stains from his face. In the reflection, he noticed the corner of the paper the officer had placed there earlier. Pulling it out, he expected it to be the name of a counselling service. He couldn't have been more surprised to see what he knew was a Bible verse and the number of a church not far from his hotel. Adam read the words again, letting them sink in, words he had heard long ago when he was a child. His grandmother had always claimed they gave her comfort. Now he remembered how he had felt as a small boy as she read them to him while she held him and told him that God loved him and was so happy he had created such a wonderful little boy. Once more he read them, repeating them out loud: "Yea, though I walk through the valley of the shadow of death, I will fear no evil; For You are with me; Your rod and Your staff, they comfort me."

He had no idea how the officer knew that of all the words in the Bible, these were the only ones he had ever remembered. He let them settle on him as he remembered a God who he had forgotten about long ago, wondering if he was really there and if he could help him.

Chapter 25

Being in her old bedroom gave Jill such a feeling of safety. Apart from the house she bought and restored with her father at the age of twenty-six, she had only lived here with her mum and dad. Beth had left home for university in Bendigo when she was eighteen and only returned for a short time between her final exams and marrying Tom. But Jill had stayed at home all through her time at uni and while she started her working career as a solicitor. Now she would have to decide if she did go ahead with the divorce if she would keep her home. Chris had never put a cent into it, so there was a chance she wouldn't have to split it with him. That would be for the court to decide, but she had already taken steps to see if that could be avoided. But if she did get to keep it, she wasn't sure if she wanted to stay anymore. It had always been a sanctuary for her when she came home at night from her hectic and often depressing job. But now, the wonderful memories of restoring the house with her father had been replaced by the memory of what Chris had done. Everywhere she looked now, she saw him. She had completely replaced everything in their bedroom when he had gone, including the furniture. She hadn't been able to bear the thought of sleeping in the bed they had once shared, and that was why it was so wonderful to be back here. She had never felt anything but loved in this house. She and Beth had been given a wonderful childhood by two people who had adored each other.

Nothing much had changed in her bedroom. Posters of bands, most long since broken up, still hung on the walls. Bon Jovi had been her favourite at the time, and Jon Bon Jovi had been the "love of her life." It seemed silly and childish now, but at the time, her whole world revolved around him.

Annie Mancini appeared in the open doorway, watching her youngest daughter. She had been delighted when Jill asked if she could join her for dinner tonight, and she had been busy making all her favourites. Most of the time, Annie didn't bother with much cooking anymore. She had always loved cooking for her family, but now with her husband gone, there didn't seem much point. She missed Joe desperately every day and had no intention of ever trying to replace him. She would rather be lonely than spend the rest of her life with someone who had no chance of even coming close to the husband Joe had been. Annie knew she had been blessed to find such a man, and she wished both her daughters could have the same happiness. Beth and Tom seemed to have achieved it, but Jill had chosen a man who had not only let her down horribly but had never been good enough for her in the first place.

"Come on, you. It's time for dinner." Jill looked up from her old bed to her mother. Her mum was getting older. If she went for more than a few weeks at a time between visits, she could see a change each time. Her mother was only sixty-five, but the loss of her husband had taken its toll. She was still short and round, the way Beth had been until recently, but she was fit. She had taken over all the work that her dad had done in the garden, keeping it like a memorial to his life. Her mind was as sharp as ever, but the creases in her face had deepened, and her skin was thinner. Jill didn't know how she would cope if her mother died too. She got up off the bed, and putting her arm around her mother's waist, they walked towards the big old kitchen at the back of the house. Annie had never wanted a formal dining room, and the family had always eaten in the kitchen at a table for ten that Joe had built for her. The girls often brought friends home for dinner, and they were always welcome. Annie used to wonder if Joan's only proper meals had been eaten here.

"Mum, this is a lot of food. There's no way we'll get through all this." A lasagne wasn't the only dish she had made. There was homemade bread and two different salads. Her mother had also cooked her wonderful chicken risotto, which was Jill's favourite. No matter how many times she watched her mother make it, she had never been able to replicate it herself and refused to eat anyone else's because it never even came close to her mum's.

"What we don't eat, we can freeze for later. And you need some fattening up. You're beginning to look like a broomstick you're so thin. And Beth's not too far behind you. I should send some of the leftovers to her so she eats a decent meal."

"There's no way Beth would eat any of this dinner. But I don't blame her. She's finally hit the magic twenty kilos she's been chasing. She looks wonderful, but she's terrified of putting it all back on again. She's bought heaps of new clothes, and I got quite the fashion show the other day. It's nice to see her so happy. It gives me hope that it's possible for marriage to work."

"Lots of marriages work, and some of them are wonderful. Your dad and I were an example of that. We were happy for nearly forty years."

"But that seems to be the exception, Mum. Look at what happened to my marriage."

"Is that why you wanted to see me tonight? You said you needed advice which I'm happy to help with but I thought you'd already made the decision to get a divorce. "

267

Jill piled her plate high with food. She'd skipped lunch; she skipped a lot of meals now. But she was unable to resist her mother's cooking. She had inherited her father's tall, lean build and never had to worry about what rice and pasta would do to her figure. It must have been torture for Beth growing up here with all the delicious food their mother served. No wonder her sister had been overweight as a child.

"Chris came to see me last night. It turns out he wasn't the father of that baby after all."

"So what?" Annie asked. "Does he think that changes anything? That boy must be stupider than I gave him credit for."

"So you don't think I should give him another chance? He was so excited last night, and he was so sure that I'd take him back."

"And are you going to? Is that what you told him?"

"I said I needed some time to think it over. I was just so surprised that it wasn't his baby. I hadn't considered that was a possibility."

"So how did he react to that?" Annie was sure she knew the answer, but she wanted Jill to understand what she was dealing with when it came to Chris. Both her and Joe had recognized early on the lack of maturity in Chris and had hoped he would be a passing faze. When Jill announced their engagement, they had both been upset for their daughter but kept their feelings to themselves. Jill was a grown woman and had to do what she thought was best. Joe had been especially angry when Chris didn't come to him and ask for permission to marry his daughter. Joe never said anything to Jill or Chris, but he never let it go, and it had created a divide between Joe and Chris, even if Chris didn't see it. Chris was so self-absorbed, he never really took notice of how people responded to him, always assuming that everyone liked him. And Joe had hated that his daughter wasn't being provided for by her husband. Each time Jill had to tell her parents that Chris had lost another job, Joe built up more resentment towards his son-in- law.

"He stormed out of the house, shouting and carrying on like a child. Sometimes I wonder if he's ever going to grow up."

Annie decided she should tell her daughter what she really thought of Chris. It might cause trouble later, but Jill had come to her, and too much had gone on for her to stay silent anymore.

"Jill, your father and I always tried to stay out of yours and Beth's marriages. It's wasn't our place to tell you what to do. But I need to speak up now."

"I wish you would, Mum. I know what I want to do, but it goes against everything I believe in and everything you taught me."

Annie put her knife and fork down so she could focus completely on Jill. "Do I love the idea of my daughter getting a divorce? Of course I don't. You're right. It does go against everything we believe in. But you're not doing it because you're bored or because you found someone you might like better. Your husband broke the sacred vows you took together. If you don't get divorced and let him come back home, I think you will spend the rest of your life looking over his shoulder. Love comes and goes at different times in a marriage, but trust is essential. Not being able to trust the people in your life is terrible but when it's your life partner, it's much worse. He is the most important person in your world, and you need to be able to count on him. If you can't trust him, then he ends up becoming your enemy, and that's no way to live. If you stay with Chris, I will support you and do my best to accept him into our family, but I won't lie to you. I'll be doing it with a heavy heart."

"Mum, what did Daddy think of Chris? I was so in love with him at the time, I was always too afraid to ask in case Dad didn't want me to marry him."

"Your father thought that you deserved better."

"And as usual, he was right. I do deserve better."

~~~

Once the decision was made, Jill didn't want to wait any longer to tell Chris. Her mother wouldn't let her leave until she'd eaten two helpings of risotto and a piece of lasagne, but Jill had got her to agree that she could take desert with her. Her mother's apple pie was the best she'd ever had, and it would give her something to look forward to later. She called Chris while she was still parked in her parent's driveway and arranged to meet him at his apartment. She had wanted to do it somewhere public in case his temper flared again, but he said he wasn't feeling well and refused to go out. She punched the address he gave her into her GPS and headed in the direction of the city.

When she pulled up to the dingy apartment building in Fitzroy, she hoped she had the wrong address. It looked like it had been built in the early seventies and was clad in depressing grey bricks. The gardens out the front had suffered from the dry summer Melbourne had just been through. The glazed foyer was locked, so she rang the buzzer for 4C. She heard the door click and pushed it open. A lift took her to Chris's floor, and she found his apartment easy enough. The building was just as dreary inside as it was outside, and she felt a little sorry for Chris. She hoped their divorce wasn't going to leave her in the position of having to sell her house and having to live alone somewhere like this. She knew her mother would take her in, but at thirty-seven, she was much too old to be going home. She knocked on the door and waited for it to be answered.

Chris took his time answering the door. He knew why she was here, and he was in no hurry to hear her final decision. If she had decided to give him a second chance, she would have just told him to come home. He tried to arrange his face to look sad, and he knew the bruising and tape across his broken nose would garner sympathy. He might not be getting his wife back, but he had no intention of leaving his marriage empty handed. He needed money, and he expected Jill to provide it.

Jill gasped when the door opened. Chris's nose and eyes were purple with bruising and swollen.

"What happened to you? You were fine last night."

"I met up with your boyfriend after I saw you. He did this to me defending your honour." Chris, twisting the truth, didn't tell her that Adam had actually been defending his own wife, not Jill. He wasn't going to tell her that. The truth would have been inconvenient and no help to his agenda at all.

"What are you talking about? I don't have a boyfriend."

"The way Adam was behaving last night gave me enough reason to think he is. He couldn't wait to stand up for you. Hit me right in the face and had to be taken away by the police. He's just lucky I decided not to make a complaint."

"Adam is not my boyfriend. No one is. The last thing I want is another *man* right now."

"Whatever you say. So what can I do for you tonight? Are you here to beg me to come home?" Chris was sneering at Jill, and she wished they had been able to meet in public. She had never seen him behave this way before, even last night when he had been angry. Bitterness was spewing out of him, and any lingering doubt about what she was about to say vanished.

"No, Chris. I'm here to tell you that I still intend to go proceed with the divorce. We can't file until June twenty-second, but I want it done as soon as possible after that date."

"I see. And where does that leave me? Do you really think I'm just going to walk away and let you keep everything? It's fifty-fifty, baby."

"That's usually the way things go. But I owned that house for nine years before we got married, and you never contributed to the mortgage, the upkeep, or any of the household bills. You paid for your car, which you still have, and all the pretty clothes you love buying. But don't worry, baby. You can keep them. I don't want fifty-fifty of those."

"I'll fight you on this."

"Go ahead. But I know how this works. If I sell my home right now, it won't fetch as much as its worth in this depressed market. And by the time the mortgage is paid out along with the real-estate costs, you might end up with *some* money. But that will all go on your legal fees. I can keep you in court for years, and it won't cost me a cent. The partners at work decided they'd be happy to represent me, and they even offered a generous staff discount. One hundred percent off, *baby*." This time she emphasised the term of endearment they had once used for each other. She wasn't angry anymore. She felt powerful, holding all the cards now, and he was going to have to do things on her terms. She felt like she was representing every woman who had been mistreated or tossed aside and left with nothing. How many times had women with children ended up living in poverty because their husbands had been able to afford expensive solicitors and found clever ways to make it look like they had nothing when the time came to split the assets?

Jill opened the briefcase she'd brought with her. She pulled out a file and handed it to Chris.

"Inside here, you'll find an agreement I took the liberty of having drawn up. I've already signed it and had it witnessed. I suggest you read it over and then sign it yourself."

"You said we couldn't file any papers until June."

"This is an agreement between you and me. It states that you will not make any claim on my property and, in exchange, I will give you twenty-thousand dollars the day our divorce is finalized by the courts. I'd sign it if I was you. It's all you're ever going to see out of me."

"I want more. If you think I'm just going to let you walk all over me and leave me destitute, then you're wrong. You going to have to remortgage or take out a loan because I want a hundred grand. I won't sign this otherwise."

"Take it or leave it, Chris. It's your decision. And don't be so dramatic. You're not destitute. You must have saved some money while we were married because you never spent a cent on me."

"I had a lot of credit-card debt when we got married. I've been trying to clear it for the past two years. I still owe about thirty-thousand dollars. You need to at least give me enough to cover those."

"Yeah, I don't think so. You're not my problem anymore. It's time you grew up and stood on your own two feet." Jill closed her briefcase and picked it up off the cluttered table where it sat. She slowly did a 360-degree turn in the middle of the room, taking it in. The furniture was old and filthy. The couch sagged and had stains all over it. She could see a small bedroom off to one side, and the tiny kitchen was piled high with dirty dishes and pizza boxes. She hoped Chris would be able to get his life together because this was no way to live, but once she left here, she was never going to give it another thought. He was nothing to do with her anymore. She walked to the door and opened it, turning before she left.

"I'm sad for us that things turned out this way. Goodbye, Chris." She looked at the pathetic man standing before her. She couldn't remember what she had ever seen in him, but she knew that if she ever let someone else into her life, she would take her time and really get to know his true character instead of falling for the false veneer people put on. She closed the door quietly behind her and walked away from the filthy apartment, sure she would never see him again.

~~~

One week later while she was going through her mail, Jill came across an envelope that was addressed in handwriting she recognized. She opened it and found the agreement she had given to Chris. It had been ripped into pieces and then taped back together, but the important thing was that at the bottom, it held Chris's signature. It was also witnessed by a solicitor. It would mean taking money out of the bank account she had never told Chris about, but it would be worth it. She was so relieved she had never told her husband about that account. He probably would have drained it if he had known the money was there. Her dad had always insisted she save 10 percent of her earnings in case of an emergency. She considered getting Chris permanently out of her life exactly that. Her wonderful dad was still helping her even if he wasn't here anymore. Jill stood up and put the agreement in the little safe she'd had installed when she had renovated the kitchen. She didn't want anything happening to that important piece of paper. She looked around the room. This was her home, and she knew she would never sell. Chris might have lived here for a while, but she wasn't going to let the memory of that time drive her out. She had exorcised him from her life, and she would do the same with her home. She could feel just as safe here as she had in her bedroom at her mother's home. He was never coming back. Finished with the mail, she picked up the TV remote and flicked through the channels. The last piece of apple pie from her mother was heating in the oven. For the first time in months, she was starving and looked forward to eating something, and Annie Mancini's pie was the best she had ever tasted. She saw that one of those romantic movies was about to start and normally she would have turned it off. But tonight she decided to watch for a while. She didn't mind that it was sappy, and everything turned out all right in the end. She could feel hope returning. Her life wasn't over. There was a chance that she could meet a man that her father would have approved of.

Chapter 26

"That's it," David said, slamming down the lid of his laptop. "I quit. We have two choices. We can get married in Mum's backyard if we can find a celebrant who will do the ceremony and order in Subway for lunch or we can wait till 2014, which I have no intention of doing by the way. There are no available dates at any decent wedding venues. Anything nice is booked out a year in advance, and anything left for hire looks dodgy." He looked at Joan sitting on the chair opposite him in his mum's lounge room. "Are you sure you really want the whole white-wedding palaver?"

"I do. Are you sure you've checked everywhere? It's not so much *where* we get married but the atmosphere. I want someplace elegant but not too over the top and definitely nothing cheesy. No red love hearts or ruffled tablecloths allowed."

"I've looked. I started at the Dandenong's and worked my way all the way down to Sorrento. Everything is booked out. Who are all these people getting married anyway? I thought nobody bothered anymore."

"Well, people must be if we're having so much difficulty finding somewhere. And as pretty as your mum's garden is," Joan said, looking out the window to the burnt lawn and a few tired shrubs that were in desperate need of some water, "I want to do this properly. I've been to enough weddings over the years to know what I want and what I don't. We agreed, not too big, only people we actually like. I don't want any obligatory invites to old aunts no one's seen for thirty years."

Joan still couldn't believe this was happening. She had waited for David to change his mind for days after he proposed. Every time he called, she flinched a little, wondering if he was calling to let her know he had made a mistake and needed to call the whole thing off. But when instead he starting searching the Internet and making calls for a place to have their wedding, Joan began to relax and sink into the joy she felt. She was really getting married.

"I might have an idea for somewhere. It's not actually a wedding venue, but we might be able to talk the owners into letting us get married and have the reception there. When you mentioned the Mornington Peninsula, it jogged my memory. Do you remember I told you about Beth's fortieth birthday party last month? It was at this beautiful property in Red Hill. It's not a winery, just a huge house with a big old ballroom. They have a cottage we could rent to get ready in, and if we wanted to, we could probably spend the first night there before we head off on the honeymoon. It's worth an ask, don't you think?"

"What's it called? " David asked, opening up the laptop again.

"Carrbridge House. The family came over from Scotland in the late 1800s and built the house. It's still owned by the original family. They built the cottage a few years ago, and they rent out the ballroom in the main house for parties. The gardens are spectacular. I got to the party early and went for a bit of a walk. There's a dam with a little jetty surrounded by willow trees and because it's high up on a hill, the view from the back porch was spectacular. You can see for miles, and there's even a view of the bay.

David brought up Google and typed in the name of the property. When the pictures appeared on his screen, he could see why Joan thought it would be the perfect place for their wedding. The ballroom was elegantly decorated in a soft moss green with white mouldings. Several huge chandeliers hung from the ceiling, and he could see what she meant about the view. A massive porch was accessible from the ballroom by huge French doors so if the weather was good, the party could spill outside. The room was easily big enough for dinner for the sixty or so people they intended to invite, and they could hold the ceremony outside in the rose garden if it wasn't too cold. The pictures of the cottage showed a quaint building covered with ivy. Inside it had a bedroom and a small kitchen and sitting room. The bathroom had a beautiful clawfoot bath and there was even an outdoor spa that looked out over the magnificent view. It was a long way from the main house, so it would give them plenty of privacy. It would be a perfect place to spend their first night as a married couple, but David would spend it sleeping in a cardboard box if he had to.

David read out the number, and Joan dialled it. She had met the owners when she was at Beth's party. They were a much older couple who looked like they should be enjoying their retirement instead of running a large property, but they said they loved it.

"Good morning. Carrbridge House. Bridget speaking. How may I help you?"

"Good morning. My name is Joan Webster. I met you last month when my friend, Beth Fraser, was having her fortieth at your home."

"Oh, yes. I remember. The Frasers. They were a lovely couple. Their party planner was a bossy one."

"Yes, she can be. The thing is, I loved your property, and I'm looking for somewhere to hold a party of my own."

"For your fortieth too, dear?"

"No, actually. I'm getting married. As soon as I can organize it. I'm having a little trouble finding somewhere to hold the ceremony and the reception."

"We don't normally do weddings, dear. We've had some for family in the past, but that's different."

"Bridget, can I be honest with you? I'm desperate. My fiancé was in a terrible accident a few weeks back and although he's on the mend now, it gave us both a terrible fright. We've had such a hard time, and we just want to get married as soon as possible."

She looked up to see David mouthing something at her. When he whispered, "That's a bit of an exaggeration," she waved at him to be quiet and tried to ignore him. If she had to embellish their situation a little to get what she wanted, then she would.

"Do you think you could consider helping us? We'll organize everything. You just need to rent us your garden and the ballroom. Oh, and the cottage if it's available. We'd like to spend our first night together there."

"Most young people prefer flying off to some exotic location or at least stay in a grand hotel in the city. Are you sure the cottage will be fancy enough for you?"

"The cottage is lovely. I've seen the pictures. And we don't want fancy; we just want private. Bridget, this will literally be the first night we spend together. We don't want any distractions. The cottage will be a perfect place to start married life."

"Ooh," cooed Bridget. "How romantic. You never hear about that sort of thing anymore. Most people live together now before they get married. It wasn't like that when I was young, but my grandchildren keep telling me I have to move with the times. I don't see why I should. The times aren't very nice."

"You're right, Bridget," Joan agreed, trying to get the woman on her side. "So do you have any available dates for me?"

"Why don't you let me check the reservation book, and I'll get back to you. You can leave me your number, and I'll call you soon."

"Can I just wait while you look? As you can imagine, I'm very anxious."

"All right, dear. Let me just put the phone down, and I'll see what's available."

Joan heard a clatter as Bridget put the phone down. She could hear the faint sound of pages turning and Bridget humming to herself. Joan could hardly breathe, she was so nervous. The wait seemed to take forever. David sat, watching her, just as anxious as she was for good news.

"Are you there, dear? "

"I am," Joan answered

"I have a date in September or one in October. Both are Saturdays, so they would be perfect for a wedding."

Joan's heart sank. That was six months away. "Are you sure you don't have anything in July?"

"We go away for all of July and August. It's much too cold down here in winter, so we fly up to Queensland for our annual holiday."

"What about before that then? Is there anything in June?"

"Let me see." Bridget turned the pages in her reservation book over and found one Saturday in June free. "I do have one day in June, but that's not enough time to organize a wedding. People can spend up to a year planning such a big event."

"Bridget, I don't need a year. I'll take it."

"If you say so. But you will have to get your own caterers and decorators. I'm just supplying the room. And what will you do if it rains dear? You can't get married in the garden if the weather's bad."

"We'll make everyone bring umbrellas."

"That's no good. The photos would be terrible. And then they'll traipse mud into my house. How many people are you inviting?"

"We only want about sixty people."

"Then I guess if it rains, we could let you use the back veranda. We used to have lovely parties out there when the children were little. They were so much fun. At one party, I think it was Alistair's fiftieth, we had a band play for the afternoon. That was a wonderful day. We have enough chairs for sixty people. But remember, you'll have to do the flowers yourself and get someone to put out the chairs. Is that all right?"

"Bridget, I'll do anything you ask. Now when can I come down and finish off the arrangements with you and pay a deposit? I'll come whenever it suits you."

"I'm free tomorrow morning. Will you be bringing your young man with you?"

"I don't think so. His leg's still in a cast the, poor thing, so it will just be me. I'll see you tomorrow. Is about ten fine?"

"It is, dear. I'll see you then. But don't you want to know what day your wedding's going to be dear?"

"Yes, I do. How silly of me. I'm just so excited, I forgot to ask. When are we booked in?"

"June twenty-second."

"June twenty-second," Joan repeated, and David gave her the thumbs up in approval. "That's perfect, Bridget. I'll see you tomorrow."

Joan put her phone down on the table, looked smugly over at David, and said, "And that, ladies and gentlemen, is how it's done."

"I could have done that if I'd known the place existed. You certainly know how to wheel and deal, don't you? I'll have to watch out for that."

"Whatever it takes, right? It's funny. That date seems familiar to me, but I can't think why."

"Is it someone's birthday?"

Joan thought back to what she had been doing that time last year. "I know what it is. That's the first time you called me."

"So we're going to get married one year from the very first time I tried to ask you out. That's certainly a fitting way to book-end the year."

"It is, isn't it?" Joan sat down beside David and laid her head on his shoulder as she thought about that first conversation they had. She had no idea it would turn out so wonderful. She'd been driving somewhere when he called. Suddenly it dawned on her where she'd been going that night.

"Oh no. Oh no, oh no, oh no."

"Oh no, what?" David asked.

Joan jumped up from beside David and grabbed her bag from where she had left it earlier on the floor. She quickly kissed David on the cheek.

"Love you, gotta go," she called as she ran down the hall to the front door.

"Where are you going?" David asked after her to her quickly retreating back.

"I'm going to talk to Caroline," she yelled back as she closed the front door behind her.

"Who on earth is Caroline?" David yelled to the empty room.

~~~

Caroline had been at the other end of the house in the laundry room when she heard the doorbell. It rang a second time and then a third before she made it to the front door. *Someone is very insistent*, she thought. She opened the door, putting on her "don't disturb me" face, but was floored to see who was standing there.

"Hi, Caroline."

"Joan. What are you doing here?"

"I'm really sorry to bother you. I needed to ask you something urgently. It's very time sensitive, so would it be okay if I came in for a few minutes to talk to you?"

"You should have called, Joan. I might have been out."

"I know. And I know you don't like people stopping by unannounced. I was in the car and halfway here before I remembered that, so I thought I'd take the chance."

"Well, you better come in then. I was just about to have a cup of coffee. Would you like one?"

Nodding, Joan stepped inside to the spacious foyer. Shutting the door behind her, she noticed the piece of timber nailed over one of the panels in the door.

"Coffee would be great. What happened to your door? You weren't robbed, were you?"

"No, it just got broken. I can't exactly replace it with regular glass. I just haven't gotten around to finding someone who can do it yet."

"I know someone who could help you. He's a third generation lead lighter, and I've used him before. His work is excellent. I can give you his number if you like," Joan offered.

"I would appreciate that. Thank you, Joan."

Joan followed Caroline through the house to the kitchen. She'd only been here once before, but at the time, the house had sparkled. Today it looked unloved. There were no flowers in vases and no lights on anywhere. When they reached the kitchen, Joan was shocked to see dishes piled in the sink and the bins overflowing.

"Are you all right, Caroline? It looks like I've come at a bad time?"

Caroline shrugged her shoulders. "It's fine. I just haven't had a chance to clean up for a few days."

"Okay," Joan said, drawing out the word. Something was not right here. Joan had never known Caroline to let anything slide, and she couldn't stand mess. Her locker at school had been arranged just so and on the first day of each term, Caroline had brought in a sponge and spray and wipe to clean it out before she put her books in. Joan had always wanted to get into her locker and put the books out of order or leave an old apple hidden in the bottom corner. That would have messed with her head. Caroline started fussing with the coffee machine and then went to the fridge. She poked around for a minute, moving jars and containers, but closed the door empty handed. She turned off the coffee machine and apologized to Joan.

"I'm sorry. We're going to have to give coffee a miss. I seem to be out of milk."

"Don't worry about it. I don't need anything. Maybe you could come and sit down?"

Caroline pulled out a chair from the table and sat across from Joan, waiting.

"I don't know if you're aware of this, but I'm getting married."

"You are? Beth didn't tell me." Well, she wouldn't, Caroline thought. Since Adam had left her, Beth was back to treating her like a child, trying not to upset her. "I guess congratulations are in order. Who's the unlucky fellow?"

"Caroline, could we not fight for a minute? This is important. The reason I needed to see you was in regards to the wedding. I have a huge favour to ask."

"Well, it's lovely of you to think of me, Joan, but I just don't think I can be a bridesmaid for you."

"What?" Joan squawked.

"I'm kidding. I am capable of making a joke you know. You should see the look on your face."

"I think I'll just get to the point." Caroline was really beginning to worry her. She seemed to have flipped her lid a little. "I've been able to find a venue; you remember Carrbridge House? They're going to let me use the house and the gardens for the wedding, but there's only one day available. I wanted to check with you if it was all right."

"I hardly think you need to care what I think about your wedding date. I can't imagine what it would have to do with me."

"The wedding would be held on twenty-second of June."

"Oh, I see." Caroline had that date engraved on her heart. She would never forget it. "Isabelle's anniversary."

Caroline got up from the table and started stacking the dishes that had been in the sink into the dishwasher. Her back was turned to Joan so she couldn't see Caroline's expression. She knew coming here had been a long shot, and she couldn't see Caroline agreeing. She could go ahead with the date without Caroline's permission, but Joan didn't want to start her marriage with discord, even if it was just with her old enemy.

Caroline stopped stacking the dishes and turned back to Joan. "I think a wedding on that date would be lovely. I don't have a claim to that day and besides, Isabelle loved weddings. She was always playing under the net curtains, pretending they were a veil."

"I wanted to ask Beth to be my maid of honour. That would mean she wouldn't be able to spend the day with you."

"That's okay. I'll manage without her. But I do appreciate you asking. It was very kind."

"Should we check if it's all right with Adam? She was his daughter too."

"I think its best we don't tell him. He's not doing very well these days, and it might make him upset. Just don't invite him, and it shouldn't be a problem."

"Well, I wouldn't ask him and not ask you. I know you don't think a lot of me, but I'm not that rude."

"You don't know what's happened? I thought Beth would have told you."

"Beth very rarely talks to me about you. We have an unspoken agreement. She doesn't tell, and I don't ask. You're a very private person, and I respect that and besides, Beth never gossips."

"I might as well tell you. You'll find out sooner or later anyway. Adam has left me. About a week before Christmas."

"Oh, Caroline. I'm so sorry. Why would he do that?"

"He said he didn't belong here anymore. He said he didn't know if he'd ever loved me and had to go."

Joan felt her heart break for Caroline. She hadn't spent much time with the Anderson family, but they had always looked so happy. Adam never gave her the impression that he was looking for something better or didn't love and appreciate his wife. Well, not until recently anyway. He had been very dismissive of her at the June dinner. And Caroline was besotted from the moment she set eyes on him. Joan still remembered teasing her about the crush she had on him. She hoped her and David would never have to face anything so tragic. She didn't think she would be able to bear it if something came between them.

"Has he said he wants a divorce?"

"He hasn't said one word," Caroline said as she wiped the bench. Some days she cleaned frantically, making sure everything was perfect. But then there were the days when she did nothing and let the mess pile up. Those were the days when she felt paralysed with fear, waiting all day for someone to knock on the door and serve her with divorce papers or for Adam to confirm what she already knew. That he was done with her permanently. So she had begun to unravel and let things go. What was the point anyway? She only had to worry about Michael, but he was easy to care for. He spent most of his time in his room studying. School had only been back for a month, but he was desperate for a high score to get into the uni course he'd chosen. He wanted to be a doctor, and he was more than smart enough. She just hoped he didn't burn out too early. And on the weekends, he spent time with Adam. He never talked to her about it, and she didn't pry.

"He rings Michael every day and sees him on Saturdays, so he's fulfilling his duty, but I haven't heard from him once."

"He might come back. The time away might be good for him."

"I doubt very much if he'll come back. He was adamant when he left, and he's a very stubborn man."

"What will you do?"

"I have no idea, Joan. I'm not going to beg him. I don't want him home because he feels guilty when he'd rather be anywhere than here. I'm worth more than that. Do you know what I mean?"

"Actually I do. I won't bore you with the ins and outs of my relationship with David, but we came close to not making it," Joan offered, but she could see Caroline wasn't listening to her.

Caroline wasn't focusing on Joan anymore. Her practical side had kicked in, and she realized Joan hadn't thought this whole wedding date thing through properly.

"Joan, how are you going to organize an entire wedding in four months? It usually takes a year to get everything done."

"I have the venue. That's got to be the hardest part."

"I helped Tom with Beth's birthday. I know they don't do any catering there. We had to organize all the food and the bar. There were no flowers or linens. They had tables and chairs, but that was about it."

"I guess I could hire a wedding planner. Are they expensive?"

"Forget about the cost. I can't see anyone decent taking you on at this late date. Is David's mum any good at planning?"

"I've only known her a few weeks, and I really like her, but no, I don't think she's much of a planner. She reminds me a lot of Beth actually."

"Well you can't have her help you with the planning then. And please don't ask Beth. I love her, but she's a complete disaster. Your wedding cake would end up being a sponge picked up at Cole's on the way to the ceremony."

"I'm sure I can organize it myself. And David will help. He's not an idiot. He runs his own very successful business, and he has a few weeks off work at the moment so he has time."

Caroline pulled a writing pad and a pen from a drawer and sat back down, the dishes forgotten.

"You can't let a *man* plan your wedding. He'll forget to do at least half of the important things, and he'll stuff up the rest of it."

"I'm sure he wouldn't."

"Joan, unless you're marrying a florist or a caterer I suggest you listen to me. What does he do for a living?"

"He's a builder."

"Fabulous. Unless you want the theme for your wedding to be "construction site," I would keep him out of it and just make sure he has a ride and a suit on the day."

"Why would we need a theme? Can't I just have what I like?"

"Yes, you can have what you like. But it all has to work together. This is your big day, and it needs to be exactly how you want it. If you leave it to someone else who doesn't know you, you'll end up with their dream wedding instead of yours. You never looked to me like a ruffle-and-lace kind of girl, but that's what you might end up with if you let everybody have a say in the day and do their little bit of the planning. You want your wedding day to reflect who you are because if you're lucky, you'll have those pictures up on your wall for the rest of your life. You don't want to regret anything about it."

"You're freaking me out, Caroline. I can't do all this. Themes, and linens, and flowers. I just want something simple."

"Then there's your theme. Quiet elegance. With a touch of vintage, I think. That's definitely you. I see you in a satin off-white gown that hugs you to the waist and then falls in soft folds to the floor. I doubt you'd want a veil, but if you do don't make it too long. And orchids would be good."

"Yes, that sounds like me, but where am I going to find a dress like that at such short notice? What was I thinking picking such a close date?" she said, the panic in her voice escalating.

"I know a dressmaker. She works from home, and she makes most of my clothes. It's one of my best kept secrets. I take in a picture, and she makes whatever I want to my exact size. She doesn't charge a fortune, and the clothes fit so much nicer and are much better quality than anything I buy in the shops. I'm her best customer. I'm sure I could get her to make a dress for you if I asked."

"Would you do that for me?"

"I would. In fact, if you like, I'll help you organize the whole wedding. I know the best florists and caterers around. You need someone to organize the invitations and handle the RSVP list. The photographer you paid for, for Beth's birthday. He's a friend of mine. And if he can't do it, I'll find someone else. You give me a budget and tell me what you want, and I'll make it happen."

"Caroline, this is very kind of you, especially considering it's us. But are you sure you should be doing this? Your life seems a bit up in the air at the moment, and the last thing I want to do is complicate it."

"You'll be doing me a favour. I'm going mad sitting here all day with nothing to do. I need to get out in the world and talk to people. Helping you plan your wedding will give me that chance. Tell me you'll say yes."

"But we're not friends. This is the sort of thing friends would do for each other. You're not suggesting our relationship changes, are you?"

"Heaven forbid. We continue on as we always have. I don't like you, and you don't like me. We're just two people in need helping each other out." Caroline shook her head and laughed. She hadn't done that in a long time. "Friends," she scoffed like it was the most ridiculous thing she had ever heard. "As if."

Chapter 27

Caroline sat at her kitchen table with her diary and her party book. The party book was her bible when she planned any kind of event. It had the name of every person or business she had ever used, and each one had a star rating from one to five. If you got a five from Caroline, that meant you were perfect. If you got a three, you might be considered if there was absolutely no one else available. If you got one star beside your name you should probably close your business and change careers because Caroline would make sure every other one of the women in her network knew to never use you. Caroline had no problem sharing which services to avoid, but it was rare for her to recommend the names of anyone who received three stars and she never, ever gave out the names of a four or a five. If someone else found them on their own, then there was nothing she could do about it, but there was no way she was going to just hand over her best finds to anyone.

When she heard the doorbell ring for the second time that day, she had already made pages of notes and set up appointments for every Saturday for the next month.

Caroline was feeling alive for the first time since Adam had left. Planning was what she did, and she was "the best." She used to dream of Isabelle's wedding and what it would be like. Her own wedding to Adam had been a rushed, quiet affair with his mother sobbing loudly in the background. Isabelle's wedding would have been a grand event, and mother and daughter used to curl up on Isabelle's bed at night and talk about what kind of dress she would wear and who her groom would be. Isabelle always had a little crush on Prince Charming from Cinderella, and she wanted to marry someone just like him. His dark hair always reminded her of her father, and she had thought her dad was the most perfect man on earth. Doing this for Joan didn't even come close to what it would have been like helping her daughter plan a wedding, but it was the distraction she needed right now.

Caroline thought she had been surprised to see Joan standing on her doorstep, but this new visitor was a complete shock. She started to shake, and her heart felt like it had turned to liquid. This couldn't be good. Why would he be here in the middle of the day?

"Hello, Caroline," he said. His voice sounded nervous, and that did nothing to calm her. This could only be bad, very bad. The final blow that she had been waiting for had arrived.

"Hello, Adam."

"Do you think I could come in?" he asked.

"Yes, of course," she said as she moved out of the doorway to let him in. "This is still your house." *For now*, she thought. He was probably here to start discussions about a divorce, and there was a good chance the house would have to go. She would only be entitled to half, and there was no way she could afford to buy him out.

Adam followed Caroline through to the kitchen where she had been working. The dishes were still half done, and the table was covered with all the work she had been doing for Joan's wedding.

"I'm sorry about the mess. I'm helping Joan plan her wedding." She started stacking up the papers into a neat pile. It gave her hands something to do and hid their shaking.

"Joan's getting married? And you're helping her? Those are certainly two things I never thought I'd hear anyone say." Adam sat down at the table, wondering if he was in the right house. He had never seen the kitchen messy before; he'd never seen Caroline messy either for that matter. She looked the same, but the polished demeanour she normally projected was dulled. He knew it was his fault.

"I guess a lot has changed in the last three months."

Caroline stopped fussing with her papers and glanced down at Adam. Seeing him sitting at the table in her kitchen was so familiar, so normal, like nothing had ever changed. It should have been a workday for him, which would usually mean that he would be dressed in a suit. But here he was in an old pair of jeans and a T-shirt. His hair hadn't been cut for a while, but she liked the extra length. It made him look a little scruffy, not as intimidating as the man he usually let the world see. He had more grey in his thick, dark hair than he had when he had left, but his eyes still looked the same. They reflected her own. Full of sadness and loss. They were rimmed in red, and it looked like he hadn't been sleeping much. Or crying. But that wouldn't be it. Adam had never cried, and it would have scared her to see that. Seeing him sitting there looking so vulnerable, all she wanted to do was enfold him in her arms and tell him everything would be all right. Despite what he had done to her, the way he'd broken her heart, she still loved him. Watching him, she realized she was always going to feel that way, and nothing he did would change that. At this revelation, a feeling of anger rose up and engulfed her. It wasn't *him* she was angry at but her *own* weakness. *Get a grip Caroline*, she counselled herself. It's over. You're not going to let him crush you ever again.

"And what did you expect, Adam? That I'd be sitting here, wasting away, pining for you."

"I didn't know what to think. To be honest, until a few days ago, I haven't thought about you much at all."

"Well, thank you for sharing that. You can't imagine how flattered I feel."

"I'm sorry. That came out wrong. What I meant is that I haven't *let* myself think about you." *This isn't going the way I planned it*, Adam thought. He had spent days practising how he was going to approach Caroline, desperate to see her but lacking the courage. He had finally managed to set aside his fears about her rejecting him, but the minute he saw her, all his carefully worded sentences flew out of his head.

"Look, Adam. I can guess why you're here. So why don't you let me say it for you and then we can get this torture over and done with? You're here to ask for a divorce. You want to tell me that we need to sell our family home and work out a settlement. You're here to suggest I find myself a solicitor."

"No, Caroline." Adam shook his head. "I'm not here for any of those things. I'm here to apologize to you for the way I spoke to you that day I left and to apologize for my behaviour for the last year. And to ask for your forgiveness."

Confusion swamped Caroline, and she needed to sit. She dropped down into the chair she had vacated earlier to answer the door, trying to figure out what was happening. This didn't make any sense to her. Unless…

"Adam, is this some sort of tactic? Are you trying to butter me up so I'll take it easy on you when we finally end up in court?"

He knew he had no right, but Adam reached across the kitchen table to take the hand that Caroline had let rest in front of her. When he touched her, she flinched and pulled her hands back and put them onto her lap. She couldn't let him touch her. She didn't trust herself not to throw herself at him and on his mercy. But last time she had done that, he had walked out and left her ashamed and humiliated. She was never going to do that again.

"I know you don't believe me," he pleaded, "but can you please listen to me? I need to say so many things but I'm afraid they won't come out right. I practised over and over, but now my words are all jumbled in my head, and it might take a little while to say what I mean. If you could please just sit for a minute and let me speak, hopefully you'll begin to understand why I'm here."

"If you must. Why don't you tell me why you came here?" Her voice was faintly tainted with bitterness.

"Is it all right if I start at the beginning?"

Caroline nodded and waited for Adam to continue.

"When Isabelle died, I thought that I needed to stay strong for you and Michael. We were both devastated but while you let your feelings out, I held all of mine in. I didn't know how I was supposed to react. After my father died, my mother used to tell me, 'You're the man of the house now. I'm relying on you.' The little boy that I was, I took that very seriously and wanted to help her anyway I could, even though I didn't have anyone to show me what being a man looked like. I got my information from my mother and the memories I had of my father. My mum and my grandfather didn't get along, so she didn't let me spend much time with him or my grandmother. My male role models came from things I saw on TV and books I read when I was a kid. I thought I was just supposed to let things bounce off me and never let them affect me. Until Isabelle's death, I'd been able to do that really well and, to be honest, nothing came along that challenged that belief. The worst thing that had ever happened to us was the miscarriage between Michael and Isabelle, but it was so early on that we hardly knew you were pregnant when it happened. I knew it made you sad, and I tried to be there for you, but I didn't let it affect me that much. And when you needed the emergency hysterectomy after Isabelle was born, it was scary there for a moment, but it turned out fine so once you were better, I hardly ever thought about it again. But Isabelle dying was just too much. I was confronted with something totally devastating, but I tried to handle it the way I always had in the past. Carry on and don't cry or show how sad you are. And I managed to keep it together for a while. I kept working and being a husband and father. I understood *your* reaction. You're a woman. You're allowed to grieve and cry openly. No one would ever think badly of you for doing that. I believed that if I did that, it would be seen as weakness."

Adam took a deep breath. He could feel the tears starting again. They had barely stopped for days, but he wanted to get through this without crying. He didn't want her sympathy; he wanted her to understand what he had gone through.

"So instead of dealing with how I felt, the only thing I could do was completely shut down. I didn't even realize I was doing it. And in the process of not grieving for Isabelle, I didn't allow myself to feel anything. I couldn't deal with anyone's sympathy or support. I didn't think I should have needed it. But the worst thing was that I couldn't love you or let you in. I didn't want to be dependent on you, and I didn't want you to see me not being strong. So I pushed you away when we needed each other the most."

Adam looked up from the surface of the table that he had been staring at as he traced his finger along a knot in the wood and settled his eyes on Caroline. She didn't look compassionate or sorry for him. Her face was cloaked in a mask of indifference he had never seen before. *I've hurt her so badly*, he thought, *that she's removed me from her heart.* "I'm sorry I did that to you."

"I tried to help you, Adam, lots of people tried to help you. I could see you weren't coping at all, and I would have done anything to get you through to the other side. You wouldn't let me."

"I know. I should have talked to you or at least someone who understood. But every time someone suggested I find a support group or went to counselling or they tried to give me advice, I took it as a criticism. I believed that everyone else was wrong, and I was the sane one. And when you started to get better, I thought it meant you had forgotten Isabelle. No, that's not right. I knew you would never forget, her but you were moving forward without her. So every time you smiled or laughed at something, I couldn't believe you thought you had the right to be happy. And that's why I pulled away from you in the bedroom. Being with you, the way you gave yourself over to me so completely and with such trust, had always made me feel connected to you like we were one person. But you became the last person I wanted to have any connection with. I felt you had let me down and you were definitely letting Isabelle down by starting to be happy again, even if it was just a little bit. After those few days when you broke down after the first anniversary, I saw a difference in you. A release, I guess. And that's when I began not only to feel cut off from you, but I began to feel like I hated you."

Caroline couldn't believe she was hearing this. Hadn't he done enough to her? She knew he didn't love her. He'd made that very clear. But to come into her home and tell her that he hated her. Why did he want to be so cruel? She was not going to sit here and listen to this. She pushed back her chair and stood up.

"I think you should go now, Adam. I don't know why you thought coming here and unloading all this onto me was a good idea, but I don't deserve it. I've done everything you asked. You moved out; I let you. I didn't ring you or beg you to come back. And for you to come here and tell me that you hate me, and in my home, in my kitchen where I cooked for you, meal after meal, year after year, what's wrong with you? I know you don't want to hear it, but you need help. And don't you dare come looking for it from me. I'm done. So just get out and don't come back."

"You've misunderstood me, Caroline. I'm not doing this right, am I? I don't hate you. I just thought I did. Please sit down and let me finish."

"I think you're already finished, Adam. There is nothing you could say and nothing you could do that could make what you just said to me all right. I might not have much pride left right now, but what I do have I would like to keep intact. I'm not going to let you destroy what is left of my life." Caroline turned her back to him, devastated. Why did he want to hurt her even more than he already had?

Adam rose out of his chair and walked towards where Caroline stood. Placing his arms on her shoulders, he gently turned her towards him. She resisted at first but just having him touch her broke down her resolve. Standing only centimetres apart, he tilted he chin up until she had no choice but to look at him.

"I love you. I know I said I wasn't sure that awful day when I left you, but that's because I never really understood what love was. I thought love, real rip-your-heart-out love, was a myth. Something made up so that people would get married and have children to keep humanity going. It was the stuff of greeting cards and romantic novels, and it was only for women. But I know now, with the deepest certainty, that I do love you Caroline."

Adam had told her over the years that he loved her. On birthdays and special occasions. Not the way that she told him almost every day, but she had cherished it when he said it. But she had believed him then, and it hadn't been true. She didn't know that she could believe him now.

"I don't know, Adam. So much has happened."

"It's not too late. Are you telling me that you don't want me anymore? That you don't love me the way you always have?"

"I… Adam, I don't know."

Standing that close to each other, Adam was able to move his hand from her shoulder where it had been resting up to the back of her neck. Looking into her eyes, he saw her confusion and her hostility, but he wasn't going to let that stop him. Moving his other hand down her body and resting it in the small of her back, he pulled her closer and put his lips to hers. Moving them slowly over hers, he felt her respond and taking that as permission, he pulled her tighter against him and let his kiss deepen. Caroline's hand reached out and lightly pressed against his chest until she moved it up his body and entangled it in his hair.

Caroline pulled away slowly. This wasn't what she had expected, and she was so angry, all she wanted to do was hit him and make him hurt the way he had hurt her. But her body had betrayed her. Her knees buckled at his touch, and she wished she could stay like that forever. Removing her hands from him, she tried to step away, but he didn't let her go.

"What are you doing, Adam?"

"I'm making the first move."

"What?"

"I'm making the first move. If I can't convince you with words how much I love you, then I want you to feel it. I am not going to move from this spot until you understand. You are responsible for all the best things in my life. Without you, I wouldn't have my son and without you, I wouldn't have known Isabelle. The time was too short, but twelve years with her was better than one hundred years without her. But most of all without you, *I am nothing*. I need you and I want you. If I have to spend the rest of my life trying to make you see that, then that's what I'll do."

"I don't know, Adam. I don't know if I can trust this. What if something else happens? I need to know that I can count on you. I can't go through this again. Your rejection was even worse than losing Isabelle. She was taken from me. She didn't chose it, and she never would have. But you chose to go. And that broke my heart."

"I can't promise that I won't ever hurt you in the future because I'm human. But I will do my best not to. But you can trust me to never ever leave you again. My life is with you, and I won't let anything come between that. I know how close I've come to losing you and our lives together. I hit rock bottom, and I made so many mistakes. If they handed out qualifications for grief and sorrow, I would have earned my degree by now. But I'm finally ready to start dealing with it now. I'm getting help. I've found someone to talk to. I've even taken some time off work so I can concentrate on letting myself heal."

"I'm glad for you, Adam. I wished I'd talked to someone earlier. I was just lucky I had a good friend to listen to me." Caroline waited for a minute, trying to let her thoughts catch up with what was happening. "I just don't know if I should believe you."

Still holding her, refusing to let go, Adam decided to tell her what had transpired in the last few days to bring him to his senses. He was still ashamed of his behaviour but if it meant she would understand and believe him, it was worth the disgrace.

"Do you know how I can be so certain that I love you? I punched someone defending your honour."

"Who did you punch, and why would you need to defend me? Trust me, my honour is completely intact."

"I saw Chris the other night. When he heard that we weren't together, he suggested that you might appreciate a visit from him. He decided that you were lonely here all alone and that some time with a man like him might be just what you need. The thought of anyone ever touching you, kissing you made me so angry, so wild with rage that I punched him. In the face! The police were even called. I could have been arrested. But it would have been worth it because it turned out to be one of the best things that ever happened to me."

"Adam that sounds like jealousy to me. Not love."

"Oh, I was jealous all right. But in that moment when I heard what he said, I saw my life laid out before me with you gone forever, and I knew. When we got married, I expected that we would be happy, but I didn't think I was in love. And I wasn't. Not then. And I don't know the exact moment that it happened, but it did. You have sunk into every part of me, and I refuse to live without you anymore. And I'll be happy to defend you anytime you need it."

"I wish you'd felt like that when your mother was alive. If you had stood up to her, it would have made my life so much easier."

"So do I. She always thought I deserved better than you, but it turns out that's not possible. There is no one on this earth more perfect for me. If she was still alive, I'd go and tell her now. She was wrong about you."

Guilt flooded Caroline. If she kept her secret to herself, then Adam would come home and their relationship would be better than it had ever been. But she couldn't keep her secret anymore. If he really wanted her it had to be the real her, and he had to know the truth.

"Adam, before you say anything else, I think there's something you should know. I should have told you years ago, but I was afraid of losing you. Your mother was right about one thing. I've kept it from you for all these years, but I need to tell you now. If we do manage to sort this mess out, and I'm not saying we will, there should be no secrets." Caroline breathed in deeply knowing that this piece of information could have him out the door again, but she wanted to know if he meant what he said. This would certainly put him to the test. "When I told you I got pregnant by accident, I lied to you. Your mother was right. I did do it on purpose and although I'm sorry I lied and I understand if you feel like I trapped you, I don't regret my decision."

Shocked, Adam dropped his arms from around Caroline and stepped back as he processed this new revelation. He had always believed Caroline and just thought his mother was bitter about her son leaving home and getting married. What Caroline had done had changed the course of his life. He had always seen himself getting married in his thirties' and hadn't been looking for a wife when she fell pregnant. When she told him about the baby, his responsible side took over and it never occurred to him to walk away. His father had died when he was ten, and he wasn't going to let his own child grow up without a dad if he could be there. Adam had instantly proposed, and he never looked back or regretted marrying her. The first sixteen years of their marriage had been wonderful, and Caroline had been the best wife a man could ask for. But here she was, telling him everything had been based on a lie. Did this change anything for him now and how he loved her? He watched her while she waited for his response, her hands fidgeting and her eyes downcast.

"I know I should be angry. It's the oldest trick in the book, and I fell for it." Caroline wouldn't return his gaze as he looked at her. "Please look at me. I want you to see that I mean what I'm about to say."

Caroline turned her face upward from the floor. She was sure she had blown it, but she couldn't live with the lie anymore. She returned his gaze and waited for him to continue. This time when he left she would have no one to blame but herself.

"What you did was underhanded and wrong. You knew me well enough to know I would marry you, and you took that decision out of my hands. That said, I'm so glad you did what you did. If you hadn't, I would have moved on. You don't know this, but I was already considering it. And that would have been the biggest mistake of my life. I don't know where I'd be now and what my life would look like, but I know I wouldn't be better off. I forgave you the minute you told me what you did."

Years of guilt and worry that Adam would find out and leave dissipated as he drew her back into his tight embrace. She felt herself sink into him. All her strength disappeared and for the first time in their marriage, she felt him holding her up and she let go.

Adam could feel her give way and heard her tears. He hoped they were good tears not bad ones. He had learnt over the last few days how cleansing it could be to let yourself cry. He stood quietly holding her while she slowly unravelled the self-imposed chains she had wrapped herself in since she was a child, looking for approval from parents who didn't know how to give it and then later hoping to be perfect enough so that Adam would love her. He hoped he had convinced her that he meant what he said. But he wasn't sure how she was going to take the last piece of news he had come to tell her. It could go either way, and he was afraid she would think he had completely lost his mind.

"Caroline" he started. "There's something so important I need to tell you. Something that has completely changed my life. And I understand if you don't get it, but I ask that you hear me out for a few minutes before you make up your mind." Disengaging himself from her, he lowered her back into her chair and then followed, seating himself and taking her hand in his.

"While I was gone I've had a revelation. About God."

"God, as in God, God."

"Yes," he smiled. "As in *the* God. Someone reminded me that he exists. I used to know him when I was little, before my dad died and my mum became so bitter. I'm ashamed to say that I forgot about Him, laughed him off as a myth. But not anymore. And the changes that you are going to see in me are because of him. I won't lie. I still don't understand why Isabelle died, maybe I never will. But I hold comfort in the knowing that one day I'm going to see her again in heaven. Because that's where I'm going. I've asked him to forgive me for my many sins, especially for my denial of him all these years, and he said yes! I know it's true because when I asked, such peace came. Like nothing I had ever known before. Caroline, I want that for you too."

Caroline couldn't have been more surprised if he had told her he had decided to shave his head and become a Buddhist monk. In fact, this was more surprising. Never once had she heard Adam mention God, and he had only set foot in a church for Tom and Beth's wedding and his mother's funeral.

"Are you serious? I mean, I don't know what to think."

"Yes, I'm serious. And I've even started going to a church. It's only been a few weeks, but the people have been so understanding, and I've found some good men to talk to. I wish I had known them before all this happened, but I know them now and I finally have someone who gets it and they are happy to answer any crazy question I ask."

"Okay. So you are serious. What does that mean for us? Are you going to turn into a weirdo?"

"No more than I always was." He laughed. "And besides who isn't weird in their own special way? It means that I love God, and I love you and Michael and if you let me, I want to share him with you, at your own pace. No pressure."

"Well, I've tolerated it from Beth all these years, and she hasn't changed my mind. What makes you think you can?"

"Oh, I'm not going to try and change your mind. I'm going to let God do that." He smiled, knowing that only God had the power to soften and heal the human heart. "But I am going to pray for you," he answered while Caroline raised her eyebrow in his direction and said "Well, good luck with that one," as she laughed.

The sound of the front door banging broke the peace in the house. "Mum, are you here? Why's Dad's car in the driveway?" They heard Michael's footsteps grow louder as he walked down the hall towards the kitchen. Adam and Caroline released their hold on each other and stepped apart. Adam brushed away the tears on her cheeks, not wanting their son to think something was wrong. And nothing had been decided. Caroline still hadn't told him he could come home. He was hopeful, but he still needed to hear her say it.

"So what do you think, Caroline? Can I tell him I'm coming home?"

"Are you sure that's what you want? I won't survive you doing this to me again. It nearly killed me."

"I'm never going anywhere ever again. I want you for the rest of my life."

"Then yes, you can tell him." She smiled then, hoping he had meant it when he said he wanted her. It had been so long.

"How long will it take you to move back home?"

"About ten minutes. I packed my car before I came."

"You were pretty sure of yourself."

"No, hopeful."

Michael walked into the kitchen and dropped his heavy schoolbag on the floor. He reached into the fruit bowl and picking up an apple took a bite. His mouth full, he looked from one of his parents to the other. He hadn't seen them together looking happy for so long, he'd forgotten it was possible. They both had stupid grins on their faces, and it confirmed for him what he already knew. Old people were weird. He swallowed his mouthful and asked "What's up with you two?"

"Funny you should ask, Son," Adam said, pulling out a chair. "Take a seat, Michael. We have something really good to tell you."

Chapter 28

Beth's heart started to beat just a little faster when she saw Tom standing at the front entrance of the restaurant. He talked to the maître'd for a moment and then headed to the table where Beth was waiting for him. It still took her by surprise sometimes how their relationship had changed in the last ten months. Over the years, time and familiarity had come between them. But they had both made changes and now they were better friends than they had ever been and they loved each other more than they ever had. Beth acknowledged that it had taken time and commitment to breathe new life into their relationship. It had started with her accepting that Tom loved her and found her desirable no matter how much she weighed. And that gave her the courage to do something for herself. By losing kilos, she had regained her self-esteem. In the past she had given up but this time she hadn't. She had persevered on the days when she wanted to throw it all in and dive into a vat of chocolate mousse and eat her way out, or when her alarm went off to get her up and out of bed before the rest of her family so that she had the time to exercise. And she couldn't deny it had all been worth it. The clothes. The glorious, beautiful clothes that she could buy. In any store that she wanted. No more trying to stuff herself into smaller sizes and then taking them home and hiding them in the back of the wardrobe. Not from Tom but herself. She had set herself a goal and she had made it. Nobody would look at her and think thin. They would see a pretty woman with a nice figure. But when she saw herself, she saw lovely curves that her husband adored and a face that shone with delight whenever she saw herself in the mirror.

But the effort had not come from her alone. After that terrible anniversary, Tom had understood that Beth wanted a change for them both and grateful that he wasn't going to have to continue in what he had considered to be a lonely existence he made some effort of his own. He started delegating more at work. Once in a while, he bought her flowers for no reason except that he thought she might like them. But the biggest change he made, and the most important, was that he backed her up when it came to their children. As a united team, there was less disobedience. Their children were far from perfect, but they knew there was no getting around Dad anymore. If Mum said "no," that was it. Dad couldn't be moved. That didn't always make for a harmonious house, but at least it wasn't one divided against itself anymore.

"Hi, beautiful" Tom said as he kissed Beth on the cheek. "How was your day?"

Beth shrugged her shoulders. She wanted to hear how his day had gone. "It was just a regular day. I think it's more important how yours went."

Tom seated himself across the table from her and picked up his menu. He glanced inside while she waited to hear if it was good news or bad.

"It went fine."

"That's all you have to say for yourself? It went fine."

"It went more than fine. Lucky I persevered and finished year twelve because if I hadn't it would have meant going to TAFE first for a year to get in."

"So they're going to take you?"

"It's not definite. I still have to fill out all the application forms, and they won't officially tell me until all placements are announced at the end of the year, but the woman interviewing me said it shouldn't be a problem."

"And you'll be able to do it at Clayton?"

"Yep. I'll be doing an Arts degree with a major in education. Monash runs that course at Clayton, so I won't have to waste time on travel."

"Well, I look forward to seeing you in your first week running around with all the other new students enjoying the 'O' week festivities. Just don't come home with someone else's vomit on your shoes after you win a drinking contest. I won't clean them for you. And please, please don't start dressing like them. It's bad enough our son wants to look like a dirty delinquent. I don't want to have to look at you with your pants halfway down your bum!"

"I promise, Beth, that I won't turn into a typical uni student. I'm going to be forty years old. I'm there to learn, not join clubs and use it as an excuse to party."

"So now we just need to figure out what to do with the business." This was the part that gave Beth the most concern. What if Tom started Uni and hated it or couldn't manage. He had been out of school for a long time and while he was smart enough and definitely committed, studying would be a big change for him.

"I rang Artie Simons on the way here. He made an offer earlier in the year, and he's still keen. I've said he won't be able to buy me out until February next year, but that suits him. He's also agreed to keep the guys on so that means I won't have to make any big redundancy payments out of the sale price."

"What happens if you find you hate uni? What will you do if you decide to quit?"

"I've gone over every scenario. What if I sell and then Monash doesn't take me? Or as you say, I don't like it? What if I turn out to be an idiot, and I can't do the work? It all boils down to this. I hate doing what I do. I've given it twenty years of my life, and I don't want to do another twenty. It's time to sell no matter what and someone is willing to give me a great price. All those years of hard work are finally paying off. And there's a big demand for men in teaching so I should have no trouble getting a job. And if I hate uni or I'm not smart enough to cope? I'll always find something to do. Artie wants a two year non-compete clause in our contract but I can always go and work for a boss. I want you to understand, if I didn't want this so badly, I wouldn't be doing it."

"And you're sure you want to be a teacher? You don't want to be something more professional like an accountant or a lawyer?"

"Beth, can you see me working in an office? I hate doing it for myself. The last thing I want is to be doing it for other people. I've been thinking about this for years, and I'm sure."

"Then I think you should go for it. I checked with the bank and the mortgage is only thirty thousand. We can pay that out and put the rest of the money on deposit in case of an emergency. And it will be a nice nest egg for our retirement. I'll keep working and if you work weekends, we should be fine. I'm just grateful we don't have a lot of debt like a lot of people do."

A waitress came over with her pad ready to take their order. Tom looked at her apologetically.

"I'm sorry, we haven't had a chance to look at the menu yet. We've been too busy chatting."

"That's fine" she said. "Can I tell you the specials and then come back in a few minutes? You two must be a new couple. I can always tell. Too busy talking to eat."

Beth and Tom just smiled at each other knowingly. They might have been married a long time, but they did feel like a new couple.

After the waitress had read through the specials, Tom and Beth made their decision about what to eat and ordered. Tom sat back in his chair getting comfortable and studied his wife.

"Beth, you're not planning on losing any more weight, are you?"

"I don't know. I seem to have got to this point and slowed right down. I think this must just be the weight that's right for my body. Is that all right? I can try to lose more if you like."

"I'd rather you didn't lose any more. You look beautiful, and I'm so glad you're healthier. But I always thought you were beautiful, and the last thing I want it to be married to a stick. I love your curves. I can't stand seeing women with their bones sticking out. I know it's fashionable, but in my eyes, they resemble chicken wings. I like being able to hug you without being stabbed by a rib."

"Then I won't lose anymore. But please don't ask me to put any on. I had my fitting for the matron of honour dress for Joan's wedding yesterday. If I add a millimetre I think Caroline will hunt me down and lock me up until the day of the wedding. She'll put me on a *no* bread and water diet until I can fit back into the dress."

Tom started to chuckle. The picture he had of Beth behind bars with Caroline measuring her everyday wasn't beyond the realm of possibility.

"It's not funny, Tom. She's taking this whole wedding thing very seriously. I think Joan's about to have a nervous breakdown. Caroline never leaves her alone, and they already didn't like each other. This hasn't helped their relationship at all. David thinks Joan should just fire her, but she can't bring herself to do it because Caroline's doing a brilliant job and the wedding is only a few weeks away."

The waitress brought over their entrée's. Beth had order the calamari fritti while Tom had gone with the fried camembert wrapped in Prosciutto. He loved cheese, and if it came fried, it was all the better.

"I like David. Dinner the other night was great. And the way he got on with the kids. It's a shame they don't want children because he was a natural. I won't mind spending more time with him and Joan."

"That's good because I have a bit of a favour to ask you. Joan needs someone to give her away. She wondered if you would do it. She has no family, and she said you were the closest thing to a brother she has." Beth mentally crossed her fingers hoping that Tom would say yes. She had already told Joan and Caroline he would do it and if she had to go back and re-neg it was going to be her in trouble, not Tom.

Tom's shoulders sagged. He knew what that meant. A suit.

"What will I have to wear?"

"Caroline wants you dressed the same as the groom and the best man. So you will be in tails. I'm sorry. I know how you hate that."

"And I guess I'll have to wear some sort of flower."

"Yep. A white orchid."

"And will I have to be in photos?"

"Only a few. You're not really a part of the wedding party, so you won't have to be in most of them like I do"

"If I put on weight after I've been fitted for the suit, will Caroline hunt me down and lock me up until the day of the wedding?"

"Oh, I guarantee it. But I promise to come and visit you in prison once in a while. I'm sure she'll allow conjugal visits," she teased.

"So who else is in the wedding party? Should I be concerned about the best man hitting on you? Isn't that why men agree to be in weddings? So they can take one of the wedding party home with them later?"

"I think that's very unlikely, Tom. His daughter will be there to. She's going to be the flower girl."

"Good, so he's married. I won't have to keep a close eye on him all night then."

"No, he's not. He was but his wife died so I guess that makes him a widower. Joan told me the whole story. He was married for about seven years, and they had just had a baby. His wife and their baby were in a car accident, and she died at the scene. The baby was fine because it was strapped into the car seat properly. She's four now and the most gorgeous thing you've ever seen. She was at the fitting too. Tiny little girl with blonde ringlets. And her dad was there with her. Don't get mad at me, but he was even more adorable than his daughter."

"I guess I got it wrong then. I won't need to keep an eye on him. It'll be you I'll have to be watching all night."

Beth leaned across the table and gave Tom's hand the lightest tap.

"Don't be silly. I have no interest in replacing you. But I did have him in mind for someone else."

"And who is that? Everyone we know is married."

"Jill won't be for long. He would be perfect for her. Joan said he hasn't dated at all since his wife died and he told David he thinks it's time to get out there. Four years is a long time alone, and he must be ready for a new relationship by now. And that little girl. Jill would eat her up, she's so cute."

"I'd stay out of it if I was you. Jill might not be ready to meet someone. And taking on someone else's child is a huge deal."

"Yes, it's a big deal, but Jill wants children desperately. She hasn't been able to have any of her own. This could all work out perfectly."

"Matchmaking is a tricky business, Beth. You could end up in trouble with your sister, and you don't want that."

"I'm not going to do anything overt like say, 'Hey, why don't you two get married and let's have Caroline plan the wedding for you. I'm just going to make sure they meet each other during the night. That's not match making I'm just doing a little manoeuvring."

"Well, while you're at it, can you make sure you manoeuver Sarah away from Michael? I don't want her making an idiot of herself at the wedding."

"Oh, that's over. She told me the other day she decided he's too 'up himself' as she put it and now she likes someone in her class. His name's Butch, although I can't imagine that's what his parents called him when he was born and he's in a band. You might want to get the shotgun out to scare that one off. He sounds like a real winner."

Every time Tom thought about some guy coming to the door to take his daughter out, he felt anxious. The thought of some grotty teenage boy touching her made his blood pressure rise. He didn't understand why fathers agreed to give their daughters away in marriage to any man.

"Have you had 'the talk' with her?"

"I tried. She rolled her eyes at me, huffed for a while and then told me she already knew everything there was to know about sex." Beth mimicked her daughter's voice "Muuum, they told us in school, and I already knew anyway. I'm not a baby you know."

"That wasn't the talk I meant. I'm talking about the one where you tell her how bad boys really are and that everything she's ever heard about them is true. They are only after one thing."

"It might have more meaning coming from you, Tom. She'll think I'm either making it up or being old fashioned. I've tried telling her but she fobs me off. You have firsthand experience anyway having once been a teenage boy. Can I leave it to you?"

The waitress bought their second course winking at them. "You two are still at it. I've never seen a couple who looked so happy." She walked away and left them to their dinner.

"She's looking for a big tip," Tom said.

Beth looked around the restaurant at the other couples dining. The younger ones still had that early love glow, but Beth knew how quickly that could pass. Many of the ones who looked like they had been together a long time appeared to be bored with each other. They were gazing off into the distance and one man was perving on the young woman at the table next to his. Beth hoped his wife didn't notice the way he wasn't taking his eyes off her. The man must have been thirty years older than her. Disgusting old pig.

"I don't think so, Tom. It looks like we're the exception here. Most people don't seem particularly happy with each other."

Tom quickly threw his glance around the room. A lot of couples did seem disinterested in each other. One old guy was checking out a youngish girl at the table next to his. His wife looked like she had noticed and was calling his name to get his attention. The man dragged his eyes away from the girl. He guessed most people would consider her beautiful, but she was too thin for Tom's taste and he looked away quickly in case Beth thought he was checking her out. Tom wished men didn't do that. It gave the rest of them a bad rap and was so disrespectful to their wives. He'd rather be looking at Beth than any of these women who held no interest for him no matter what they looked like. He was a one woman guy. And that's what he wanted for Sarah. Someone who would love her as much as he loved her mother. He was going to do his best to make sure that happened.

"So you think I should talk to Sarah? Father to daughter. She might not listen to me, and that will be one uncomfortable conversation. I hated talking to Lochie about sex and girls, but talking to Sarah will be even more embarrassing."

"Tom wouldn't you rather be uncomfortable now than have her pregnant at sixteen. The best thing you can do for her is give her your time and let her know she's too special to waste herself on losers and jerks. I think she will listen to you—she already knows that you think she is lovely."

"I'll do it then. Can I wait until tomorrow? I might need a day to work myself up to it."

"That's fine. And I promise to cross my fingers for you."

Chapter 29

"She wrote back! She wants to meet me!"

"Good morning, gorgeous. How did you sleep?" David asked his very excited fiancé on the other end of the phone. He could only imagine that the 'she' Joan was talking about was her half-sister and she must have finally written back. Joan had sent a letter to Abby Fisher two weeks ago and had been anxiously waiting for a response for the last week. She had almost given up hope of receiving a reply thinking that maybe she had scared the woman or perhaps Abby thought it was some kind of con. The Morgans had been a wealthy family, and Abby may have thought Joan was after money. She had been vague in the letter not wanting to tell her the whole truth before she met her. She wrote that her mother and Abby's father had known each other forty years ago and she suspected that Jonathon might be her father. In an effort to convince Abby that they were related, she included a recent photo of herself.

"I slept fine, but I wish I'd been doing it beside you."

"Only one month to go, and then that's exactly what you'll be doing. Now who wrote back?"

"Abby did. She wrote, and she wants to meet me." Joan was busting with excitement at the thought of meeting her. She finally had a relative. She was part of a family. "Will you come with me? She said she's free on Saturday morning. "

"Of course I'll come. But do you mind driving? My leg is still a bit sore and the drive will take well over an hour."

"I'd drive to Sydney to meet her if I had to."

"Well, thankfully we don't have to go that far. Can I hear her letter?"

"Yes. Sorry, I'm just so happy.

> *Dear Joan,*
>
> *I was surprised to receive your letter last week but on reflection I shouldn't have been. My father had a bit of a reputation when I was growing up. I guess it caught up with him. I can see from the photo you sent me that we look very much alike and you look like Dad. I'm an only child and always wanted a sister and now I guess I have one. If you are free this weekend and can make it to Ballarat we could meet. If that doesn't work we can make it another time. If you were wanting to meet our father it would be best if we did it sooner rather than later. He's not well and he deteriorating quickly. I'll wait to hear from you.*
>
> *Abby*

She's given me her home number. I'm going to call her and tell her we're coming."

"Question? Do you think our wedding planner extraordinaire will let you go? She's had you every Saturday for months."

"She's already told me she doesn't need me this weekend. All the planning is finished and there's nothing more to do for a few weeks. And then it's just another fitting and visit to the hairdresser so they can practice a week before. Totally unnecessary, but I don't dare argue with her. And Tom's agreed to give me away so that's sorted. The most important thing now is making sure we show up on the day dressed. As long as you've written your vows, that is?"

"I'm working on it. Are you still sure you don't want to go with traditional? I have no problem with you agreeing to honour and obey me. And in return, I'll do the cherish thing until one of us dies."

"David, get writing, and I'll see you tonight. Don't make me bring Caroline with me to sort you out."

"I'm getting a pen right now. Don't bring that woman here. She doesn't know where I live, and I'd like to keep it that way."

~~~

Joan picked up David at nine on Saturday morning and with the light weekend traffic they were in Ballarat right on time. Joan talked the entire drive about all the plans that had been made for their wedding. David loved hearing how happy she was with the way all the details were coming together. David had only met Caroline a few times but that was enough. She had insisted coming with him to his suit fitting, fussing and tugging at his shirt. He was afraid she would show up at his house on the day of the wedding to make sure he'd showered correctly and had matched his underwear to his tie. But he had tolerated everything she did silently because according to Joan their wedding was going to be the most perfect one ever held. When Joan pulled up outside Abby's house she fell silent for the first time that day.

"So are we going in?" David asked. "My leg needs a stretch."

Joan turned to face him white with fear. "I can't do this. What if she doesn't like me? What if she doesn't believe me?"

"Joan, everybody likes you. And if she doesn't believe you then that's her problem. Why don't we go in and meet her before we make a judgement about her."

"Are you sure it'll be all right?"

"I am. But if it's not we can leave. No harm done." David placed his hand on her arm to steady her. Joan took a deep breath and turned the car off.

David and Joan made their way up the path together. Abby lived in a beautiful period home set well back from the street. The path to the front door was lined with roses and the garden beds were surrounded by lavender. Each side fence was hedged with camellia's that were in full flower. It was one of the most beautiful gardens Joan had ever seen and she wondered if it was her sister's work. If it was then that was one thing they didn't have in common. Joan loved looking at gardens and being outside in them, but she had no interest in digging or planting. It felt like too much work to her. The house reminded her a lot of her own. It was probably three times the size of Joan's small terrace but it was painted in the same cream with heritage green trim that Joan had chosen when she had the house painted over summer. A bullnose veranda wrapped around the front and sides of the house and a beautiful old rocking chair looked out over the street. The house sat on a wide street not far from the centre of town and was complimented by other houses just as old and beautiful. Before they even reached the door it swung open and Joan saw a woman so much the image of herself that it was like looking in the mirror. They had both let their long dark hair fall in soft waves around their face and both were wearing jeans and similar coloured jumpers. But it was their piercing blue eyes that matched each other's perfectly. They both had the eyes of their father.

Abby held her hand out to Joan in greeting and then shook David's hand as well. Introducing themselves, Joan turned back to the garden.

"Your gardens are lovely. Do you do all this work?"

Abby laughed and shook her head. "No. This is all my husband's handiwork. I enjoy the garden, but he won't let me near it. He's convinced that if I touch a plant it will die, and I'm quite happy to let him think that."

"Me too. I'm hopeless with plants." Joan felt her nervousness disappear as she found a connection with this stranger.

"Come on in. I've already put the jug on. I saw you pull up. Were you nervous? You took a long time coming in."

"I was. This is all very strange. And seeing you now, I feel like I'm looking in the mirror."

"I know exactly how you feel. I don't think there's much doubt that we are sisters."

The ice broken, the two women began comparing their lives over coffee. Abby had grown up the pampered daughter of a rich father and a doting mother but it turned out all hadn't been well behind the closed doors of the family home. Rumours of her father's infidelity reached Abby's mother Emily's ears often. Sometimes it was long term affairs but he had no problem with cheating on those women either. Abby's mother had stayed with Jonathon until Abby had married. She came home from her honeymoon to find her mother had kicked her father out of their home and filed for divorce as soon as was possible. When Joan was little she had longed for a father. She could see now that having him around would not have given her the fairy-tale life she had dreamed of.

David sat back and quietly watched the two women. Their voices were so similar, it was hard to tell which one was talking if he didn't follow the conversation carefully. He might as well not have been there they were so engrossed with their conversation. He stood, wanting to stretch his leg and wandered around the lovely lounge room. He couldn't believe how similar in taste these two were, even though they had been raised separately and came from completely different economic backgrounds. Most of the artwork and furniture in this room would fit perfectly into Joan's house. And Joan's furniture, while not of the same quality, wouldn't look out of place here.

All Joan's anxiety about meeting her sister had gone. They hadn't stopped talking since they sat down and Joan had taken an instant liking to her. An hour had passed in the blink of an eye as they filled each other in on their childhoods. Joan sugarcoated her past a little, not wanting to overwhelm Abby with just how differently they had been raised. But as they talked, she knew she needed to broach the subject of their father. It was one of the reasons she had come today, and she had learnt that Abby was aware her father wasn't always a good man.

"Abby. I'm wondering if the police ever came to speak to your father. I know it's a personal question, but if you don't mind?"

"Our father, you mean. You're going to have to get used to saying that." She shook her head. "I never saw the police talk to Dad. But Mum told me a story once. She probably shouldn't have, but she was so angry and hurt by all the years of his infidelity, I guess she wanted me to know what he was really like. When I was growing up she protected me from the truth but once they were divorced I heard all sorts of awful things. She did say that when I was about four the police came to the house and asked him about a girl that had been working for him. Mum didn't remember the name of the girl, but she had made some accusations about Dad forcing himself on her. Mum said the police never came back and dad denied the accusations. She thought the girl must have been making it up to get money. She didn't doubt they had slept together, but she never believed he had raped her. No one wants to think that about someone they love. When the police didn't pursue it and the girl never showed up she figured she had been right. How did you know the police had talked to him?" As she asked the question Abby's face changed from mild surprise to disgust. "Are you telling me that story was true? That he raped some poor girl that worked for him. I always knew he had a bad side, but he was always a good father." She clapped her hand across her mouth as she gasped with the sudden realisation. Are you saying that girl was your mother?" Tears sprung to Abby's eyes and she stood up and started to pace around the room.

"Oh, Daddy, what did you do?" she continued, speaking quietly to herself. She turned back to look at Joan, who wished she could take her question back. Abby's father was dying, and Joan had hurt her by disparaging his character.

Joan stood up from the couch to face her sister.

"I could be wrong, Abby. Maybe your mother was right and mine made it up to try and get money out of him. My mother never said a word to me about him. That's why I didn't know about you. I only found out recently when I was going through some papers of hers and found the police report that she had filed. I'm very, very sorry to have upset you. We should go and leave you alone."

"Don't go" Abby spoke through her tears. "I want to know the truth, and there's only one person who can tell us that. Will you consider coming with me to see him?"

"Do you really believe he'll tell you the truth? If he's kept it a secret this long wouldn't he deny it?"

"What you don't know, Joan, is that he has Alzheimer's. He's had it for several years now and soon he won't remember anything. But sometimes he tells me things from when I was little. He doesn't associate the little Abby he remembers with who I am today, but he still talks to me. I think it's worth asking."

"I don't know. I don't want him to know about me."

"We won't tell him who you are. He may not even notice you. If you give me the details I'll ask the questions. But I want you to be prepared. Seeing him isn't very pretty. I'm used to it now but it can be a shock if this is the first time you've come in contact with Alzheimer's." She looked at her watch. "It's visiting hours now. I was going this afternoon, but I'm happy to go now. Actually I need to do it now. Bring your own car and that way if it's too much you can leave."

Joan looked towards David wanting his council. "What do you think?"

"I think it's a good idea, Joan. I'm here for you if something goes wrong, and if there's a way to find out the truth, I think you should do it."

"All right," Joan replied, but that didn't mean she wasn't apprehensive. She had not intended to meet her father today and hadn't prepared herself for it. But she did understand the urgency of doing it now. She knew very little about Alzheimer's, but she was willing to take Abby's word for it. She reached inside her bag and took her keys out. David gently pulled them from her grasp.

"I think I should drive." He looked at Abbey. "We'll just follow you." She nodded in agreement as they left the house and she pulled the door closed behind them.

"You can't drive, David. Your leg's still bothering you."

"It'll be fine, Joan. We'll see you there Abby."

As he followed Abby's car, David glanced across at Joan. He could see she was scared and he couldn't blame her. Her father might be an old man now, but what he had done in the past had been evil, and Joan saw him as a monster. Now she was going to have to face him. Joan remained quiet as they followed Abby's Mercedes for a few kilometres out of town and turned into the driveway of what looked like a small hospital. They followed Abby inside and after she entered a number on a pin pad, they were able to enter a locked wing.

"They have to keep it locked. It's safer for the patients. If you decide to leave, please make sure no one follows you out. Sometimes they escape that way, and it's dangerous for them to wander the streets. That's why I had to put Dad in here. He lived with me for a bit, but he kept disappearing. My husband, Terry, insisted we put him here."

David and Joan followed Abby halfway down the long hall until they reached room seventeen. The name Jonathon Morgan was attached to the door, and Abby looked through a small window.

"He's dressed. I thought I better check. Sometimes I've found him in various states of undress, and I'm thinking that might not be the way you want to see him for the first time. Do you want to come in or stay in the hall?"

"I'll come in. As long as you don't mind if I leave."

Abby shook her head. "No problem. Any time it gets too much, you leave. David, I think you should stay out here. If there are too many people, he gets agitated."

"It's okay with me. Just look after my Joan."

Abby smiled. She hadn't said much to David since they had met because she had been focused on Joan, but she approved of him. He was very protective of her new sister, and that was a quality in a man that she admired.

The women entered the room together, but Joan moved to the corner with her back to the wall. It was a small space and consisted of a hospital bed with a bedside table beside it. A small TV hung from the wall and the midday movie was on quietly in the background. There were two large matching arm chairs, and Abby lowered herself into one. The other was occupied by an old man. Joan knew her father was in his early seventies. This man looked much older than that. His face was covered in stubble, and his grey hair was cut short, but it didn't look like it had been combed today. Because he wasn't standing it was hard to tell just how tall he was but Joan could see even though he was sitting he was still slim like he had been in the photos she had seen. His eyes were the same blue as hers, but the colour was the only thing they had in common. While hers always reflected what she was thinking, his were vacant. It surprised her how much of a difference that made to someone's whole expression. She had always thought it was a person's mouth that brought life to his or her face. But his empty eyes told her he wasn't really here anymore.

"Hi, Daddy. How are you today?" Abby waited a few moments for a response. She took the old man's hand in an attempt to rouse him, but he seemed unable to respond. Abby directed her attention to Joan, who looked like she wanted to disappear into the wall.

"He seems to be having a bad day. These are happening more and more. Terry thinks it won't be long before he can't manage to get out of bed anymore. This is a high-care facility so he'll be able to stay until he passes." Joan nodded her understanding to Abby but didn't respond. This was a horrible way to meet someone. He was close to death but completely unaware of it. He would never have the chance to put any wrongs right or say goodbye to his family. He was already gone. His body lived on, but the very essence of who he was, his ability to love and reason, had disappeared. Joan desperately hoped she would never end up like this. With her mother's early death, she had never had to worry about being faced with the burden of caring for an elderly parent. But seeing her father like this, it occurred to her that one day she might be the one being a burden to her loved ones.

Abby could see that Joan was deeply troubled by what she saw, but they had come here for a reason. "What was your mother's name? It might jog a memory for him."

"Margaret Webster."

Abby was still holding her father's hand and stroked it trying to get his attention. She called out "Daddy" a few more times and then changed to Jonathon. When he heard his name, he tipped his head towards Abby, and for the first time, Joan heard her father's voice.

"Hello."

Abby smiled. "Hello Jonathon. Do you remember me? I'm Abby."

"I know a little girl called Abby. Do you know her?"

"I do. I was also wondering if you know a girl called Margret Webster. She works for you." Abby saw how confused Joan was by the way she phrased her question. "He has no idea about the present. If I can put him in the past, we might have more chance at getting an answer." At first, Jonathon didn't react so Abby continued to talk about Margaret, telling him the story Joan had told her. When she mentioned the police, she thought she might be getting through to him.

Jonathon pulled his hand back from Abby's and started to become agitated. His hands were shaking, and he kept running them up and down the top of his legs. Abby asked again if he knew anyone called Margaret, but he didn't respond. A few minutes passed, but he didn't speak again. Abby looked over to Joan, understanding what she was feeling. Alzheimer's was an awful disease—the way it robbed a person of themselves. Abby was used to it now and had seen the slow progression as her father became more ill. But Joan was seeing all the damage that had been done suddenly. Everyone dies, but Abby prayed daily that this wasn't in her genes. She never wanted her children to see her like this.

"I don't think we're going to get anywhere with him today. I can try again later and let you know if he says anything. I can't promise anything though. He's slipping away very quickly now."

"That's all right." Joan spoke for the first time since entering the room. "I've seen enough. Do you mind if we go?"

"I think that's a good idea. But please come back to my house for lunch. Terry should be home by now with the kids. I sent him out this morning so we could have some time alone."

"I'm looking forward to meeting them. How did you explain me? I don't want them to know anything bad about their grandfather."

"They are aware of what their grandfather was like. He never let age slow him down. I'll just tell them that Dad had an affair with your mum when he was younger. They don't need to know the details."

The sisters exited the room, closing the door. Joan took one more look through the window. The old man, she found it hard to think of him as her father, had calmed down and was sitting still again and staring at nothing. David had been leaning against the wall outside the door and pulled her into a hug when she came out.

"Did he say anything?" he whispered into her ear. Joan shook her head. "I'm sorry."

Joan pulled away a little and smiled at David. "It's okay. I believe my mother. She wouldn't have been the way she was and chosen to avoid any intimacy with men if something hadn't happened to her. He did get agitated when we asked him about it. It would have been good to have some actual confirmation. I'm glad I faced him, but I don't think I'll be seeing him again."

"I agree. Coming here today was important. And brave."

"It was horrible, David. What if I end up like that? I don't want to do that to you."

"If it happens, and you have no reason to believe it will, I will take care of you. That's what we do when we love someone."

Joan nodded as they followed Abby back down the hall. Joan could hear people chatting in the distance and one woman screaming. She could make out the sound of another voice over the screaming, trying to calm the patient down. The people who worked with these patients every day must be some of the most special people on earth. She knew *she* could never do it.

~~~

When David and Joan left hours later, they were both exhausted but happy. Joan had loved her niece and nephew. Terry was a bit reserved with David at first, but they had soon fallen into football talk and the universal language of sport that most men speak gave them something in common. They had been delighted to be asked to the wedding and promises were made to spend more time together in the future. It wasn't until they were almost home that Joan could share what she was feeling. After an hour of silence, David was surprised to hear her speak.

"I think I can finally forgive her."

"Who?"

"My mother. It won't give me the childhood I should have had, but it will give me a chance in the future. Not holding on anymore to the hate I've had all this time. I can move forward. Let all the baggage go."

Looking over, David could see that she did indeed look lighter, less burdened.

"I'm glad then. Glad we did this today, and glad we did if before our wedding."

"Me too. It's time to move on and move forward. Together," she said, grateful that she had waited for him. There was no one else on earth she wanted to do this thing they called life with.

Chapter 30

"Hello Dear. It's Bridget."

Caroline sighed. Bridget and her husband were lovely people, but the way they couldn't manage to follow her instructions was driving her crazy. They had been on the phone to her countless times this week with tiny little problems that most halfway competent people could solve themselves. Because the wedding was being held at five in the afternoon, she had hired a professional company to light the back of the property to make the most of the spectacular gardens and the porch where the wedding would take place. The lighting specialist had called Caroline in a state yesterday after Bridget's husband, Alastair, who insisted on supervising any work done, had tripped on a cable and knocked over a spotlight. It had been repairable, but Caroline had to insist Alastair leave it to the professionals before they agreed to continue working. She had Bridget give him a whiskey and sit him in front of an episode of *Midsummer Murders* to keep him out of the way. Caroline had no idea how they managed to run their business. They were some of the most inept people she had ever met and Caroline knew if she wasn't overseeing every detail, Joan's wedding would have been a disaster.

"Good morning, Bridget. Everything's under control, I hope?"

"Er, not quite, dear. I was going to call Joan, but I remembered just in time that you told me I wasn't to bother her today. She will have to be told what's happened, but it might be best coming from you anyway."

Stay calm Caroline she told herself. Never yell at the elderly. You'll be old one day too.

"What's happened, Bridget? Don't tell me Alastair's been at the champagne again. I told you to keep him out of the kitchen. "

"He only had one bottle, and that was an accident. He thought it was ours."

"I know that, Bridget. It's just a shame that it was the vintage bottle of Moet meant for the bridal table. Why don't you tell me what the problem is, and we'll see what we can do to sort it out?"

"Well I'm afraid it's a bit worse than a missing bottle of champagne. Alastair was out in the garden doing some planting this morning. We bought a lovely maple on Thursday and it was delivered today. Remember how you said for us to go out and leave all the work to you that day? Well we've been looking for a tree like this for a long time, and we had the perfect spot in the garden for it. I thought it would be best to get Alastair out of the house this morning and out of the way of all the people swarming around here. I had no idea there would be so many of them here today. So anyway I sent him outside to keep out of the way, and he got out his little digger and started to dig a hole for the tree. One of the boys from next door had come over to help him get the tree in the hole because it's very heavy and Alastair's not as strong as he used to be."

Caroline thought she better interrupt Bridget's rambling before the old lady forgot why she'd called in the first place.

"Bridget what's the problem. And quickly please. I've got a lot to do today."

"There's no need to snap, dear. I'm getting to it. Alastair dug the hole in the wrong place."

"Well then, have him fill it in and dig another one."

"I will. But first we need to fix the pipe."

"What pipe, Bridget?"

"The one that brings the water from the dam up to the house. I'm afraid he hit the main water pipe with his digger. You should have seen it. It looked lovely. Water just shot up straight out of the earth and into the sky. I think I might get a water feature put in next summer."

"Can you turn the water off so our guests don't get wet Bridget?"

"We've already done that, dear. Francis from next door who was helping with the tree ran down to the dam and turned off the main tap."

"The,n Bridget," Caroline asked, completely exasperated with her, "what's the problem?"

"We have no water in the house."

Very un-Caroline like she screeched down the phone. "What?"

"All the water for the house comes from the dam. So when we turn off the tap, we have nothing."

"Then call a plumber and get him out there immediately."

"I have. I've called lots of plumbers. But it's Saturday. They all said they were booked up for the day, and no one will come. The earliest I could get was Monday.

"Then we will have to go without water. What do we really need it for, Bridget? I have sparkling water for the tables and the caterers can take all the dishes away dirty."

"That's all well and good, dear, but I think that with all that champagne and fancy water you insist on serving you might be wanting the toilets work-ing for the guests. And without water, you can't flush them." Bridget's voice trailed off, and Caroline barely heard her as she finally reached the reason for her call. "We'll have to cancel the wedding."

Bridget was lucky she was an hour's drive away because if Caroline had been in the room with her, she would have cheerfully strangled her.

"Listen to me, Bridget. Under no circumstances are we cancelling this wedding. If I have to bring up buckets of water from your blasted dam for people to use to flush the toilets, I will. But this is your lucky day, because I know a plumber, and I'll have him there in an hour. Don't do anything until he arrives and then have Alastair show him what he's done. Do you understand me?"

"Well, what am I supposed to do about a toilet until then? I've already arranged to stay the night with a friend, and we were leaving as soon as I finished talking to you."

"You rang her before you rang me?" Caroline yelled into the phone. Never in all the years that she had been organizing parties had she come across someone so incompetent. They might have a beautiful house, but they wouldn't be earning any stars from her.

"I had a whole pot of tea this morning to calm my nerves. This has all been very stressful. If I don't find a toilet soon, I'm going to be in very big trouble. Things don't quite work the way they used to dear. I'm quite old, you know."

"Bridget, you either cross your legs or find a tree, but don't you dare leave."

"I'm not sure I like your tone, Caroline. You shouldn't be talking to me like this."

Caroline closed her eyes and breathed in and then out and then in again.

"Bridget, is the cottage also hooked up to the main pipe?"

"Sort of. When we built it, the council made us pay for huge water tanks. If they get empty water pumps up from the dam, but they should be full. We've had a lot of rain here recently."

"Then why don't you go down to the cottage and use the toilet there?"

"Oh, I never thought of that. Aren't you a genius?"

"I'll have a plumber there as soon as I can. Just don't make a mess in the cottage. I spent two hours getting that ready yesterday. And under no circumstance are you to mention any of this to Joan."

"If you say so, dear."

~~~

When Beth saw the caller ID on her phone, she wondered if she should pretend she hadn't heard it ring. But she knew she would be in serious trouble, and she didn't want any conflict today. Joan was finishing off her breakfast after spending the night at Beth's house. They weren't due at the hairdresser's for an hour, and they had been enjoying a leisurely morning.

"Hi, Caroline," Beth alerted Joan. Not wanted to think about any problems that might have arisen since yesterday Joan started flailing her hands about and mouthing I'm not here.

"I need to speak Tom now," Caroline ordered down the phone. "But be discrete. I don't want Joan knowing I need him," she barked at Beth.

"Sure." This could not be good. Caroline never lost it. Beth carried on talking as she walked through the house looking for her husband who had gone into hiding this morning. "Of course everything is fine here. And Joan's perfectly calm."

"Beth, stop your asinine rambling and put your husband on the phone now!"

333

Beth found Tom in the back shed where he usually went when he needed to get away from his family. Beth held her hand over the speaker on the phone.

"It's Caroline," she whispered, holding the phone out to him.

"So?"

"She wants to talk to you."

"Tell her I'm not here."

"I can't. She's hysterical. Did you forget to do something?"

"Not that I know of. Can't you handle it? I'm already nervous enough without being yelled at by her," he whispered back. "Just tell her I went out." He waved Beth away and went back to mentally practicing walking down the aisle without tripping and making a fool of himself.

Beth returned the phone to her ear. "I can't find him, Caroline. I think he must have popped down to the shops for some milk. Would you like me to give him a message?"

"I can hear him, Beth. I don't care how nervous he is. You put him on the phone right now or I swear I'll come right over."

"I tried," Beth said, shrugging her shoulders and handing the phone to her husband.

Tom scowled at Beth as he took the phone from her. "What's up, Caroline?" he asked wondering what he had done that had got him in trouble.

"I need you to listen to me very carefully, Tom. I want you to get your suit and your shoes, get in your truck, and get down to Carrbridge right now."

"But the wedding's hours away. I'm not ready yet, and anyway, aren't I supposed to be arriving in the limo with the girls?"

"There's been a change of plans. You're going to get ready there. So remember your razor, hairbrush and anything else you might need. There's been a plumbing emergency and I need you to go and fix it now."

"Can't someone else do it? It's my day off."

"Tom. There is no water at Carrbridge. That means no toilets, and no toilets means no wedding. So stop complaining and get a move on."

"Gee, Caroline. You really need to work on your manners."

"I don't have time for manners, Tom. If you don't go now, this whole day will turn into a disaster."

"Fine, I'm going. What should I tell Beth?" he said as he saw her concerned face, trying to figure out what was happening."

"Just tell her you'll see her at the wedding later. And whatever you do, don't say anything about this to Joan."

~~~

Adam lowered the newspaper he had been hiding behind while he finished his coffee, smiling at his wife.

"Poor Tom. I hope you didn't make him cry."

"Not yet, but I will if he doesn't get that pipe fixed." Crisis averted, Caroline felt her blood pressure begin to return to normal, and she rechecked the list she seemed to have surgically attached to her hand all week, making sure she hadn't missed anything.

"Do you want me to go down and see if I can give him a hand?"

Caroline couldn't imagine Adam knee deep in mud with a pipe in one hand and a wrench in the other while wearing his best suit. Yes, he had changed so much since he came home and only for the better but imagining him in the dirt was beyond the realms of possibility, although, what she had always thought was possible kept changing. He hadn't convinced her yet that God was real, but it was getting harder to deny that there was a chance it was true. Because she had never seen such a transformation in one person and never wanted him to go back to the way he had been. Something or someone had made him different, more sure of who he was and more kind, but not in the weak way that she had always imagined a Christian man to be. She no longer knew what to think.

"Thanks, but that's okay. Tom will be fine, and there are still hours before the wedding. I'm sure he'll get it fixed."

"So what time are you off this morning?"

Caroline checked her watch. She was already dressed but was going to have her hair and makeup done with the wedding party.

"I'm leaving in half an hour. I'll be going straight to Carrbridge from the hairdressers so I can check on the caterers. The florist rang earlier and told me all the flowers had been delivered, so that's one thing off my list. I just want to be there to make sure everything's perfect."

"Are you sure you have to leave so soon? Michael's not here. We could pop back upstairs for a bit."

Caroline smiled, remembering how Adam had woken her up a few hours ago.

"What's gotten into you, Adam? You're an old man of forty. Shouldn't you be slowing down a little?"

"What's got into me is you," he flirted with his wife, "and I have no intention of ever slowing down. We have a lot of catching up to do."

"Well, it'll have to wait till later. Say about midnight. I'll be all yours then." Caroline got up from the table, taking her breakfast plate with her, but stopped to drop a kiss on the top of her husband's head.

"Thank you again for the flowers. They meant a lot to me. We have a busy day ahead of us, but it's important for us to remember. I thought we might go to the cemetery together tomorrow."

"I'd like that. I wish we could go today, but we did tell Joan it was all right to have her wedding on this date." This year's anniversary was going to be very different than last year's. They weren't any less sad, but they were together this time.

"I'll see you at Carrbridge later then. Seven o'clock, was it?" he teased, knowing full well the ceremony started at five.

"I'm going to ignore that. Please don't forget to make sure Michael's ready and wearing his suit. I really don't want to see him later with a dirty pair of jeans drooping down past his backside. And remember, not a word to Joan."

~~~

The guests began to arrive at half past four for the wedding. It was already chilly but thankfully there had been no rain, so people were able to wander around and admire the gardens. The outdoor heaters would keep people warm during the ceremony. The back porch was already lit up, and it looked like a thousand tiny stars had fallen just for David and Joan. As dusk fell, it would look even more spectacular. Seventy chairs had been wrapped in white organza, and attached to the back of each one was a single white orchid. Barely noticing his surroundings, David paced back and forward, trying to burn off some of the nervous energy that had plagued him since the limousine had arrived at his house to bring him here. He'd been fine all day until he'd seen the car pull up outside his house. That's when it all began to feel very real for him. It wasn't that he was regretting his decision. He only hoped that he never gave Joan reason to regret hers. And the anticipation of tonight after everyone had left and they were alone together had him breaking into a sweat every five minutes. This was going to be their first time, and what if he was no good? The anticipation had been building for months, and he didn't want her to be disappointed.

"David," his best man, Matthew, called, trying to get his attention. David stopped pacing for a second and turned his attention to his oldest friend.

"What?"

"You're wearing a hole in the floor. And you're going to end up soaking through your suit if you keep that up under these heaters."

"I can't stop. I just wish it was already over. I can barely remember my vows, and what if she doesn't turn up?"

"So read them off the card. Problem solved. And Joan is nothing like the other one. You know she's already here. You need to stay calm. If she saw you behaving like this, she'll be the one thinking you've changed your mind." Matthew had been the best man for David and Charlotte's abandoned wedding so he was knew how devastated David had been and understood his nervousness. But Joan was a different kind of girl from Charlotte, and Matthew thought she was an excellent match for David. "Do you want a drink? It might help calm your nerves."

"No, thanks. I doubt it will help and then I'd have no chance of remembering my vows. Besides, I'd be surprised if there was any left." Caroline had sat old Alastair in the corner with a bottle of scotch and told him not to move on pain of death. He refused to leave the porch; he still hated having strangers in his house, but Bridget had insisted on renting out his ancestral home to help cover the cost of its upkeep. David watched as Caroline kept sending dagger looks at the old man who looked genuinely terrified of her. *I wonder what that's all about,* he thought. The old guy was a bit of a pain, but he wasn't that bad.

~~~

"I thought she'd never leave," Joan exhaled. "Not that she hasn't been wonderful, and I can't believe how smoothly this day has gone, but I was afraid she was going to insist on checking my underwear to make sure it matched and run her hand up my legs to make sure I hadn't missed a spot when I shaved them this morning."

Beth was only half listening. She kept running back to the mirror to make sure it was really her in the reflection. She knew the day was all about the bride, but she was so thrilled with herself she couldn't resist feeling special too. Caroline had steered them away from choosing a colour for her dress that was "on trend," like mint or the fluro colours that might look all right on someone younger but wouldn't suit Beth at all. She was wearing a plainer, shorter version of Joan's dress. Pale copper in colour, it complimented the caramel tonings in Beth's hair that she had kept since her make over last year. The hairdresser had pulled it back into a low twist against her neck and a few loose curls framed her face. She was wearing the tear drop pearl necklace and earrings that Joan had bought her as a thank you for being her matron of honour.

"Beth, you look beautiful, but you need to stop running to the mirror every five seconds. Focus on me please." Joan didn't realize that she was experiencing the same nervous concerns as her groom. What if they weren't compatible in bed? She knew he loved her, but how long would he hang around if she disappointed him? She didn't know what he liked or what he expected. What if he was into something weird and he'd kept it a secret from her? Then what would she do?

"Beth. Talk to me. Tell me I've done the right thing by waiting to sleep with David."

"Joan, I've already told you twice today. He's not some kinky guy. He's your David, and he's kind and he loves you. If there's something he does that bothers you tell him. And not months later, but at the time. It'll save a lot of heartache. And besides, I don't think this is the time for this conversation." Beth tilted her head towards Zoe, the flower girl. She was adorable with her blonde ringlets and dressed in the palest of pink. She was sitting on the couch, constantly smoothing out her dress. Beth saw a future Caroline in the making. They hadn't had to tell her once to behave, and she had stayed pristine while they had taken the photos in the garden.

Beth heard a knock at the door, and Tom poked his head through the doorway.

"Everybody decent?"

"Yes," Joan called out. "You can come in."

Tom shut the door behind him and walked into the small lounge where they were waiting.

He took a moment to admire the bride but thought his own wife was much more beautiful. She looked amazing.

"It's time, girls. The car's outside waiting." He gave Joan a serious look and asked. "As your stand-in father, are you absolutely sure this is what you want to do?"

"Yes, Dad, it is," she replied, playing along. Taking one last look at herself in the mirror recently vacated by her matron of honour, she decided this was the most beautiful she had ever looked. She took a deep breath and picked up the simple bouquet of white orchids that matched Tom's button-hole. He held the door open for the three girls and waiting for them outside was a beautiful silver limo with a chauffeur standing by the open door to help them into the car. While Joan got herself settled, Tom pulled his wife back into the privacy of the porch.

"You look amazing," he said while his eyes took in her face and then travelled down the rest of her. "David might think he's the luckiest man here, but I have to disagree."

Beth adjusted the orchid in Tom's buttonhole and smoothed his jacket. "You still haven't told me what you got up to today."

"I promise to fill you in later. We don't have time now."

"You'd better. By the way, you in this suit is a very good look. I'd kiss you now if I could, but I don't want to smudge my lipstick. I guess it'll keep for later. "

They heard the sound of a man clearing his throat loudly behind them. The chauffeur stood beside the car door waiting for them, and Beth could see Joan motioning them into the car.

"Come on, you two. I've got a very important date."

~~~

By the time Jill arrived at Carrbridge, she was exhausted. Beth's children had fought with each other most of the way, and her mother had been no help. Caroline came over to greet her, and Jill was complimenting her on how romantic the porch looked when she stopped midsentence.

"Oh, my," she whispered under her breath. Caroline followed the direction her eyes had taken. "*Who is that?*"

"He's David's best man, Matthew. "

"And is he here alone tonight?"

"No. His daughter is the flower girl."

Jill felt a rush of disappointment. This was going to be her life now. Any man she was attracted to would be taken, and the ones left weren't worth bothering with. Joan had snagged the last decent unattached man in Australia.

"He's not married if that's what you're asking. I'm not sure of the situation, but he doesn't have a wife. I could ask Joan later if you want."

"Yes, please. I'd like to know everything about that man."

Caroline looked at him, not sure why Jill was swooning like a schoolgirl.

"Really? Him? I lost interest in him the minute I had him measured for his suit." She saw Adam across the room with a very glum-looking Michael in tow. He had begged to be allowed out of coming to the wedding, worried about having Sarah following him around all night. "I guess it's hard to notice anyone else when you already have perfection," she said to herself as she hurried to kiss her husband hello.

~~~

Joan hadn't seen the ballroom or the foyer yet today. Caroline had wanted it to be a surprise and when Joan took in how beautiful the room was, she gasped with delight. Tiny fairy lights were strung from the ceiling and then covered in sheer organza. Simple flower arrangements graced the tables along with what appeared to be hundreds of candles. Joan had insisted there be no traditional wedding cake, and instead there was a tiered stand of the most beautiful cupcakes ever created. Caroline was waiting for them at the French doors that led out to the porch where all the guests were waiting. After giving all four of them a final check, she motioned to the quartet, and they began to play Pachelbel's Canon in D Major.

Zoe led the way down the short aisle followed by Beth. The flower girl couldn't resist giving a little wave at her father, who stood beside David. When she reached the small alter she looked back towards the French doors as everyone rose for the bride and then looked towards David. She always loved seeing the groom's face when he saw his bride for the first time.

David had to restrain himself from running down the aisle to meet his bride. He didn't think there could be anything in nature that could match her beauty. She was wearing a floor-length gown in champagne satin. The neck fell in a deep V, and the fitted sleeveless bodice was encrusted with hundreds of tiny pearls that had been hand sewn on by Caroline. The pearls graduated away at the waist and the shimmer of the fabric reflected the thousands of lights that adorned the huge porch. Joan had chosen a simple tiara covered in tiny pearls that held back her hair, which tumbled down her back in loose curls.

The walk towards David seemed to take an eternity. She fixed her eyes on his, and when she saw the way he was looking at her, any concerns about whether they would be compatible evaporated. The celebrant waited patiently for the two of them to look away from each other and towards him but eventually, he gave up and motioned the guests to sit.

Joan could hear the celebrant talking and tried to concentrate on what he was saying. She dragged her focus towards him realising she was in danger of missing her own wedding if she didn't concentrate. Beth read out the Bible verse she had asked to be included in the ceremony and then it was time for their vows. David reached into his pocket for the notes he had made afraid he wouldn't be able to remember on his own. He could see his hand trembling as he tried to hold the piece of paper still.

"My lovely, Joan. You have brought to my life the kind of love and hope that I didn't think was possible. You are my first thought when I wake up in the morning, and you are my last thought before I fall asleep at night. My days are consumed by thoughts of you, and every time something good happens to me, you are the person I want to share it with and when something bad happens you are the person who knows the right words to say to make my sadness disappear. I wish only for you for the rest of my days, and I will endeavour to love you with every part of my heart, my soul, and my body. I am yours forever."

Joan took a deep breath and blew it gently through her lips. How was she ever supposed to follow David's words without crying? Beth handed her the vows she had written, but she knew them by heart and didn't need to look at the card.

"David. With you in my life, I gain your strength and your wisdom. You are my champion and my soft place to fall. Fear of the future no longer exists because whatever happens, I have the comfort of knowing that we will face it together. I promise to listen to you and consider your needs and feelings in every decision I make. I give my whole self to you and for the rest of our lives, my eyes will never turn from you. I love all of you with all of me."

Still shaking, David listened to the celebrant and when asked the obvious question he responded, "I do." He slipped a diamond encrusted band on Joan's finger, refusing to let her hand go. Joan hardly waited till the same question was asked of her before she agreed to take David as her husband. When they were announced as husband and wife, the room full of people disappeared as David and Joan kissed the only person they were ever going to touch in that way for the rest of their time on Earth.

~~~

Dinner was everything and more than Caroline had promised. She had created an atmosphere where people danced and laughed. The speech from Matthew didn't give away too many of David's secrets but still managed to keep everyone in fits of laughter. In her speech, Beth gave David a friendly warning about looking after her friend but everyone knew it wasn't really necessary. He hadn't let her go once all night. Caroline fussed and bossed behind the scenes until everything that needed to be done was. She stood away from the crowd watching seventy happy people enjoy each other's company. She loved the sense of accomplishment she felt at what she had achieved tonight. Across the room, she could see a new romance beginning. Matthew had left the bridal table some time ago and was sitting with Jill, his Zoe asleep on his lap. She saw Jill reach out and stroke the little girl's hair. Caroline couldn't be sure who she was more enamoured with. It didn't really matter. Anyone could see those two came as a package pair. Sarah had spent the entire night pretending to ignore Michael while taking covert glances in his direction. Caroline could see heartbreak in her future because Michael was completely unaware she was even in the room. Sarah's parents had hardly sat down all night, Beth refusing to let Tom stop dancing. He didn't seem to be minding the slow songs.

Caroline felt a touch from behind, and Adam circled his arms around her.

"Care to dance?"

"I don't know. What if someone needs me?"

"Look around. Everyone is having a wonderful time. The only person here who needs you is me."

He spun her off towards the dance floor as Michael Bublé crooned about love.

~~~

"You know, this could go on all night." David said as he kissed his wife's hand for the hundredth time that evening. "I don't think anyone would mind if we snuck off."

"I think you're right. And all I want is to be alone with you. Why don't we say our good-byes and thank yous, and I'll meet you by the door in five minutes?"

"Oh, no. I'm not letting you out of my sight." David stood up and tapped his glass with a fork. People turned towards the sound and the DJ turned the music down so he could be heard.

345

"On behalf of myself and Mrs. Saunders." He paused while the guests clapped. "I would like to thank you all for coming tonight. Each one of you is here because you are part of our extended family and you are important to us both. Special thanks go to my best man, Matthew, who seems much too busy to care whether I thank him or not." David held up his glass in Matthews's direction, and Jill blushed as all eyes turned to the pair who had both felt an instant attraction to each other and hadn't stopped talking and flirting once since Matthew had approached her and asked her to dance. "I'd also like to thank my parents and sister who got to put up with all my woeful whining when I thought I'd lost Joan forever and have accepted her into the family like one of their own. And to Abby, Joan's sister, and her family for coming out and celebrating with a room full of strangers. We look forward to getting to know you better." David scanned the room and found Beth and Tom sitting with their children. "Thank you to Beth, who's interference has brought me the most wonderful gift. My wife. Without her, we probably wouldn't be here tonight. And to Tom, who stood in as family for Joan today. But our last and most important thank you tonight goes to Caroline. She took what could have been a disaster and turned it into a night for us all to remember. I've never been so afraid of anyone in my life before, but she was exactly what we needed." David raised his glass again, and those who knew Caroline well laughed.

"Now that said it's time for us to leave. You can stay as long as you like, but I've decided to start my honeymoon a little early. Goodnight." David pulled Joan up to meet him and kissed her again while their guest looked on. After one more wave good-bye, David and Joan didn't stop for anyone as they left the room, but they could hear the shouts of well wishes behind them. The foyer was empty, and suddenly they felt shy with each other in the quiet. David removed his jacket and put it around Joan's shoulders to protect her from the cold, but when they stepped outside, he saw it had been unnecessary. The limo had been replaced with a small enclosed carriage and sitting in charge was Bridget.

"Alastair was supposed to do this, but he fell asleep hours ago. Besides, with all he drank tonight, he might have driven you off into the dam," she grumbled.

David helped Joan into the carriage and heard Bridget order the horse forward. After the noise of the evening, the silence made him feel like he and Joan were the only two people on earth. When they reached the small cottage, David held Joan's hand as she stepped out of the carriage, and they waited outside until the noise of the horse clip-clopping on the drive receded.

David opened the unlocked door and saw that the room was bathed in the dim light from what looked like hundreds of candles. Kissing her deeply as he reached down, he collected his new wife in his arms and carried her over the threshold.

Joan hadn't been expecting him to do that until they returned to her home. where they had decided they would live together.

"Aren't you supposed to do this when we get home?"

"Wherever you are is home," he said as he kicked the door shut behind him.

Epilogue
Five months later

When Tom had said all he wanted for his fortieth birthday was a quiet party at home with their friends and family, Beth wasn't sure she believed him. But watching him from the kitchen window, laughing with Adam and David, she saw that today was exactly right. He was having a wonderful time. She put the last candle on the cake and hoped it tasted as good as it looked. She might have improved in the cooking department, but she knew she would never have been able to make something this good. Caroline had given her the name of a new bakery that she had discovered and that made the most delicious cakes possible, but only after Beth swore to never divulge to anyone where it had come from. Beth was going to have a piece, but just a little one. She didn't need to be quite so vigilant anymore, but there was no way she was going to let all her hard work go to waste, so she kept an eye on the scales at least once a week.

"Come on, you two. Time for cake." Michael and Lochie were hunched over the new laptop Beth had bought Tom for his birthday in anticipation of university next year. Tom had taken one look at the manual and handed it to the boys to set up for him. They both looked relaxed after finishing their exams a few weeks ago. Lochie still had another year of high school, but Michael was done and just waiting for his scores. He had every hope of getting into medicine next year. Lochie still hadn't decided what he wanted to do, but he had announced that whatever it was, it wouldn't be at Monash with his Dad watching over him.

"Would you like me to carry that for you?" Matthew asked from the sliding door that led outside. November was shaping up to be a lovely month, not too hot yet, and everyone had congregated outside under the pergola.

"That would be great. I'll get the lighter for the candles." Matthew and Zoe had become familiar faces around her home, and Beth was hoping for an announcement any time now. Jill and Matthew both said they were taking it slow, and Jill was still waiting for her final divorce papers, but they were always together.

Matthew loved it here. It wasn't the quiet life he had known with his late wife. She had been a very steadying influence after his wild teenage years, and he had loved and appreciated her deeply. Jill and her family were the complete opposite. They laughed loudly and told silly jokes to each other. Beth, in particular, was chaotic and didn't care about the mess in her house as long as everyone was having a good time. Jill's mother had grilled him for hours about his life before she gave him the nod of approval, but he hadn't minded and understood why. He was going to be the same with his daughter. Zoe had blossomed around these people and had gone from being a very sedate serious little girl, with only her father for company, to a fun-loving child. He was grateful to them, especially to Jill, who had accepted instantly that where he went, Zoe went. He hadn't been able to stop himself from falling in love with Jill and after seeing how happy Joan and David were, he was beginning to believe that he might have another shot at a happy life. Being a newly married man, David felt obliged to give out advice and told Matthew that waiting to have sex until he was married was the best thing he had ever done. Matthew thought it sounded a little extreme, but maybe it was worth thinking about. It certainly hadn't done David and Joan any harm.

"Okay, everyone. It's time to blow out the candles, and then Tom's going to make a speech," Beth yelled over the din of clinking glasses and laughter.

"No, I'm not," he yelled back. Beth pinched him gently on the arm and gave him "the look"—the one every husband and child knows, he one that lets you know she's not kidding, and you'd better do what she said.

Tom blew out the candles while everyone sang "Happy Birthday."

"I've been ordered by the boss to give a speech, so I will but I promise to keep it short. Thank you all for coming out today. I thought turning forty wouldn't mean much. It's just another day. But I was wrong. All of you have made it special, especially my family. I have a wonderful wife whose going to stand beside me as I embark on a new chapter in my life and my three children who keep me from getting much sleep from worrying about them. I love you all. To friends old and new, I look forward to the next decade with you."

Adam called out "hear, hear," and about thirty people responded in kind and raised their glasses to Tom. As Beth started to cut the cake, Joan asked everyone if they would be quiet for a moment. She took David's hand while all eyes watched on expectantly.

"David and I just wanted to let you know we are going to be building a new house. We've been collaborating on a few projects, and we need a house with more space. After the success of our first project together, the Beacon Street Medical Centre, we decided to work together more. And we have a secondary project that we started about five months ago that's going to need a lot of room."

Joan pulled the loose top that she had been wearing tight and turned sideways to reveal a small baby bump. The women clapped and called out congratulations, while the men looked confused until their wives explained. Jill couldn't help the flash of jealously that shot through her, but it only lasted for a second. She was happy for Joan and David, even if it wasn't what anyone had been expecting. She wondered if it had been planned. Joan had always been adamant that she didn't want children. Matthew saw the look of pain cross Jill's face at the news and then saw her quickly rearrange her features into a smile call out congratulations. He leaned over and whispered in her ear. "I hope that will be us one day. Married and with a baby on the way."

Jill replied under her breath, saying, "But what if we get married and I can't get pregnant? History tells me it might not be possible."

"Don't worry about history. Just focus on the future, our future."

Jill knew that wasn't a proposal, but it was a promise of one to come when she ready. He had made his intentions clear, but she had asked him to wait until her divorce was final. She didn't want to begin an engagement before her failed marriage came to an official end, and she wasn't in a hurry this time. Matthew was nothing like Chris, but she needed to be certain before she jumped in again.

Beth threw herself into Joan's arms, hugging her so tight, David started to worry she might break the baby. He couldn't believe how happy he was. When Joan first came to him in terror, holding one of those life-changing sticks, he'd wanted to vomit. This was not what they had planned. And worse, it was his fault. In all the wedding chaos, Joan had forgotten to pack her birth-control pills. Caroline really should have put that on the list. And maybe once or twice on their honeymoon, he hadn't been as careful as he should have, but seriously, they were *old*. It just never occurred to him that Joan would be able to get pregnant, and so easily. The doctors on TV were always saying how fertility drops off in your forties, and the chance of an unassisted pregnancy was rare. But after a few days, he stopped thinking about the two pink lines on a stick and started thinking about a tiny pink baby with Joan's blue eyes and maybe a little of him too. He was gone after that and was planning a whole tribe. He hadn't let Joan in on that secret yet. Let her deal with the first one, and then he would bring it up. Joan had taken a little longer to come around to the idea, but when she heard the heartbeat for the first time, she knew she could do this with David. And her baby would have all the love that she had missed out on.

After Tom separated Beth from Joan, they stood back a little from the crowd. Beth was beaming from ear to ear.

"You look happy for them. I hope you're not getting clucky. I don't want to have to do uni with a screaming baby in the house."

"Don't be dense. At my age, I can't think of anything worse. I'm on the homestretch now. There's no way I'd start again. I am happy for them, but those two idiots have no idea what they're letting themselves in for. I can't wait to see it."

"It wasn't so bad, was it? And there's hope for our lot. Lochie did much better in school this year, and Sarah seems to have calmed down a bit. She's decided she wants a fairy-tale wedding just like Joan's and realizes someone like Butch might not be her ideal prince." Tom looked over at Nate who was sitting in a corner with his iPod. "We might need to surgically remove that thing from son number two's hand but when he actually notices the other people around, he's good company."

"You're right. It hasn't been all bad, and the good days made it all worthwhile. But I couldn't have done it without you," Beth said, leaning into Tom.

Caroline couldn't help herself and was in the kitchen clearing plates and stacking the dishwasher. She hadn't seen Joan since the wedding, and she could see married life suited her. She just hoped she was ready for motherhood and the good and bad that came with it. Seeing someone pregnant always reminded her of being pregnant with Isabelle and how easy it had been to protect her before she was out in the world.

Joan saw Caroline inside through the window and decided this was as good a time as any to approach her. No one was around, and if she said no, they could keep the discussion between them. She slid the door closed behind her so they would have privacy. Joan picked up some used napkins from the table, threw them in the bin, and then walked over to the bench where Caroline was working. She saw Joan approach and told herself to be nice. This wasn't the place to start a fight.

"Congratulations. You kept that a secret for a long time."

"We decided we wanted to be through the danger period before we told anyone. But I'm five months now, and the doctor says everything is progressing perfectly. And I was starting to get bigger, so people were going to guess anyway."

"Have you had your scan yet?"

"Last week. Don't tell anyone yet, but it's a girl."

"Well, congratulations again," Caroline said as involuntary tears sprung to her eyes. "Boys are wonderful, but having a daughter is very special. You know that means David will want you to try for a boy."

"I know. I'll cross that bridge when it comes. The reason that I wanted you to know it's a girl is because I'd like your permission. We want to call the baby Bella. It's a name I've always loved, but it also reminds me of Isabelle. But if you think that will be too hard for you, we can come up with something else."

Caroline thought about Joan's request, appreciating how she always considered her feelings when it came to Isabelle. *Maybe Joan isn't so bad,* she decided.

"I think Bella is a perfect name, and Isabelle would be thrilled. I wish you and David all the luck in the world. I think you'll both make wonderful parents."

"Thank you, Caroline. It wasn't planned but once the shock wore off, we were both thrilled. David blames you for it. He thinks if you'd written us a honeymoon list, it would have had birth control on it, and I wouldn't have forgotten."

"Typical man. He could have taken responsibility himself. How about I write you a list of all the things you'll need to buy before the birth to make up for it? And if you need help with the baby shower, give me a call. With Michael off to uni next year, I'm at a loose end. Maybe I should take up professional party planning."

"That's very kind of you. I think Beth might want to have a hand in the planning if you can stand working with her and her disorganized ways… and as long as you don't think this makes us friends. I might be pregnant, but I haven't lost my mind. You're still a complete pain in the neck and a snob to boot."

Caroline smiled at Joan, enjoying their exchange. "Don't worry. I have enough friends, and I'd never pick someone like you. You're still the same as you were in high school. I didn't like you then, and I don't like you now. Besides no one would believe us anyway."

"Agreed. Let's promise to never be friends."

"Done. You and I will never be friends." Caroline smiled as one stray tear slipped down her cheek. Bella—it was a beautiful name, and Joan choosing it for her baby was so kind. She didn't understand how Joan had ended up in her life after all these years, but Caroline was glad she had, even if she never let on to Joan. "We should join the others. It sounds like they're having too much fun out there without us."

Joan nodded, and the two women left the now tidy kitchen, going in search of their loved ones arm in arm. The sound of laughter coming from the Frasers' backyard could be heard long into the night.

www.ingramcontent.com/pod-product-compliance
Lightning Source LLC
Chambersburg PA
CBHW032228010726
47494CB00002B/403